D1707530

LUCKY BALDWIN

Lucky Baldwin

The Story of an Unconventional Success

by C. B. GLASSCOCK

RENO NEVADA

SILVER SYNDICATE PRESS

Post Office Box 71226 Reno, Nevada 89570

The Silver Syndicate Press wishes to acknowledge the most gracious and generous support and assistance provided by Stanley Paher and the staff of Nevada Publications. Without their help, LUCKY BALDWIN would never again have seen the light of day.

Copyright © 1993, Silver Syndicate Press.
All Rights Reserved.
ISBN 0-913814-27X

Proudly printed in the United States of America.

CONTENTS

INTRODUCTION

From 1860 to the early 20th century in California and Nevada, there were a number of men who actively cultivated the entrepreneurial dream. They built railroads and other transportation systems, established ranches, banks, and various industries, and created stock companies and other enterprises, starting them all from persistent dreams and with practically no capital. In the end most of these individuals acquired great wealth and fame.

What common characteristics did these men of ingenuity and explosive energy possess? First, they had an uncanny ability to recognize opportunity where the fearful saw only confusion. They were more than willing to take even the largest of calculated risks, rising above even the greatest uncertainties and obstacles. Demonstrating lightning-quick reasoning under stress and pressure, these hard-workers threw themselves into their endeavors, bringing to them intense commitment and wheel-to-the-grindstone perseverence. Though many of their projects failed, they never quit. Never! With them, optimism sprang eternal.

It is easy to be fascinated by these competitive, restless

individuals, especially those who traced their origins to Nevada's gold and silver mines and who succeeded in stock market speculation and manipulation. While all of them have passed over the Great Divide, these men and the business and financial monuments they left behind are still quite familiar to the general public as names and as institutions synonymous with great influence and power.

Among these doers and shakers were Darius Ogden Mills, William C. Ralston, and William Sharon of Northern California's Bank Crowd; John W. Mackay, James G. Fair, James C. Flood, and William S. O'Brien, of Virginia City's Bonanza Firm; John P. Jones and Alvinza Hayward of the Nevada Union; and certainly, at a later date, the "King of Nevada," George Wingfield, who, among many other enterprises, developed the Goldfield Consolidated Mines. A man also belonging to this group, among the most spectacular of them all, is Elias Jackson "Lucky" Baldwin.

Before I even knew that there was a Baldwin, his name seemed to always cross my path. When I was a boy growing up in the suburbs of Los Angeles, our family often drove through a nearby community called Baldwin Park; as a student in high school, it was not uncommon to skip the last afternoon class in order to catch the final race of the day at the Santa Anita Racetrack. Inside the track, at the clubhouse entrance, was a large Maltese cross; in front of that were several brass plaques which proclaimed the site the final resting place of four great American Derby racing champions: Volante, (1885); Silver Cloud, (1886); Emperor of Norfolk, (1888); and Rey El Santa Anita, (1894). One of the plaques noted that these horses were "Raced by E. J. (Lucky) Baldwin."

When I first visited Virginia City in the late 1940s, I heard that the Ophir, first great mine of the Comstock, had been the source of many millions for an individual named Baldwin:

INTRODUCTION

in 1978, when my family began operating Meeks Bay Resort at Lake Tahoe, I learned that Tallac, one of Tahoe's most historic recreation destinations, was yet another creation of the man, Baldwin.

EARLY YEARS IN THE MIDWEST

E. J. Baldwin was born April 4, 1828, on a farm in the village of Hamilton, Ohio. He was the fourth of five children and was of pure British ancestry. When he was six, his family moved to Terre Coupee, Indiana, ten miles west of South Bend.

Although his schooling was minimal, by the age of sixteen he was already recognized for his native shrewdness and for his expertise with horse-flesh. Not long after winning $200 on his own horse in a race at South Bend, he married Sarah Ann Unruh, a girl from a neighboring farm. He was just eighteen years old and she was his first wife.

Soon after, he moved across the state to Valparaiso, where he opened a grocery and saloon. His first daughter, Clara, was born there on May 14, 1847. After a brief stint in the hotel and general store business in nearby New Buffalo, and a venture in canal boat transportation, he moved to Racine, Wisconsin, where he opened still another hotel and grocery.

THE EMIGRANT TRAIL

In 1853, imagined opportunities in the booming mining districts of the Mother Lode in northern California led Baldwin to sell his businesses and move West. He sensed possibilities not only in gold mining itself, but in support businesses which supplied the miners. On his westward journey, he carried wagonloads of brandy, tobacco, tea, and coffee. His five-month trip was by way of Council Bluffs, Laramie, Fort Bridger, Salt Lake City, Ragtown, Placerville, and Sacramento, ending in San Francisco.

Along the way he once got lost while tracking an antelope; friendly Indians brought him back to his party. In Salt Lake City, he had dinner with Brigham Young and ended up trading much of his brandy, tobacco, tea, and coffee to the Mormons in exchange for horses. On leaving Salt Lake, his party was attacked by Utes; Baldwin always maintained that Brigham Young's brother had instigated the raid. Nine Indians were killed in the skirmish. Later, near the Humboldt River, Baldwin encountered more Indians and had to fight off a band of Piutes.

Early Days in the West

Three days after he arrived in San Francisco, Baldwin purchased the Pacific Temperance Hotel with funds obtained from the sale of his horses. Thirty days later he sold it, doubling his money, and purchased the Clinton Hotel. It proved a failure, and after a brief stint in the brickmaking business, he opened a livery stable. It was during this period that he first met Adolph Sutro and began to develop an interest in the buying and selling of mining rights as well as an appreciation for the value of accurate, first-hand information. With his livery stable profits, he also purchased a few business lots on Market Street.

In the spring of 1860 he visited Virginia City to verify the truth of the Comstock Lode stories. On this trip, he got caught in deep snow just out of Strawberry, in eastern California, and was rescued by the famous "Snowshoe" Thompson. Eventually, Baldwin sold out of his San Francisco livery business and opened a lumberyard in Virginia City. He spent much of his spare time studying the mines and learning how to trade effectively in their stock.

Baldwin sold his lumber business in 1862 and returned to San Francisco, where he re-rentered the livery business. During this time he finally divorced his first wife, ending many

[x]

years of domestic strife. With monies earned from his business, he began seriously trading in Comstock shares. By 1867 he was able to sell his interests in the Savage, Chollar-Potosi, and Yellowjacket mines at prices that made him a small fortune. He then decided he needed a vacation.

His first trip was to India, where he hunted tigers and elephants. Next, he traveled to Japan. In what amounts to an incredible success story, he assembled a Japanese vaudeville troupe and brought them back to America. Opening on Broadway, they were an immediate success. Baldwin brought the show out West and eventually sold the company when it reached San Francisco.

Origin of the Name "Lucky"

There are many stories of how E. J. Baldwin came by the nickname "Lucky." Perhaps it came about in the following way. Before leaving for his hunting trip to India, Baldwin left his shares of the Ophir, Crown Point, and Hale & Norcross in a locked safe under the care of his broker. He left specific instructions that the broker was to sell Hale & Norcross when the stock reached his original purchase price of $800 a foot.

But the broker was unable to sell, for Baldwin had taken with him the key to the locked safe. Upon his return from Japan, Baldwin found that the stock had advanced more than 1000%. He sold out at prices ranging from $8000 to $10,000 a foot, building yet another fortune.

He married the widow Mary Cochrane in 1869, and returned to the Comstock. By establishing a pattern of reasoned investment, of timely buying and selling, he became a bull in that borrasca year, accumulating shares of the Ophir. Returning once again to San Francisco, he watched closely the behavior of individuals with Comstock connections and soon began to buy heavily in the shares of the Crown Point.

INTRODUCTION
Making it Big

When boom times returned to the Comstock in the early 1870s, Baldwin was able to sell his Crown Point positions to Jones and Sharon for $2.5 million. Later, his profits from the sale of his stock in the Ophir were estimated at $5 million. To fully appreciate the magnitude of that fortune, it should be noted that a dollar was worth approximately twenty times what it is today; at age 47, Baldwin had become a legitimate financial titan.

On June 5, 1875, his success with stocks was formally recognized by his peers when he was made the first president of San Francisco's Pacific Stock Exchange. In that same year, working with William Sharon and others, he provided funds which made it possible for the defunct Bank of California to reopen its doors.

C. C. Goodwin, a former editor of the *Territorial Enterprise*, once described Baldwin as ". . . .tall and strong, and swarthy, his eyes sometimes blazing like a fiery Spaniard's sometimes deep and sullen as a Pottawattamie; not much faith in the average man, looking on most women as schemers . . . ." Goodwin knew each of the leading figures of the Comstock and characterized Baldwin as a man with ". . . a wondeful brain, immense sagacity and solid judgment . . ."

With cash in hand from his successful stock operations, Baldwin returned to his loves of an earlier era, the hotel business and horse racing. It was a time to thrive on the challenge of largeness and bask in the glow of superlatives.

Still in San Francisco in 1873, he began the construction of what would become the finest hotel west of New York. It was called—what else?—the Baldwin. Although the hotel's opening was delayed by the temporary failure of the Bank of California in 1875, the theatre part of the enterprise opened later that year. The hotel finally began operating in 1877. The world's best actors and actresses performed in the

[xii]

INTRODUCTION

Baldwin Theatre. Designed in an ornate French Renaissance style and erected at a cost in excess of $3 million, the spectacular hotel was famous until fire claimed it in 1898. Even today, pictures of this magnificent structure inspire awe and admiration.

During the mid 1870s Baldwin also purchased 1000 acres on the south shore of Lake Tahoe from Ephraim "Yank" Clement. Eventually increasing his holdings to 8000 acres, he built the Tallac Hotel, with the capacity to accommodate 400 guests. About this time, Baldwin traveled to Saratoga, New York, where he bought two thoroughbred stallions (GRINSTEAD and RUTHERFORD), the primogenitors of what later became his prized racing stable.

Perhaps none of Baldwin's ventures proved so meaningful to him as his purchase of the historic Rancho Santa Anita in southern California in 1875. With the San Gabriel Mountains as a backdrop, the unsurpassed beauty of this fertile area attracted Baldwin on his first visit. He bought the first 8500-acre parcel from a Los Angeles merchant for $25 an acre. Baldwin gradually acquired surrounding properties until his holdings reached about 46,000 acres. The tract included large sections of present-day Arcadia, Pasadena, and Monrovia, as well as parcels in San Marino and Sierra Madre.

Taking great pride in its agricultural experiments, his Rancho, at its height, was one of the showplaces of southern California. With 3,000 walnut trees, 500 acres of orange trees, 3,000 head of cattle, 500 horses (70 of them thoroughbreds), and vineyards producing 384,000 gallons of wine and 55,000 gallons of brandy anually, it was yet another mammoth Baldwin enterprise.

After the tragic fire of 1898 destroyed the uninsured Baldwin Hotel, California newspapers often portrayed Baldwin as a man beset by economic troubles. It was rumored that the panics of 1893 and 1897 had hurt him. He was now referred to as the "former" millionaire, an impression he did nothing to dispel by paying his bills only when nearly forced to do so. Although heavily indebted and extended, land rich and money poor, he left an estate valued at more than $10 million when he died in 1909. Clearly, Baldwin was not in such bad economic straits as some of his creditors were led to believe.

North to Alaska

In 1900 the seventy-two-year-old Baldwin boarded the *S. S. Valencia* in San Francisco, bound for Nome, Alaska, in what would be portrayed by the contemporary press as an attempt to recoup his fortune. He took with him portable buildings, wagons, horses, hay, brandy, and the set-up for a complete gambling house. As he did when he journeyed to California nearly fifty years before, he saw potential profit not just in mining but especially in the secondary business activities that supported the miners. But he was too late to get in on the ground floor, and ended up selling all the materials he had shipped. Even then, it was said, he made a profit of somewhere between $50,000 and $60,000.

Closing Days

Baldwin returned from Alaska and settled down on his ranch at Santa Anita. He was still seen in the company of beautiful young women when he shopped in nearby Monrovia. He even had time for reminiscing when he entertained John Mackay, the richest and most famous of the Bonanza kings, in 1904.

Still craving action, Baldwin decided to build a racetrack on the Santa Anita Ranch. After carefully surveying the potential for profit, he planned a first-class plant. It was to be the finest in the West—nothing less would do. After a few delays, the track opened in December 1907. It was the fulfillment of Baldwin's fondest dream, and he considered it his greatest accomplishment.

Even after he died at his ranch on March 1, 1909, "Lucky" Baldwin did not drop from the public eye. Many would-be heirs suddenly surfaced, making vain attempts to grab some of the Baldwin fortune. One surprise did emerge from the reading of the will: Baldwin had a daughter, previously unacknowledged. The following is offered to clarifiy the relationships between Baldwin and the known women and children in his life.

WIVES

Sarah Ann Unruh—Married, 1846. Divorced, 1862.
   Daughter, Clara.
   Daughter, Elizabeth (1854-1855).
   Son, E. J., Jr. (Born 1857, lived two weeks).
Mary Cochrane—Married, 1869. Divorced, 1875.
Jennie Dexter—Married, 1879. Died, 1881.
   Daughter, Anita.
Martha Agnes Fowler—(marriage and divorce undocumented. 1882-1883?)
   Daughter, Rozella.
Lillie Bennett—Married, 1883. Wife at time of Baldwin's death.

RELATIONSHIPS THAT MADE HEADLINES

Lennie McCormack—late 1870s.
   Accused Baldwin of indiscreet behavior and ended up in jail in the process.
Verona Baldwin—1880s.
   Baldwin's cousin, she shot him in the arm and later accused him of ruining her in body and mind and of fathering her child.

INTRODUCTION

Louise C. Perkins—Trial in 1887.
$5 million suit for alleged breach of promise.
Lillian Ashley—1890s.
Accused Baldwin of seducing her and fathering her child. Her sister attempted to kill Baldwin by shooting him in the head during the courtroom proceedings. She inadvertantly jerked the barrel of her revolver and the bullet went harmlessly into the wall.

RANCHO SANTA ANITA

After Baldwin's death, his daughter, Anita, took over the lakeside cottage and 3,500 of the surrounding acres, running it more as a ranching concern than as a farm. In 1934 she sold 214 acres to the Los Angeles Turf Club, which built the present Santa Anita Racetrack on the parcel. Two years later she sold her remainng 1,300 acres to a syndicate headed by Harry Chandler of the *Los Angeles Times*. During the late 1930s and the 1940s, parts of several motion pictures were filmed on the Chandler portion of the ranch, notably *African Queen* with Humphrey Bogart and *Road to Singapore* with Bob Hope and Bing Crosby.

In 1947 the State of California and the County of Los Angeles jointly purchased the 111-acre heart of the original rancho as a site for an arboretum. Open to the public and supported in part by the California Arboretum Foundation, these key historical structures from Baldwin's past may be visited:

The Queen Anne Cottage, which in Baldwin's day accommodated visitors to the ranch.
The Coach Barn, built in 1879, now restored with Baldwin's 1876 coach, the Tally-Ho, on display.
Santa Anita Train Depot, built in 1890, relocated to the arboretum grounds, and renovated in 1970.

INTRODUCTION

THE AUTHOR

Carl B. Glasscock's classic *Lucky Baldwin: The Story of an Unconventional Success* has long been out of print. Anyone desiring a copy had to search the shelves of antiquarian book dealers or libraries. This new edition, which faithfully reproduces all of the original photographs, will again make this fascinating story available to the general reading public.

I first encountered Glasscock's writing in the *Death Valley Chuck-Walla,* written and published by Glasscock and his partner Court Kunze in Greenwater, California, from January to June of 1907. Original copies of the *Chuck-Walla* are now very rare; only the Bancroft Library at UC-Berkeley has a complete set. In that charming, diminutive news magazine, the early twentieth-century newsman first displayed the light good humor that permeates all his later work.

Glasscock published ten books during his lifetime, and each one met with an excellent public response. This volume presents his authentic, vivacious style in an undocumented, unencumbered, no-index format. I know you will relish Glasscock's rendition of the life and times of a true California and Nevada pioneer.

DUKE HUBBARD
Meeks Bay Resort
Meeks Bay, California
April 15, 1993

LUCKY BALDWIN

CHAPTER I

A NEW SPIRIT IN AMERICA

IN THE year 1828 occurred two incidents which should be considered together in justification of this story of an unconventional success. One, known to the twelve million persons who then constituted the population of the United States, was the election of Andrew Jackson to the presidency. The other, known only to half a dozen families in the village of Hamilton, Ohio, was the birth of Elias Jackson Baldwin.

The election of Andrew Jackson signalized the birth of a new spirit in the development of this country. In Elias Jackson Baldwin that spirit was incarnated.

The spirit of America was such as to put into control of the nation's destinies an energetic, fighting individualist, a "man of the people," indifferent to culture and convention, wholly devoted to the advancement of materialistic success without restriction. Baldwin was both a product and a personification of such spirit and such times. Three generations of American forebears, themselves molded in the hard life of the frontier, had contributed to that product.

The life and character of Elias Jackson Baldwin's great-grandfather, grandfather and father were the common life and character of the great body of Americans who had been pushing westward from the colonies since before the Revolution. It was a life that had taught them, of necessity, self-reliance and self-sufficiency. They could build their own houses, make their own clothing, provide their own food, defend their homes from the savages, furnish their own entertainment, preach their own sermons, and for the most part govern themselves. This experience through several generations had bred a notable spirit of individualism.

The so-called West, then reaching to the Mississippi, had brought this spirit of individualism contending for equality of opportunity into control of the national government for the first time in the year of Elias Jackson Baldwin's birth. In an environment in which that spirit was dominant he was to pass the most of his eighty-one crowded years.

It was an environment in which there was little thought of the refinements of life. The mere task of making a living occupied most of the waking hours of the people. They had elected Andrew Jackson to the presidency because they believed him to be an honest courageous frontiersman, one of themselves, unhampered by cultural or other theories, who would make life easier and more prosperous by assuring them the individual opportunities which they craved. Their action was instinctive rather than reasoned.

So, on April 3, 1828, Elias Jackson Baldwin, in the fourth generation of his line in America, added his first howls to the voices of those millions of Americans who were howling down the cultural and intellectual integrity of John Quincy Adams. His life began with the new American régime of unrestrained individual opportunity.

He was as well equipped as the most exacting infant could hope to be for the tasks and accomplishments before him. Probably the home into which he was born was superior to that of most of his neighbors. At least his father, William Alexander Crooks Baldwin, had had time to make it so. He also had been born on that farm. Apparently less restless than most frontiersmen, a point which may account for the stability of some features of Elias Baldwin's character, William Baldwin had remained on the farm.

There he had taken his bride, Elizabeth Nancy Miller, daughter of a neighboring farmer, and there he remained while five children, George Washington, Sarah Ann, Elizabeth, Elias Jackson and Evaline, were born. William Baldwin was a preacher as well as a farmer, and was honored and respected among the villagers of Hamilton.

The baby, Elias Jackson, came into a home where he was welcomed, though three other children had preceded him. He was a bright strong child, filled with nervous energy, curiosity and a tendency to mischief. Naturally affectionate, he submitted readily to his mother's kindly corrections, although too frequently the intensity of his emotions and desires made him go straightway and do the same thing or something similar again. In the same fashion he arose superior to the more emphatic and painful corrections administered by his father.

Neither a pat on the head nor a slap on the bottom seemed to have any permanent influence on the small Elias. That fact is attested in family reminiscences and proved in the character of the man into which the boy was to grow. Elias Jackson Baldwin was born an individualist in a nation of individualists which had just come into this birthright and was prepared to take advantage of it.

By heredity he had the strength of mind and body, the resourcefulness developed through three generations which had fought for life and independence in the wilderness. The influence of his environment, the spirit of the times into which he was born and which he was to personify, was tremendous. The simplicity, the opportunity, the freedom of the West, which had been expanding with the frontier for a third of a century, had brought the nation back to the principles of its founders: liberty, equality, opportunity.

With strong, rude, unconventional men promoting such principles and opportunity in control of the government, a new wave in the rolling tides of advancement upon the frontier was inevitable. The Erie Canal recently had greatly stimulated the western movement. The Ohio and Mississippi Rivers were dotted with flatboats and rafts bringing thousands of Americans from the grinding hopeless labor of the eastern mills and shipping centers to the cheap lands, the free life, the greater opportunities of the West.

Ohio became as densely populated as New Jersey. To the western Americans of 1828, that seemed crowded. The Baldwin family chafed under such close contact, thereby revealing their frontier spirit. William Baldwin decided to move. In Indiana there would be less than half as many neighbors. Land was just as good, and far cheaper. Opportunity was correspondingly greater. And in 1834, when Elias Jackson Baldwin was six years old, his father sold the farm on which he and his father before him had been born, loaded his household goods and family into two wagons, each drawn by four horses, and set out on the newly surveyed trail which promised to be a road from southwestern Ohio to northwestern Indiana.

Doubtless the boy was overjoyed at the adventure. He was that sort of boy. From the time he had been able to walk his eager curiosity and abounding energy had carried him into every activity of the farm. He was always under foot, investigating the mysteries of the stable, the secrets of the henhouse, the family life of the pigs. When his father had warmed his small posterior for stealing apples stored in the loft, the boy had not waited for his tears to dry before setting out on a tour of exploration of the woodlot and the creek bottom.

He had stocked the horse trough with tadpoles, pulled hairs from the horses' tails and immersed them in the expectation that they would grow into hair snakes, hounded his father for a bow and arrow to hunt rabbits in the corn-field, and had generally made a nuisance of himself. His older brother,

Washington, had revealed no such abounding energy. William Baldwin compared his sons and with some intelligence attempted to divert young Elias's energy to useful purpose.

The child had been learning to dodge the stamping feet of the stabled horses since his creeping days. He had no fear. As soon as he was tall enough to reach to the bellies of the horses he had been given a currycomb and told to go to work. He was delighted. No crusted mud or stable litter remained thereafter on the hocks and legs of the Baldwin farm horses. His father could complete the job swiftly where Elias could not reach, and gain time to go into the woods for a mess of pigeons or an occasional deer or wild turkey. And Elias might go with him, lugging bow and arrows and longing for a gun.

To such a boy the prospect of a three weeks' journey by wagon across the wilds of Indiana to a new land which his imagination had peopled with Indians, trappers, wild horses and game, must have been a foretaste of heaven. To sleep under the stars, to cook upon a camp-fire, to ford the creeks and ferry the rivers, to fish with his brother, to hunt with his father; could anything be finer? The pioneer spirit bred into him through three generations of frontiersmen soared. And soaring, it realized and justified itself, however subconsciously.

The hardships were nothing to the boy. Probably he had never heard the word. He was accustomed to rough fare, a hard and lumpy bed, to the sting of sleet upon his face in winter and the sting of insects in summer. His mother and sisters might complain; his brother Wash, more stolid, would not; his father, a man, would not; he himself, eager and interested, would not. It seemed a glorious adventure.

It was in fact, though of course the boy did not suspect it, a typical event in mankind's glorious adventure of settling a continent, of building a new nation dedicated to the principle that all men should have equal opportunity in the pursuit of what they believed to be happiness. The Baldwin wagons were not alone on the ruts of the trail from the Ohio River to Lake Michigan. Others were before them, others behind them, others to the north and south, all rolling, ever rolling westward.

For Elias it was but the first great adventure, the first stage of a journey that would carry him as it would carry the nation simultaneously to undreamed accomplishments. At the moment each day was sufficient unto itself.

Each sunset found the little party twenty or thirty miles farther on its way. William Baldwin, driving the four horses of the lead wagon, would cast about him for a camping place combining the advantages of feed and water for the stock, fuel for the camp-fire, and dry ground a little removed from the mosquitoes of the creek bottoms. If there were woods near by which might yield pigeons for the pot, or a stream which might furnish a mess of catfish, so much the better.

William Baldwin would guide his team from the road to the selected camp site. Elizabeth Nancy Baldwin, with Elias on the seat beside her and the little girls disposed upon the bedding in the rear, would follow. Quickly the horses were unhooked and led away to water. Then they were staked out upon the best feed available. In the meantime the mother and children gathered sticks sufficient to start a fire. The father might take his muzzle-loading shotgun and move out in search of some small game. Wash would cut a willow pole, dig some grubs and fish the holes of the meandering stream. The little girls would hunt for berries in the thickets or for watercress in the shallows. To Elias always fell the task of grooming the horses—as far as he could reach.

For the first time in his brief life he sensed injustice, and protested. The protest netted him about as much as do most individual protests against injustice. He was told that grooming the horses was the only way in which he could do his part of the necessary work. Wash, less nervous and more lazy, was a better fisherman. His father needed the time to bring in game to supplement the family larder. His mother had to cook and wash and mend and nurse the baby, Evaline.

Driven back to the task which he had learned so well and so eagerly on the farm where adventures did not beckon on every hand, the boy swallowed his protests but did not change his mind concerning the injustice. But he did not sulk. He curried frantically to finish his work and be free. At last it was done, but the day was almost done with it. Too late to go fishing. Elias looked around for something else to do. A rabbit was sizzling in the frying pan.

The boy watched his chance, seized a leg when his mother's back was turned and dodged behind a wagon. There he consumed the leg, and felt better. Virtue might be its own reward but a fried leg of rabbit was far more comforting to a hungry boy.

The family gathered around a pot of hominy and the pan of fried rabbit in the dusk while the mother dished out the food upon tin plates and placed a slab of corn pone upon each. There was only one rabbit, and six persons to eat it. Elizabeth Baldwin was quick to note the absence of one leg. Her suspicions instantly and accurately alighted upon Elias.

The little boy drew back, wide-eyed, but fearless. He was hungry. He had curried all the horses while Wash and his father were having all the fun, fishing and everything.

The mother's indignation cooled. Not so the farmer-preacher father's. He'd have no thieving in his family. He picked up the willow switch upon which Wash's catfish had been strung, and grasped his son by one shoulder. The boy shivered, blinked and turned appealing eyes to his mother. His father laid on the switch. Welts arose under the thin cotton shirt. The boy's teeth came down upon his lip. Tears squeezed between tight-shut eyelids, but he did not cry out.

The correction administered, he was ordered to bed without his supper. Suppressing a sob, he went to the rear end of the wagon, pulled out a roll of "kivers," spread them upon the ground beneath the wagon and hid himself within them. There he listened to the succulent sounds of the vanishing supper, and comforted himself as best he could with the memory that he had had at least a leg of rabbit before all the trouble started.

Supper over, father and Wash moved away to the creek, leading the horses to water. Sairy and Liza were put to work washing up the plates. Elias felt a gentle hand upon his shoulder, and thrust his head from the "kivers." It was his mother, with a generous slice of corn pone spread thickly with molasses. The child ate, and was comforted.

But all days were not the same. Far from it. There were some when he was permitted to go with his father at daybreak in search of a deer or antelope for the depleted larder. When he happened to be first to spot the game in some thicket and his father had bagged it, Elias was as elated as if he had brought it down himself. Then, with his father in good humor, he would plead for a gun of his own, always to be put off with the assurance that he could have it when he earned it.

There was the day on which he had gazed upon the marvels of the city of Indianapolis, a city of several hundred population, the largest the boy had ever imagined.

There were long afternoons on the jolting wagon seat beside his father in which the boy's eager curiosity doubtless prompted the man to reminiscence and prophecy. William Baldwin had had some advantages over most frontiersmen, and at heart was a kindly man though with a heavy hand against "sin" as he conceived it, and a firm belief that to spare the rod was to spoil the child. Doubtless such a man would warm to the child's interest and tell him something of the background of his family and of his country, and of the future for which he hoped. Probably the father told the boy of his own childhood experiences when he was kidnapped and held for months by marauding Indians. Probably the boy longed for such an experience himself, and plied his father with questions concerning the possibility.

Indians still roamed the Indiana prairies, though their numbers had been greatly reduced and their menace virtually eliminated since the famous battle of Tippecanoe, twenty-three years earlier. But if William Baldwin explained this to his adventurous small son he must have disappointed the child with the further information that most of the savages had been moved northward and westward under government pressure, and that the government was planning to move them all northward into Michigan Territory and west of the Mississippi.

Probably he told him also that even the Indiana country was being rapidly settled, that it was rich farm land, and that some day there would be many big towns there, as big as Indianapolis which he had seen. Already other towns had started. Logansport, Lafayette, Terre Haute and others were already on the crude map by which William Baldwin was setting his course. Soon there would be regular stage-coaches running between them, and growing business which could not thrive among hostile Indians. Even the bears and wolves, and perhaps the deer and antelope which roamed the unfenced miles, would be killed off or driven away.

Most of the better land had already been taken up. It was hardly pioneering to move from Ohio even as far as northwestern Indiana in 1834. The real pioneers had arrived fifteen or twenty years earlier. William Baldwin expected to pay as much as four or five dollars an acre for the farm he planned to buy near Terre Coupee Town, a few miles west of the settlement of South Bend.

It must have been disappointing to the boy to be told that there were to be no more such opportunities of adventure as his father and grandfather had enjoyed. But if the character of his later life is any criterion of the character of the child, he comforted himself with plans for other activities and adventures suggested by his father's forecasts. Elias Jackson Baldwin was a child of action. He did not brood.

Jolting along over the ruts he pictured stages dashing from town to town in the Wabash Valley through which the wagon was moving slowly day after day. Perhaps he would be a stage driver. He had never heard of a railroad.

CHAPTER II

TERRE COUPEE TOWN

THE road from Cincinnati to Lake Michigan, surveyed and marked by an act of the Indiana General Assembly passed in 1828, was a well-defined but otherwise little improved route when the Baldwin family traveled it in the first stage of Elias Jackson Baldwin's preparation for a checkered career.

The village of Indianapolis, boasting ninety families in 1832, had more than doubled its population when the Baldwin family passed through it two years later. Its streets were crowded with men, women and children, wagons, horses, cattle, hogs and sheep, looking eagerly or wearily as the case might be to the founding of new homes and the making of new farms and cities in the wilderness.

Still, when the wagons and stock scattered out toward Crawfordsville, Terre Haute and Logansport they did not crowd the routes. But there was a sense of suppressed excitement, of concerted movement, of a flowing stream of humanity, of indomitable purpose aimed toward the building of a greater nation.

At swampy creek bottoms the heavily laden wagons frequently mired so deep that men and women and children had to join in the labor of cutting brush and saplings to corduroy a way through the mire. Other emigrants, halted behind the bogged wagons, lent a hand. The roads were built by those who used them more consciously than the present concrete highways are built from the funds of the gasoline burners who cover in a day a distance which then consumed weeks. Elias Jackson Baldwin learned so to build, to his own purposes.

Whatever else it may have been it was not a dull nor unproductive journey to the boy. Neither was Terre Coupee Town, the family's objective some ten miles west of South Bend, a disappointment, although he had been hearing about it for months at his father's home in Ohio.

He gazed from the wagon seat with the appraising but proud eye of an owner. It was not much of a town as towns went, even in the Indiana of that early day. Even its name was soon to be changed from Terre Coupee Town to Hamilton. But it thrilled Elias's farm-bred soul.

Scattered along the dusty street between trees and vacant lots were two general stores, a blacksmith shop, a tinshop, a carpenter and cooper shop, a stable and feed yard, and at one end a rambling structure with the odor of a tannery. A sign, "Doctor," hanging from a tree in front of a small white cottage thrilled the child's mother with its evidence of metropolitan advantages. She looked in vain for a church, however, and decided that Terre Coupee must be a heathen town. That she decided promptly to correct that condition, and carried her plan through as the Baldwins usually carried their plans through, was indicated a year later when a church was built.

Elias could get along nicely without the church. He was far more interested in the stores, and demanded to know if they couldn't stop and buy something. When told that they might come back after supper he subsided, despite his excitement, careful not to risk a definite refusal.

The little caravan drew out beyond the village, and William Baldwin turned his team out from the road to make camp. The children swarmed down from the wagons and Elias made himself useful in an effort to maintain himself sufficiently in the good graces of his parents to be permitted to inspect the wonders of the village after the chores were done. His industry and eagerness were rewarded.

Supper finished, the boy trudged happily through the dust to the village in company with the entire family. The two general stores were marvelous in his eyes. He entered the first on the heels of his father as eagerly as he might have stepped into Aladdin's cave.

A counter of whip-sawed planks, worn smooth by use, extended along one side. Behind the counter was a wall striped by shelves, gaudy calicos on one, "bunnits" filling another with color in the gardens of flowers which formed their "face trimmin'," gay shawls and bandannas, men's shirts and beaver hats, shelf above shelf to the top. There a row of gleaming tinware erupted against the ceiling and spread out half-way across the room with pots and pans and pails hanging in an indiscriminate jumble, giving starry reflection on high to the light of two coal-oil lanterns and half a dozen tallow candles.

At the rear the counter turned the corner to form the grocery department, with several uncut cheeses on the first shelf behind it, and firkins of butter, baskets of eggs, stacks of yellow soap bars, crocks of honey, bags of tea and coffee, piling up and up to the top shelf where slabs of bacon, hams and strings of dried apples and onions erupted against the ceiling in competition with the tinware.

We can hardly go wrong if we picture Elias climbing on one of the flour barrels which buttressed the counter and feasting his eyes. Immediately before him were three fly-specked glass jars, one of which contained mysterious brown lozenges, one striped sticks of red and white, and one black sticks of strange promise. The child's experience with sweets had been confined to wild honey, molasses and an occasional lump of maple sugar. But the sure instinct of childhood must have told him that those three jars contained horehound drops, peppermint sticks and licorice. He tugged at the skirts of his mother, watching the storekeeper weigh out flour on the steel-yards suspended from a beam above the counter.

The mother shook him off, and questioned the storekeeper

concerning matters of more vital interest to her. She learned that hens' eggs were selling at three cents a dozen, duck eggs at two cents, and turkey eggs at three cents. It was a mite high, but most folks were setting their eggs just then. She could get setting hens for seven or eight cents apiece.

Elias tugged again, and indicated his overwhelming desire for one of the red and white sticks in the middle jar. The storekeeper grinned, thrust a floury hand into the jar and presented the child with a peppermint stick. Mrs. Baldwin thanked him, and negotiated for the purchase of a few hens as soon as the family was settled on the new farm.

The storekeeper beamed at the news that the Baldwins were planning to join the community and settle on the Joseph Galloway farm of eighty acres a little beyond the village. Here was a potential steady customer. He presented Mrs. Baldwin and the little girls each with a stick of peppermint. Washington chose the darker delights of licorice.

The storekeeper assured the woman that Joe Galloway was certainly aiming to sell his farm. Getting too crowded for him. Going out west to Illinois or mebbe Iowa and take him up some new land. Restless sort of feller, Joe. Reckless, too. Was there something else Mrs. Baldwin needed?

Yes, a jug of molasses. Elias produced the jug from beneath his feet, and the storekeeper filled it slowly from a barrel. William Baldwin was summoned from conversation with a group of loungers to pay the bill, which he did with a few cents' worth of silver. Then he was himself formally welcomed to Terre Coupee Town with a tin cupful of whisky poured from a wickered demijohn under the counter. A competent man could sustain his spirit with both prayer and hard liquor in the America of 1834.

On the way back to the wagons for the night, Elias decided that perhaps he had better be a storekeeper than a stage driver. He made the announcement with the added observation that

Lucky Baldwin's horses, driven by C. C. West, bringing home the thrills in one of the Roman holiday events which were a feature of the turfman's last years.

"The Cottage," on Santa Anita Ranch, built for a club house but generally
used by Baldwin as a private retreat.

Between pine and eucalyptus. A scene revealing some of the improvements
under Baldwin on the famous Santa Anita Ranch.

Santa Anita Depot, built in 1890 by the Santa Fe on Baldwin's ranch. The furnishings of the relocated and renovated depot are authentic of the late 1800s.

FOUR GENERATIONS
E. J. Baldwin, center; Clara Baldwin Stocker, right; Rosebudd Doble
Mullender, left; Joseph Mullender, lower left.

The Coach Barn, built in 1879. Its interior is decorated in cedar and redwood paneling and iron work. It housed the Tally-Ho coach and several carriages.

Jennie Dexter, Baldwin's third wife and mother of his daughter Anita.

At forty-seven when he was first president of the Pacific Stock Exchange.

At fifty-seven when he was being sued by the nineteen-year-old Louise Perkins.

Near the end of his career.

Nearing seventy and near the height of his racing career.

E. J. BALDWIN.

The Baldwin Hotel and Theatre, San Francisco, 1877-1898. This was Baldwin's pride and monument until it was destroyed by fire.

Indian attack on the Baldwin party near Salt Lake City in 1853, as pictured by artist Cross, from Lucky Baldwin's description.

Lucky overlooked no bets. He even marked the cards—with advertising of his ranch lands.

The ornate barroom in the Baldwin Hotel as it appeared between drinks in the '80s.

The Oakwood Hotel, near the Santa Anita Ranch. It was famous as a roadhouse in the '90s, and burned without insurance in 1912.

Baldwin's Tallac Hotel on Lake Tahoe.

MRS. ANITA BALDWIN.

LOUISE C. PERKINS.

A session of poker in Lucky's private quarters in the Baldwin Hotel. Lucky is at the left.

Anita Baldwin with Rey el Santa Anita, of the strain of Lucky's Derby winners.

the storekeeper was a smart man. Questioned by his father, mellowing under the influence of his quarter pint of whisky, the boy explained that he had heard a man laughing in the group of loungers and saying that the storekeeper had raised the price of molasses enough to pay for the peppermint sticks he had given away. It looked like good business to Elias.

And that was an era in which good business in America was fast coming to be its own justification. Elias Jackson Baldwin was absorbing the ethics of his time and place. Into the active, independent self-sufficiency of mind conferred upon him by three generations of frontiersmen, such ethics fell as seed into prepared ground. Promptly they were cultivated by his ambition, watered by his intelligence and warmed by his eager observation of the men and life about him.

America was booming in the second term of Andrew Jackson's administration. To the rough and ready westerners who had been largely instrumental in putting him into the presidency, that was sufficient evidence that their theories of government and of the promotion of equal opportunities for every man were correct. Their contempt for the conventions of the East and South increased with their prosperity and independence.

The spoils system had been established in national politics. Success, which they measured in terms of money-making, was the god of the people. Any business methods which led to success justified themselves. As industry became the greatest virtue, idleness became the greatest vice. The old-fashioned virtues of honesty, sobriety and chastity were of minor importance.

Western lands had doubled in value—at least in appraised value—since Jackson's first election. The sale of federal lands to settlers and speculators, financed by eastern capital, was multiplied by five in the first two years of the Baldwin family's residence in Indiana. Even the federal treasury had more money than it knew what to do with. The last instalment of the national debt had been paid off in 1835, and the tariff was bringing in more money than Jackson believed the government had a right to spend under the constitution. The country, ripe for an orgy of speculation, proceeded to speculate.

That was the dominating spirit of America, the spirit of the West, the spirit of Terre Coupee Town, of a thousand similar villages taking root in the Mississippi Valley in 1834. In that spirit came William Baldwin at the age of thirty-four, and his family including Elias Jackson Baldwin at the age of six, to Terre Coupee Town, and in that spirit he was welcomed. Any man who added himself and his family to a new settlement in those days was welcomed. Each village looked upon itself as a potential metropolis, a center of trade, travel and industry.

Two days after little Elias Baldwin had noted that a storekeeper could make up the gift of half a dozen sticks of candy by the simple process of raising the price of a jug of molasses, and had thereupon decided to be a storekeeper instead of a stage driver, he was installed with the rest of his family in the house vacated by Joseph Galloway. It commanded eighty acres of farm land, a young apple orchard, a log barn, pigpens, and a fox- and skunk-proof hen-house. The home was what was then known as a double cabin, containing two goodsized rooms and a loft, solidly built of fitted logs, with whipsawed plank floors and a substantial slab roof.

The house was furnished comfortably enough with furniture brought from the Ohio home. The Baldwins were a family of more cultivated tastes and somewhat better education than the average frontier stock. They were proud of an ancestry which they traced back to a pure British strain. They made their influence felt quickly in their new environment. Within a year a church was built, and a schoolhouse soon followed.

Elias and his brother Wash, though small children, labored almost as diligently as did their father on the farm and their mother and sisters in the house. In the winters they attended the village school. In the spring they hoed the truck patch, cleaned the hen-house, milked the cows, drove the wagon to the village to exchange farm products for such necessities as they did not produce on the farm. In the summers they hoed the corn, raked hay and tended live stock. In the autumns they husked corn, helped with the butchering and piled the winter's fuel.

For recreation they advanced quickly from mumble-peg and marbles to fishing and hunting. In this they were aided and abetted by their nearest neighbor, Jeremiah Garoutte, on the adjoining farm to the eastward. Young Jerry, evidently considered more dependable than most lads of his age, was the proud owner of an old flint-lock muzzle-loading shotgun. Elias trailed him admiringly for miles along the creek bottoms and through the thickets in search of bob-whites, foxes, anything that might be dignified as game.

When, after a long period of such service during which Elias had been permitted to lug the heavy gun over such areas as promised no shooting, he was allowed to fire at a crouching rabbit, the gun kicked him flat, but he arose grinning, thrilled to the depths of his being. He had killed the rabbit. The friendship between the two boys was sealed.

Elias Baldwin never forgot that favor. Many years later he proved the endurance of this boyish admiration and affection. Neither did Jeremiah Garoutte forget. When he had become prosperous, settled and respected, and Baldwin was a multimillionaire, unsettled and notorious, Garoutte was the best potential source of anecdote concerning Baldwin's boyhood until gossip concerning the latter became so scandalous that Garoutte's reminiscences were frowned upon by a conventional wife. Baldwin's affairs became known to hundreds of thousands; Garoutte's respectability to hundreds. Each was content.

But in the meantime another boy came to the little community of Terre Coupee. His name was Schuyler Colfax, a serious-minded but active lad, older than the other boys, but nevertheless an addition to their group. Schuyler also owned a gun, and was generous. Elias knew more places where wild turkeys might be found than any boy in the district. He was tough, tireless and uncomplaining, and was always permitted to go along, and sometimes to shoot. He grew to be almost as fast a friend and admirer of the Colfax boy who was to become vice-president of the United States as he was of Jerry Garoutte. Not quite.

Occasional shooting of another boy's gun was not sufficient for Elias Baldwin. He wanted a gun of his own, and determined to have it. It was in the winter of 1837, the time of the nation's first great financial panic. The Baldwin family fortunes were in a sad way. Elias, in common with the nation, was absorbing painful lessons in economics.

The economic difficulties of 1819 had been to the panic of 1837 hardly more than the difficulties of 1921 were to the depression beginning in 1929. The displacement of such substantial moral values as honesty and sobriety by the virtue of money-making had produced a national orgy of speculation.

The stock-market was unheralded, but the developments of those years proved beyond question that when men wish to gamble or to speculate they will find or develop a medium. In that period, land, banks and transportation agencies were the medium. Land valuations generally throughout the twenty-five states which then constituted the union had doubled and trebled, and in some areas multiplied by ten during the Jackson administration.

The experience of the nation in the decade from 1830 to 1840 appears to have been strikingly similar to that in the decade from 1923 to 1933. Under Andrew Jackson the country as a whole had prospered, just as it did during the administration of Calvin Coolidge. Speculation swelled to heights of madness. The bubble grew and grew. Hardly had Jackson been succeeded in the White House by Van Buren when the bubble burst, just as a similar bubble was to burst in the face of President Hoover.

Banks throughout the country suspended specie payments or failed entirely. Private and public enterprise was suspended. Valuations which had been built on inflated credit vanished. Farms and plantations were put up for forced sale at one-tenth their valuations of the previous year. Half the workmen and clerks in New York, Philadelphia and other important cities were thrown out of employment. Nine-tenths of the factories in the country closed. Shipping was paralyzed. The rich became poor and the poor destitute.

Indiana, the home of the Baldwins, was hit as hard as any, and harder than some. Only a year before the bursting of the bubble the state had undertaken a great transportation development, including several hundred miles of canals which were designed to put its farm products into world markets at a tenth of earlier prohibitive costs. Millions of dollars' worth of bonds had been authorized and some millions sold. With the panic all market for the bonds vanished, and the state defaulted its interest. Most of the projects were abandoned. Creditors took over improvements already completed. The state's credit was ruined. Its farmers were without a market.

Beef sold at retail for two cents a pound, pork at one and one-half cents, lard at three cents. Butter, salted down in firkins and freighted all the way to Cincinnati brought only six cents. Corn was virtually valueless, and the whisky into which it was distilled could be purchased for nineteen cents a gallon.

LUCKY BALDWIN

William Baldwin was being hounded to pay the two-hundred-dollar mortgage on his eighty acres, owed to Hormal Reed and Martin D. Clark, and could not. Little Sarah Ann Baldwin died that year. The situation had not improved the father's temper, and he became more certain than ever that to spare the rod was to spoil the child. In such circumstances life on the Baldwin farm was not conducive to the happiness of a nine-year-old boy.

His ambition for a gun and a horse of his own had been too long thwarted. He had done what seemed to him to be a man's work about the farm and his reward had been an increasingly heavy hand from his father, and only an occasional bit of comfort from a mother wearied by labor, worried by want and strained by the agony of watching a little daughter die.

But the boy's ambition had waxed rather than waned in the face of disappointment and denial. He was willing to work for that horse and gun, but he wanted the reward of his labor. Perhaps the spirit of speculation and adventure which was to move him throughout a long and checkered career also was at work.

He gave the matter thought, and decided that he would run away and make his fortune. With only his school lunch of corn bread, fried salt pork and an apple for supplies, he started for the Mississippi, determined to go to St. Louis and become a fur trader. But it was in the dead of winter, and after spending a night in an abandoned cabin in a snow-storm the adventure ended as such boyish adventures usually end.

CHAPTER III

INDIANA IN THE '40S

Two more monotonous and disappointing years passed on the farm. For young Baldwin they were only slightly relieved by such stimulating talk as he heard among his elders at home, at the Colfax farm and at the Garoutte farm concerning a new wave of emigration which was flowing over Indiana. Wagons such as those in which he himself had moved from Ohio were again passing almost daily along the rough country roads. Their drivers or their children explained that they were going into Michigan, into Illinois, or on to the Territories of Wisconsin and Iowa.

The panic of 1837 had started a vast new wave of emigration. The spirit of America was again seeking in the West the freedom, opportunity and independence which it had lost temporarily in the economic collapse of the East. Elias listened eagerly as he heard it all explained by his elders.

In the West lay opportunity. The memories of prosperity in the preceding decade were still vivid. The spirit of the nation had been chastened but the ambition and code of its individuals had not been greatly altered. In the West, just beyond the Mississippi, any man could take up a farm, start a store, make a fortune. And under the demands of the time, boys were men at the age of puberty.

They did a man's work, developed a man's self-reliance, traded with a man's shrewdness, and dreamed the American man's dream of making a quick fortune. Elias Baldwin was typical. He worked from dawn to dusk outside of his few hours in school, and had nothing to show for it. Stimulated by the talk of prospective fortunes which he heard, he decided again to branch out for himself. This time, however, he chose the summer, and formulated a definite plan.

One job at which a boy with stamina could be as useful as a man was that of driving hogs to the packing houses at Cincinnati. The price of hogs in recent years had been so low that it had not paid to move them to the distant market. The Baldwin drove had grown to nearly two hundred. Elias broached his idea to his father.

He would take the hogs and join one of the big droves that would soon be going out of South Bend. He would get a good price for them. He was a good trader.

William Baldwin considered. It was a long drive. The hogs would lose a lot of weight. But he needed cash badly, and he had faith in this upstanding son with the shrewd hazel eyes. Elias argued. There were so many hogs that they could not feed them until the next corn crop came in. With all the hogs out of the way he would not be so badly needed on the farm.

The father wanted to be convinced, and agreed to think it over. Elias felt that he had won his point. He was certain of it next day when his father told him that Tom Libby and Isaac Brundage were planning to take a drove in from the Libby and Colfax places. There might be others from east of the Bend.

Elias was delighted. He assured his father that he would get a good price, and that he'd be careful to keep up the weight of the animals by the strictest attention to the task of putting them on the best feeding-grounds at every stop. They would be earmarked so that he could keep them more or less separated from the others for that purpose. They would average one hundred and fifty pounds each at the packing house. Could he have what they weighed above that?

But the father was a shrewd trader also. He couldn't accept the first proposition made. At last he agreed to give the boy whatever he could above one hundred and sixty pounds average on the hogs at the slaughter house.

Elias took the road joyfully with the hogs, Wash following into South Bend with the farm wagon containing Elias's roll of "kivers" and his grub-box to be loaded upon the drove wagon. Grunting and squealing in a cloud of dust the dozen small droves which were to take the road assembled on the outskirts of the town and moved slowly southward. Elias trudged, caked with dust and perspiration, doing the best he could to keep his own hogs sufficiently segregated so that he could move them out to the best roadside pasturage at each stop. Stopping to camp each night he ignored his own weariness and hunger while he cut out his own hogs and urged them into stretches of meadow where the grass grew richest and into bits of woodland where the mast lay most thickly.

But the journey was not all labor. On the evening of the third of July the dust cloud which covered the drove and drovers settled down at the edge of open fields two or three miles from Logansport. They had been on the road for several days, and were weary and dirty. Tom Libby, as captain of the drive, had ridden on to the next farmhouse and returned beaming and redolent of corn liquor to announce that there was a wedding going on, and that he had received permission to pasture the hogs not only overnight but for two days, and in addition an invitation for the drovers to join the wedding party. Some of the drovers could go to the wedding feast and dance, and the others remain with the hogs. On the following day Logansport was to have a rip-snortin' Fourth-of-July celebration, and those who missed the wedding could go to the celebration.

Quite naturally, young Elias wanted to do both. But he gave the matter thought. The wedding, he suspected, would mean large quantities of food, which he could enjoy, and larger quantities of whisky, which he could not enjoy. The attendant dancing and horseplay might or might not be enjoyable. The Fourth-of-July celebration, on the other hand, probably would offer an equal amount of entertainment in the way of food, and much more in the way of fireworks, games, parades and so forth which promised a real thrill to a youngster. And last but not least, in the absence of competition he could maneuver his hogs into the best pasturage in the neighborhood. He decided in favor of the Fourth-of-July celebration for himself.

While the young men went whooping away to the wedding, and the older ones sat and smoked, the boy segregated his ear-marked hogs to the best of his ability and herded them into a stretch of woodland where the rooting was most succulent. Then he rolled in his "kivers" and awaited the dawn. At day-break he was awakened by the returning wedding guests who told mouth-watering tales of the feast of roast wild turkey, saddle of venison, a vast assortment of vegetables, bowls of wild honey, pies of a dozen varieties, and great pots of coffee with the "fixins" of cream and maple sugar, not to mention a barrel of corn whisky and drinking gourds conveniently placed. They had drunk and eaten through the night and danced to a lone fiddler's repeated rendition of *Leather Breeches* until they could eat and drink and dance no more.

It had been a gay night, but Elias, clear-eyed and eager for his own day, was glad that he had chosen as he did. He breakfasted on cold corn pone, herded his hogs into fresh pasturage and trudged away to Logansport to the celebration. The village was gay with flags and bunting, and crowded with an assemblage of farmers, storekeepers and mechanics from miles around. Elias had missed the sunrise cannon salute and flag-raising, but was in ample time for the parade. He scuffed bare feet in the dust of the village street and gazed wide-eyed at the line of marchers, headed by a fife and drum corps, followed by school-children with red, white and blue sashes, politicians in plug hats, and "highly respectable citizens and a few venerable worthies of the Revolution still surviving," according to the local newspaper account of the day's program.

Elias fell in with the other spectators behind the procession and followed to the grove for the ceremony of another flag-raising, the reading of the Declaration of Independence, and a florid address by a rustic orator. Probably it would have been a sad bore to a twelve-year-old boy of this day, but it was a tremendous and never-to-be-forgotten spectacle to the farm-bred child of 1840 who had never seen such a vast crowd—perhaps a thousand persons—in his life. He thrilled alike to the perfervid oratory and the punctuating boom of cannons, and glowed with the first realization of his birthright as an American citizen.

When the feast was set out at the conclusion of the ceremonies the boy was almost too excited to eat. And it must have been a greater day for the orators than it was for the child. Reading a current account of it nearly one hundred years after the event, we find a list of ten formal toasts, each doubtless accompanied by sufficient words and music and punctuated by cannon shots and volleys of musketry.

Reproduction of the list may not be amiss in the effort to reveal how little the nature of after-dinner speakers has changed in a century. They include (1) The day we celebrate—the sixty-fourth anniversary of our country's freedom; (2) The memory of those illustrious patriots who, etc.; (3) In memory of George Washington; (4) Officers and soldiers of the Revolution; (5) The President of the United States; (6) The Vice-president and heads of Departments; (7) The Constitution of the United States; (8) The People; (9) Our Flag; (10) The American fair.

By that time excitement, food and corn liquor were not to be denied. Volunteer orators demanded recognition from the toastmaster, and offered: To the Sovereignty of the People; Our Farmers and Mechanics; The Militia of Indiana; Wisdom, Strength and Beauty; General Lafayette; The Love of Country; The People's Servants.

When those toasts also had been drunk probably the orators were no longer able to orate or the assembled crowd to hear. The celebration was ended. Elias, as drunk with excitement and pride in his Americanism as were some of his elders with whisky, marched back to his hogs as if to take command of an army. The toast to the officers and soldiers of the Revolution especially had thrilled him to the marrow. He remembered that he had heard his father say that seven Baldwin brothers, among whom was his own great-grandfather, had come from England and settled in America about the year 1700. Surely with so many of the name in the colonies his own direct ancestors must have risen to the need and covered themselves with glory in the Revolution. Elias thrilled at the thought. The perfervid periods of the rustic orator were addressed to him personally as the descendant of a family without whose services the country never would have been free. The Revolution became his Revolution, the Nation his Nation.

For the first time in his life he realized the nature of his birthright. And realizing it he determined to take full advantage of it as all Americans worthy of the name were doing. To him, as an upstanding American boy, it meant freedom, independence, the opportunity to make a profit, to work out what he then conceived to be a glorious destiny, just as the nation appeared to be working out a glorious destiny, hewing to the line of success, let the chips fall where they might.

It was the beginning of a life of extraordinary independence of thought and action, an independence of character which was to make him an outstanding figure of his time, utterly defiant of public opinion or convention. At the moment it was an inspiration which put even hog driving on a higher plane. But it was tempered by his realization of the immediate necessity for work—to get his drove of hogs to the slaughter house with an average weight of more than one hundred and sixty pounds each.

When the drove skirted the town of Indianapolis and stopped in neighboring fields for rest while Tom Libby went to purchase supplies, the boy secretly bought a large bag of salt and secreted it in his bed roll. After that he had time to admire the displays in the store windows and upon the plank sidewalks under the wooden awnings of the stores.

Indianapolis had more than doubled in population since his first stop there with his migrating family in 1834. It was now a city of approximately three thousand population. The stores into which the boy wandered were a veritable museum to his eyes. The Indianapolis Clothing Store displayed a startling assortment of brown and white "grass coats," linen coats, Holland and gingham coats, muslin and gingham shirts, satin, valencia and marseilles vests, and other summer raiment "just received from Baltimore." Another store displayed hoopskirts and basques and shawls in varied patterns, and bonnets with bright-colored birds nesting in flowers beneath the brims. In another were quill pens and inkhorns and writing paper and books.

Elias was not much interested in books, but he knew that his sister Elizabeth was, and he memorized the titles with the thought of repeating them to her. There were the works of Patrick Henry, Collins's Poems, Lockhart's *Burns, The Life of Wilberforce, The Pirate's Own Book, The Sentiment of Flowers, The Language of Flowers.*

If he had arrived a week earlier he might have seen Hume's *History of England,* Johnson's *Lives of the Poets, The Federalist* and some others. But those classics of the time had just been purchased from the bookseller with a fund of fifty dollars appropriated by the General Assembly to establish the Indiana State Library. Elias merely marveled that there were so many books in the world, and went on to complete his inspection of the town and its wonders before returning to his business affairs.

The drove of hogs moved slowly onward. The boy continued to keep his own animals on the best pasturage at each stopping place in so far as he could. The fourth week of driving found them within easy reach of the stockyards. He lugged his sack of salt to his grunting charges. The animals abandoned their pasturage to take the salt, in such quantities as they had never before enjoyed. At the first watering-place they drank to the bursting point. Elias beamed, but kept his counsel. And when the hogs were weighed in, each animal hoisted, squealing and kicking in canvas breeching upon steelyards, the Baldwin consignment averaged ten pounds above the run of the drove. The boy's personal profit, according to his agreement with his father, was thirty-two dollars. Now, at last, at the age of twelve, he was rich.

Home again at the farm, he became a figure of importance. Even his father admitted that the hogs must have been put through with care, skill and judgment. The gifts for mother and sisters were received with thanks and enthusiasm, and the second-hand shotgun which he had purchased for himself was properly admired. And still he had money of his own. Elias Jackson Baldwin could no more allow money to waste in idleness at the age of twelve than he could at any later period in his acquisitive career. He promptly bought a horse.

It wasn't much of a horse, as horses went in Indiana in 1840, but it had possibilities. The boy developed them. Probably no horse in history was ever groomed and fed and tended with greater care. Within three months the animal had so far improved in both appearance and usefulness that it was sold for double its cost. The boy was launched in a business that was to make his name known among horsemen as long as printed records exist and horsemen gather to swap lies, truths or horseflesh.

In 1844, when the family moved to Crawfordsville, then the largest town in northern Indiana, to give the children better schooling than was available at Hamilton, Elias was recognized as an expert in horse-flesh and a trader whose shrewdness belied his youth. He was already, at sixteen, a capitalist with investments of several hundred dollars. His was a native shrewdness, carefully exercised. Perhaps that was why he took little interest in the dry details of reading, writing, arithmetic, geography and so forth which constituted the curriculum of a small-town school in the Middle West in 1844. In business he was a man among men, and shrewder than most, he knew. In the work of the farm, which was the business of all of his associates, he was better than most men. It was contrary to his character to sit at a desk, memorize and "recite." The family experiment in the higher education offered by the Crawfordsville Grammar School lasted only a year.

The Baldwins returned to their farm, and Elias and Washington and their father returned to the plow and harrow, the hoe and the scythe, and to the delights and profit of horse-trading. Also, as a more practical experiment in education William Baldwin allotted a few acres to each of his sons to cultivate and manage as they wished for their own profit.

Elias took a new interest in farming. At about this time too he began to reveal another characteristic which was to be perhaps as great a factor in his life as was his interest in horses, adding even more to notoriety, if not to fame. The boy who could be thrilled by the grace of a high-stepping filly had become a youth who could be similarly enchanted by a neat ankle, momentarily exposed beneath a swaying crinoline.

Apparently when youth began to notice such attractive feminine beauties there was little more to be done about it ninety years ago than there is to-day. Indiana has changed greatly in a century; adolescence little. Nature takes her course.

On a neighboring farm lived Sarah Ann Unruh, a pretty girl with large dark eyes, a smiling mouth, and such feet and ankles as even the voluminous skirts of the time could not conceal completely from young Baldwin's inquiring eye. The Unruhs and the Baldwins were good friends as well as neighbors. In the brief intervals of labor on the farms Elias Baldwin and William Unruh, brother of the delectable Sarah Ann, occasionally hunted and fished together. Returning with strings of fish, or partridges, or perhaps a deer, Elias frequently was a guest at the resulting feast in the spotless kitchen of the Unruh farmhouse.

In addition to a warmly welcoming smile and an alluring ankle, Sarah Ann possessed exceptional skill as a cook. Young and strong, she was never too tired to stroll through the warm twilight evenings with the visiting young man after the meal had been consumed and the pots and dishes washed and put away. The outcome was inevitable.

Talk of war with Mexico and even some tentative business speculation based upon the likelihood of war were increasing at the time. The price of horses was going up and the market was active. Young Baldwin made several profitable deals. With money in his pocket, and a growing confidence in his ability to make more money, he felt that he was in truth a man. A man should have a wife. He was more and more convinced of it when he sat with Sarah Ann beside the open fireplace of the warm and fragrant kitchen after the rest of the Unruh family had gone to bed.

At about this time also young Baldwin acquired additional and more tangible evidence that he was capable of supporting a wife. It took the form of two hundred dollars, won on his own horse in a race at South Bend. There, if a man wanted to use it so, was honeymoon money.

But though he was a man in his own eyes, Elias Baldwin was only eighteen years of age. Early marriages were common enough, but the laws of Indiana were a bit ahead of their time and the consent of parents was required for the marriage of minors. With Sarah Ann's hand in his and her warm red lips upon his lips, this difficulty for Baldwin faded in a purple haze. He hitched his fastest trotter to a new red cutter, bundled the girl in buffalo robes, and drove across the state line to the village of Bertrand, Berrien County, Michigan, a few miles north of South Bend. There he gave his age as twenty-one and Sarah Ann's as eighteen, and attained his greatest ambition since the acquisition of his first horse and gun. Similar ambitions were to run parallel throughout his life.

Returning with his bride to his father's home, he quieted the remonstrances of both families by buckling down to his work with even more energy than in the past. How effectively he did so is indicated by the fact that members of the Unruh family remained his friends throughout a long and checkered career, even at times when friends were sadly lacking.

Through the remainder of that winter and spring he worked as in the past upon his father's farm, drawing no wages, but taking a small profit from the few acres assigned to him and from his shrewd trading of horses. In the summer he rented a small farm adjoining his father's, and made a home of his own. In the autumn he bought a threshing-machine in partnership with his brother-in-law, William Unruh, and made so much money that he was able to sell the second-hand machine at a further profit.

In this variety of activities, farming, threshing, horse-trading, young Baldwin had accumulated nearly two thousand dollars—an impressive capital in the hands of a boy of nineteen in the '40s. Half a century later he was to be widely quoted as saying that it was not the first thousand dollars but the first hundred that were hardest to accumulate, but there is nothing in the early record to show any slackening in his steady acquisition.

But two thousand dollars merely stimulated the youth's ambition. He sought greater opportunity, just as the nation was seeking to expand through the arbitrary war with Mexico. New territory extending to the Pacific was opened to exploitation through that war. Elias Baldwin felt the same urge.

The spirit of the new West, supported by the industries and banks of the East, was aggressive, immoral, indomitable, dominant. America's westward expansion in half a century was perhaps the greatest movement of humanity in recorded history. Baldwin was part and parcel of that movement, the personification of its spirit. His character through half a century was the character of the nation. After that it was the nation that changed, not Baldwin.

For the moment he felt only the urge to expand, to profit from the labor of the less shrewd. He abandoned the labor of the farm and moved with his wife to Valparaiso, Indiana, then a community of four hundred population, until that year known as Porterville.

There he established a small grocery business in the center of the village, and a saloon in a dirt-floored cabin near the end of the main street. The grocery business he conducted with the assistance of William Unruh, and left the saloon to the management of a hired bartender, upon whom he called regularly, twice a day, to collect the receipts. In a village of four hundred population, center of an area where most of the residents produced the bulk of their food and sometimes even their whisky on their own farms, neither branch of the business was conspicuously successful. Young Baldwin's profits in Valparaiso were chiefly in experience.

In Valparaiso his first child, Clara, was born, on May 14, 1847, when the father himself was less than twenty years old.

Shortly thereafter a man was killed in a drunken brawl in the saloon. Baldwin himself was not present at the time but William Unruh witnessed the shooting, and on the strength of his report Baldwin decided to abandon the saloon business. The little grocery alone gave no promise of providing sufficiently for his increased family, and he sold it to another optimist. William Unruh returned to the farm, and Baldwin packed his wife, baby and household goods into a wagon and moved to New Buffalo on the Michigan Road, where he opened a so-called hotel and general store.

Once again William Unruh joined him in the management of the business. The hotel proved a disappointment in a community where two transients a day was a high average of travel. It was closed after a few months. Business of the store was just sufficient to maintain the family. Baldwin was not a man to be satisfied with a mere living. Neither his natural energy nor ambition could tolerate idleness.

The Illinois Canal was then being completed to give the first cheap freight transportation from Chicago to St. Louis. Baldwin recognized its possibilities. His childhood experience in the long journey by wagon from Hamilton, Ohio, to Terre Coupee Town, Indiana, and his later experience with the hog drive from South Bend to Cincinnati were vivid memories, emphasizing the waste and delay of overland transportation. The possibilities of canal freighting appeared tremendous. Baldwin found time between the measuring of sugar, tea and calico for Hoosier housewives to buy lumber, hire workmen, and superintend the building of three canal boats to take advantage of the new transportation route.

His boats were the first upon the new canal. Baldwin loaded them with grain taken on contract from neighboring farmers, and using his own horses on the tow-path moved the freight through the canal to the river and manned a steering sweep on to St. Louis. The grain, moved more cheaply than freight had ever been moved in the Middle West, was sold quickly at a good profit, and Baldwin returned to New Buffalo with a pocketful of cash for himself and the farmers.

LUCKY BALDWIN

The venture, however, though financially successful, had been otherwise unsatisfactory. The long days and nights on canal and river had been too monotonous to satisfy a young man of Baldwin's energy. In St. Louis he had heard of the great gold discoveries in California and had seen scores of adventurers starting out with wagon-trains for the hazardous journey across the western plains, mountains and desert. That was something more to his liking.

Even in his enthusiasms, however, Baldwin was cautious where money was concerned. Contrary to the development of most character, his daring was to increase with age, his recklessness always to be greater in his loves than in his business. Now his inclination was to join the rush to the California gold-fields, but his judgment promoted delay.

His brother Washington, and his boyhood friend and neighbor, Jeremiah Garoutte, were restrained by no such caution. They joined a party setting out for the placer diggings. A "local History Scrap Book" in the library at New Carlisle, Indiana, states that Wash Baldwin "is said to have died with his boots on as a result of a dispute over the stakes in a card game." Jerry Garoutte lived to attain independence and respect in the development of California, and a renewal of his friendship with Elias Baldwin.

In the meantime the young man controlled his eagerness while he awaited first-hand reports from reliable sources on the possibilities of the golden West. Neither New Buffalo nor the store business was flourishing. With the profits of his venture in canal-boat transportation and something from the sale of his store, Baldwin moved to Racine, Wisconsin, opened a hotel called the "Racine House," and bought a grocery business.

Racine was the largest town in which Baldwin had lived. Both the hotel and the grocery business made money. But again life became monotonous. The young man's energy fretted for an outlet. Reports of the richness of the California placers, and of other opportunities in the booming mining districts came back from Jerry Garoutte. Quotation of prices of a dollar apiece for eggs, a dollar a pound for bacon, and other foodstuffs in proportion in such gold camps as Rough and Ready, Red Dog, Brandy City and Angels, indicated to the farm and hotel experienced Baldwin that possibilities of wealth were not limited to the use of shovel and gold pan.

He decided to go. He had waited three years since the first news of the great gold discoveries had reached him, but he would wait no longer. He sought and found a buyer for his hotel and grocery business in the person of Horace Wormer, a resident of Racine.

The business was transacted without haste, as was Baldwin's habit, and with profit, as was also his habit. Two more months were consumed in preparation for the journey and in organization of the party which was to make it. Baldwin's outfit consisted of more than a score of horses, and four strong wagons, one of which was loaded entirely with brandy and another with tobacco and tea for trading purposes. The other two carried his household furnishings, personal property, miscellaneous goods for trade with the Indians to be encountered on the way, and last but not least his wife Sarah and his daughter Clara, not yet six years old.

The party which set out from Racine in March, 1853, included Rachel Wormer, the eighteen-year-old daughter of Horace Wormer who had purchased Baldwin's business; W. F. McHenry, a grocer and friend of Baldwin; Dr. J. L. Page, a physician who had lived in Baldwin's hotel; Reuben M. Norton, first mayor of Racine and a partner in Norton & Durand, freight forwarders and warehouse men; Justine Cartwright and Thomas B. Wright, local blacksmiths. William Unruh wished the party good luck, and returned to Indiana.

They were to need all his good wishes.

CHAPTER IV

ACROSS THE PLAINS

FRESH, strong and eager for the adventure, the party traveled steadily across southern Wisconsin and Iowa to Council Bluffs, some five or six hundred miles on the tortuous roads of that period, without adventure. It was hardly a foretaste of what was to come, though the roads were deep in mud, and the river crossings difficult.

Horses were in fine condition, however, and the food supply ample and sufficiently varied. Baldwin, already known as a man of more than average stamina and resourcefulness as well as the chief man of property in the outfit, had been elected captain. The journey of a month from Racine to Council Bluffs was hardly more than a training jaunt for the coming trek across the plains, mountains and deserts of Nebraska, Wyoming, Utah, Nevada and California.

The wagon-train pulled up at the Missouri River with every member, even to the six-year-old Clara, toughened rather than tired by the first month of steady exercise, ample food and nights of sound sleep in the shelter of the wagons. Though the great rush to the California gold-fields had dwindled greatly in the past two years there was still a steady movement of emigrants to the West. Council Bluffs was crowded with wagons, horses, oxen, cattle, men, women and children, awaiting accommodation on the feeble ferry service across the Missouri.

The emigrant route to California had been clearly marked by four years of travel, and every intelligently managed party knew quite well the difficulties and hardships which confronted it. Baldwin had few illusions and encouraged none among

[50]

his associates. When they chafed at delay, awaiting ferry service, he counseled them to get all the comfort they could from the enforced rest. They were already four years late for the easy money of the first gold diggings, and four days now could make little difference. Their opportunity, he advised them, lay in the business possibilities of the new state rather than in the gold-mines.

Awaiting ferry service, Baldwin spent much time among the other emigrants, collecting all the information he could concerning the routes and problems to be encountered. So he met a man named D. A. Shaw who was making his second overland trip to California. Shaw looked over the Baldwin party's stock and equipment, and decided that it was in good condition and well selected. It should have comparatively little trouble. He offered to act as guide and councilor. Baldwin was quick to accept, and the train was increased to thirty wagons under Shaw's direction.

With new energy and enthusiasm they at last drove their wagons upon the ferry scows, landed near the single log cabin which then marked the site of what is now Omaha, and took to the Carson Trail across what was to be defined by Congress a year later as Nebraska Territory.

It was mid-April. The melted snows and spring rains made the wagon trails a slough of mud. The Brule and Ogillallah Sioux, who ranged the territory from the Black Hills to the Republican River, were inclined to be hostile. These Indians had been dealing with emigrants for four years with mutual suspicion and disadvantage. Organized Indian war-parties were uncommon but raiding bands frequently descended upon the wagon-trains, stampeded the loose stock, and when the action seemed safe, murdered the men, kidnapped the women and stole the supplies.

The Baldwin party drew up its wagons in a circle on the prairie at night and camped within the shelter, with a guard maintained outside. By day they plodded slowly onward through the mud. The rivers were in flood. Frequently it was necessary to swim the horses and float the wagons across streams which in mid-summer would hardly have wet their tires. But for all this they were prepared. The wreckage of wagons along the way, the rusted tires thrusting up like brown bones in the sand of the crossings, were more than wrecks. They were the tragic experience of thousands of emigrants, from which had grown wisdom. American ingenuity had developed wagons which might hope to escape such an end. The wheels had been made larger to surmount the chuckholes, the tires wider to tread the dust or mud, the bodies watertight to float the deeper streams where no ferry-boats were available. The Baldwin party was equipped with the best. The miles rolled steadily behind them.

On two or three occasions small parties of Indians attempted to stampede the horses grazing near the wagons in the evening or early morning, but prompt action corralled the animals, and the Indians who were mostly armed with bows and arrows were too cautious to risk coming within gunshot of the emigrants.

The first test of Baldwin's fitness to lead his party came at the crossing of the Elkhorn River, swollen to flood proportions. Acting on information obtained from earlier emigrants, he had provided several hundred feet of rope in his equipment. With a light cord tied to his waist, he swam the swollen stream and pulled across a length of stout rope. This rope was stretched to prevent the wagons from drifting down the stream. Another rope was brought across, and horses were forced to swim. A team was hitched to the end of the rope, attached to a wagon on the opposite bank and driven forward. The wagon rolled into the stream, floated to the other bank and amid the cheers of the party rolled up upon the sand. One after the other, the remaining wagons and teams followed until the entire party and equipment were safely across.

On they plodded, across plains which to-day are checkered with fenced corn- and grain-fields, orchards, towns and comfortable farmhouses but which then were a weary expanse of grass, just showing green in the spring sunshine, and marked only by wavering lines of willows in flooded creek beds. On and on, day after day, seeing many more wrecks of earlier caravans than they saw human beings.

Occasionally two or three Indians, peacefully but gainfully inclined, would approach the evening camp-fires, begging food, or anything in the way of gifts which the party might produce. Baldwin invariably gave them food, and occasionally gifts of cheap jewelry or a trade knife with which he had stocked himself for the purpose.

At times the train caught up with another party, moving more slowly than their own because of inferior stock or a larger outfit which delayed progress. On such occasions the groups would make adjacent camps, and a fiddle or an accordion might help to give the evening variety with such tunes as *O Susanna, Don't You Cry.*

Summer was approaching, and the weather was finer and the trail firmer under foot. They were in buffalo country now, and fresh meat was plentiful. The grass was green and thick. The horses were well fed and strong. The going in general was greatly improved, and the little train speeded up. So they approached Fort Laramie, Wyoming. Baldwin knew that the post existed, but was not quite certain of its position.

Going into camp early one evening after an unusually good day's journey, Baldwin looked up to see a lone rider approaching. Even at a distance the figure was arresting. Apparently he was not an Indian. As he approached, holding his pony at an easy lope, a battered plug hat could be made out on his head. Baldwin's suspicions were disarmed but his curiosity was increased. The visitor rode like an Indian, and evidently without a saddle. Nearer, it appeared that he might be an

Indian, but such an Indian as none of the party had ever seen. Baldwin looked to his gun and waited. The plug-hatted visitor pulled down to a walk, and came to a stop beside the wagons.

"Whoa, haw, God damn you," he greeted cordially.

Baldwin laughed, and extended a hand to shake that of his visitor. He had been told that many of the plains Indians had adopted these words, frequently heard among the bull-whackers of '49, as a conventional salutation. This unexpected guest appeared harmless. Baldwin invited him to stop and eat. The Indian spoke no more than a dozen words of English, but "eat" was one of them, and he dismounted with alacrity and handed Baldwin a soiled and crumpled bit of brown paper, extracted from a fold in his breech-clout. Baldwin opened the paper and read:

"This is a no-good Injun. He won't fight or work, but watch him or he'll steal your shirt."

Baldwin grinned. The incident appealed to his sense of humor which ran strongly to practical jokes, as did much of the humor of pioneer days. "Where you get?" he demanded.

"Eat," said the buck.

"Oh, all right," Baldwin agreed. The women of the party had already gathered enough buffalo chips to make two or three small fires, and a supper of buffalo meat, corn bread cooked in a Dutch oven, and stewed dried apples, was soon ready. The Indian ate enormously, but conversation was difficult. Trading his few words of the Cheyenne dialect with the savage's few words of English, Baldwin at last made out that he was only a few miles from Fort Laramie, one of the important posts on the long journey. With luck they should arrive next day.

The entire party was warned to keep an eye on the Indian to prevent the thieving of which he had unwittingly brought word from the Fort. A double guard was placed for the night. Despite the precaution, at daybreak the Indian was gone and with

him a potful of stewed dried apples, inadvertently left un-
guarded beside the remains of the camp-fire.

Another point of information brought by the self-invited
guest was accurate. At noon the wagon-train pulled into the
settlement at Fort Laramie. About three weeks more of
travel should take the party through South Pass, where the
first Mormon emigrants from Nauvoo, Illinois, had turned
from the Oregon Trail six years earlier to found Great Salt
Lake City.

For three days the party rested in camp at Fort Laramie
while Baldwin traded a small part of his two wagon-loads of
brandy, tobacco and tea for a few such supplies as dried buffalo
meat and horseshoes. Refreshed, they set out again, encouraged by information that the various tribes to be encountered between Laramie and Salt Lake were for the most
part reasonably friendly, though they might try to stampede
and steal the grazing horses.

The Indians at that period were more interested in warring
with one another and stealing and begging from the whites
than they were in keeping the peace with one another and
uniting against the invaders. Their experiences with the whites
had been greatly varied in the six years since the first great
Mormon invasion had opened their eyes to the fact that there
might be as many white men as Indians in the world.

The explorers, trappers and traders who had preceded the
Mormon hegira had been hard tough men of the frontier
school, men who understood the instability and childishness of
the savage character. Many of these men had been willing
to cheat the savages, while others had treated them honestly
and still others had taken squaws and become Indians themselves in their habits. Nearly all had brought guns, knives,
trinkets and trade goods which had been wealth to the Indians.
Occasionally they had murdered and scalped or been murdered
and scalped, but in general the Indians had looked upon them

as potential benefactors. The Mormons had understood and profited by this attitude, had treated the Indians well and had aroused no wide-spread antagonism.

Individual savages and a few villages dominated by chiefs who were vain, boastful, greedy, treacherous and unstable, had murdered trappers and trading parties, usually for purposes of robbery, but occasionally for revenge. This situation in general had remained unchanged even through the pioneer rush of '49 and '50. The western prairies and lower slopes of the Rocky Mountains still swarmed with buffaloes, providing food, shelter and raiment for the savages. The emigrants brought luxuries, biscuits, blankets, knives, guns, beads, tobacco,whisky. They seemed to be an addition to and an improvement upon savage life. In general they were welcomed, though at a cost of a heavy tax of gifts to their hosts.

But two or three years of the heavy immigration which began with the gold-rush demonstrated two or three things to the Indians. Some of the whites were as cruel and treacherous as the savages themselves. Others could be intimidated. They were not supermen, as had at first been feared. Why trade them furs or buffalo robes for blankets, knives, horses and luxuries when it was so much cheaper and more exciting to raid, murder and rob? Raids, murder and robbery grew more common as emigration increased.

Raiding and robbery were more in keeping with the Indian character than open warfare. The Indian preferred to shoot from ambush, to tomahawk a sleeping victim, to steal from a helpless one. Not until the westward flood of white emigrants, hide hunters and settlers actually began to make serious inroads upon the vast buffalo herds which were the assurance of life to the savages did the latter start the greater wars which ended in their downfall simultaneously with the extermination of the herds which had sustained them. This was to be some fifteen years or so after the passage of the Baldwin party.

That party left Fort Laramie hopeful in the assurance that if they watched their live stock, were generous to individuals or small groups of savages whom they might encounter, and put on a bold front against larger parties, they could pass in safety. Their food supplies were ample, their horses in fairly good condition, and their trail through South Pass to the Great Salt Lake well marked and of reasonably easy passage.

Baldwin usually rode in advance of the wagons to watch for Indians, to scout for the best creek crossings, and to kill fresh meat which would conserve the staple supplies of the party. Thus a few days out from Fort Laramie he met with his first serious misadventure.

Stopping on a high creek bank, perhaps half a mile ahead of the creeping wagon-train, he studied the region for an easy crossing. An antelope, with the curiosity of its kind, thrust its head up among the bushes on the opposite bank. Baldwin jerked up his gun and fired. He was never a notably good shot, and the bullet missed. The antelope dashed away through the brush. Baldwin was piqued. He was never a man to submit quietly to failure or ridicule. The antelope's white rump, flirted almost in his face, suggested both. Baldwin spurred his horse and followed.

Up one creek bottom and down another, across flat stretches of brush-clad desert and over hills he rode, occasionally sighting the antelope again, but never coming within gunshot. At last he traced the animal to refuge in a clump of trees in a wide creek bottom. This time he would make no error. He tied his horse to a bush and crawled cautiously toward the group of trees. Fifty yards away he made out the animal, half hidden in the undergrowth. He sighted carefully and fired again. The animal leaped, and disappeared over a rise, but running upon three legs only. Well, he had hit it. That was some comfort. It couldn't run far on three legs. Baldwin followed on foot, expecting to bring down the animal within a few hundred yards. Occasional blood spots drew him on. But the few hundred yards extended to a few thousand, and still the wounded antelope was not seen. Darkness was coming on.

Against his inclination, but moved by his better judgment, he abandoned the hunt and started back to his horse. He could not find it. He found the clump of cottonwoods, or one very much like it, where he had wounded the antelope, but no horse was near it. He climbed a tree but could see no sign of life. Twilight was deepening. He figured his position to the best of his ability and struck out on foot toward what he believed would be the night camping-place of his party. Pitch darkness descended. He stumbled over bushes, stepped into prairie-dog holes, and finally discovered from the north star that he was walking in the wrong direction. He abandoned the effort for the night and stretched himself upon a bed of sand, hungry, thirsty and cold.

At daybreak he was on his feet again, plodding toward the place where he hoped to encounter the wagon trail. It was a rough wild region of almost desert land, cut by dry gullies, paved with rock and sand, and sparsely grown with brush. Wearily he stumbled onward, rolling a pebble in his mouth to keep his thirst from mounting. A spot of green appeared on the horizon to the westward. That might mean trees, water, even a shot at some game, food. The thought quickened his pace. The trees were more cottonwoods in a wide gully beside a trickle of water. He drank gratefully, but there was no game in sight.

Strengthened though disappointed, he took up the march. The sun was high and hot. A rabbit bounded through the brush and stopped upon a knoll at Baldwin's shrill whistle. But before he could take aim it leaped away. All day he plodded, until his boots were cut to shreds on the rough footing, his tongue was dry and swollen, and his empty stomach seemed to cling to his backbone. The sun dropped again toward the mountains, and the man spurred himself to new effort. If he could not find water again before night he might never rise on the morrow.

He left the gully down which he had been walking, and struck off at right angles in the hope of finding a watercourse less dry. In that, at least, his judgment was sound. Before twilight had faded to darkness he stumbled upon a trickling stream, drank his fill, and captured two small frogs which he skinned and toasted over a fire of twigs, and bolted, half raw.

His night's rest, the second without blankets or shelter, could hardly have been called rest. It was tormented by dreams and discomfort. When daybreak came he could hardly stand, but he struggled up, filled himself with water, searched vainly for more frogs, and plodded on.

"By gad, I'm not beat yet!"

The midday sun saw him still lurching on, stopping more frequently now to rest in the shade of a dense bush, but always struggling to his feet and setting his eyes toward any landmark which he could choose to keep himself from circling on his path. Mid-afternoon brought him within sight of more trees in the distant heat shimmer. He set his teeth upon cracked dry lips and lunged onward. An hour passed and he was still a mile from his goal, but he spurred himself onward, reeling now but determined that he would succeed.

A hundred yards from the high bank which concealed the base of the grove he stumbled into the hole of a prairie-dog and fell. Just a minute's rest, and he would make it. Suddenly he was conscious of sounds, the yelping of dogs, the shrill cries of children, the guttural voice of a man. Indians!

Well, better a tomahawk in his brain than the death by thirst and starvation which had been coming closer with each step in the last two days. He struggled to his feet, seized the gun to which he had clung in the hope of killing some game, and with his best assumption of strength strode toward the hidden encampment. Even in his weakness he remembered that a savage should be approached with confidence, if at all. At the top of the bank he paused for an inspection. Three teepees of buffalo hide thrust up from beside a slender stream, shaded by cottonwoods. Two or three bucks lolled upon buffalo robes before the teepees. Squaws pottered about. Children and dogs played and quarreled.

"How!" Baldwin raised a cracked voice from his dry throat.

The bucks leaped to their feet and the squaws screamed, while the children scuttled into the lodges like prairie-dogs into their holes.

"How!" said Baldwin again, and strode down the slope into the camp and thrust out a hand to the nearest buck. The Indian shook hands. The other bucks stepped forward and also shook hands. "How!" they grunted.

Baldwin walked boldly between them to the stream, and drank. Then he returned, rifle in hand, and seated himself calmly on a buffalo robe. He was weak to the verge of fainting, and the scene swam before his eyes, but he tightened his self-control one more notch and handed his tobacco pouch to the nearest Indian.

The buck filled a stone pipe from the pouch, lighted it with an ember, and handed it to the starving man. Baldwin puffed and handed it to his neighbor. When the pipe had gone around, Baldwin spoke again:

"Eat," he said. "Long hunt; no get. Plenty sick. Eat!"

A buck grunted a few words and one of the squaws brought a wooden bowl of meat from a pot simmering over the fire. Baldwin consumed it ravenously. Then he walked again to the stream and drank. The pipe was filled and passed again. Evidently there was to be no immediate trouble here. Baldwin's assumption of confidence and friendship had been wise. After the second pipe the Indians began to speak. Baldwin understood only a few of their words and they were familiar with only a few words of English, but between the two, supplemented by signs, each told his story.

The Indians, for some reason not made clear, had remained in this camp while the main village had moved on toward the Black Hills country in pursuit of buffalo and to cut lodge poles for their next winter's lodges. The tribes had been at peace for months, and this group was a day's travel from the emigrant trail. This doubtless explained the absence of a lookout who, ordinarily, would have discovered the wayfarer long before he discovered the Indians.

Baldwin explained his difficulties as best he could, and promised gifts if the Indians would lend a horse and guide to take him back to the emigrant trail and his party. He indicated that his friends were rich and strong and generous. The Indians grunted agreement.

On the following morning, after Baldwin's strength had been almost fully restored by numerous bowls of antelope meat, topped off by a fat puppy, boiled and served as a feast of ceremony in honor of the extraordinary occasion, the traveler indicated his wish to be gone. The chief of the group grunted a word, and the squaws set about the task of dismantling the lodges. Baldwin protested that he wanted only one man as guide, and a horse for himself, which could be brought back laden with gifts. The protest was ignored. The entire party would conduct him. With gifts promised, every Indian wanted to assure himself of a full share.

The grazing ponies were herded in by a naked boy. Squaws stripped the coverings of hide from the lodges and lashed the lodge poles to the sides of the more sedate animals which were to drag the *traineaux*. The trailing poles were heaped with the lodge hides, cooking pots and other possessions of the savages, and the caravan set out. The bucks bestrode their horses in proper dignity, with squaws, half-grown children and dogs on foot, and under foot. The distance which Baldwin had hoped to cover in a day with a single guide required more than two days with this heterogeneous escort. But at last they reached the main line of emigrant travel, and by consulting members of a plodding ox-train eventually found the Baldwin party, which had dropped out of the main train in the hope of his return. It was just about to break camp in the sad conviction that Baldwin had been killed by accident or Indians.

Baldwin was welcomed back as a man from the dead. His Indian friends stared with unwinking curiosity at the excitement in the camp at the wanderer's return. Kisses, embraces, hand-shaking, back-slapping, shouts, tears and laughter moved the savages only to silent wonder. But even their stoicism was not proof against the riches which Baldwin heaped upon a buffalo robe as reward for their help. Knives, beads, tin pots, gay cotton ribbons, a box of dry biscuits, and several pounds each of tobacco, tea and sugar were included. The bucks grunted with satisfaction and the squaws and children screamed with delight. The group promptly set up their lodges and settled to noisy enjoyment of their new-found wealth. Baldwin and his family prepared to move on with his party.

It had been their first close contact with the savages of the West, but it was to be by no means their last. Contacts far less happy awaited. In their ignorance they plodded on.

CHAPTER V

FRIENDLY MORMONS AND HOSTILE INDIANS

NEAR the junction of the Sweetwater and the North Platte the Baldwin wagons caught up with those of D. A. Shaw's train which had left them to wait and pray for the return of "E. J." The train was further increased by another group which had been encamped for several days at the mouth of the Sweetwater, resting and feeding its stock for the difficult march through the semi-arid region from the North Platte well into the Rockies, where the California trail branched through South Pass on the route of the Mormon emigration to the Great Salt Lake.

Travel was difficult, with a steady drag up the long slope toward the continental divide. Feed was sparse. Horses and oxen grew thin and weak. In order to find sufficient grazing to keep their stock alive the long train under Shaw's direction found it necessary to break up, so that they might camp at scattered spots where some bunch-grass would be available. Thus Baldwin's party, though nominally still a part of the larger train, was left again to his direction. Baldwin was quick to take advantage of the superior condition of his horses and pass the plodding ox-teams and weakened horses of the others. Soon he was well in the lead where he could have first choice of whatever feed was available.

Shaw, who also had exceptional horses and two strong but light wagons which he had had built to his own specifications, was also well in front. His position as guide and captain of the train was only an honorary one, due to the fact that he was the one man in the party who had covered the route previously. It entailed no responsibility beyond that of giving the best advice of which he was capable. Though two or three routes through the mountains had been opened since the first gold-rush, Shaw advised following the Mormon trail across Green River, through Fort Bridger and Echo Canyon, with which he was familiar from his first journey.

The semi-arid nature of the region, with its consequent lack of forage and game, had resulted in a wide scattering of the Indians, and the groups which were seen occasionally with their ponies, *traineaux,* squaws, children and dogs dragging across the country were too small to be a serious menace, even though they might attempt a raid. Few had guns, and fewer still had powder and bullets. Most of them preferred to beg rather than to risk attack with bows and arrows upon the well-armed emigrants.

Advised of this, the Baldwin party, which included eight tried men, struck out boldly across the Little Sandy, the Big Sandy, and on through the magnificent scenery of the Rockies to Green River, flowing swiftly, deep and wide. Two be-whiskered men, owning a flat-bottom scow, offered to ferry them across. Baldwin negotiated. The price seemed high.

"I'll float my wagons over, and swim my horses," said Baldwin. "I've done it before."

"Them wagon beds have got cracks in 'em I can stick my finger through," said one of the ferrymen. "They'll sink half way acrost."

Baldwin shook his head, and retired to deliberate. Soon his face brightened with a grin.

"By gad, I'm not licked yet."

Explaining his purpose, he set about with his associates to unload the wagons. As each was cleared it was rolled backward down the slope into the stream, a rope attached to the tongue. Water poured into the deep bed. By the time the last wagon stood in the stream the first was filled. Horses were hitched to the rope, and the wagon was dragged up far enough to drain. Less than half the water ran out. The cracks had swollen tight. The remaining water was bailed out, and the wagon reloaded.

The saddle stock were forced into the stream and swam across, leading some of the harness horses. The other wagons were bailed out and reloaded. With long ropes attached they were ferried across under their original power. Half a day's labor had saved E. J. Baldwin fifty dollars, and made him two bitter enemies in the persons of the two ferrymen.

"That's been the way all through life," he told a friend fifty years later. "Getting money begets enemies. Saving money is the same as getting it. The more money, the more enemies. A man with money is game in any season for any one. His only safe course is one of self-defense."

But at that moment Baldwin did not stop to philosophize. He waved a derisive farewell to the ferrymen swearing upon the opposite bank, and turned his wagons toward Fort Bridger. The mountain nights were cold and clear, with stars hanging almost within touch of the peaks. The trail was reasonably good, and, to the great relief of the horses, was mostly down grade. The little train rolled into Fort Bridger in far better condition than most emigrant trains.

Fort Bridger in reality was more a trading-post than a fort, having been established by the famous mountain man and scout, James Bridger, without government assistance or garrison, as a base for his own operations. It was merely a group of adobe buildings, surrounded by an adobe wall. Bridger's influence with the Indians had tended to promote peace in the region, and as there was rich grazing in the near-by meadows the fort was a popular resting-place for the emigrant trains.

Another route from the headwaters of the Arkansas River joined the main trail at this point, adding more pack- and wagon-trains to the general western movement. Before reaching Salt Lake City another stretch of desert country with little feed and less game was to be encountered, and Baldwin rested at the fort for several days to put his animals in the best possible condition for this next hard pull. With this preparation he passed the dry area without great difficulty and rolled through Echo Canyon at the high speed of twenty-five miles a day into the Mormon settlement.

Salt Lake City was then six years old. It was the first town worthy of the name that the party had seen since leaving Council Bluffs, nearly a thousand miles and two months back on the twisted trail. The sight was welcome, though a welcome from the Mormons was by no means assured. The Latter-Day Saints had been ejected summarily from their head-quarters at Nauvoo, Illinois, and from Council Bluffs, Iowa, and were believed to have neither respect nor love for the "gentiles," as they called all persons who were not of their faith. Brigham Young, their efficient prophet and leader since the mob murder of their original prophet, Joseph Smith, in 1844, was a shrewd man, however, and had controlled his disciples sufficiently to take a goodly profit from the swarms of emigrants who had been passing through his city since the start of the gold-rush.

Reports of the Mormons' hard bargaining and treachery had traveled back and forth from coast to coast. Other reports of their kindness to sick and needy travelers had not succeeded in relieving wide-spread distrust. But Baldwin had been well advised, as he usually was before any venture. Trade with the emigrants, he knew, had come to be an important feature of the prosperity of the Mormon stronghold. Their farms, the first greatly successful development of the science of irrigation in the United States, were richly productive. Food was available at lower prices and in greater variety in Salt Lake City than at any point between the Missouri River and the Sacramento River.

Manufactured goods, tools, tea, coffee, tobacco, brandy and luxuries in general were not so cheap. But the Mormons had become well-to-do through the sale of food supplies to the emigrants, and were able and willing to buy some of the luxuries for themselves. Baldwin knew this. Hence his two wagon-loads of brandy, tobacco, tea and coffee. They assured him a welcome.

Three years earlier, before the federal government had created the Territory of Utah and appointed Brigham Young its first governor, or four years later, at the time of the so-called Mormon rebellion, such material wealth as Baldwin's might have been looked upon as a sufficient prize for confiscation, but in 1853 Brigham Young was prospering too greatly from the emigrant trade to imperil it. Baldwin conducted his party to camp in the "River Jordan" meadows, a short distance from the city, and then arrayed himself in his best costume to call upon Brigham Young. He was received with courtesy, questioned about the latest news from "the States," advised to consult Walker Brothers about the sale of his goods, and invited to return for dinner, an invitation which was to be repeated and accepted and enjoyed with considerable merriment some twenty-two years later.

Baldwin thanked the prophet-governor, and made his deal with the general mercantile firm of Walker Brothers. They purchased his tobacco at one dollar a plug, and his tea and coffee at a similar price. The merchants referred him to Brigham Young's brother for the sale of his brandy, and the liquor was cashed in at sixteen dollars a gallon. Baldwin counted a profit of between three thousand and four thousand dollars. Elated, he purchased a few luxuries and new boots for his wife, daughter, his temporary ward, Rachel Wormer, and himself, and returned to his camp.

Travelers returning from the California gold-fields had told him that good horses were bringing high prices west of

Salt Lake City, where the rough travel and insufficient grazing of the deserts were taking heavy toll of the emigrants' stock. Baldwin's penchant for horse-trading was stimulated. He promptly invested a part of his profits in horses which he selected with the greatest care. With these extra animals he hoped to cover the seven hundred miles of desert and mountains which lay between him and his goal in record time. Grain and water could take the place of tobacco and brandy in the two emptied wagons. It would be needed on the desert.

The few days of rest, with good feed for the horses and such luxuries as fresh milk, butter and fruit for the human beings, had strengthened them again for hardship. They set out with new energy, ahead of the scattered sections of the Shaw party with which they had been in contact from time to time ever since leaving Council Bluffs. That independence proved a costly and almost tragic error.

Perhaps no better illustration of the isolation of Salt Lake City at that time can be offered than two quotations from *The Deseret News,* the official Mormon newspaper and the only publication then printed between the Missouri River and California. *The News* was supposed to be published every two weeks, but its issue of July 30, 1853, stated: "The absence of paper prevents our knowing when the next number of *The News* will be issued." It was not issued for two months. On October first it came out with the following note: "Sept. 28, 4 P.M. Our friends will rejoice with us that a fresh supply of paper has this moment arrived and we lose no time in putting a sheet to the press. . . . Our type was mostly set for this number some six or eight weeks since, hoping for an earlier arrival; we do not feel disposed to change the plan of our history, but to bring up arrearages in future numbers as fast as possible."

That delay perhaps accounts for the fact that there was no current report of the arrival, departure or subsequent trouble of the Baldwin party. And with such evidence of the irregularity and uncertainty of communication there is little wonder that the party, apparently rich in money, equipment, supplies and horses, was headed for trouble when it turned into the desert wastes west of Salt Lake City.

Two records, however, exist. One is in an interview given by Baldwin to *The San Francisco Call* in 1900, forty-seven years after the event. The other is in a painting of the scene made by A. A. Cross, a leading artist of the day, on commission from Baldwin, who took him to the spot some twenty-odd years after the battle and described the incidents to him in detail. The two records are somewhat contradictory. The Cross painting shows the battle to have taken place while the wagon-train was moving through a region of barren rocky buttes, which were picturesquely described by a lawyer in Cross's subsequent suit for his fee as "these biscuspid mountains."

There are some evident errors in Baldwin's interview describing the battle, such as his statement that his daughter was then two years old, when in fact she was six, but his own account in general probably is more accurate than the other.

"At Salt Lake our party broke up," he said, "some buying their wagons from me and going in different directions. I had brought along a wagon of tea and tobacco that I sold to Walker Brothers for a good profit. Two other wagons were loaded with brandies and wines. Brigham Young sent his brother out to our camp to bargain for these. I sold them to him for my own price.

"Brigham Young's brother visited us often and urged us to take a different road from other travelers, insisting it was easier, and more feed for horses. I took his advice. It was just after the famous Mountain Meadow massacre by the Utah Indians, and we were fearful of the same fate. Brigham Young's brother assured us we would avoid all danger by following his advice.

"The second morning out we were preparing breakfast. A shot from the rocks above pierced our coffee pot. Women, children and all made for our wagons. Then a fusillade followed. There were wild Indian yells.

"Mrs. Baldwin put our two-year-old baby in the most sheltered spot in the wagon, and gamely stood out of cover, loading guns for me. One of my shots killed the chief, and wild with rage the Indians came closer. One Indian grabbed a girl and was dragging her off when one of our party shot him, just in time.

"There were cries in the distance. The Indians retreated to join another band. There were nine dead Indians. We had several wounded.

"I always believed that Brigham Young's brother caused the attack and was with them, disguised as an Indian. . . . Young knew I had several thousands from sales, and he incited the Indians. The girl the Indian attempted to steal married a man named Shaw and lived in San Berdoo.

"In later years I sent Cross, the famous painter, to the exact spot in Utah and had the scene painted. The survivors each have a photo of the painting."

So much for Baldwin's memory of the battle. It is corroborated in part by D. A. Shaw's record of his own overland journeys, stating that the Indians were believed to have been instigated by some of the Mormon officials who, having obtained Baldwin's goods, were anxious to recover the cash paid for them.

In any event the battle was fought and won. The Ute Indians, of a lower order than many of the easterly tribes, were like the general run of red men in that their courage was largely dependent upon superiority of numbers and other advantages in attack. Wise perhaps, stoical certainly, in the face of torture and inevitable death, they could never maintain unity of purpose or action in the face of determined or unexpected resistance. The Baldwin party's defense had been both determined and unexpected. The Indians fled before it. The emigrants bandaged up their wounded, and moved on, getting back as quickly as they could to the main route, from which they had been diverted by the advice of Young.

The desert rolled slowly behind them, the route still marked by the bones of oxen and horses, the wreckage of wagons and pack-saddles, and occasionally by the graves of the earlier emigrants who had succumbed to its hardships. But this party was well found. The luck of Lucky Baldwin, he insisted throughout his life, was usually due to careful planning.

Certainly that was true at this point. The barrels of water and grain for his horses which he had loaded into his wagons in place of the brandy, tobacco and tea sold in Salt Lake City, made the passage of the desert comparatively swift and simple. They reached the Humboldt River in good order, followed it toward its sink, and there again encountered hostile Indians.

Baldwin was driving some distance in advance of the main train, accompanied only by Rachel Wormer and one or two men, when they were attacked without warning. But the Piutes of this region were even more stupid and less warlike than the Utes of the previous encounter. Evidently, unaware of the following train, they expected the attack upon the single wagon would be as simple as stealing a pine-nut from a papoose. Baldwin later declared that he believed their purpose was to take the young woman, Rachel Wormer, alive. In view of the known character of those western Nevada Piutes, it seems more likely that they thought they could shoot down the two or three men of the party from a safe distance, and loot the single wagon at their leisure.

But like most Indians, they were extremely bad rifle shots, and their bullets went wild. As they started to close in, Baldwin managed to turn his team, and drove through the scattered Indians at a run, pistols and rifles keeping time to the beat of hoofs, until the main party was reached. Quickly they drew their wagons into the circle of defense and prepared to withstand an attack in force. Fortunately, they were close to water, and were able to maintain the camp for several days while three or four more trains arrived, bringing the caravan up to a strength of one hundred members and about fifty wagons.

With this formidable demonstration they moved on through the Piute country without meeting the slightest trouble from the Indians. The worst of the desert and the greater part of the weary journey were behind them when they came to Ragtown, near the Carson River. A contemporary description of Ragtown as of that date has been left to posterity by *The Placerville Herald* of August 6, 1853, almost the precise date of Baldwin's arrival. "This town of the desert," it says, "consists of one clapboard house, five cloth houses, a log cabin and two willow shelters. The six houses give meals at $1 each; and the meal consists of bread, fresh beef, thin coffee and sugar."

The Baldwin party could do better than that for themselves. They moved on to Mormon Station on the Carson River. There they suffered their first loss of a human life, though even that did not occur until after Baldwin's guiding hand had been removed.

T. B. Wright, one of the blacksmiths who had been in the original party from Racine, quarreled with one John O'Meara, another emigrant, over the picketing of a mule. O'Meara was dissuaded from killing Wright only because Wright was unarmed. Wright announced that the next time they met he would be armed. He was. And O'Meara, safe with a plea of self-defense under the code of the time, shot him to death.

Before that occurred, however, Baldwin had gone to the Mormon settlement of Genoa in the hope of selling the horses which he had bought for that purpose with part of the profits of his brandy, tobacco and tea sales in Salt Lake City. On the way to Genoa, for the third time he encountered hostile Indians, and lost two of his animals in the encounter.

Horse-buyers from Sacramento were coming across the Sierra at the time, as Baldwin had been advised in Salt Lake

City, to purchase animals from incoming emigrants, many of whom were reduced to dire need. But Baldwin was not reduced to need. Also he was advised of the value of good horses on the California roads and trails to the mining camps. Therefore he was in position to drive as hard a bargain as the horse-dealers themselves. His stock was in far better condition than most of the emigrant stock. Horses for which he had paid one hundred and fifty dollars each in Salt Lake City brought him six hundred dollars each in gold. With the horses he sold wagons and harness, and retained only such animals as he could use under saddle in the small pack-train with which he planned to cross the Sierra.

Ill advised as to the best route across the mountains, he headed with his party, now reduced to six, with saddle horses and pack-horses, through what was known as Johnson's Cut-Off. Fortunately a day or two of extra travel was the only ill effect of his routing. The route took him up Gold Canyon, where two or three itinerant prospectors were already scratching with their picks at low-grade gravel, and where six years later the Comstock Lode was to be discovered with a profit of millions eventually for the man who then traveled indifferently over its vast but unsuspected riches.

Chapter VI

CALIFORNIA IN '53

HANGTOWN, aspiring to a new fame with the change of its name to Placerville, sprawled perspiring in the August sunshine. It was as hot on the western foot-hills of the Sierra Nevada as in the best corn-growing weather of Indiana. A rambling street stretched up the slope like a grimy finger beckoning to another and older world.

Answering the summons which had called him more than two thousand miles, a lean and sunburned man, ragged and barefooted as he had been as a boy on an Indiana farm ten years earlier, came trudging down the dusty ruts of the emigrant trail from the crest of mountains blue and white in the eastern sky. It was E. J. Baldwin.

The mid-western prairies, the Mississippi and Missouri Rivers, the Rocky Mountains, the great American desert, the thrusting peaks of the Sierra, and twenty-five busy years of life lay behind him. California, and a new life, stretched away before him. Five months of hardship had been occupied in a journey which one may make now in three days of luxury.

Looking back upon that scene in an August afternoon of eighty years ago it seems that all of Hangtown's two thousand inhabitants, red- and blue-shirted miners, bartenders, merchants, blacksmiths, gamblers, Chinese, Chilenos, Mexicans, bull-whackers and mule-skinners with a sprinkling of dance-hall girls and a few weary wives and unkempt children, should have been out with flags and firecrackers, fifes and drums, to welcome the newcomers. To-day the accomplishment would command such an ovation. Consider: A man barefooted after a two-thousand-mile journey because he had lent his last pair of boots to a girl whose shoes had worn to shreds; a woman who had driven a team, fought Indians and cooked on fires of buffalo chips for months; a child of six, nourished upon buffalo meat, corn-meal and molasses, but still as strong and gay as any product of any present-day scientific diet and training; a string of horses, saddled and packed; and a new world at their feet.

That was the picture. Nineteen hundred and thirty-three might be impressed. Eighteen hundred and fifty-three was not. Perhaps no better indication of Hangtown's own character could be suggested. It was accustomed to such cavalcades. It had been built by them. Its people had accomplished the same or similar journeys. The town was growing old—four years old—and sometimes weary, and a bit blasé. The first bloom of its excitement had worn away. The unpainted frame buildings along its main street were weather-beaten by winter storms and summer suns. The shake roofs were curling and cracking. The wooden awnings were beginning to lean sadly against the false fronts of stores and saloons. Even the deep dust of the street in the hot still air stirred but lazily under the feet of the Baldwins, E. J., Sarah Ann and Clara, and their temporary charge, Rachel Wormer.

Women at the doors of outlying cabins looked them over casually, and nodded indifferent greeting. Percentage girls on their way to the saloons gave hardly a glance. They did not suspect the possibilities latent in that barefooted sun-tanned Indiana farmer which other women were to discover as time went on. Gamblers, manicuring their nails with bowie-knives on the shaded plank sidewalks before the saloons, did not even look up. Miners, ruminating in patches of shade, between drinks which yesterday's pannings provided, commented briefly.

"Good-lookin' horses that feller's got."

"Damn good."

"Must be from som'ers in Nevady. Couldn't of come fur, an kep' his stock like that."

"Prob'ly one o' them Mormons. They're hell on horse-tradin'. See he's got two wimmen, a old 'un an' a young 'un."

The group broke into coarse laughter. Baldwin looked them over, his eyes level and cold. They lapsed into silence, and he passed on.

A sign thrust out from the square front of a two-story frame building proclaimed the El Dorado Hotel. The party stopped, and E. J. walked into the bare front room which opened upon a plank sidewalk. It was furnished with benches around the walls, a huge pot-bellied stove in a box of sawdust littered and stained by tobacco quids, and a narrow plank counter at one side with a rack holding a dozen keys behind it.

"Yes, reckon we kin fix ye up," said an indifferent clerk in a soiled gingham shirt and dingy linen trousers. "How many?"

"Two rooms. Myself and wife, and my little girl and a friend. How much?"

"Two dollars apiece, the rooms. Meals is a dollar apiece."

"That's high."

The clerk straightened belligerently. "Where ye from?" he demanded. "This is a gold camp. If ye don't like it ye kin move on. An' if ye're from Utah, with two wimmen, ye kin move on anyhow. We don't like Mormons here."

Baldwin knew when not to argue. "I'm from Indiana and Wisconsin," he said. "I'll take the rooms for a night or two anyhow. Where can I put up my horses?"

"Livery-stable down the street a piece. Supper's at six o'clock," said the clerk, respect mounting at Baldwin's unruffled dignity and cool inspection.

Negotiations concluded, the women and child entered, one of the pack animals was unburdened of their immediate necessities, and E. J. moved the others to the livery-stable. There he interviewed a lazy proprietor, examined the quality of hay and grain provided, and decided not to stable his animals. Conference with a near-by storekeeper gave him the name of a farmer who might provide good pasturage at one-fourth the cost of stabling, and only half a mile away. He drove the animals to the farm and made a deal.

He reached the hotel again just as a greasy-looking China-man appeared upon the sidewalk and began to beat a dishpan loudly with a long-handled spoon. Half a dozen men, seated upon the edge of the sidewalk, came to their feet and hurried inside. Baldwin grinned, walked to his room and found his wife, daughter and Rachel Wormer waiting impatiently.

"Hurry, Pa; supper's ready," the child shouted.

"How d'you know?"

"I heard it. Hurry, Pa. I'm hungry."

"You're always hungry." He grinned again. "Reckon if Eve had beat a dishpan Adam'd known it was time to come to the apple tree. There's some'p'n about that noise that jest naturally means supper's ready, in any language. Wait a minute now, till I wash."

The dining-room was hot, crowded and noisy. The Baldwin party found places together upon a bench near the end of one of the two long plank tables. Fried pork, fried potatoes, sourdough bread, were placed before them on tin plates. Thin and bitter coffee from grounds evidently boiled to extinction was provided, with molasses for sweetening. They ate hungrily, without speaking, as did all those about them. The tin dishes banged upon the bare tables, flies buzzed, rough boots scraped upon the floor, both food and drink were con-sumed noisily, but there was no conversation. As fast as the men finished they pushed back their plates, glanced sidewise at the only two women in the room and stamped out.

"A dollar's too much for a meal like that," said Baldwin when he had washed down the last bit of sourdough bread with a last swallow of the deadly coffee.

[77]

"A dollar? My gracious, E. J.!" said his wife, shocked. "Why, we gave a better meal than that at the Racine House for a quarter."

"We did, at that," he agreed. "But we got to remember this is California. There might be money in the hotel business here at that. I'll look 'round some."

For ten days he looked around, cheering himself up for the expense of the sojourn by the knowledge that his dozen horses were gaining needed rest and sleekness upon cheap pasturage. Placerville had passed the peak of its boom but it was still an active and prosperous town, catering to a dozen camps in the Mother Lode country where men with claims on rich bars were taking out sometimes as much as a thousand dollars' worth of gold in a day by their own efforts with shovel and rocker.

Into Placerville they came, buckskin pokes heavy with gold-dust, to drink, gamble and carouse away their taking, or to ship their gold by Wells Fargo to San Francisco and thence to their families in the East, and buy for themselves what they needed in the way of new boots, shirts and trousers, and grub supplies of bacon, flour, potatoes, coffee and molasses. Freight wagons arrived and departed at frequent intervals with loads of groceries, hardware, clothing and whisky for the more distant camps. Life was hard, but colorful with hope, disappointment and accomplishment.

Disappointed himself at his first observation of the town and its possibilities, Baldwin began to thrill as conversation with miners and merchants gave him a clearer idea of the extent and riches of the gold-fields. Almost every one, he realized, was making money. The fact that a trembling weazened little man in clay-smeared boots and ragged cotton shirt begged him piteously for a dollar near the door of the El Dorado meant nothing. He had seen that same man, gloriously drunk, stake a whole pokeful of gold-dust upon the turn of a card only two nights before. He glanced around to see that he was unobserved as the beggar pleaded, and having made sure that no public precedent was being established, slipped the man a coin. Two days later he saw the same man hanged for knifing a bartender who had refused to treat delirium tremens with one more free drink.

The victim had not yet ceased to jerk at the end of his rope when two other men dashed up the street on horseback and vanished around a turn in the road. Three days later they too were distributing dust upon the gold scales of saloons and gambling places, and Baldwin learned that they had jumped the claim of the alcoholic little Sidneyman and taken out a thousand dollars each in twenty-four hours.

Baldwin expanded to the atmosphere of a country where such things could happen. The gambling spirit in his own blood was strangely stimulated. Yet the shrewd caution which was a more powerful factor in his character moved him to look into every possibility before determining his own course. So investigating, he decided that the business opportunities of Placerville were distinctly limited by its size. Also, he wanted first-hand information from a man whom he could trust, a man who had been in touch with this hectic life since the first great gold-rush, four years earlier. Such a man was his boyhood friend, Jeremiah Garoutte, whom he hoped to find in Sacramento. He would visit Jerry, learn the truth about the mines, the farms, and the whole business of the rich new state. If Sacramento were sufficiently promising, he might locate there. In any event he would go on to take a look at the metropolis of San Francisco before settling down.

His horses sleek with rest on good pasturage, Baldwin trekked out of Placerville with his family. In Sacramento he was disappointed not to find his old friend, Jerry Garoutte, and to discover that the town itself had only some three thousand population and was recovering but slowly from a fire which

had destroyed six hundred of its houses a few months earlier.
Sacramento was the chief transfer point for supplies shipped
up the river from San Francisco to be distributed by wagon-
and pack-trains through the dozens of gold camps scattered
through the western slopes of the Sierra, but its history of
floods and fires did not recommend the place to Baldwin's
judgment.

San Francisco, however, won his interest and approval
promptly. It boasted twenty-five thousand population. Despite six disastrous fires which had swept it in the four years
of its importance since the start of the gold-rush, it was by far
the most promising city Baldwin had ever seen. Wharves
developed into planked streets bordered by frame buildings on
piles or upon the hulks of grounded sailing ships stretched
eastward into the bay from approximately the line of Montgomery Street. On these planked streets and on the sandy
streets to the west and south were stores, warehouses, saloons,
and other frame structures innumerable.

Telegraph Hill hoisted its signal flags when incoming ships
were sighted through the Golden Gate. The Parrott Building,
a three-story structure made of stone brought from China in
the preceding year, was the city's most imposing edifice, though
the Niantic Hotel, built upon the hull of the grounded ship
Niantic at what is now Clay and Sansome Streets, commanded
admiration. The Jenny Lind Theater, also a three-story
structure, on Kearny Street, had recently been purchased and
converted into a city hall. The Monumental Fire Engine Company's bell had only temporarily ceased to summon vigilantes
for salutary hangings of murderers, bandits and arsonists.
The few scattered street lights were burning whale oil, and
most of the city's water supply was furnished by pedlers who
measured it out from hogshead tanks mounted on horse-drawn
carts.

And yet, it was a city. There was business in plenty, and

adequate promise of far greater business to come. This was what Baldwin had hoped to find. Already, at twenty-five, he was a man of confidence and self-assurance equal to his tremendous energy. This self-assurance moreover was nicely balanced by a native caution which moved him to plan his future upon his experience. He knew he was a business man, not a miner. It was that knowledge which had kept him in the hotel and grocery business in Wisconsin when his friends were stampeding to the placer diggings four years earlier. The same trait now kept him from rushing away to the gold-fields, and moved him to study the business opportunities at hand.

Half a day in the teeming streets of San Francisco convinced him that here lay his opportunity. He looked up the largest livery-stable and freighting concern in the city and sold his horses. Why buy horse feed at a dollar a day for each animal when he was already paying three dollars a day each for food for himself and family, and three dollars for a bedroom in an uncomfortable hotel? His first move had been to turn Rachel Wormer over to the care of her brother, a brickmaker, to whom she had been sent by her parents in Racine.

That responsibility, and his horses, off his hands, and some seven thousand dollars safely deposited in the Wells Fargo office on Montgomery Street, Baldwin looked for a business opportunity. He had not only paid the expenses of his five months' journey from Racine to San Francisco but had more than doubled his Wisconsin capital.

The expense of living in the Pacific Temperance Hotel on Pacific Street not only irked his thrifty soul but suggested a profitable use for his idle capital. With his experience in the hotel business in Valparaiso, New Buffalo and Racine, he believed he could operate a hotel in San Francisco with profit both to himself and the community. Half a dozen meals at one dollar each in the fly-infested dining-room of the Pacific Temperance Hotel confirmed him in that belief.

The meals, the furnishings and the inefficient service convinced him that the proprietor, named Hyde, was not an experienced hotel man. The cost of his accommodations convinced him that a goodly profit would be certain under efficient management.

He made himself acquainted with the easy-going Hyde, and engaged in casual conversation. Baldwin was a man trained in the circuitous methods of trade and barter of New Englanders whose descendants controlled the small business of the Middle West.

"You have a nice little business here, Mr. Hyde," he suggested, remembering the price of his meal of boiled mutton, boiled potatoes, dried apple pie and thin bitter coffee.

"Well, mebbe," said Mr. Hyde, leaning against the counter with its fly-specked case of cigars and plug tobacco. "Can't always tell. They's times when business is so good that I feel like I was straddle o' the roof, an' every shingle was a gold riffle. An' mebbe next week word drifts in of a strike somewheres, an' they ain't half a dozen customers left in the house."

"You get good rates."

"Yeh; when I get 'em. Trouble is, I got to charge enough to carry me through the lean times. Right now the house ain't half full."

"Too bad. Well, I'll be lookin' around the city."

"What line o' business you figurin' on, Mr. Baldwin? Minin'?"

"Haven't made up my mind. Store, mebbe; or a livery-stable or something. Mebbe a freightin' business. I had a hotel back in Wisconsin, but I've done 'em all."

"Hmm; I see. Well, I wish you luck."

"Thanks. I've gen'rally had good luck if I worked hard enough for it," said Baldwin, and strolled out to the muddy water-front at Battery and Pacific Streets, a few steps from the hotel. Then he walked more briskly to Clay Street and down the wharf which served as a continuation of the street to the Niantic Hotel. There he engaged the proprietor in conversation until he had learned that there were only half a dozen hotels in the city, and most of these were operated by men of little experience. Also he learned that for many months there had not been a new gold strike of sufficient importance to have much effect in temporarily depopulating San Francisco. That suggestion by the proprietor of the Pacific Temperance Hotel evidently was fiction designed to explain present lack of business. Baldwin decided that the man might be willing to sell. He made further inquiries as to the sources and wholesale costs of food supplies. Then he returned, primed, to deal with Hyde.

Casual conversation in the bare office lobby followed after supper.

"I hear the Adams Hotel's for sale," Baldwin suggested tentatively.

"Oh, that?" Hyde's tone dripped with contempt.

"I've been lookin' around," said Baldwin. "I think mebbe I'll buy it."

Hyde studied him. "You'll be makin' a mistake, Mr. Baldwin. The Adams is all run down."

"I'd aim to fix it up some. Mebbe give you some competition, Mr. Hyde."

Hyde looked worried. "How much they askin'?" he questioned.

"Haven't gone into that yet," said Baldwin. "I'm lookin' around."

A lounger stepped up to buy a plug of tobacco, and Baldwin moved away to allow his planted seed to germinate. The next morning Hyde approached him.

"How much you figurin' to invest, Mr. Baldwin?" he asked after a few preliminaries.

"Depends," said Baldwin. "Mebbe five thousand or so in cash."

"I been thinkin' it over," said Hyde. "I'd kinda like to get back to minin' myself. I don't like to see a stranger come in here an' lose money on that Adams place. It's all run down." He paused, and ruminated. "Tell you what I'll do, Mr. Baldwin," he announced as with a sudden happy thought, "I'll sell you my furniture an' all here an' my lease for six thousand cash. You can see for yourself it's a good business."

Baldwin shook his head. "I'd rather pay less for the Adams an' fix it up to suit me," he said. "I aim to get it for forty-five hundred an' put mebbe five hundred into improvements."

"Well, I'd like to get back to minin'," said Hyde, weakening. "I'll let you have this for fifty-five hundred, an' you won't need to spend anything for improvements."

Baldwin looked about him with a critical eye. "That stove," he pointed to the great rusty heater in the middle of the office, "won't last through another winter. An' the beds could be better. I haven't been in your kitchen yet, but my wife has. She was boss of the kitchen in my Racine House, an' she says you'll need a new range, come next winter; an' some other things."

"Well, say fifty-two hundred an' fifty," said Hyde.

"Let me look it all over, an' check up on your lease, an' I'll consider it for five thousand cash, mebbe," said Baldwin.

By nightfall the agreement was being written.

"Date that three days back," said Baldwin. "Just like to show the folks back East how snappy business is done out here. Hotel bought the same day I struck San Francisco."

Hyde obligingly complied, the agreement was signed, the money paid and the receipt delivered.

"Well, you've bought a nice business, Mr. Baldwin," said Hyde. "You'd ought to do well here. I wish you luck. Here's the key to the safe. Now I've got just time to catch the night boat to Sacramento. I'm going up into that Nevada City country. There's good claims up in that neighborhood yet."

"Thank you, Mr. Hyde. I don't believe in luck. I'm a business man. And before you go, there's just a little matter of three days' board."

"I swan! You are a business man, Mr. Baldwin. I'd clean forgotten that you owe me three days' board an' room for yourself an' family. That'll be; let's see, your little girl's six, ain't she? We'll make it half price for her meals. That'll be thirty-one dollars and a half, altogether."

"Oh, no." Baldwin smiled pleasantly. "It's not my board. It's yours. According to the date on that agreement we've just signed I've been proprietor of this hotel ever since I've been here. It's you who owe me for three days' board an' room. I think your rates are a little high, but according to what you were going to charge me, you owe eighteen dollars. Just pay the clerk an extra dollar as you go out an' I'll send your baggage down to the Sacramento boat for you."

Hyde stared. "By God!" he said at last. "You don't need luck, but if you'll take my advice you'll carry a gun."

"Got one," said Baldwin pleasantly, and produced a small pearl-handled pistol from a side pocket.

Hyde gasped, and moved away. Baldwin grinned, and turned to his new business. In thirty days he had improved it to such an extent that he sold out for a net profit of five thousand dollars. In the San Francisco of 1853 that was an achievement worthy of note. Most local business was extremely bad. The sensational prosperity which had followed the sensational gold-rush of '49 had been dwindling sadly through the two years which had followed the necessity for organization of the first Vigilance Committee under Samuel Brannan in the summer of 1851.

State government and courts reeked of the graft which was

the precursor of the racketeering of three-quarters of a century later. The criminal element, organized and intrenched in politics to fatten on the millions in gold coming into San Francisco, had demoralized the business of the state's center of supplies and trade. The vigilantes, hanging eight notorious criminals and deporting fifty in the summer of '51, had brought only superficial order out of chaos.

Before Baldwin arrived in San Francisco crime and graft together were growing again. The first rich placer claims on the western slopes of the Sierra seemed to have been stripped. Men were turning to deeper mining, which required both more capital and more skill. It was no longer common for a New York shipping clerk, a New England farmer or a New Orleans waiter to trudge to some mountain creek and return with a thousand or five or fifty thousand dollars' worth of gold.

Eggs which had cost three dollars a dozen in 1850 were down to a dollar and a half in 1853. Chickens which had brought five dollars apiece could now be purchased for two. Pork had dropped from fifty cents to thirty cents a pound. Onions had fallen from seventy-five cents to twenty-five cents, and everything else in proportion. Judged by standards of 1932, prices were still high, but judged by the standards of 1850 the merchandising profits of 1853 had been reduced to the vanishing point.

With many of the placer streams worked to exhaustion, and with gamblers, robbers and political grafters taking the profits of those still producing, a definite exodus from the state had started. More persons were leaving, broken in spirit and in pocket, than were coming in. The state's only product of any importance was gold. When that diminished, business failed. An editorial comment from *The Alta California* of February 12, 1853, reveals the depths to which San Francisco had fallen and in which it still struggled when the Baldwin fortunes were cast with it:

"There has never been so deplorable an exhibition of mendicancy in our streets as may be witnessed daily at this time, . . . hundreds of destitute men and scores of women and children besieging the pockets of society in public and private, in doors and out. . . . Little girls . . . are to be found in front of the city saloons at all hours of the day, going through their graceless performances."

That was the situation when E. J. Baldwin revealed a business ability sufficient to improve a five-thousand-dollar investment to the extent of a five-thousand-dollar profit in thirty days. At the age of twenty-five he had not yet acquired the penchant to hold on to property, especially real property, ignoring an immediate profit for the sake of a greater increment, which was to be a dominating characteristic of his later, greater, years.

He was still the trader, the Indiana farm-boy who would buy a broken-down horse, feed and groom it into higher value or appearance of value, and sell it at a profit. With the assistance of an industrious wife he saw to the cleaning, repairing and grooming of the Pacific Temperance Hotel, and the feeding of its patrons with better food and service until the hotel prospered despite the general business depression. Then he sold, and took his profit.

And then too he made his first business error in the new land. The development and sale of hotels promised a greater profit than the operation of hotels. He started a new one on Jackson Street which he called The Clinton. But its location, chosen for its cheapness, was too far from the long wharf which was the traffic center of the San Francisco of that day. Even clean rooms and superior board failed to lure the transients coming in on the Sacramento River steamers and going out to board ships for Panama or around the Horn. The hotel languished. In five months the five-thousand-dollar profit of Baldwin's first venture in the new land had vanished, but he succeeded in selling the hotel to a man named Corbett.

It was the first business reverse of his career, but he accepted it philosophically. "I'm not licked yet," he told his wife, when he had settled his family temporarily in a frame cabin. "Good thing I got rid of The Clinton. You're lookin' kind of peaked, Sarah Ann. You been workin' too hard, mebbe. Now you can take it kind of easy here while the baby is on the way, an' I'll go out an' make us a livin' some way so's we won't have to cut into our capital any more till business seems to pick up."

Jobs were hard to get in San Francisco, but Baldwin was energetic and resourceful. He was still a notably good hand with horses, and managed to pick up enough money to feed his family without drawing on his reserve. Between jobs he managed to investigate business possibilities as far away as Stockton and Sacramento, but found nothing of promise.

More miners were coming into the city in 1854 without funds than with funds. The organized crime and graft which had been checked temporarily by the vigilantes' ropes and "tickets of leave" in 1851 and 1852 were making themselves obnoxious again in 1854. The small farms which had supplied the gold camps with staple foods were being abandoned in direct ratio to the abandonment of the worked-out placer bars, and their owners were drifting back to the city, broke. Business was rotten.

And in that situation, on August 25, 1854, Baldwin's wife gave birth to Baldwin's second daughter, named Elizabeth, for his mother. Mrs. Baldwin was very ill. The baby was puny and fretful. The mother's strength returned slowly and with it her temper, which was as quick as that of her husband, and now under poorer control. Perhaps this, and perhaps the uncertainty of Baldwin's small trading ventures and intermittent employment accounted for the fact that he was seldom at home.

It was not, at the moment, a happy family. Baldwin was

on better terms with his little daughter, Clara, then seven years old, than with either his wife or the new baby. Clara was a strong, upstanding, handsome little girl with a temper that refused to bow either to her mother or father. Her small rages amused the father, and occasionally he found time to play a bit with her, or to take her on walks through the brush and scrubby trees which sheltered flocks of quail and innumerable jackrabbits in the neighborhood of what is now the civic center of San Francisco.

Affairs drifted rather unhappily along into the next year. "I'm not licked yet," was Baldwin's reiterated answer to the complaints of his wife and the wails of his baby.

He spoke the truth.

Chapter VII

THE VIGILANTES CLEAN UP

Rambling around the edge of the city, at Powell and Union Streets, on a day when the business outlook seemed as gray as the sky overhead, Baldwin happened upon a small building bearing a crudely painted sign: Wormer Brick Company. He had not seen the son of his Racine friends since the day two years before when he had consigned young Wormer's eighteen-year-old sister, Rachel, to his care. So he entered the office smiling, and was received with courtesy.

The accidental renewal of acquaintance was the start of a new deal for Baldwin. He had expected to stay perhaps five minutes. The visit extended for two hours. When Baldwin departed he carried with him a signed partnership agreement and a receipt for a payment upon the price fixed. And Baldwin was never a man to part easily with money. Young Wormer's boastfulness of his business success, backed by figures on costs and sales, had proved to be an astonishing sales talk, perhaps because he had no idea of making it so.

"I tell you, Mr. Baldwin," he said, "if San Francisco is to go on growing, it has to grow with bricks, and I make the bricks. Why, the first year I was here, 'forty-nine, there were two bad fires that almost destroyed the town. In the next three years there were four more bad ones. Most of the buildings in town then were just thrown together with rough lumber. Of course we all use oil lamps and candles. A lot of the cooking a few years ago, and some even now, is done over open fires in back yards littered with packing cases and scraps. About our only water supply was in barrels at back doors, and still is.

Sydneymen and a lot of other criminals who flocked in with the first gold-rush found it was easier to set fire to a few buildings and loot them and others in the excitement than it was to work.

"It cost a lot of money and was bad for business. It has held the town back. Now every one with brains as well as money and confidence in the future of the town is building with brick instead of wood when they build at all. It's the best fire insurance they can get. I tell you some day San Francisco is going to be a city of a hundred thousand people, and I'm going to get rich making brick for its new buildings."

"How much do you make?" Baldwin asked.

Wormer, proud of his success, produced records of costs and sales. Baldwin was convinced. When he left the little office he was a partner in the brick business. In the next two months he sold more bricks than Wormer could manufacture. In intervals of salesmanship he worked in the yard and fired the kilns to speed up production, to fill his orders. Potential profits were not being gathered. Baldwin could never stand that. He had learned enough of the manufacturing end to feel that he could make bricks as good as Wormer's. When he had decided that he searched the region for another clay deposit, and having found one on a country road called Lombard Street, he purchased it and dissolved his partnership with Wormer.

By night he studied the theory of brick-making in every book and pamphlet he could find on the subject. By day he practised in the clay pit and drying yard. To rest between jobs he carried samples of his bricks to potential builders and took orders. Business was booming for E. J. Baldwin, if not for San Francisco in general.

"I told you I wasn't licked yet," he told his wife, nursing the infant Lizzie.

"The baby's sick," said Sarah Ann harshly.

"I'll send in a doctor to-morrow, on my way to the yard."

"You better."

Next day the doctor came, looked the little one over and shook his head. "Puny," he said. "Nothing special I can see wrong. Just puny. She's past a year old now. You'd better give her some cow's milk three times a day."

"There's no cow's milk to be had in San Francisco, Doctor."

"Oh, yes, there is. There's a dozen people living in that nice district over south of Market Street, and some in other places that keep their own cows. Some of 'em are my patients. I'll find one with a boy to bring a quart or so over to you every day. It'll be expensive, maybe four bits a quart, but the baby ought to have it. She's puny."

The milk came the next day, and regularly thereafter. But the baby took little of it. Little Clara profited, and became huskier day by day as Lizzie faded. Baldwin was too busy to notice except when his wife demanded his attention. Then he picked up the wailing infant and examined it closely.

"Poor little brat," he said. "I'll send the doctor again."

A week later, despite daily visits by the doctor, the baby died. It was October 30, 1855. For a time the loss, their first real grief in nine years of married life, brought husband and wife more closely together. But Baldwin was busy and prospering. He had come into touch with the builders of San Francisco, and had absorbed some of their certainty of a great future for their city. He had invested in half a dozen pieces of property. The federal government was recognizing the importance of the port of San Francisco with plans for a fort to guard the Golden Gate, and a structure on Alcatraz Island, in the bay.

Baldwin obtained the job of superintending the government's brickyards at a salary of four hundred dollars a month. That did not meet his desires. Both by nature and by the independent experience of all his adult years he was an employer, not an employee. He arranged a contract with the government to board the fifty men at work in the brickyard. In this his hotel experience again became of value, and was further extended. The contract netted him six hundred dollars a month.

The total income of one thousand dollars a month was needed to carry and expand his real-estate investments, including several sage-brush lots on Market Street. He was working day and night. The resurgence of crime and graft which had followed the disbandment of the first Vigilance Committee and accompanied the business depression of the early '50s was a serious threat to the growth of the city and the value of Baldwin's investments. He was troubled, and with good reason.

Riding out one day to look over a recently purchased lot on the newly surveyed McAllister Street, he discovered a tent on the property and a ramshackle fence around it. Squatters were common in the outskirts of San Francisco at the time, and Baldwin recognized the sign. Also he knew that appeal to the authorities to clear these squatters from his newly purchased lot would be futile. It was possible that the authorities had even conspired with the squatters to establish themselves there in the expectation of securing title through some corrupt court procedure. So Baldwin made some inquiries. His suspicions were confirmed when he learned that the fence had been thrown up by city firemen.

"There was nothing to do but fight for it," he told a friend, years later. "So I went back to town, obtained men and guns, and went out again to the lot. We surrounded the place and shouted to the squatters to come out. Two men who looked as though they might have been products of the British prison camps in Australia, the type generally recognized in San Francisco as criminals, stuck their heads out of the tent. I had ten men, armed with muskets and shotguns and pistols. The squatters realized that they were licked. In ten minutes the tent was down and the lot cleared. Not a shot was necessary, though shooting among the squatters was common in those days.

"I built a cabin on the lot and put in a man named McHenry as guard. He was a man who had come out from Racine with me, and I knew he could fight. But he didn't have to. Neither the authorities nor the Sydneymen did anything about it. Probably they didn't think the lot was worth gun-play when there were so many others to be grabbed from owners who wouldn't fight. McHenry stayed there until I sold the lot at a profit.

"If he hadn't already been a loyal friend he would have been after I rescued him from the worst scare he ever had in his life. There was a big Chinese graveyard out in that direction, and the city grafters who wanted the land decided it would have to be moved. So a gang of Chinamen went to work to take out the coffins and ship the bones back to China. One night I happened to drive McHenry out in a buggy. The streets were nothing but ruts through the brush, and there wasn't a light for a mile, and I dropped him at a wrong corner. Instead of getting to his cabin he stumbled over a shovel, fell against a pile of coffins stacked up beside an open grave, and finally managed to fall into the grave and dump the bones of half a dozen Chinamen in on top of himself.

"He let out a yell that almost made my horse run away. I jumped out of the buggy and stumbled through the dark toward the yells. Even in the dark I could see I was in that graveyard and I didn't care much for it myself, but I went on, thinking something terrible had happened to McHenry. When I reached the grave I could just make out by the starlight that it seemed half full of white bones and skulls and waving arms and legs, and most God-awful yells.

"When I realized what had happened I had to sit down on the edge of a coffin and laugh. That seemed to scare the live man in the grave worse than ever. He let out a shriek that even stopped my laugh.

" 'Wait a minute, Mac,' I said, 'it's E. J. Give me a hand an' I'll pull you out.'

"Well, I dragged him out, an' he was as white as a skull himself. But grateful? You never saw such a grateful man in your life. It was pitiful. I didn't dare laugh again till I got him over to his cabin. Then I got back to my buggy, an' my horse must have thought I was crazy, going home."

But even such rough comedy could not compensate for the seriousness of the crime situation. Members of the first Vigilance Committee, which had operated so effectively with the hanging of eight men and the deportation of fifty, met after four years to discuss reorganization. The criminal element failed to see the handwriting upon the wall, and when the prominent and influential James King publicly denounced one James Casey as a thief, extortionist and fire-bug, Casey murdered King in cold blood. Then he boasted that the courts would acquit him. Probably the courts would have done so, but the more honest business men who had organized and operated the first Vigilance Committee would not.

The erstwhile executives of the committee met at once, reorganized, and voted to punish Casey. The murderer's arrogance vanished abruptly when he heard the news, and he took refuge in the county jail. A call for new members of the Vigilance Committee brought twelve hundred men together in twenty-four hours. Fully armed, they closed in upon the jail, removed Casey and another murderer named Cosa, tried them and hanged them. Eight days after his murder of King, Casey dangled at the end of his rope. The vigilantes went home for a few days of peace. Their action was salutary but insufficient.

Less than a month later David S. Terry, Associate Justice of the State Supreme Court, stabbed an officer who was arresting a notorious grafting politician who had supported Terry. The tolling of a firebell promptly summoned the vigilantes. The so-called legal authorities who called themselves "law and order men" also called their cohorts. The vigilantes seized Terry almost from under the guns of the "law and order men" and carried him to headquarters. They were not quite ready, however, to hang a justice of their highest court, and were satisfied to hold him until the victim of his bowie-knife was on the road to recovery. Then they released him.

Terry was a fire-eater, an adventurer, a man of violence. The fact that a man of his type could have been elevated to the Supreme Court bench was in itself the best evidence of the depravity of state and city government. A native of Kentucky, he had served under General Sam Houston in the Texas war and in the war between the United States and Mexico. He had come to California with the first gold-rush and had discovered more possibilities of wealth and power in the devious politics and court methods than in the placer mines. He was still to figure in two of the most famous killings and in one of the most famous court cases in the history of California, but this first stabbing affray was of importance only in so far as it resulted immediately in the recruiting of the new Vigilance Committee to a membership of eight thousand armed men.

The eight thousand were organized into companies of infantry and cavalry, drilled and disciplined. The venal "law and order men" were worried. They appealed to the governor to break up the organization, and the governor accepted their mandate and ordered the vigilantes to be dispersed, by force of arms if necessary. California was threatened with civil war.

But the vigilantes were backed by the force of public opinion. Such men as Baldwin, who had staked their small fortunes and their labor upon the orderly growth of San Francisco, realized that only by the elimination of organized crime and graft could the city attain the high destiny which they hoped for it. They supported the committee with arms and money, and urged it to do its duty. The committee barricaded its headquarters with sand-bags, winning the name of "Fort Gunnybags," and defied the half-hearted attacks of the so-called authorities. Members policed the streets, arrested offenders, uncovered evidence and conducted trials. Before the summer was over it had hanged two more men, and deported twenty-five. More than eight hundred notorious criminals hastily left the city. The courts and constituted authorities themselves took notice and began to enforce more rigid justice.

San Francisco was cleaned, and the entire state was chastened. On August 21, 1856, the committee, eight thousand strong, paraded the streets with fife and drum corps, and announced its disbandment with its work accomplished. Business, relieved of the strangling grasp of crime and corruption, began to recover strength. Baldwin heaved a sigh of relief and turned to his labors with new energy.

Another baby was on its way. The child was born in March of 1857, a boy. He was christened Elias Jackson Baldwin, Jr. Baldwin was delighted. But the new happiness ended quickly in a deeper sorrow. The baby lived but two weeks. That death marked almost the end of domestic happiness in the home of E. J. Baldwin and his wife Sarah Ann.

No one who was old enough to be observant at that time remains to testify as to who was at fault. Baldwin himself, though an active business man, was not of sufficient importance in the San Francisco of 1857 to have entered the public record. The amours which made his name as notorious as did his horses, his millions and his luck in later life probably had not begun. The evidence of this may be deduced from the close parallel of later scandals and growing wealth.

In 1857 he had neither time nor money to spend promiscuously upon women. He was engrossed in his business, and probably close with his money, every cent of which was needed to carry his investments in San Francisco real estate. And Sarah Ann Unruh, though she had been a faithful and indus-

LUCKY BALDWIN

trious wife for eleven years, had a temper and ideas of her own. Testimony to that effect is available in records made many years later.

Between a close-fisted business man and a violent-tempered wife there was little peace. Perhaps if the two babies had lived the outcome might have been different. But they had not lived, and the breach widened. The home was not happy. Baldwin buried himself in business.

The brick-making contract with the government had been completed, and shortly after the death of his infant son Baldwin established a livery-stable business in San Francisco. Horses were, as they had been since childhood and were to continue through life, one of his chief delights. But such a business could provide neither sufficient outlet for his energies nor sufficient profits for his ambition. He continued to extend his real-estate trading and to take his first lessons in the speculative possibilities of mining deals.

In his real-estate operations Baldwin took no man's word. He rode far and wide to examine possible purchases. Thus it happened that he was an eye-witness to one of the most famous killings in the history of the West—the Terry-Broderick duel. He described the scene thirty-odd years later to the historian, H. H. Bancroft.

David S. Terry, the same fire-eating justice of the State Supreme Court who had precipitated the second organization of the Vigilance Committee by stabbing an officer who was about to arrest a notorious political knave, had been unchastened by his narrow escape from death at the hands of the aroused vigilantes. He had gone his swashbuckling, bulldozing and violent way until he had run afoul of Senator D. C. Broderick, a man generally respected in the community and in the Senate. Broderick had refused to back down before Terry's violence and had told the Kentuckian where to head in. Terry had challenged him to a duel. Even in the rough-

and-ready government of California formal duels were not looked upon with favor, but Broderick evidently felt that acceptance of this challenge was his only honorable course.

The affair was quietly arranged, and the principals and their seconds repaired to an outlying and very thinly settled district near what was known as Seven-Mile House. Baldwin, ignorant of the impending tragedy, happened to be riding through the district examining land which was for sale. His first intimation of trouble was when he broke through the scrub and discovered two men facing each other with pistols in their hands.

By the time he had pulled up his horse and recognized the two men, both of whom were known to every resident of San Francisco, Broderick's bullet had kicked up the sand at his feet and Terry was aiming his own gun with deadly eyes.

"Broderick's pistol went off accidentally, and Terry simply murdered him."

That was Baldwin's statement thirty-odd years later. If he had made it public at the time he might have precipitated another reorganization of the vigilantes for the hanging of Terry, for the town was humming with threats by the time he returned to his livery-stable. But Baldwin was a man unique in his ability to mind his own business. He kept his mouth shut.

Terry lived on to greater notoriety, greater scandal and more bloodshed, ending with his own. He led a heavily armed party of claim-jumpers in the early days of Virginia City and held off all opposition until he abandoned the ground voluntarily to return to Kentucky to fight in the Confederate Army in the Civil War. He fought spectacularly as counsel for Sarah Althea Hill in her famous suit against William Sharon, Comstock multimillionaire. Having lost the case he married the fair Sarah Althea and threatened to kill Justice Field, before whom the case had been tried. In the end he fell before the gun of Justice Field's body-guard, who pleaded self-defense and was freed.

In the meantime E. J. Baldwin was going quietly about his own affairs. Expanding his real-estate speculations to include mining, he learned that the exhaustion of the placer bars along the Sierra streams had turned the energies of the few mining engineers of the day to search for the sources of the placer gold. A new and golden promise of deep mining had developed. But this required capital.

Instead of attacking a gravel bar with shovel and rocker, the owner of a claim now had to sell a fractional interest for enough cash to install machinery for development of his holdings. Miners with claims and rich samples of ore were crowding every barroom, every hotel office, and patrolling Montgomery Street in the neighborhood of the Wells Fargo office, trying to sell interests to develop their claims. The mining stock exchange had not yet been conceived. Baldwin began to learn about both mining and mine speculation. The few small speculations that he tried turned out poorly. He sought further information.

One of his acquaintances was Adolph Sutro, a German Jewish immigrant of about his own age, and of similar ambition, industry and persistence, but of superior education and intellectual attainments. Sutro had arrived in San Francisco in 1850, three years before Baldwin, but too late to find the easy riches of the first placers. He had been forced to engage in whatever business offered to maintain himself, but he had not been content. He had spent every available hour in the study of the best works on mining and metallurgy available. He had supplemented this study with experiments in a laboratory of his own and with talks with all the practical miners and engineers he could meet. Incidentally he had familiarized himself with the promotion methods of the day as they developed.

Sutro came occasionally to Baldwin's livery-stable to hire a horse or a rig. The two men were sufficiently alike in their ambition and the indomitability of their characters to develop a mutual respect. Baldwin recognized the superiority of Sutro's learning. When opportunity offered, he questioned:

"What do you think of this deep mining that seems to be taking the place of the placers, Mr. Sutro?"

"It is the inevitable development," said Sutro. "That placer gold has been washed down for centuries from decomposing quartz. Most of it has been panned out on the surface. But other ledges are there, hidden. They will be found. But it takes money to sink shafts and hoist ore and extract the gold from it. It will be a bigger business than the placer mining was at its best."

"I bought a little share in a mine at Grass Valley the other day," said Baldwin. "Here's a sample." He displayed a bit of quartz, shot thickly with gold. "What do you think of it?"

Sutro examined the specimen, and his eyes brightened. "It's rich," he said. "It's what they call free gold; that is, free milling gold. All that's needed to work ore like that is to crush it and run it through a mill. If crushed, it could even be washed in rockers like any placer gold. If there is a big body of it in the mine you're interested in, you've got a good thing."

"I've been offered more than I paid for it," said Baldwin.

"Then you've got a certain profit if you take it now," said Sutro. "There are two ways to look at this mining business as it is developing in California now. Some men will make money out of owning, promoting and developing deep mines. Others will make it out of buying and selling interests in the mines, regardless of whether the mines themselves ever produce dividends in gold. In a year or two, I suspect, the way things are going now, we will have a regular exchange organized for such buying and selling."

Sutro was correct in his forecast, but a little premature in the date. The San Francisco Stock and Exchange Board was not to be organized for four years, on September 11, 1862, and then upon the demand of great promotions on the Comstock Lode, discovered in western Nevada in 1859. But in the meantime the buying and selling of fractional interests not yet dignified as shares of stock continued from hand to hand in San Francisco.

Baldwin discovered that there were profits in shrewd trading of such fractional interests even before the mine involved had hoisted a single bucket of ore. His interest in actual mining for profits waned with this discovery and his interest in the buying and selling of mining rights and shares expanded. But at the same time he discovered that accurate first-hand information as to the potential value of claims offered for promotion was invaluable. The men who had such information almost invariably profited at the expense of those who did not have it.

So, when a heap of silver bars appeared in the window of the Bank of California late in 1859 with the announcement that they were the first product of the newly discovered Comstock Lode, in the Washoe district of western Nevada, Baldwin sat up and took notice. The town seethed with excitement over reports that there were thousands of tons of ore available assaying up to two thousand dollars a ton in gold and five thousand dollars a ton in silver. The excitement which stirred not only San Francisco but all the towns of northern California and the dwindling gold camps of the Sierras to such frenzy as they had not known since the original gold-rush, ten years earlier, communicated itself to Baldwin.

He was not a man to go off half-cocked, except occasionally in matters of temper. In matters of dollars and cents he was invariably cold and calculating. He had witnessed several stampedes out of San Francisco in his six years of residence and knew that most of them were false alarms. So he investigated and found satisfactory evidence that the first assays of this Comstock ore had been made from ore carried to Grass Valley, California, and given to Judge James Walsh of that town.

The certified assay reports showed $1,595 in gold and $4,791 in silver to the ton of ore. When he had obtained that information from satisfactory sources, Baldwin was convinced.

He decided to go and look over the ground himself and buy up some interests for promotion. But by that time the mountains were impassable with snow, and hundreds of would-be stampeders, like Baldwin, were forced to wait through the winter. Even then, Baldwin had no great faith in the actual value of the discovery. He himself had never been inoculated with the fever which changes a man's whole life and character from the moment he first sees a line of yellow dust appearing at the edge of the wet sand in a gold pan in his own hands. But he knew that reports of six-thousand-dollar ore in vast quantities would make a great boom camp from which he should profit in the promotion and sale of claims.

He had an advantage over a great many of the excited Californians in that he was acquainted with the topography of the region involved. Gold Canyon on the slope of Mount Davidson, where the vast new riches were reported to have been discovered, loomed clear in his memory. He had traveled its whole barren length of sun-bleached stone, wind-driven sand, gray sage-brush and darkly twisted piñon trees only seven years before.

When excited men crowded into his stables to hire or buy horses for the long trip to the latest El Dorado, Baldwin knew what they were facing when they spoke of Johnson's Cut-Off, Gold Canyon, Washoe Lake and Carson Valley. He could furnish information and directions as well as horses. The information he gave freely. The horses suddenly increased one hundred per cent., two hundred per cent., three hundred per cent. in value.

"No, I can't hire out a horse for that trip. It's too far, and too tough. I've been over it, coming this direction. Yes, I'll sell you a good one, broke to pack or to ride. The price has gone up a little. Looks like the demand was going to clean out my stable soon as the snow goes out, an' leave me without anything to accommodate my local trade. I've got to look out for that."

It was good business for Baldwin, and he sat back in comfort to count his first indirect profits from the Comstock Lode. In the early spring he was away with the others to take more direct profits.

He came again to Placerville, now seething with business and the excitement of the stampeders preparing to defy the mud, snow, avalanches and bitter cold of the high mountains. With a man named Howard and another whose name has been lost from the record, he climbed the long slope to Strawberry, a snowbound and meager shelter on the old emigrant trail. The proprietor of the station and the few members of the advance guard of the Washoe rush who were there warned the party not to go on.

Baldwin never took kindly to warnings. His egotism and self-confidence were too great. Though a man of little more than average size he was built of steel and whipcord, and knew it. He led his companions out from Strawberry flat to the steep climb to the summit of the western divide. It was a cold gray day of lowering clouds and threatening storm. Two or three miles out from Strawberry the snow began to fall again. Baldwin and his companions struggled onward, upward. The storm increased in violence. They fought onward, pausing occasionally to rest in some temporary shelter of fallen trees or overhanging rock.

Perhaps eight miles up the slope, Howard collapsed. Even Baldwin began to feel the strain, and decided that they should make camp and wait out the storm. They found a windfall which promised some shelter, and gathered twigs and sticks with which to start a fire. The first match flared and faded. The second match did likewise. Baldwin took stock. He had but one match left. Howard had two. The other man had none. And without a fire they would sleep at a temperature below zero that night. It meant that they would not awaken.

The three shivering men gathered close in the snow, spreading their coats to shield the tiny flame of the next match from the gale. The match sputtered, flared and faded. There were two matches left between them and death by freezing. Neither Baldwin nor the others were praying men, but we may suspect that they prayed then. If they did, the prayer was answered. The flame held until the twigs ignited. A fire soon blazed. They huddled together between windbreak and fire, boiled a pail of coffee, and drank it scalding between bites of hardtack and half-frozen salt pork.

In the midst of the dreary meal, Baldwin suddenly laughed aloud. His companions looked up in amazement. "What t'hell?" they demanded with one voice.

"Nothin'." Baldwin laughed again. "I was just thinkin' about another time I had to eat pork in a snow-storm. Only I had to kill that myself, and it wasn't salted. I was about ten years old then, and now I'm past thirty. I had run away from home to make my fortune and had got stuck for the night in a deserted cabin with a half-wild pig. Well, I still got a long ways to go."

He arose and built up the fire. Throughout the night he made that his responsibility. Daylight found the little group miserable but alive. The snowfall had stopped and the crust was frozen just enough to make walking almost impossible. They debated over a meager breakfast. Baldwin was for going on. The others demurred. A hail from a distant ridge settled the argument.

It was Snowshoe Thompson, even then famous in the West for his accomplishments in carrying mail through the snow-bound mountains. He had been sent on the trail of the fool-hardy trio by the proprietor of the station at Strawberry, where he had arrived in the midst of the storm the previous evening. In an interview many years later, Baldwin told of the rescue.

"When Snowshoe Thompson showed up there was no more argument about whether we should go on. He told us we just couldn't make it on that light crust without snowshoes, and we had sense enough to believe him. He had a reputation. And besides, Howard was a wreck. He went back first. He put his feet on the back of Thompson's snowshoes and his arms around Thompson's neck, and away they slid, down the eight miles to Strawberry.

"It was slow work for Thompson to come back, and our hopes were just about down to zero when his 'Hello' brought us back to life. Thompson made those three round trips without a kick. I've traveled all the ways there are to travel, from elephant-back in India to jinrikishas in Japan and the fastest coach and eight in California, but that ride on the back of Thompson's snowshoes was the fastest and most exciting in my life."

The journey to the Comstock was delayed, but not discouraged. Baldwin arrived in time to see the victims of the Pyramid Lake Indian massacre of the Ormsby punitive expedition, some eighty men, carried into the rambling new camp of Virginia City. He himself joined in the expedition organized to chastise the Piutes for that unfortunate affair. Also he made what investigation he could of the first mines opening on the lode, convinced himself that they had a future rather than a profitable present, bought a few "feet" here and there, and returned to San Francisco prepared to deal with any promotions that might be suggested.

San Francisco had a new lease on life. Luxuries had been added to its necessities. The overland stages were coming in on regular schedule—three weeks' drive from St. Louis. The first pony express brought mail from St. Joe, Missouri, in ten days in 1860, and the first steam-driven street-car moved on

Market Street.   The first steam fire-engine appeared and demonstrated its efficiency.   Gold and silver from the Comstock mines began to supplement the diminishing streams of gold from the California placers.

The city had almost doubled in population in the seven years of Baldwin's residence.   Business was picking up, and Baldwin was prepared to make the most of it.

CHAPTER VIII

THE COMSTOCK EXCITEMENT

BUSINESS picked up with a rush in San Francisco in 1860. It was a city of attainment as well as of promise, a city of gay sophistication, effervescent in its youth, astonishing in its energy and ambition, eager, alive, unconventional. It was delighted with itself and its possibilities.

The newly established pony express had brought its business men and its newspapers into real contact with the world. The overland stage service was bringing new fashions and luxuries from the East in three weeks or less. The city's streets were gay and its restaurants were beginning to attain the distinction and charm which were to grow in fame throughout the world.

New wealth was pouring in from the Comstock and from the improved mining methods on the Mother Lode. New residents, business men and investors were arriving from the East. The outlook was bright. E. J. Baldwin's resolution to take his profit from the city's expanding business weakened in the general excitement. Why be satisfied to hold a pail under a faucet when one might dip it in the reservoir at the source?

Adolph Sutro, coming to the Baldwin stables to buy new horses for his second journey to the Comstock, spoke with stirring enthusiasm. "It is going to be the greatest mining district in the world," he said. "It will be the greatest field for capitalists. That deposit is a true fissure vein. It runs down for thousands of feet. There will be millions of dollars spent for promotion and machinery."

Baldwin was impressed, but cautious. "How much are freight costs running now?" he asked.

"Anything," said Sutro, "anything at all. A packer may take a load out of Placerville at five cents a pound. He may lose half his mules in the mud within fifty miles, or see them slide off the grade. Another man may take what is left of the freight if you are there to arrange it, and charge you fifty cents a pound to deliver it in Virginia City."

"I see," said Baldwin. Such business was a little too speculative to suit him. He decided to wait and watch. In the meantime the business of buying and selling horses for the growing lines of Washoe freighters was highly profitable. Before the summer was over the first toll roads were being opened across the mountains. Baldwin learned that lumber prices in Virginia City had fallen from four hundred dollars to eighty dollars per thousand feet. Substantial business houses, hotels, restaurants and cabins were displacing the first tangle of tents and shacks upon the slope of Mount Davidson. Still Baldwin waited.

Returning travelers told him that the business of the Comstock was continuing at fever heat, with an impromptu curb exchange operating twenty-four hours a day for the sale of "feet" in various claims. The excitement was reflected in San Francisco. Bartenders, stable-boys, business men and society women were speculating blindly in the Washoe promotions. Baldwin continued to hold off.

He was still sticking to his business when the first reaction set in. Speculators discovered that they had been buying "feet" in claims located miles from the first producing mines such as Ophir, Chollar, Corsair and Washoe. Values crashed. Even the richly producing mines slumped to a fourth of their best prices of that first hectic year. San Francisco awakened from its debauch with a sad financial headache. Baldwin congratulated himself upon his caution.

But despite himself he had been inoculated with the fever. When the wild excitement and mad speculation settled down to more rational production, Baldwin was susceptible to its promise. The livery business was not so good. Baldwin's home life since the death of the two babies had become less and less satisfactory. He dragged through another year with small profit and less enthusiasm. When his daughter Clara was sent to Mills College, already a girls' school of note, across the bay from San Francisco, there was little to keep him tied to the treadmill. So, in 1862, he sold out his livery business, reserving a few teams and wagons, and headed back over the trail to the Comstock.

At a sawmill in the Sierras he loaded his wagons with lumber, and moved on past Lake Tahoe to the Carson Valley, and once again climbed Gold Canyon. It was nothing like the scene he had first looked upon so indifferently nine years before. Where his saddle and pack-train had followed a narrow rocky trail, his heavily loaded wagons now rolled smoothly over a well-tended road, wide enough at every point for ore and freight wagons to pass. Where two or three itinerant prospectors had been seen scratching with their picks at surface gravel, two or three thousand men were now swarming.

Over the ridge at the head of the canyon, whence a lone Piute squaw had looked down on the first Baldwin party, a town of ten thousand souls now clung to the mountainside. Ore wagons rolled in an almost unbroken line down Gold Canyon to the reduction mills on the Carson River. Freight wagons dragged in a similar line up the grade to the twin camps of Gold Hill and Virginia City.

Baldwin and his skinners guided their teams over the ridge where James W. Nye, first governor of the newly created Territory of Nevada had passed "under a splendid arch made by the ladies of the city," and had been greeted by cheers and rifle salutes in the preceding year. Baldwin stopped at a real-estate office for information, and was directed to an area where he might leave his teams and wagons temporarily.

Before the day was out he had purchased a lot below the town and established a lumber-yard. As usual, he conserved his resources and contented himself with a tent and his own cooking on a corner of his lot until he could look into the possibilities of the town.

But business in Virginia City, though still active, was slackening. The pony express, unsupported by the government, had been abandoned after a year and a half of spectacular service. The mad speculation which had brought vast sums of money into the development of the Comstock had been greatly reduced by the failure of innumerable wildcat companies. The richest mines had worked out their best ore to a depth of two or three hundred feet and were encountering great and costly difficulties in the steaming floods and caving stopes of lower depths.

Such battles as that promoted by the fire-eating Judge David S. Terry, who had brought a group of henchmen to the district, squatted on a disputed claim and fought with knives, guns and clubs to hold it, had passed. Court battles had taken their place. Terry had met William M. Stewart, most spectacular of mining-camp lawyers, in the great legal battle between the Ophir and McCall companies for title to disputed ground, and had carried the trial to a disagreement of the jury in a court-room crowded by three hundred armed men. The case had been dropped with the Ophir's purchase of the McCall claims, and Terry had left the Comstock to join a Kentucky regiment in the Civil War. Senator Stewart and others were continuing to pile up legal fees which aggregated ten million dollars. Such drains as that were sapping the prosperity of the district when Baldwin arrived. In fact Baldwin's caution had cut him out of the big money of the first stampede, just as it had made him late for the big money of the California gold-rush, and was to make him late for the big money again in the Alaska gold-rush forty years later.

Building operations were almost at a standstill. Lumber prices were dropping. Baldwin could not dispose of his wagon-loads wholesale at a profit. He decided to sell them retail. "There's more ways of killing a cat than choking it to death on pudding," was one of his favorite aphorisms. This seemed to be a good time to apply it. There was no immediate urge to return to San Francisco. His interest in life with Sarah Ann had been on the wane, by mutual consent, for several years. There was no reason why he should not remain in Virginia City until he could dispose of his lumber at a small profit, and at the same time take advantage of the opportunity to study the city, the mines and mining business in general.

The Comstock Lode was a tremendous laboratory for such research. *The Territorial Enterprise,* soon to be the first journalistic school of Mark Twain, provided a directory and curriculum for the student. If he were interested in sociology and criminology there was a murder or two a week in the boozing kens, gambling houses and segregated district, or a wildcat and bulldog fight in Piper's Opera House, or a traveling stock company's melodrama at the same theater to be enjoyed. If he were interested in finance and promotion there was the curb-exchange on C Street, and the record of prices and production in the newspaper. If he were interested in mines and metallurgy there were the producing mines and the pounding reduction mills, ably described and reported by Dan DeQuille.

The bonanza kings, Mackay, Fair, Flood and O'Brien, were as yet unheard of. The coming financial magnate, William C. Sharon, was still in the real-estate business in San Francisco. The indomitable promoter and tunnel-builder, Adolph Sutro, had just seen his highly profitable mill on the Carson River go up in smoke. That most spectacular of mining-camp lawyers, William M. Stewart, was still only a lawyer-politician, though perhaps the leading man of the district. Baldwin himself was only a keen-eyed, hard-drawn man with an unfailing instinct for the main chance. That chance, he decided after a few weeks of study and inspection in the intervals of selling out his lumber stock, lay in the trading of mine shares rather than in the actual working of the mines.

On several occasions when Adolph Sutro rode up from his place at Dayton on the Carson River, looking into the possibilities of promoting the great tunnel which was to make him a leading figure in the West for many years, Baldwin met and talked with him. In that contact he learned something of the geological formation of the lode. At other times he managed to gain entrance to the workings of the Ophir, then the greatest mine in the district, and to the Mexican, the Savage, the Chollar and others. By the time his lumber was sold off he felt that he knew more about the Comstock and its possibilities than did most of the men who were trading in its stocks. So he returned to San Francisco to cash in on this knowledge.

But at the moment the mining business was dull, and to find an outlet for his energies and investment for his idle capital he reentered the livery business with J. N. Killip in the Commercial Street Livery-Stables.

The first wild gambling in Comstock shares with its heavy losses to wildcat investors had brought the mining-stock business into ill repute. Money that should have been going into the basic trade and industries of San Francisco and the agricultural development of the West had been sunk and lost in Washoe stocks. Eastern funds which had been available for investment in western mines at the start of the Comstock boom were cut off by the Civil War. When the stocks collapsed, legitimate business was swamped in the chaos.

Forty leading brokers who had been trading from hand to hand along Montgomery and Pine Streets decided to organize an exchange where stocks could be listed and traded with better regard for their true values. The San Francisco Stock and Exchange Board was organized on September 11, 1862. This

improvement in trading facilities stimulated the market temporarily. In the resulting excitement the result was evil. The
forty members of the original board soon became known as
"The Forty Thieves."

Business men who dabbled in stocks frequently found themselves in difficulty and occasionally in bankruptcy. *The San
Francisco Bulletin,* reporting the failure of one such business
man, commented that it was due merely to a report that he had
been gambling in Comstock shares. Baldwin watched his
step. But probably he was not happy about it.

It was at this point that his first domestic troubles, the fore-
runner of many such troubles, reached a climax. Sarah Ann
Unruh Baldwin went her own way. Clara Baldwin, at the age
of sixteen according to her own later testimony, left Mills
College and was married to J. Van Pelt Mathis, an assistant
clerk in the San Francisco Customs House.

There is no record available of either the divorce of Sarah
Ann from Elias J., or of the wedding of Clara to Mathis.
Perhaps both records were burned in the San Francisco fire of
1906. That there was a divorce is sufficiently attested by the
fact that Sarah Ann married one Richard C. Alden, chief clerk
in the Customs House, and left one daughter by that marriage,
Edith Alden. This daughter, half sister of Clara, married a
man named Daniels and later a man named Johnson. While
Edith was still an infant, however, Sarah Ann Baldwin Alden
died, May 27, 1872. She was buried in Laurel Hill, later removed to the Masonic cemetery and finally came to rest in the
Baldwin mausoleum at Cypress Lawn.

In the meantime, with neither wife nor daughter to require
any of his attention, Baldwin turned his entire energy to business. San Francisco then had a population of seventy-five thousand. It was the largest city west of St. Louis. Some three
weeks' hard and dangerous journey from the Civil War zone,
California had escaped the immediate devastating effects of

the war. For years it had mined and minted its own gold, circulating fifty-dollar octagonal gold slugs even before the government mint was established in San Francisco. Perhaps no better illustration of its wide separation from and independence of the rest of the nation could be found than the fact that its business was maintained on a gold basis when the East went to greenbacks. Federal currency sold in San Francisco at thirty-five cents on the dollar. Banks were demanding and getting one and one-half and two per cent. a month on commercial loans. Among brokers two to three per cent. was being paid.

The Central Pacific had just started to lay its rails for the western end of the first transcontinental railroad. A local railroad was operating from San Francisco to San José. Another ran from Sacramento to Folsom. Telegraph lines were operating to Virginia City, and to a few points in California. The telegraph company was preparing to build the first transcontinental line.

That was all interesting business, but Baldwin had been infected with the Comstock fever. He had watched the quotations at the San Francisco Stock and Exchange Board since the opening, and had seen his own small purchases of Ophir, Mexican and Savage shares recover from the slump into which they had sunk in the general disrepute of mining stock speculation in 1862, when he had picked them up at bottom prices.

So he continued to put the small profits of his livery business into such Comstock shares as his investigation on the lode had convinced him were sound investments. Occasionally he took a profit on one of the three or four stocks in which he was interested, and invested it in another. He did not trade on a margin.

The mining-stock gambling as conducted on that exchange was transacted under a system which allowed buyers and sellers to make their deals with a ninety-day delivery clause. Shares in the Ophir, for instance, might be quoted at "64 S-90." That meant that the seller had ninety days to deliver. In other words, an operator could sell stock which he did not own, just as a bear on the present-day exchanges may sell short, but with the important difference that there was a definite time limit for making good on the short sale. Similarly, a "B-90" clause gave the buyer the right to demand delivery at any time within ninety days.

But that system was either too complicated or too speculative for Baldwin. He stuck to his livery business, and the cautious investment of available funds in what he believed to be prime stocks at low prices. Through 1864 the business of the Comstock continued somewhat discouraging. Most of the first rich mines seemed to have exhausted their treasure. Gould & Curry was producing richly, but the district in general was suffering from over-expansion. The Bank of California's Virginia City branch under the direction of William Sharon had lent so much money on various Comstock securities that it was in grave danger. Eighty-two reduction mills had been built with a capacity of sixteen hundred tons of ore a day, and only one-fourth of that amount of ore was being hoisted. One sixty-thousand-dollar mill sold for three thousand dollars.

William C. Ralston, cashier and leading director of the bank, was worried, but Sharon had got in too deep to retreat, and plunged more deeply. Baldwin, with his own account in the Bank of California, probably did not know the vast extent of the bank's commitments, but he did know Sharon, and Sharon was wise enough to encourage Baldwin's continued investment in Comstock shares to help support a market on which the bank's fate now depended. Probably Sharon was wise enough also to give Baldwin an occasional bit of inside information on which to take a profit. Adolph Sutro also was an enthusiastic bull on the future of the lode, and one in whom Baldwin had great confidence. Baldwin continued to buy.

When the Civil War ended, and the nation faced its tragic era, Baldwin in common with most of the capitalists and business men of the time found himself in difficulties. He needed ready cash, a need which was to press him to strange activities at times throughout the rest of his life. He owned two livery-stables. He decided to sell, and devote his attention more strictly to real estate and mines. How he accomplished it is set down here as told years later by Jules Cavalier, the buyer.

Cavalier was a recent arrival in San Francisco, and had a few thousand dollars to invest. He became acquainted with Baldwin and was advised that the livery-stable business was a good one.

"But I have two stables," Baldwin explained, "and I can't give the personal attention to both that I should give. I'll tell you what I'll do. I'll give you an option on either one for ten thousand dollars and let you run it for a month. Then, if you want to buy it, you can have it for the ten thousand dollars."

Cavalier couldn't see a thing wrong with that proposition. He accepted, and took over one of the stables. The business flourished. There were more demands for buggies, double rigs and saddle horses than Cavalier could supply. Profits were correspondingly high. Cavalier never thought of Baldwin's other stable. At the end of the month he paid over his ten thousand dollars for the one he had been operating. Business promptly dropped away.

Baldwin's profit had been such that he could dispose of the other stable, revived with the return of the business he had been deflecting to Cavalier, at a lesser price, and still mark up another successful trade. To-day that might be looked upon as a dirty trick. It was considered a smart one in those days.

Since the administration of Andrew Jackson, America, growing like a weed under the stimulus of the expanding frontier, had taken on some of the noxious characteristics of a weed.

Growth was its own justification. Methods were of little importance. It was accomplishment that counted. The nation had proved it in the Mexican War and in its treatment of the Indians. Baldwin had been born and reared in that atmosphere, and had helped to develop it as he had taken part in the expansion and development of the nation.

With a conscience made easy by consciousness of success, he turned to the mining stock-market. In that year (1867) the Savage mine was the best in the Comstock, producing $3,737,100. Savage was one in which Baldwin had bought "feet." The price was up. Baldwin sold. Chollar-Potosi, another producing $200,000 a month, was up. Baldwin sold his interest. Yellow Jacket produced $1,729,276 in that year. The price was up. Baldwin sold.

The famous Ophir was not producing a cent. The price was down. Baldwin held on. Crown Point and Hale & Norcross offered no profit. Baldwin held on to his interests there.

"To be a success you've got to keep your eye on two ends—when to go into a deal and when to go out—and don't waste any time in doing either," said Baldwin thirty years later.

The sales of Savage, Chollar-Potosi and Yellow Jacket had made him a rich man as riches were counted prior to the big bonanza. He decided to step out and see a bit of the world and of the life which he had been too busy for thirty-nine years to enjoy. Where should he step?

A group of British sportsmen with whom he had become acquainted answered the question.

"India."

They had recently finished an exciting summer hunting buffalo through Kansas, Nebraska and Wyoming, and were planning to finish a couple of years of sport with some tiger and elephant shooting in India. They would be glad to have Baldwin go along.

Instantly his childhood ambitions, long smothered by work

and business activity, revived. The Englishmen told him exciting stories of the rare sport to be found in the great jungles where the British government had recently established itself as the ruling power. Little was known in America of the India of that day. Big-game hunting was a business for Americans, not a sport, as the buffalo hide hunters were proving.

Baldwin listened, and made up his mind to go. They might even visit Japan, just coming to the attention of the world as a result of the treaty which had first opened its ports to American commerce a few years earlier.

Baldwin settled up the tag ends of his business, locked his remaining Ophir, Crown Point and Hale & Norcross shares in a safe, left instructions with his broker to sell if they happened to reach the price he had paid for them, and started out with his British friends for a new view of the world.

CHAPTER IX

BIG GAME IN INDIA

SINCE childhood on the Indiana prairie, Baldwin had been fond of shooting. Pigeons, prairie chickens, and occasionally a deer had fallen before his old muzzle-loading guns from the time he had been big enough to aim one. He had never become a notably good shot but he made up in enthusiasm and luck what he lacked in skill.

In illustration is a tale by David Unruh, son of H. A. Unruh who managed the Baldwin estates in southern California. Baldwin and Dave Unruh had gone together into Bear Valley in the San Bernardino Mountains to look over a disputed boundary-line between some two thousand acres owned by Baldwin and a similar range owned by Gus Knight. On the disputed line they encountered Knight, widely known in those mountains as a tough old desert cattleman.

Knight was armed, with a rifle across the horn of his saddle. When Baldwin and Unruh approached him he stopped his horse and waited. Baldwin passed the time of day, and led up to the subject of the dispute in the roundabout manner in which he generally approached matters of business. Knight grunted surly answers to his remarks and questions, all the while keeping his rifle aimed casually at Baldwin's midriff.

"I was pretty nervous," said Unruh. "I was only a kid, just out of Stanford, and I believed all I had heard about Knight's willingness to shoot first and argue later. Sitting as close as he was, he would have blown E. J. clear out of the saddle if he had touched that trigger. Finally E. J. got a little nervous too.

" 'I wish you'd turn that rifle the other way, Gus,' he said to Knight. 'It makes me nervous. I've got my hand on a gun here in my pocket and if I get to trembling it might go off.'

"Knight laughed at that. 'Why, you old scoundrel,' he said, 'you couldn't hit a barn from the inside with that little two-barreled pop-gun you pack.'

" 'By gad, I'll show you,' E. J. said. 'You see that squirrel up in that tree?' He pointed up into a big sycamore. 'If you'll agree not to shoot me while I'm doing it, I'll knock him down for you.'

"Knight laughed at that, and agreed. Baldwin pulled out the little old derringer that he always carried in his coat pocket—one of those old-timers with one barrel above the other—and shot up through the leaves. Down tumbled the squirrel.

" 'By God, I didn't think you could hit a barn,' Knight said. 'I'll turn the rifle the other way.' And he did.

"That put them both in a better humor, and they joked a little and settled the dispute right there.

"As we rode away I said to E. J., 'You surprised me more than you did Knight with that shot.'

" 'Shh!' he said, leaning over toward me. 'Don't tell a soul, but that wasn't the squirrel I shot at at all.' "

That was Baldwin's reputation in the '90s, when he was seventy years old. Probably he was better in the '60s. Crossing the plains with his covered wagons in 1853 he had thrilled to the shooting of buffalo and had perfected a steady hand and eye in brushes with hostile Indians. In the Rocky Mountains he had killed elk and bears. Even within what is now the center of San Francisco he had maintained his gunnery practise and taste for the sport in hunting quail and rabbits.

So when the English sportsmen stimulated his imagination with tales of the rare sport to be had in India, Baldwin was tempted. And the whole history of his life indicates that he was usually ready to follow the advice on moral issues given by a famous character of literature: "When tempted, succumb at once, and avoid the struggle." Baldwin succumbed.

Hunting big game in India in those distant days was not the common sport that it later became. It was not only far more dangerous, but far more uncomfortable. It required strength and courage, and the very fact that Baldwin was eager to go is sufficient evidence that he possessed both those characteristics. He was to need them.

From Baldwin's personal reminiscences handed down by word of mouth in the forty-odd years during which he became a colorful and familiar figure throughout the sporting world, it is possible to reconstruct the story of his hunting achievements. Though a reticent and even a shy man among strangers, he liked to talk with friends. Also, it seems, he was not a man to spoil a story of good sport by a too strict adherence to accuracy of detail.

In illustration, one of his hunting tales, recounted to his niece, Mrs. L. H. Rush, whom he had entertained and thrilled from childhood, may be cited. This story concerns his buffalo-hunting adventures during his first trip across the plains from Wisconsin to California.

Baldwin, as captain of the covered-wagon-train moving westward through the buffalo country, frequently took upon himself the duty of providing meat for the party. That duty afforded a break in the deadly plodding monotony of the slow journey. So, riding far ahead of the wagons one day, Baldwin sighted a great dark blur upon the distant prairie. He had already seen enough buffalo to recognize this mass of color as a herd of tremendous size. He spurred forward, shielding himself as far as possible in a low draw which ran in the general direction of the herd.

The wind was toward him and he managed to approach within a hundred yards of the scattered outposts of the herd before they became alarmed. Then, following the methods of the Indians who had hunted the buffalo with bow and spear long before the hide-hunters had organized their slaughter by shooting from a hidden rest with the great Sharps buffalo gun, Baldwin spurred his horse toward the herd. The animals promptly stampeded. Baldwin raced his horse beside the herd, seeking the fattest of the young cows and calves for a shot at close quarters that would leave meat in the path of the on-coming wagon-train.

One, two, three fat young cows fell before his guns as he galloped so close that he could not miss, even from a running horse. In the excitement of the chase, and seeking only the most promising game, he gradually worked his way into the edge of the herd. By so doing he turned the course of the panic-stricken animals a little, so that he himself was running within the arc of a vast circle. And at this critical moment his horse stuck a forefoot in a prairie-dog hole, and took a header, with Baldwin somersaulting over its head.

E. J. was young and tough, and had been spilled from a running horse before. He struck the ground rolling, and came to his feet on the run, without injury. But all around him were running buffaloes, and his horse was lost in the herd.

"What did you do, Uncle?"

"Why, I did the only thing there was to do. There must have been ten thousand of those buffaloes, and they'd started to mill, so I couldn't get out. Lucky for me they weren't so thick right where I landed in the edge of the herd, so I just straddled a young bull on the run and held on, slapping him on the side of the head with my hat till I managed to get him out beyond the edge of the herd. By that time the stampede was about run out and pretty well slowed down, and I slid off. It was about five miles back to where the wagon-train would cross the line of the stampede, and I had to walk it. But I got there before a wagon came up. By the time they got there I had all three of my slaughtered cows skinned, and one of them half cut up. We had boiled buffalo tongue for supper that night. Good, too, I remember."

The stories of the big-game hunts in India which were experienced fourteen years later, and recounted from time to time through the next forty years, perhaps should be considered in the perspective of that buffalo ride. In any event, they do Baldwin credit as a raconteur as well as a big-game hunter.

The party, directed by the experienced British sportsmen who had invited Baldwin, landed at Calcutta, outfitted from the British stores which were just then beginning to provide for such parties, and headed into the Assam district, south of the Brahmaputra River.

One of their first experiences was as spectators at a scene which must have given the American not only a thrill but a most illuminating idea of the possibilities of sport in a land of wild elephants and tigers. With the demonstration there made, it will always remain a mystery to those who knew E. J. Baldwin best, why he did not include elephant labor in his later pioneering development of southern California ranch land, as some of his contemporaries attempted to use camels in desert transportation in the West at about the same period.

Baldwin and his friends were visiting the superintendent of the government keddahs and watching the great variety of constructive labor which was being performed by the tamed elephants—work such as in this country at that period required ten-ox teams—when one great bull went *must* or temporarily crazy. The great beast killed its mahout and several villagers, and escaped into a near-by jungle. From this retreat the animal proceeded to raid the crops and native villages over a large district, killing every native with which it came into contact, and doing incalculable damage to property.

The British superintendent, believing that the rogue's wildness was merely temporary as is usually the case with elephants in the *must* period, decided to catch it alive rather than kill it. Trained elephants were valuable. When the next report of the rogue's raid upon a village came in, the superintendent took a famous old tusker which had long been used for the punishment, control and training of newly caught elephants, and with two well-trained females and plenty of ropes and chains, journeyed to the ruined village. Baldwin and his friends went along as spectators on thoroughly reliable elephants obtained from the keddah.

Near the ruined village, which lay upon a plain bordered by jungle, the *must* elephant was caught in the act of destroying the last of the native crops. The veteran superintendent of the keddahs promptly advanced upon his big tusker, leaving the two female elephants in charge of their mahouts within signaling distance, and the spectators a little farther in the rear.

The trained tusker came within a hundred yards of the rogue before that animal took notice. Then it charged. And when a bull elephant charges it has something like the destructive possibilities of a six- or seven-ton gravel truck traveling at the rate of one hundred yards in ten seconds flat. But instead of retreating, the trained tusker advanced at a walk, trunk curled tight between his tusks, and head down.

The shock almost hurled the superintendent from the pad girthed to the tusker's back, but he managed to cling to handholds made for the purpose, while his trained beast did its work. The charging elephant, crazy with rage, was in the situation of a rough-and-tumble fighter against an equally powerful scientific boxer. It had struck the trained elephant a glancing blow on the low-swung forehead. The latter, with head down, caught the rogue under the trunk, with a tusk on each side of its neck, and lifted with all the power of seven tons of bone and sinew. The rogue's front feet were literally lifted from the ground, and the trained tusker promptly twisted and threw it upon its side. With another deft movement, it pinned down the fallen beast.

The superintendent signaled the female elephants in reserve, and himself slipped to the ground and secured the rogue's legs with a tremendous hobble of chains. With the arrival of the others the roping was completed, and the *must* animal was led away between the two females while the tusker assisted when necessary by prodding the rogue from behind. Later the party saw the animal, entirely recovered from his temporary insanity, going quietly and efficiently about his labors. In the meantime their respect for such elephants as the huge tusker was unbounded.

When the actual hunting began it was difficult to get Baldwin to hunt in any other manner than on elephant back. In that decision he was wiser than one of his more experienced associates. The latter, whose name has long since been forgotten in the retelling of the story, left his mount while the party was hunting an elephant that had been doing great damage to native villages in the district south of Dhubri on the Brahmaputra. He followed the trail of the rogue into a jungle of matted creepers and thorns so thick that he would have been brushed off the back of his mount if he had tried to ride. Baldwin and the others protested, but the man was an experienced hunter and a cool and accurate shot, and insisted that he could enter the jungle safely on foot and dispose of the rogue, which would certainly escape them if they waited for it to come out.

He had gone perhaps three or four hundred yards along a narrow game trail into the tangled mass of vegetation, accompanied only by one native gun-bearer when a great trumpeting of elephants reached the party waiting in the open. The sound of a shot followed, with more trumpeting, and another shot. From their points of vantage on their own elephants the friends could see the trees and vines within the jungle swaying as if moved by a small tornado. Soon, a quarter of a mile away a herd of a dozen wild elephants burst from cover, circled in a short arc and rushed back into a more distant area. One huge bull, however, was in evident distress, and stumbled and fell as the others vanished.

The party moved up to examine the huge animal, and found it dead, with a bullet hole through the trunk and into the lungs. Perhaps ten minutes later the native gun-bearer who had accompanied the hunter on foot, ran from the game trail, panic-stricken, and told the story of the tragedy. A quarter of a mile within the dense tangle of trees, reeds and vines, they had come upon a dozen animals where they had expected but one. The big bull evidently had winded them and had charged at once. His master had fired twice, but as he seized the extra gun to shoot again the whole herd was upon them. The native had leaped behind a huge tree, but the white man had been caught and hurled into the air, to be trampled to death when he fell.

There was no more hunting on that day. The party followed the path broken through the jungle by the stampeding elephants to a point where they found the body of their companion, literally flattened into the earth. Baldwin had seen violent death before, upon the western plains and in the first wild days of Virginia City, and the tragedy served merely to confirm him in his decision to do his hunting in India from elephant back rather than under elephant foot. The bad bull had been killed, and the party decided that they would hunt no more elephants. Anyway, the government preferred to have them hunt tigers. Elephants, in general, were an asset. Tigers were a liability.

The body of their friend was returned to the nearest British post for burial, and the assistant superintendent of the government keddah was induced to direct their search for tigers. Baldwin's personal tales of his jungle adventures claim no elephants among his trophies. He did, however, bag not one but two tigers.

It was always possible in India at that time to obtain the help of British government servants to hunt down any beasts which might be terrorizing the native villages and damaging their property. The government sixty or more years ago had already recognized the value of wild elephants as potential tame elephants capable of being trained to do a vast amount of constructive labor. The government service therefore was devoted to the task of catching rather than killing the huge beasts, but could always be depended upon to assist in hunting down the rogues which terrorized and demoralized the natives.

Tigers, on the other hand, had absolutely no potential value except as trophies. Those that kept to their jungles were a menace to the building of roads and the general development of the country under British rule. They were therefore legitimate game. Those which had discovered that wandering natives and native cattle were an easier prey than the wild hogs and buffaloes of the jungle must be hunted down as robbers and murderers. When a man-eater appeared in any district, therefore, the officials not only were glad to cooperate with volunteer sportsmen in the hunt, but offered rewards for the destruction of the killer.

Word of such a killer came to the Baldwin party on the day they were attending the burial of their companion killed by the stampeding elephants. Fed up with elephant hunting, they moved at once to the raided village. The natives explained that the tiger had been dragging down a bullock or cow from the edge of the grazing herd on an average of about twice a week for several months, and had also killed five herders, and two women coming home from the fields in the early evening.

The beast's latest victim, struck down on the preceding evening, had been dragged into a small open space just within the edge of the jungle, half consumed and left hidden beneath a windfall. The natives, investigating on elephant back, had discovered the remains, but had been afraid to dismount to recover it. They would, however, lead the white men to the spot, assuring them that the tiger would return during the night to eat the remainder of the hidden body.

It was past midday when the party reached the scene. The native shikari or huntsman explaining that by building mucharns or platforms in the trees surrounding the body the white men could spend the night safely until the beast returned to its kill, and then shoot it from their perches. The government agent who had accompanied them assured them that this was common practise. The mucharns were quickly—too quickly—built. At sundown the three whites climbed to their platforms and the shikari, armed with his old smooth-bore match-lock, took up his place in a fourth tree.

Hours passed in extreme discomfort. The rooting of wild hogs in the jungle, the howling of jackals, the distant scream of some hunting cat served merely to tighten the nerves and make the cramped watchers more distressed. Midnight had come and gone without a single sign of life in the comparatively open glade between the trees when a crash was heard in the direction of one of the mucharns. A single scream followed, and then a thrashing and snarling in the undergrowth and the noise of some bulk evidently being dragged.

After that the nearer noises died away. The jungle was almost silent except for an occasional muttered curse and the sound of a watcher moving stiffly and cautiously on his too-hastily built and uncomfortable platform. At dawn they climbed stiffly down—all except the native. His tree was empty. On the ground below was his ancient match-lock, a rag of loin-cloth and a stain of blood upon a trodden spot of grass. Bent grass and broken brush indicated the trail over which the unfortunate native had been dragged. Two hundred yards away lay the remains of his body.   Other natives explained the signs.

The shikari evidently had sighted the tiger approaching noiselessly in the darkness, and had moved on his flimsy mucharn to obtain a shot at the beast.   Either the edge of the platform had given away or he had missed a hand- or foot-hold, and had dropped directly in the path of the man-killer. The tiger had sprung, raked his scalp clear from the skull with one stroke of a paw, and had killed him instantly with a grip of the jaws over the top of a shoulder, piercing the chest simultaneously from front and back.   The remains of the body, of which only the upper legs and buttocks had been consumed, made that hasty autopsy easy.

Two men had been killed in his first two hunting efforts in India, and Baldwin began to show his character.   He had plenty of physical courage.   Also he had a temper, which grew hotter with interference.   He was determined now to kill that man-killer.   But he realized fully the danger of the hunt and his own lack of knowledge and experience in jungle shooting.   He conferred with the most experienced government agent available, with his British companions and with the best native shikaris in the neighborhood.   The white men preferred to sleep after their uncomfortable night.   Baldwin was rarin' to go, and did so.

The party, mounted on dependable elephants, explored the jungle until they found a single water-hole in a drying nullah or creek bed, perhaps a mile from the scene of the last night's tragedy.   The fresh footprints of the tiger in the surrounding mud were sufficient evidence that the beast had drunk there after its night's gorge.   In all probability it would be sleeping in the neighborhood.

A hundred natives directed by several experienced shikaris lined out through the jungle to beat the tiger up and move him in the direction of the last night's kill.   Baldwin returned to his mucharn, dismissed his mahout and elephant and waited. The yells of the beaters, the crashing of undergrowth, came faintly to him through the jungle, slowly increasing in volume. The sportsman searched the ground and undergrowth as far as he could see, perhaps fifty yards here and less than ten yards there. The beaters were circling in, still at a distance of half a mile.

Dry yellow grass moved at the edge of the glade. Baldwin's grip tightened on his gun. But this tiger was a veteran of many beats. He had moved far in advance of the beaters, but hesitated to show himself in the open. Instead he slipped through the tall yellow grass at the edge of the glade, so well hidden in the natural camouflage of his black and yellow striped hide that the waiting sharpshooter could hardly be certain that a tiger was there. But E. J. had shot foxes in the Indiana cornfields in his youth, and coyotes and wolves slipping in and out among the patches of sage-brush on the plains. He noted the direction taken by the beast in the swaying grass, and spotted a small break through which the animal must pass if it did not turn back in an attempt to break through the line of beaters.

His calculations were accurate. The grass ceased to move at the edge of the small break, and a great black and yellow head peered forth, followed by one tentative forepaw. Baldwin followed up the line of the leg with the sight of his heavy rifle, and touched the trigger as the sight reached the half exposed shoulder.

A screaming roar answered the shot, and the great beast made one spring into the open, stood a moment, snarling viciously, and toppled over upon its side. Baldwin, elated, scrambled down from his mucharn and advanced. Inherent caution, however, made him pause a few paces from the beast and place another bullet directly through its head. The tiger did not move. The first shot had passed through the lungs and the tip of the heart.

That sport was almost too tame, though the natives who had

been relieved of the killer were profuse in their thanks and praises. Baldwin wanted to hunt the beasts, not to have them driven up to him for slaughter. So a drive by elephants was organized in an area some miles to the north, where villagers had suffered severe losses from tigers and leopards.

A young buffalo was tied as bait within the edge of the jungle, with the double purpose of locating a tiger and of providing it with food which might be expected to keep the killer within hunting distance for a couple of days. On the next day a native runner reported that the buffalo had been killed, partly eaten and the remains dragged into a thick covert of wild rose. This was an area peculiarly adapted to hunting on elephants, as the growth was too dense to be beaten by men on foot.

Forty elephants had been obtained from the nearest keddah for the hunt, and with the keddah superintendent, Baldwin and the British sportsmen each mounted on an experienced beast they were lined up to drive this covert. But the tiger in this affair was also an experienced and wily beast. Three times he broke back through the advancing line of elephants rather than expose himself in the open. And the three successful breaks taught him that he could throw an advancing elephant or two or three of them into such confusion by a direct charge that he could pass safely behind the line. The shikaris, however, were as experienced as the tiger, and the mahouts always managed to calm their animals and return them into line for the beat back.

On the fourth advance Baldwin was riding near the center of the line. Most of the elephants had grown more nervous and panicky than the tiger. The covert had been beaten down into such a dense low tangle that a crouching tiger might lie within ten paces of an approaching elephant without being seen. And that was precisely what this beast did.

Baldwin's mahout abruptly checked the advance of his

elephant and pointed to a tangle of vines, perhaps thirty feet
ahead. A blur of black and yellow was just visible through
the cover. Unable to distinguish a vital spot, Baldwin fired
into the mass.

The result was spectacular. A roar that frightened the
elephant into a quick turn was followed promptly by the tiger,
in person, springing directly toward the animal's shoulder.
Baldwin's second shot from the remaining barrel of his double-
barreled rifle caught the gigantic cat full in the mouth, in mid-
air, not six feet from the cringing mahout. At that short range
it literally blew off the top of the tiger's head.

"That was a thrill," said Baldwin. "That was sport."

"And what did you do then, Uncle?"

"I stopped hunting tigers, and went to Japan."

CHAPTER X

PIONEERING IN VAUDEVILLE

JAPAN in 1867 was not the Japan of to-day. That was the year in which the rule of the Shoguns came to an end and the Imperial Court was restored to power. The country had been theoretically open to world trade only since the advent of Commodore Perry and the United States fleet fourteen years earlier. It had been actually in contact with the rest of the world for only nine years, since the Shogun's Prime Minister had signed a temporary agreement with the United States, England, France, Russia and Holland.

Prior to that it had been a land almost unknown, barring its people from emigration, and refusing admittance to the ships of other lands. Under the Shogunate, prior to the advent of Perry, the Occidental countries knew virtually nothing of Japan. Jesuit missionaries and commercial explorers alike had been expelled and persecuted as a menace to the country. Even with the opening of Japan to commerce, the policies and prejudices ingrained in its people for twenty-five centuries bound them sufficiently to prevent any wide-spread travel or attempt at colonization. They were satisfied with their own civilization, and distrusted the Occident, though now willing to accept its proffered advantages.

Baldwin found a people so different from any he had ever seen, with customs and habits so novel to his Indiana mind that he looked about with acquisitive curiosity to find a profit. Silk and tea were going out in the few American ships that had brought in cotton, lumber, tallow and kerosene. Such trade seemed pretty well organized. Its possibilities did not appeal to him. He devoted himself to sightseeing, with an eye out incidentally for any deal that might net a cash profit on his trip. Thus he happened to see a group of Japanese jugglers and wrestlers tossing knives and human beings around in such a whirl of glittering blades and arms and legs as left him marveling that one could survive to collect the tiny fee for which they seemed to risk their limbs and lives.

Here was an idea, an opportunity. So far as he knew, no Japanese had ever been seen in the United States at that time. He had never seen one in San Francisco, where the streets swarmed with pig-tailed Chinese. In their colorful native costumes the Japanese should draw a crowd even if they did nothing but sit to be stared at, like a bearded woman in a side-show. With their skill as jugglers, keeping seven deadly knives in the air at a time, whirling themselves and each other in gaudy disks of color or glistening wheels of bronze arms and legs, and doing other stunts more incredible, they should attract thousands.

Their takings, Baldwin discovered, amounted to a few cents a day each. Immediately he engaged an interpreter and negotiated with their manager. The Japanese refused to go to an unknown land, even at double the rate of pay they were then earning. Baldwin appealed to the American consul, the British consul, the French consul for help in his argument. The Frenchman, he found, was in urgent need of money for some personal purpose. Baldwin agreed to lend the money, on adequate security.

In due time he was to get it back, with an added gift of an odd Oriental ring which indirectly was to net him an added additional profit of one hundred thousand dollars—the only bit of luck he ever admitted in his accumulation of millions. But that will be chronicled in its place. In the meantime the consular assistance overcame the fears as it aroused the cupidity of the Japanese. When Baldwin departed he took with him one of the first vaudeville troupes to tour America. It had almost everything that a vaudeville troupe should have— geishas, novelty, color, action. If a song and dance act or a buxom blonde in pink tights were needed to lend variety they could be picked up in New York.

The show opened at the New York Academy of Music, according to Baldwin's memory, at Niblo's Theater on Broadway near Crosby Street, according to J. B. Marvin who was then a clerk at the famous old Fifth Avenue Hotel, and later a trusted employee of Baldwin. Both memories agree that it was "a natural," that it "knocked 'em dead," and that it played to crowded houses for two months. That was a new record of theatrical success in the New York which then centered at Fourteenth Street, boasted a population of about one million, and had not yet built either the elevated or subway lines.

When Boss Tweed was strangling the city, already hard-hit by the depression following the Civil War, when residents as far away as Harlem had to use steamboats and a few horse cars to reach the theater district, a two-months run on Broadway was really something to boast about. Baldwin boasted, cleaned up, and took his show on the road.

It was thus, perhaps, that he met the woman who was to become his second wife, Mary Cochrane, a widow, of New Orleans. There is little in the available record concerning her— not even the date or place of marriage. There is, however, a family tradition that a few years later Baldwin was so fearful that the woman was planning to poison him that he refused to eat any food prepared in his home until she herself had eaten of it.

They had not yet been married when, on his westward tour, Baldwin visited his old home at Hamilton, Indiana, for the first time since his departure nearly twenty years before, and stopped for a few days with his youngest sister, Evaline, then married to a neighboring farmer, Thomas B. Fawcett, near New Carlisle. His pockets were bulging with the profits of his vaudeville adventure, and the money was rolling in from the show in Chicago. Baldwin spent a part of it for a monument at the graves of his father and mother who had died within a year of each other, in 1865 and 1866, and were buried in Hamilton churchyard.

They were married before Baldwin took her on one of the first transcontinental trains ever to run, in 1869, on his second visit to his sister. Probably that trip was a wedding journey. It must have been a great experience for a man who had trudged the same route through five dangerous and weary months, sixteen years before.

In that same year Baldwin's first daughter, Clara, began at the age of twenty-two to follow in her father's footsteps, matrimonially speaking. She divorced J. Van Pelt Mathis after five years of married life, and immediately married her second husband, Albert Snyder, with whom she was to live for three years before divorcing him. She had had no children by Mathis, but one son, Albert Snyder, Jr., was born of her second marriage.

In the meantime, however, Baldwin had completed his tour as a vaudeville impresario, ending in San Francisco with an incident typical of his character. In those days of immature press-agentry it was the practise of showmen literally to drum up trade. Traveling stock companies selected their troupers as much for their ability to "double in brass" as for their histrionic ability. The man who might be going to play Romeo or Simon Legree upon the stage was likely to be playing a cornet or base drum upon the street corner or before the theater half an hour earlier.

Baldwin's Japanese jugglers and wrestlers could parade in their colorful kimonos with invaluable publicity, but they could not tootle a horn. Therefore it was Baldwin's practise to engage a local band in each city for the alluring overture in front of the theater. Also at that time his business education had progressed to the point where he believed it to be more profitable to stall off his employees than to pay them promptly. It was a theory and practise that was to mark his later life with various complications. He had not paid the musicians in San Francisco at the end of their first week.

The bass drummer, seeing Baldwin in front of the theater one evening, ceased to beat the drum and demanded his wages. Baldwin argued. It seemed cheaper to argue than to pay. The drummer felt that it might be more profitable to argue than to play. Neither person was getting anywhere, and the band was sadly weakened by the silence of its bass drum. Baldwin could see that that was poor business. He promptly ended the argument by seizing the drummer's drumstick, running the man off the sidewalk, and proceeding to beat the drum himself. That was a good many years before Eugene Schmitz, president of the San Francisco Musicians' Union, was elected mayor of the city. The city was still ununionized. Baldwin got away with it.

He continued to beat the bass drum in front of the theater until the show closed a few days later and the musicians were paid off—in instalments. Baldwin wanted all his cash for something more profitable than the payment of wages. The Japanese troupe which had made him a small fortune as well as a pioneer's place in the vaudeville business of America was sold to Gilbert of Gilbert and Sullivan fame, according to an interview with Baldwin published in *The San Francisco Call* many years later, and taken across the Atlantic for a tour in which they appeared before the crowned heads of Europe.

Baldwin was free to inform himself again as to the situation in the Comstock and the possibility of more profits in the trading of its shares. The first information he was able to pick up around the Stock and Exchange Board and in Flood and

O'Brien's bar was that the Comstock was in a bad way. The lode was at almost its lowest point of production. Many of its most famous mines were substituting assessments for dividends, with disastrous effect upon their shares on the exchange.

Baldwin congratulated himself upon having sold out most of his holdings before he started to India in the preceding year. But what about Hale & Norcross? He had owned some "feet" of that, and had left it with his broker to sell if it happened to reach the purchase price of eight hundred dollars a foot.

"Oh, haven't you heard about Hale & Norcross?" said the friend with whom he was talking. "It's suspended from the board."

"Suspended? Why? I left instructions for my broker to sell mine at eight hundred dollars if it ever got back up to that. That's what I paid for it."

"Well, you played out of luck there." The friend laughed. "Hale & Norcross is the only thing that's been showing any signs of life. There was evidently a corner in it. They struck a rich pocket and it went up to one thousand dollars a foot. Then a lot of the boys with information that the pocket would be cleaned out in a few weeks sold it S-90, thinking they could make their deliveries after the pocket had been cleaned, at maybe two or three hundred dollars a foot.

"But the pocket was a bonanza. It's still producing, and their time is up, and they can't deliever. It was $2,925 a foot on February eighth, and hopped to $7,000 on the fifteenth. Then it went to $8,000 and was suspended from the board pending an investigation, and to save the shorts. I hear some of them are paying as much as $12,000 a foot for it off the board to make good on their commitments. If you had stayed here and watched your business instead of playing around the world you could have got $12,000 a foot for it just as well as $800."

"By gad!" said Baldwin. "Well, there's no use crying over

spilled milk. Anyway I made a lot of money on that show tour, and at least I got my money back on Hale & Norcross. Let the other fellow worry."

With that comforting philosophy he went to call on his broker. "I think I'll buy a few feet of Crown Point and Savage," he said. "Let me see my account. What's my balance? What did you get for that Hale & Norcross?"

"Your balance is all right, but I didn't sell any Hale & Norcross for you. I got your order to sell, but you took your safe key with you, and when I got to the wharf your ship had sailed. How much have you got? It's worth twelve thousand dollars a foot."

"By gad!"

There was really nothing more to be said. Baldwin went to his safe, extracted the almost forgotten shares of Hale & Norcross, and sold them at from eight thousand to twelve thousand dollars a foot.

A fortune, which legend has put as high as five million dollars, was tossed into the lap of E. J. Baldwin. The figures, unquestionably, are far too high. Even at twelve thousand dollars a foot, the entire Hale & Norcross mine would have been worth only six million dollars, and Baldwin's interest was a small fraction. But he did make a fortune. The story spread swiftly through the financial district of San Francisco. The luck of Baldwin was established in the popular mind, and with it the name of "Lucky" Baldwin, which was to cling to him through life. He resented it always, insisting that his real financial successes were due to hard work and perseverance rather than to luck.

Various other incidents have been cited as the basis of the famous nickname. E. J. White, a friend and associate of Baldwin, many years later told Joseph L. King at the time of the latter's research for a history of the San Francisco Stock and Exchange Board, that Baldwin won the nickname in his southern California land ventures in the '70s. Here is White's story as quoted by King:

"Baldwin had to his credit the sum of $40,000 with the banking house of Workman & Temple, in Los Angeles. On the suspension of that firm he was compelled to accept for his $40,000 a deed to an extensive tract of land. The railroad, in 1875, had only reached Bakersfield, and land was of little value in Southern California, so Baldwin held on. In time the railroad was extended to his vicinity. Land became in demand and advanced to $100-$200 an acre, and in the end the ranch, since known as the Santa Anita Ranch, became one of the most valuable in the state."

That explanation of the name and fame of "Lucky" is not sustained by the evidence, which will be offered in its proper place. Other sources of information, chiefly journalistic, sometimes ascribe the nickname to Baldwin's luck upon the race-tracks where he gained a more wide-spread fame than ever he did in his mining-stock activities.

Baldwin himself, in an interview many years later, ascribed the nickname to a deal in the Crown Point property on the Comstock in which he bought shares as low as eight dollars each and sold out to William Sharon and John P. Jones for two and one-half millions. That story, however, is so parallel in detail to the better-substantiated record of a more famous deal in Ophir, that it might indicate that Baldwin's memory had confused the names of those two great mines.

Whether or not he confused them, it is certain that he attributed his trading successes in mining stocks to his personal knowledge of the mines and his courage in pushing a deal in which he was interested—never to luck. In an interview on his racing career, many years later, he answered the question: "Where did you get the name of Lucky?"

"That's a hard one. I've worked hard for everything I've gotten in life."

But there is other testimony, in direct quotes from Baldwin, in *The San Francisco Call* of January 14, 1900. "I lent a foreign consul in Japan a large sum of money. He returned it with the gift of a strange ring. This ring was much admired in San Francisco but I never thought of it bringing me luck. At that time Canton & Everetts were dealing in stocks. Everetts took a fancy to the ring and wanted to buy it but I would not part with the gift. One day he offered to carry 500 shares of Crown Point for me if I would let him wear the ring for six months. I told Everetts he was childish, but let him wear the ring. I forgot all about my five hundred shares until Crown Point began to boom. I sold out with a clear profit of $100,000. Now that was luck, pure and simple, and the only luck I ever had that I didn't work for."

Perhaps also the recollection of that luck resulted in later life in Baldwin's ascribing his Lucky nickname to a deal in which he sold Crown Point holdings to Sharon and Jones for two million five hundred thousand dollars. His memory was somewhat similar to his temper. It flared.

But whatever the incident that caused the name of Lucky to be applied to E. J. Baldwin, it clung, and was repeated so frequently by business associates, sporting writers, court reporters and the public at large that it became as much a part of the man as the black Stetson hat, the black frock coat and the pearl-handled pistol which he adopted as uniform costume for office, ranch, race-track and court-room.

With the first great increase in cash capital attributed to the luck of the Hale & Norcross deal, Lucky Baldwin became a notable and a powerful figure in the material development of the West, in the history of the American turf, and in some of the most notorious scandals in the court records of seduction, breach of promise, and gun-play.

Perhaps the story of the lucky deal in the forgotten Hale & Norcross stock is not accurate in detail. Perhaps the story of the one-hundred-thousand-dollar profit from a Japanese luck ring is not accurate. Perhaps the two-million-five-hundred-thousand-dollar deal in Crown Point has become confused with a five-million-dollar dramatic clean-up in the famous Ophir stock. Regardless of accuracy, the fact that such incidents have grown into legends attests the personality of the man. Lucky Baldwin had become a notable figure in the dramatic history of the West. He was on his way to wider fame, if not infamy.

It is sufficient for the purpose of this narrative at this point to know that in the year 1869, when the Comstock Lode was at the lowest ebb of production since its discovery ten years earlier, Lucky Baldwin, forty-one years old, once divorced and twice married, was a rich and lucky man in the opinion of his associates. That year marked the beginning of a new era in the history of the West in which he was to have an active and influential part.

On May 10, 1869, the first transcontinental railroad was completed. San Francisco's dependence upon stage-coach, freight wagon and steamship was at an end. California ceased to be an outpost of civilization, a region of raw mining camps, a land of adventure, and began to develop into a state more substantial in the production of its farms than it had been in the production of its mines.

Still the spirit of America was the spirit of the frontier, although it had been subdued east of the Mississippi by the Civil War. One aftermath of that war was a new flood of western migration. And still Lucky Baldwin was the personification of that spirit, with its worship of success, its contempt for conventions and its overwhelming energy. He was prepared with plenty of cash to take advantage of the new opportunities.

Again he visited the Comstock, taking with him his second bride. And where a lone Piute squaw had stood staring stupidly down upon his little pack-train sixteen years before, there now spread a city of fifteen thousand souls. Within sight of the spot where he had rolled himself in a blanket on the sand, Lucky Baldwin now occupied the bridal suite in the imposing and luxurious International Hotel. Where he had been forced to be content with a supper of fried mush and bacon, he could now order fresh oysters, filet of beef, roast capon, hearts of lettuce with Roquefort dressing, French pastry, fruit and champagne.

Virginia City, surrounded by sun-bleached desert, provided all those delicacies, and more—for the lucky. And Baldwin was more than lucky. He was shrewd, persistent, indomitable and not always scrupulous. Also now he had a reputation. Even William Sharon, dictator of the Comstock, guiding spirit of the Bank of California, leading financier of the Pacific Slope, president of the new Virginia City railroad, chief of the Union Mill and Mining Company's monopoly, wired to his bank in San Francisco for a report on Baldwin's balance, and gave him recognition and every courtesy.

The Bank of California was in serious straits. A check drawn by Baldwin for the full amount of his deposits might have wrecked it. It was Sharon's job to see that no such check was drawn. It would be smart to entangle Baldwin sufficiently in the monopoly's affairs so that he must be an ally in a crisis. Baldwin did not know of the danger, but probably he suspected it. *The Territorial Enterprise* was filled with columns upon columns of legal notices offering for sale delinquent stocks upon which the owners had declined to pay assessments.

A disastrous fire in the Yellow Jacket and Crown Point mines had caused a loss of millions, and had cut off their production. Collapse of the Hale & Norcross corner in which Lucky Baldwin had sold at the peak had been followed by a rapid slump in the price of its shares from eight thousand dollars to forty-one dollars. It was bargain day on the Comstock. Baldwin had the cash with which to pick up bargains. He enjoyed a reputation which won him entrance to the mines. He talked with the best-informed men in the district and verified their information by personal inspection.

Sharon apparently was as optimistic about the great future of the lode as he had always been. Had not the Bank of California and his monopolies ridden out a similar if minor depression five years earlier? Baldwin listened to his arguments and inspected the mines involved. He looked into the Hale & Norcross, now again in borrasca after the exhaustion of the small bonanza which had inspired the corner. There he found a young man named John Mackay and an older man named James Fair tracing a stringer of ore. Mackay and Fair told him that it was a rare bargain at its present price, and that they were buying all they could carry.

Baldwin investigated Mackay and Fair instead of looking deeper into the mine, and found that they were practical pick-and-shovel miners of the California diggings who had graduated into equally practical engineers in the Comstock. He talked to John P. Jones, superintendent of the recently burned Crown Point and a practical mining engineer with a reputation for success earned in the first deep mines of California. He talked with his old friend, Adolph Sutro, who was just preparing to break ground for the mining and drainage tunnel which he had been trying for years to promote.

Sutro had nothing but hard words for Sharon, for the bank ring, for the milling monopoly, but a greater enthusiasm than ever for the Comstock Lode. "It's the greatest true fissure in the world's history of mining," he said. "Any competent geologist will verify that. Scores of them have done so. It extends deeper than man can ever work. When my tunnel is finished it will cut the present terrific mining costs in half, and increase the depth to which the lode can be worked by two thousand feet. The only reason the bank and Sharon and the monopoly's mills are against it is that they are afraid it will cut them out of their graft."

Baldwin tore himself away, rudely, knowing from experience that Sutro would hold him all day for promotional argument. But he had faith in Sutro's knowledge. He stored the information away, and went down into the depths of the Ophir to look into its stopes and galleries and examine the stringers of ore that were being traced toward the barren ground of the worthless California. A thousand feet away, in that direction, he descended into the steaming shaft of the Best & Belcher, one of the richest of the early producers, and noted the trend of its workings.

Thus primed with information, he wired to San Francisco for the purchase of a considerable amount of Ophir and others, all at bed-rock prices. There was no luck in that. If luck figured at all it was in the prior acquisition of the money necessary to make those purchases. The decision to buy was based upon the best judgment of which Lucky Baldwin was capable.

He himself was neither mining engineer nor geologist. Neither did he greatly trust the good faith of those who were. But in the mining business, as he was to be to a sensationally successful degree in the racing business, he was a player of form. He had checked up on Mackay, Fair and Jones, and had found that though none of them was as yet either very rich or very successful, their records were sound and their energies tremendous. He had discovered that they were investing in the depressed stocks of the mines in which they were working. He had faith in deeds if not in words.

In the meantime, however, the word that Lucky Baldwin was in Virginia City, personally examining the mines, spread swiftly. Promoters, brokers, prospectors and beggars beseiged him. He was not the greatest man in the territory but at the moment he appeared to be the greatest opportunity. The stories of his luck had preceded him from San Francisco. The amount of his fortune had been multiplied in the telling.

Men who had seen him a few years earlier peddling lumber through the town presumed to identify themselves as old friends, to sell him claims or stocks, to plead for a grub-stake, to interest him in the promotion of a horse-race or a prize-fight. Pasty-faced miners sobering up from a jag besought him for a dollar. If there happened to be no one looking, they got it. Otherwise, not. He established no precedents for indiscriminate philanthropy. Sharpers who expected him to be easy picking were brushed aside, rudely, physically.

He was in the prime of life, of medium height, but with high-crowned black hat and long frock coat giving him an appearance of height above the average. The costume also gave him a deceptive appearance of slenderness which made his strength surprising when he knocked down any too-importunate nuisance. Within a few days he was known by sight to almost every resident of Virginia City.

It was the beginning of a new phase of life, a phase in which publicity, sycophants and women—especially women— were to distort and harden his character into lines which became sometimes almost grotesque. The manner in which they hurled themselves upon him, or upon his buckskin poke of gold, in those early days of his notorious riches was but a feeble forecast of the years to come. But at that time he had a bride. Perhaps her influence had not yet waned.

Still honeymooners, they boarded a train at Reno for extension of the honeymoon to the East. Again he visited his sister, Mrs. Evaline Fawcett, at the farmhouse near New Carlisle, Indiana. There he played with his two small nieces, chatted with boyhood friends around Hamilton, and otherwise enjoyed himself with the simplest of entertainment. After a few days of that he journeyed on eastward to give the bride a thrill in the New York theaters and at the Saratoga races.

CHAPTER XI

BIG MONEY

BALDWIN returned to San Francisco with two new ambitions aroused by his luxurious tour of the East. In New York he had been impressed by the furnishings, the service and the food of the famous Fifth Avenue Hotel. The solid walnut dressers, haircloth sofas, hair mattresses and running water of the Fifth Avenue Hotel were something to stir the admiration of a hotel man who had operated the barnlike Pacific Temperance Hotel with its wooden benches, corn-husk mattresses and agateware bowls, pitchers and slop buckets. He would give San Francisco a hotel of which it could be proud—when he had the money.

At Saratoga he had been impressed with the color and excitement of the sport of kings. To a lover of horses who had won his first stake of two hundred dollars on a dusty country road in Indiana, the jockeys in gaudy silks on satiny horses before a grandstand gay with flags and the gowns and parasols of beautiful women were something equally worthy of emulation. He would give to the world race-horses and a track and grandstand to outshine Saratoga—when he had the money.

The few hundred thousand dollars and a few hundred shares of stock in the depressed Comstock mines were not enough. He looked again into San Francisco real estate and bought the unimproved property at the dusty corner of Powell and Market Streets, where he had hunted quail a few years earlier. There, he thought, would be a fine site for a great hotel— when he had the money.

He looked again into the Comstock situation, and found it

still sad. He spent a great deal of time around Flood and O'Brien's bar, lunching on Mrs. Flood's famous corned beef and cabbage, and occasionally lifting a glass with James R. Keene, General John W. Gashweiler, James B. Haggin, John T. Bradley and others of equal fame in the mining stock-market. At times he enjoyed a little personal chat with Flood himself across the mahogany. From each he learned something, and tucked it away for future use.

He gathered that Flood and O'Brien had become affiliated with Mackay and Fair in a few deals in which Flood had negotiated extensive purchases of stock on information furnished by Mackay and Fair. It was the beginning of the world-famous bonanza firm of Mackay, Fair, Flood and O'Brien, though none suspected it at the time.

Incidentally, he learned that the Bank of California was extended to the breaking point in the Comstock and was maintaining itself only through its monopolistic control of the milling business, the transportation business and a few of the mines. Although D. O. Mills, Sharon, Ralston and a few others of the so-called bank ring virtually controlled the lode, their outlook was not too bright.

Neither was Baldwin's for that matter. The Crown Point stock which he had purchased at a low ebb in the previous year was down from the eight dollars a share that he had paid to two dollars. His Ophir and Hale & Norcross also were down. Baldwin dropped in to the Stock and Exchange Board each day to hear these stocks called and quoted. The news was invariably bad. He searched for something better.

And thus he discovered that some sales of odd lots of Crown Point were being made outside the board rooms. He was instantly curious. Why should any one want to buy Crown Point, apparently ruined by the disastrous fire of the previous year, unless they had inside information.

The fortunes of the Comstock, he knew, had been won

largely on inside information. William Sharon, for instance, had bought control of the Belcher at $6 a share and sold it at $1,525. Only inside information could have directed such a deal. Now if Baldwin could only find out who was buying Crown Point at $2 and $3, he might deduce the source and value of the inside information which he suspected. He offered a few shares of his own outside the board as a bait, and was rewarded. The buyers, working through agents, were John P. Jones and Alvinza Hayward.

Baldwin decided that it was enough that an engineer of Jones's reputation was secretly buying up the stock of the mine in which he worked. The fact that the bank ring was showing no apparent interest might mean merely that Jones and Hayward were not advising their associates until they could grab as much of the stock as possible. Lucky decided to go along with them, but without their knowledge. He sent out his own secret agents to buy odd lots outside the board. The price rose slowly to eight dollars a share. There was now a fair demand for the stock on the exchange, though buying was still cautious.

Then, abruptly, news of a new bonanza discovered in the Crown Point by John P. Jones spread through the Comstock and the San Francisco financial district. The stock leaped upward. It halted and hung for a day or two at fifty dollars, but was so closely held that no sales were made. At that time, according to an interview given by Baldwin to H. H. Bancroft, the historian, years later, James R. Keene who was to become the most famous stock-market operator trained in the West was on his uppers.

"I wanted to help him out," said Baldwin. "I told him to buy Crown Point, and when he wanted to sell I would buy it. I saw Keene and Jones together at the race-track, and figured Jones was trying to buy Keene's stock. Sure enough, next day Keene was offering one thousand shares at sixty dollars. I took them, and a lot more. A recent decision in a New York court had held that a majority could shut down a mine, and they were planning to shut down the Crown Point, presumably to counteract the report of the bonanza and hold the price down until they could buy more.

"So I got all the available lawyers, McAllister, Burgess, Stow, Thornton and all those, and a group of armed men to whom I paid thirty dollars to forty dollars a day, and sent them up to keep the mine open. So Sharon and Jones bought me out for two million five hundred thousand dollars. At that time I could have broken the bank, and the state."

Prior to that sale, however, the price of Crown Point had made a sky-rocketing ascent on the exchange from less than three dollars to more than one thousand dollars a share. That deal, according to a later interview with Baldwin already cited, was the basis of his nickname of Lucky. But, he insisted, there was no element of luck in it. In any event he had the name, the fame and the money.

Adventuresses, of which San Francisco had some as alluring, clever and unscrupulous as any in history—Cleopatra, Du-Barry, Lady Hamilton, Lola Montez—began to take an interest in his money, and in him. They found him susceptible, and not always discriminating. He could tell a beggar to be gone. He could knock down and kick out an offensive promoter. He could not resist the charms of a pretty woman with a dainty ankle and alluring eyes. Court records, newspapers and personal reminiscences over nearly half a century bear witness.

And only a small percentage pressed their adventuring to the point of gun-play, lawsuits and attendant publicity. Two who were most intimate with him in later life have talked with me about him. They did not defend his morals or lack of morals, but each revealed a warm spot in her heart for his memory. Others, not adventuresses but women who knew him well for many years, have told me frankly of this phase of his character. But they insisted upon what has generally been overlooked in the scandals, that it was only one phase.

"Mr. Baldwin loved pretty women. You can not reveal his life and character without bringing them in. But also he loved fast horses, fine trees, rich farm lands, and success or the evidence of success in any form."

It should be kept constantly in mind in the study of his life, character and accomplishments that he was an outstanding representative of a period in American history notable for its aggressiveness, individual independence, personal accomplishment, defiance of restriction and scorn of convention. His material success, to his own mind and to the minds of many if not most Americans of the time, justified his practises just as American development of New Mexico, Arizona and California justified the United States' high-handed seizure of that vast territory through a trumped-up war with Mexico.

This is no defense of his defiance of moral conventions. He did defy them, and was looked upon by the conventional as an ogre. But there is no evidence that it worried him. He revealed no moral or spiritual scruples or evidence of a painful conscience. He became a professing disciple of Ingersoll and a practising disciple of Casanova. Pretty women with an eye to his money, or charmed by his notoriety, sought his society. Some were thoroughly sophisticated adventuresses. Younger ones were willing to be. Some, perhaps more innocent, were thrust upon him by unscrupulous older women who were acquainted with his susceptibility and his wealth. Some merely took a chance.

He enjoyed their society and was willing to compensate them in various ways, generally, it may be believed, to their satisfaction, though court records indicate that not all were satisfied. To some, under pressure, he gave thousands of dollars. Some he helped into advantageous marriages. One, who has been named to me by the milliner who witnessed the incident, was made at least temporarily content by the gift of a hundred-and-sixty-five-dollar hat.

He was not, in most instances, a gay deceiver. As he said in answer to one suit, his public reputation was such that every woman who came near him must have been warned against him in advance. Pride in such a reputation might be looked upon as further evidence of complete moral depravity. Yet Baldwin was proud.

He was Lucky Baldwin. His character, for better or for worse, was his own, as his success was his own. The rest of the world could go hang. He would do as he pleased, and did. If he was a sinner, he would be a glamourous sinner. He was no hypocrite.

In all the stories of the gay San Francisco of bonanza days, so far as I have been able to discover, there has been no printed reference to a famous upper floor in the eminently respectable Occidental Hotel, or to certain suites in the equally respectable Russ House across the street, long since burned to ashes. There has been no printed reference to the parties that went on there. The names of California millionaires whose power extended across the continent half a century ago were protected.

San Francisco had a way about such things. As a sentence now classic described one of the most famous of the old French restaurants, "On the first floor Society dines with her husband; on the second she trifles with her reputation; and the third is not mentioned."

Just so a certain floor of the Occidental Hotel of those days was not mentioned—in print. But men who have lived in San Francisco since those days have told me of it. They do not want to be quoted. They are respectable in a way that Lucky Baldwin was not. But from their stories it may be gathered that nothing more Sybaritic has existed in America. The parties in such environment in the San Francisco ruled and colored by bonanza millions were famous among the initiated.

But their fame was whispered—never sung. The gossip of Baldwin's affairs, on the contrary, was shouted. He did not care. Chiefly in that did he differ morally from many of his contemporaries.

The point to be made here is that San Francisco in the '70s offered not only temptation but example and opportunity to Lucky Baldwin. And Lucky Baldwin throughout eighty-one years was never a person to slam the door in the face of opportunity. He welcomed it, clasped it to his breast, kissed it warmly upon the lips, and took it to live with him.

His ambition was equal to his energy. Two millions, three millions of dollars could not satisfy him for life any more than two or three women or two or three race-horses could satisfy him. He wanted more, and more, and more, and set forth to get it.

The Crown Point bonanza was ushering in a new era on the Comstock. All the stocks moved up in sympathy. The Bank of California came out of its difficulties. Crown Point reached $1,825 a share. Belcher, adjoining, struck pay ore. Baldwin tried to interest Mackay and Fair in buying control. They declined. He bought. The stock mounted from $2 to more than $1,500 a share.

In popular opinion Lucky Baldwin was a greater man in 1871 than Mackay, Fair, Flood or Jones. He was more spectacular. With his wide black hat and his long black coat, his reputation for fabulous good luck, and the fast horses and handsome women with which he appeared in public, he was the sort of figure to take the eye and appeal to the imagination. His picturesque appearance and reputation won him recognition even in the lobbies of the leading New York hotels and theaters and in the paddock at Saratoga.

Being good copy, his reputation for luck increased, and his more valuable characteristics of energy, persistence and intelligence were overshadowed. He was indifferent to publicity, and just a little shy with strangers and reporters, thereby stimulating their interest in his affairs. He disliked the reputation for luck, and being himself convinced that he was not lucky but shrewd he continued to extend his operations on the basis of whatever inside information he could pick up.

Thus he discovered that Flood and O'Brien in San Francisco were buying up odd lots of stock in the presumably barren ground stretching between the Best & Belcher and the Ophir. If Flood was buying, Baldwin knew it was on information furnished by Mackay and Fair, who knew more about the underground workings of the lode than any two men in Virginia City.

But Mackay and Fair had declined Baldwin's proposal to buy control of the Best & Belcher. If they were interested in the thirteen hundred feet of hitherto unproductive ground between that and the Ophir it must be because of something they had discovered at the Ophir end.

Baldwin hesitated a while in an effort to decide whether to compete with Mackay, Fair and Flood in the buying of the adjoining ground that was not being worked at all, or to buy into Ophir where he believed there must be indications that were prompting the Mackay-Fair-Flood secret purchases. At last he decided to buy into Ophir.

It was his first great mistake. It was to net him only an insignificant five million dollars when he might have had fifty millions if he had bought into the barren ground from which the big bonanza firm took one hundred and five million dollars in dividends alone. Perhaps he was right in insisting that he was never lucky. If so, he was wrong in insisting that he was always wise. And he still had a battle before him to collect the five millions.

Mackay, Fair, Flood and O'Brien obtained control of the despised Virginia and California ground between Best & Belcher and Ophir for a total of one hundred thousand dollars.

Then they assessed themselves another one hundred thousand dollars and went to work. Their underground search lasted two years, and cost them several hundred thousand dollars more, but they persisted. And they were rewarded with such magnificence as mankind would like to believe should always reward such faith and energy. In March of 1873 they opened the big bonanza which lifted the market value of the stock in two mines alone from less than two hundred thousand dollars to more than one hundred and sixty millions.

Perhaps Lucky Baldwin was shocked and grieved by his ill luck in having decided to purchase Ophir stock instead of Con-Virginia stock. But he consoled himself. Ophir too was moving up in sympathy with the big bonanza. He found that his purchases of Ophir at an average of about eight dollars a share had brought him a substantial fraction of the total shares. Why not go ahead and acquire control? There were two or three reasons. The most important seemed to be that control was held by the bank ring, headed by William Sharon, and Sharon had a reputation of being a buzz-saw to fight.

So he tried to buy quietly, and succeeded in accumulating about half the stock of the mine. But something seemed to be wrong. Despite the steady demand which he fostered and supported, the price of Ophir failed to reach the height of several other mines. Superficially that could be explained by the fact that Ophir was still levying assessments instead of paying dividends. But Baldwin was not satisfied with superficial reasons. He thought he saw the devious hand of Sharon and the bank ring in the situation. He knew their methods. So he obtained fifty samples of Ophir ore and had them assayed privately. Only one out of the fifty revealed sufficient gold and silver to justify milling. It was too bad to be true, especially with the big bonanza producing ore worth six hundred and thirty dollars a ton next door.

Baldwin was satisfied that the true riches of the Ophir were being concealed in the hope of depressing the stock so that he would be squeezed out and the bank ring could buy it back at a much lower figure. But now he had sufficient stock to take control—or thought he had. The doubt was due to a recent court decision which had decreed that any one holding stock, even when already sold for future delivery, could vote it.

At that time James R. Keene was operating on the exchange for Sharon and against Baldwin. In that capacity he was buying Ophir for cash and selling it at the same time, "seller ninety," that is with ninety days to deliver. Such transactions would give the bank ring control during the ninety days in which they could vote the stock.

But Baldwin consulted with other stockholders, and on the basis of their ownership decided to run things himself. With the support of these stockholders, some of whom had paid for but not yet received their certificates, Baldwin put his own superintendent, Samuel Curtis, in charge of the mine with instructions to take out any ore which would pay dividends, if such ore were available as he believed it to be.

Then he discovered that A. H. Lissak, president of the Ophir, had been instructed to call a special meeting of the directors to throw Curtis out of his job. A report reached Baldwin that Lissak was acting under orders from Flood and his partners in the bonanza firm. If that were true, Baldwin was fighting not only the entrenched bank ring but the rising bonanza firm. The odds seemed all against him, but he held stock that had cost him a million dollars or more and he did not intend to lose it.

He consulted his attorney, Reuben H. Lloyd, one of the most brilliant lights of the San Francisco bar, and decided to obtain an injunction against the meeting on the ground that Lissak was planning to swing the meeting illegally by casting two votes, one as president and one as trustee. The meeting had been called for eleven A.M., in the San Francisco office of the Ophir Company. Lloyd informed Baldwin that the papers could not be obtained in time to serve before eleven-fifteen. That would be too late.

"All right," said Baldwin. "I'll take care of that fifteen minutes. You have an officer there to serve the papers at eleven-fifteen, and it will be all right."

Baldwin went to a friend, George G. Grayson, a minority stockholder, and suggested that he put a pistol in his pocket and go along to the meeting. Grayson did so, and Baldwin explained his plan on the way.

Arriving at the meeting, a minute or two before eleven o'clock, Baldwin and Grayson entered the room and Baldwin locked the door behind him. Lissak protested. Baldwin argued, playing for time. Still Lissak protested, and started to unlock the door. Baldwin promptly knocked him under a table. Other directors dragged him out and put him on his feet, and then turned their attention to Baldwin. All this took time. He was grinning now, and continued to spar with them, verbally and physically, until a peremptory rap came upon the locked door. Now if Reuben Lloyd had done his stuff, the battle was won. Baldwin pretended to submit. The clock had moved on to eleven-fifteen.

"Very well, if you are going to make such a point of it, unlock the damned door."

Some one unlocked it. A deputy sheriff stepped in, to Baldwin's welcoming grin and the chagrin of the opposition. The injunction papers were served and the meeting was stopped without having accomplished anything.

But a few days later notice was served on Baldwin's man, Samuel Curtis, that he had been dismissed from the superintendency of the Ophir and Lissak's brother had been appointed in his place and demanded immediate possession of the mine. Curtis, happening to be in San Francisco on business, reported immediately to Baldwin.

"Wire your assistant in Virginia City to shut down the mine and hide enough essential parts of the hoisting engines to prevent reopening until you get there," said Baldwin. "I'll round up some guards with Winchesters and plenty of ammunition, and you can take them back on the first train and reopen the mine. And work it for all there is in it."

Two days later, Curtis, back in Virginia City, reopened the mine. A small bonanza was encountered. Baldwin, now definitely on the inside, was advised ahead of the public. Keene, offering to sell Ophir at sixty dollars, seller ninety, presumably to depress the market at Sharon's or Flood's orders, was snapped up by H. H. Noble, Baldwin's chief broker. Within a year the stock was quoted at an advance of more than five hundred per cent. on that figure.

That Baldwin knew when to sell as well as when to buy is revealed in a story by Joseph L. King, historian of the San Francisco Stock and Exchange Board. Incidentally it reveals a sidelight upon James R. Keene who was later to gain fame upon the New York exchange.

"H. H. Noble was broker-in-chief for E. J. Baldwin," according to King's chronicle. "Noble watched the board in the interest of his client every minute of the day. At the height of the market, probably January 7, 1875, Keene bid $315 for 10,000 shares of Ophir. Baldwin was not in the board and Noble passed his book of orders to another broker, requesting him to execute the orders of the stocks yet to be called, and quickly hied himself to Baldwin's office.

"A broker must be quick about a business of this kind, and on opening the door of Baldwin's office he hurried up to his desk, saying: 'Keene is bidding $315 for 10,000 shares of Ophir.' Here was the long awaited opportunity to get the best of a large trade.

" 'Sell it,' said Baldwin, rising in his excitement.

"It was a $3,000,000 order and Noble naturally hesitated a moment. Baldwin saw the hesitation, and in his eagerness

to make the sale and beat Keene if possible, said to Jules Cavalier, his bookkeeper: 'Give me that box of stocks.' When
handed the box Baldwin grasped a bunch of certificates, rolled
them up without looking at them and handed them to the broker
with the remark: 'There is enough security. Hurry up!'

"When Noble arrived in the board room Keene was still
there, but Mr. James R. Keene was one of the brightest of
brokers. He knew when to bid for $3,000,000 worth of
Ophir, and he knew when to cease bidding. The bid was not
repeated. The securities were returned to Baldwin and we
learned afterwards that they totaled more than $3,000,000."

A brief digression may be permitted here to note that Jules
Cavalier had evidently failed to make good in the livery-stable
that he had purchased from Baldwin through a true Baldwin
deal some ten years earlier. But he had not been left to starve
on that account. Having taken his ten thousand dollars,
Baldwin gave him a job. Later he was to appear again as a
Baldwin employee on the great Santa Anita ranch, and finally
to be buried by Baldwin when he died penniless.

Similar side-lights on this same phase of Baldwin's character
may be found in numerous incidents of his life. Repeatedly
he was able to turn a shrewd deal, amounting to what many
persons would call a dirty trick, and later take the victim into
his employ and even into his friendship. It is a more common
trait in human nature to avoid the person whom one has injured. But Baldwin, whatever his shortcomings, was an individualist.

With the exception of his brief partnership with Wormer
in the brick business and his subsequent brief partnership with
Killip in the livery business, he was always his own man, in
profit and in loss, in prosperity and in depression, in business
and in private life, regardless of reputation, indifferent to
public opinion—especially if it were bad. In his Comstock
operations he never joined a pool or otherwise hampered his
independence in the market.

In the big deal in Ophir he had, he thought, been fighting Sharon and the bank ring, though word had come to him just before the meeting in which he had checkmated Lissak, that Lissak had called that meeting at the request of Flood, representing the bonanza firm. Though several of the records mention Flood as the man who requested that meeting, it seems more probable in the light of history that it was Sharon.

The bank ring's monopoly under Sharon had been weakened by the defection of Jones and Hayward with the Crown Point bonanza, though the bank had been saved from collapse by that same bonanza. Then Sharon's powers had been further threatened by the rise of Mackay, Fair and Flood with the opening of the big bonanza. It seems very doubtful that Sharon would have cooperated with Flood.

Though the detailed records were destroyed in the San Francisco fire of 1906, enough is known to students of the melodramatic history of the Comstock to serve as a credible guide to the facts. If we accept such guidance we may find our way logically to what appears to be the truth among the contradictory reports concerning Baldwin's acquisition of millions in Comstock trading.

Reports may be found which will contradict each other and offer details contradictory to this history, but unquestionable facts contradict some of those reports and furnish guide-posts to accuracy. For instance, H. H. Bancroft, the historian who left an extensive sketch of Baldwin's life in *The Chronicles of the Builders,* says that after the successful fight for Ophir control recited above, Baldwin waged another successful battle over Ophir against the bank ring. At that time the price of Ophir stock was fluctuating wildly to the extent of a million dollars total gains or losses within forty-eight-hour periods.

"Hoping to find him unprepared," says Bancroft, "the bonanza firm sent word one day to his broker to make good his account at the Nevada Bank by 3 P.M. At the moment the market was demoralized; but not so Mr. Baldwin, who, so far from being forced to sell at a sacrifice could at one time have netted a profit of many millions, though to have done so would have produced a panic. Finally, however, he retired from the fray with $5,000,000 added to his possessions; and to the defeat inflicted on Ralston and his colleagues, coupled with the fact that Ophir's promised bonanza did not materialize, was mainly due the collapse of the greatest financial institution on the Pacific Coast."

That story has been widely circulated as the accurate account of Baldwin's greatest killing on the Comstock. It has even been used in the preparation of court cases in which heirs of Baldwin's millions have been involved.

But with all due respect to H. H. Bancroft, it should be analyzed. Baldwin himself was perhaps the heaviest single depositor in the Bank of California at the time its failure precipitated a panic on the Pacific Coast in the summer of 1875. At that time he had a balance variously stated at from one million to two million five hundred thousand dollars. It does not seem credible that he would have helped to wreck a bank which held so much of his money. Impeaching the accuracy of the Bancroft report even more definitely is the fact that the Nevada Bank, owned and controlled by the bonanza kings, Mackay, Fair, Flood and O'Brien, was not in existence at the moment of which the historian writes. The Bank of California failed on August 26, 1875. The Nevada Bank opened for business first on October 4, 1875. The Bank of California reopened under its new organization on the following day.

Perhaps all that is of minor importance, though it seems worthy of a place in these pages as indicating the extent and diversity of Baldwin's operations and perhaps explaining the variety of legends which grew up about his Comstock operations and the acquisition of his first millions.

Bancroft has left us other stories, probably based in part

upon his interview with Baldwin. One of these is to the effect that in his first big deal in Ophir, Baldwin carried a number of friends with him to sensational profits. "To one man, as appears on his books," Bancroft writes, "he gave a check for $570,000, and to others from $50,000 to $100,000 as their profits on stocks bought for them with his own money and at his own suggestion."

If that is true it is virtually the only time in his life that Baldwin stepped so far out of character as to appear an altruist. His business and social dealings before and after the accumulation of millions reveal few such tendencies and no such gifts. "His books," cited by Bancroft, are no longer available.

A statement dictated in 1891 by H. A. Unruh, who had then been his confidential man for twelve years, stated that "when Mr. Baldwin sold his stock in the bank (of California) he started in and made a great losing through trying to make Rube Lloyd rich." But that statement too is unsupported by any documentary evidence, as is Baldwin's own statement that James R. Keene "was going about on his uppers" at the time of Baldwin's first profitable Crown Point deal, and that he (Baldwin) "wanted to help him out," and did so by promising to take off his hands at a profit any Crown Point stock that Keene could buy.

But whatever other traits of character Baldwin's busy years of operation in the San Francisco stock exchanges may reveal, a few points stand out clearly and beyond dispute. He was a shrewd and extensive operator, relying upon accurate information and backing his judgment to the extent of millions. He was a real power in the market for several years, and that in competition with some of the most successful and spectacular men that this country has ever known.

He was honored in that business, and looked upon as a leader. In proof is the fact that on June 5, 1875, he was elected president of the newly organized Pacific Stock Exchange Board, which he himself had promoted. In his inaugural address as first president of the new board, he said:

"Let this be a place where every mine will have to stand upon its merits, where no rings shall exist, where no man or set of men will be allowed to foist a worthless stock upon the market, where wash sales will be frowned down, and quotations can be relied upon as showing the real market value. Then, gentlemen, we will gain the public confidence; prosperity will smile upon us, and the country and ourselves be proud of our institution."

At the age of forty-seven he was a rich and powerful man. The evidence indicates that his net takings from operation in Comstock shares in the ten years after his return from his tiger hunting totaled between five million dollars and seven million five hundred thousand dollars.

Several years before the exhaustion of the big bonanza in 1877 he had accumulated sufficient money to start gratification of the two great ambitions with which he had returned from that honeymoon trip to New York and Saratoga in 1869. As fast as the cash became available he proceeded to gratify them.

CHAPTER XII

BRANCHING OUT

WHEN George Kennedy, veteran mixologist in the most luxurious bars of the West for nearly half a century, told me that Lucky Baldwin had more things to do in an hour than any man he ever saw, "and did them," he suggested the picture, but hardly completed it. And Kennedy had known, served and observed such men as John Mackay, James G. Fair, James C. Flood, William Sharon, Collis P. Huntington, Leland Stanford, and others as energetic in the development of the West.

Compared to the diversity and energy of Lucky Baldwin's activities in the half-dozen years from 1871 to 1877, the steady advances of his famous contemporaries along their individual lines of mining, banking and railroad building might appear to have been almost lives of idleness. It is true that they accumulated fortunes far greater than his, and died in the odor of comparative sanctity. But it is doubtful that any man ever lived who engaged successfully in as great a variety of activities as Lucky Baldwin did in those years.

The abbreviated history of his operations in the Comstock market, which has filled the preceding chapter, would seem to have been enough to occupy the days and nights of even an extraordinary man to the exclusion of all other interests. But despite the fact that these activities gave Baldwin his first millions in the face of bitter opposition from such powerful experts as Flood, Keene, Mackay and Sharon, he found time between rounds of that fight to do a score of things, each of which might have been expected to crowd his every waking moment. And Baldwin, it must be remembered, was an individualist. Always he conducted his own affairs, giving subordinates little authority.

Still, in those few years, he found time and energy not only to accumulate millions in the mining stock-market but to build and operate one of the two finest hotels west of New York, to acquire and develop the most spectacular rancho in southern California, to start a racing stable which was to make his name famous in the sport of kings, to promote an irrigation project far beyond any precedent of its time, to become the first great subdivider in what was to become the paradise of realtors, to grow into a power in the financial affairs of the West, and to add to his reputation as a Don Juan with another divorce, another marriage and incidental scandals.

Vast and varied as his activities were in those hectic years, Baldwin was merely keeping pace with the country whose spirit he personified. The spirit of America was still the spirit of the frontier, although its people had leaped the barrier of the western plains, mountains and desert to the Pacific Coast, and were now flowing in from both sides for the settlement of the vast areas obtained by purchase from France, by war with Mexico, by treaty with Great Britain.

With the end of the Civil War a new era of speculation and disregard of moral conventions had been ushered in. The Tweed Ring had looted the New York City treasury of an amount estimated as high as two hundred million dollars. The great era of railroad building had netted the promoters, including Huntington, Hopkins, Stanford and Crocker in the West, some one hundred and thirty million acres of government land and more than twenty million dollars of public funds. Jay Gould, Jim Fisk and associates had looted the Erie railroad of ten million dollars and engineered the gold corner which was the disgrace of the Grant administration.

In the panic of 1873 the nation as a whole crashed from inflated affluence to dire poverty, just as it had done in Baldwin's early youth in 1837, and as it was to do again in 1893 and still again in 1929. Eighty-nine railroads went bankrupt, throwing half a million railroad builders out of work. Nearly half the iron and steel plants in the country closed. Forty-six thousand commercial houses failed in the tragic era while the population was considerably less than half what it is to-day. And still the nation struggled to its feet, and turned its hand to whatever it could find to do—the formation of the first great organizations of business into trusts, the formation of working men into unions to defend their wage scales, the continued settlement of the vast unoccupied public domain.

The nation was indomitable, immoral, unscrupulous. Lucky Baldwin typified, as far as any one man could typify, the spirit of the nation. To be sure, he enjoyed some advantages in his situation. California had been hit less heavily by the panic of 1873 than was the rest of the United States. It had the advantage of the millions in gold and silver coming out of the neighboring Comstock Lode. It was isolated. It had even maintained its circulation of gold while the rest of the country was forced to use greenbacks, depreciated sixty-five per cent. But it was soon to suffer its own more or less private but none the less demoralizing panic with the exhaustion of the big bonanza. Yet through it all Baldwin's energy never lagged, whatever may be said of his morals.

So extensive and involved were the mazes of his activities that it is practically impossible to recite them in chronological order. With the profits of his first big Crown Point deal available, his greatest ambition at the moment was to build a hotel that would be a monument to his name and fame. That purpose had been in the back of his mind while he was still dabbling in San Francisco real estate, before entering the Comstock as a leading operator. The site had already been selected—virgin ground at the corner of Market and Powell Streets. In 1870 it was looked upon as being far up-town.

But Lucky Baldwin visioned a city of ten times the population which San Francisco then boasted, and planned accordingly. Perhaps there was a bit of vanity in his ambition. This magnificent hotel would make his name known throughout the civilized world. San Francisco lacked a hotel worthy of its riches. The Palace had not yet been projected, though it was soon to be. The most modern hostelry in the city at that time probably had not cost half a million dollars. Baldwin planned to spend three millions.

Such expenditure should produce a worthy rival of the finest hotels in the world. Baldwin would be satisfied with nothing less. He engaged John A. Remer, the best architect he could find, and ordered him to spare no expense in the line of towers, cupolas and so forth, not to mention grand staircases, mural decorations by Garibaldi, famous scenic artist, pillars, chandeliers and mahogany finish. Then he signed a contract with Alex MacAbee, the leading builder in San Francisco, and paused a moment to await the result.

Work upon the hotel was started in 1873 and pushed steadily into the following year. Baldwin's local fame spread with the newspaper reports that he was building the finest hotel west of New York. At the same time his name was appearing more and more frequently in the news of fortunes being won and lost on the mining stock exchange. His reputation of being a shrewd and successful trader and his reputation of being a genial host to adventuring women grew side by side. His second venture in matrimony was not flourishing. No children had come of that marriage. His daughter Clara that year married her third husband, Budd Doble, still famous as one of the greatest drivers in the history of trotting races.

Doble again stimulated Baldwin's interest in horses and went with him to the opening meeting at Saratoga. There Lucky purchased two Kentucky-bred stallions, Grinstead and Rutherford, as the start of his racing stable.

Returning to San Francisco he received word from a pros-
pector whom he had grub-staked that there was a promising
gold property to be had in Bear Valley in the far-away San
Bernardino Mountains of southern California. Baldwin had
never been in southern California. He decided to go.

There was neither railroad nor decent highway from San
Francisco to Los Angeles. The Southern Pacific was building
slowly southward through the arid wastes of the San Joaquin
Valley. Baldwin had his choice of three routes: by stage from
the southern end of railroad construction through the San
Joaquin Valley and over the Tehachapi Mountains, by stage
from San José down the coast, or by the sea.

A little coasting steamer plied from San Francisco to San
Diego, stopping at Monterey, Santa Barbara and Wilmington.
If he took that he could ride on the only railroad in southern
California, a narrow-gauge line from Wilmington to Los
Angeles. But the steamer had just departed, and he was in a
hurry. He found a little freight schooner that would stop at
a rickety wharf a few miles up the coast from Wilmington, if
weather permitted. Probably it would permit. Southern
California climate, though not yet publicized, was already
recognized.

Baldwin boarded the schooner. It tied up three days later
below the bluffs of the Rancho San Vicente. There the city
of Santa Monica more than half a century later was to look
over the palatial seaside homes of Marion Davies, Douglas
Fairbanks, Jesse Lasky, Joseph Schenck, Louis Mayer, Norma
Shearer and others similarly famous.

But where tens of thousands of persons now crowd the sands
and surf on summer holidays, Baldwin could see no life except
the sea-gulls. Where a lovely park adorns the bluffs only a
few long-horned cattle grazed, knee deep in the wild oats.
Where luxurious buses, electric trains and private cars beyond
counting now carry gay parties daily to and from the beaches

only a few freight teams and a "spring wagon" serving as a stage to Los Angeles, greeted the traveler. For twenty dusty miles he rode through the ranchos, past the hills that now bear his name and contribute to the wealth of his heirs, to the village of Los Angeles.

There he stopped at the Pico House, the leading hotel, three stories high with a bathroom on each of the two upper floors, claiming to be modern and luxurious in that some of its rooms were lighted by flickering gas-jets instead of kerosene lamps and candles. The streets were deep with dust. Flies buzzed in the hotel dining-room. The only street-car, horse drawn, ran from the Pico House on a meandering course to the car barn at Sixth and Figueroa Streets.

Baldwin saw only dirt and laziness where modern writers picture a charming indolence. Probably Baldwin was right. In the next two years, according to the reminiscences of Jackson Graves, nearly half the population of Los Angeles died of smallpox. "One could not go out in the street, at any time of the day or night, without a hearse rushing by with a smallpox corpse in it."

Baldwin started out promptly for Bear Valley. Half a day's ride from the dusty town he found himself in what, by contrast, seemed to be paradise. The rich lands, the rolling contours, the great oaks of the San Gabriel Valley, backed by the steep slopes of the Sierra Madre with the snow-capped peak of San Jacinto etched against distant blue sky, checked him in amazement.

"By gad! This is paradise."

The wild oats, thick among the scattered oaks, reached to the bellies of the grazing cattle. For an instant Baldwin was again the practical farmer that he had been on the Indiana prairie. He waded into the high grass beside the road, pulled a clump and examined the soil around its roots.

"This will grow anything," he told his traveling companion,

and his eyes were shining with a light that they had seldom revealed in twenty years of business. "I'm going to buy this
country. Who owns it?"

His companion shrugged. "Oh, I don't know; maybe Juan
Sanchez, maybe Morillo and Romero, maybe Temple and
Workman, maybe Harris Newmark. They all own a lot of
land out in this direction. Come on; let's go. It's a long trip
to Bear Valley."

They continued their journey, through San Bernardino, then
a sleepy village only occasionally stirred from its siesta by the
arrival of stages over the Santa Fe route from the distant East
to Los Angeles. Coming into Bear Valley, Baldwin's interest
in the mining property which he had been traveling for days to
examine was again checked by the agricultural possibilities
which his imagination pictured. Oranges, grapes and amazing
garden products growing in every cultivated spot where sufficient water had touched the desert stirred him as free gold in
a chunk of ore might have done.

The mining claims which he examined appeared to be of low
grade, though with great quantities of ore which promised long
and profitable work if proper milling facilities could be provided. The prospect was not exciting. But the possibility
of seeing the thousands of desert acres of Bear Valley blossom
into rich gardens, orchards and farms under an irrigation
scheme which had already flashed into his mind was stimulating. He remembered the marvels wrought with irrigation by
the Mormons in the desert around Great Salt Lake as he had
seen them twenty-odd years before. He made the necessary
arrangements to hold the mining properties, but with only one
eye upon those properties and one upon the far more fascinating land. Then he returned to Los Angeles, making a further
inspection of the San Gabriel Valley en route.

A new ambition had been added to his earlier ambitions of
making a fortune in the Comstock, of building a hotel that

would be a monument to his greatness in San Francisco, of developing a racing stable that would build him a greater fame and even more profitable thrills on the race-tracks of the country. His vision of such a ranch in the San Gabriel Valley as would make the old Spanish haciendas appear as ill kept barnyards by comparison, demanded realization.

But back in San Francisco Baldwin had hardly time to inspect the rising walls of the new hotel when all thought of a vast new estate in southern California was swept from his mind by a sudden panic sweeping down from the Comstock with the rumor that the big bonanza, opened in the preceding year, had been exhausted. Consolidated Virginia, then the chief of the two big bonanza mines, dropped two hundred dollars a share. California, its companion, lost sixty per cent. of its valuation. The two together dropped twenty-four million dollars almost overnight. All the others crashed in sympathy. Baldwin's Ophir holdings lost a million dollars in two days. The Bank of California, where Baldwin's cash for building the hotel was on deposit, trembled. All business felt the shock.

"By gad, I'll see about this," said Baldwin, and hurried to Virginia City. There he convinced himself very quickly that the rumor which had caused the crash was a false one. He found Mackay and Fair smilingly superintending the development and production of their mines, and blissfully unconcerned.

"It's no affair of mine," Mackay said. "I am not speculating in stocks. I make my money here out of the ore."

He was almost too unconcerned. His apparent indifference aroused Baldwin's suspicions. He knew John Mackay. Back again in San Francisco he made inquiries which convinced him that Mackay, Fair, Flood and O'Brien were again quietly buying the depressed stock of the Con-Virginia and California. Baldwin immediately bought some too. Within a few weeks his judgment was justified. He recovered the million depreciation in Ophir almost as quickly as he had suffered it. The market again climbed swiftly.

And it was at this point that Baldwin promoted, organized and was elected president of the Pacific Stock Exchange. He cashed in some of his latest purchases and ordered his hotel builder to push ahead with construction. At the same time he was gaining new recognition in the sporting circles of San Francisco by his appearance in the rôle of an owner at the race-track. Fine horses and fine equipages were outstanding badges of success in the San Francisco of the '70s.

The Comstock millionaires and the new railroad millionaires were building magnificent homes and laying out estates of feudal grandeur along the peninsula south of the city. A new railroad extended to San José, affording them adequate transportation to their offices in San Francisco, but though some hooked their private cars to the local trains for commuting purposes, others preferred to drive their fast horses, direct from their palaces among the oaks to their offices among the five- and six-story skyscrapers of the city.

William C. Ralston, cashier and chief power of the great Bank of California though D. O. Mills was its president, maintained relay stables at ten-mile intervals between his mansion at Belmont and his office, and drove horses selected for their ability to hit a two-twenty gait on the road. Leland Stanford was using some of the millions he had extracted from the Huntington-Stanford-Crocker-Hopkins railroad contracts to start the stock farm and race-track at Palo Alto, on what was to become the site of Stanford University. Herbert Hoover, who was to be the most distinguished graduate of that university, had just been born.

The stables of the millionaires rivaled the magnificence of their homes. Tiled stalls and mahogany woodwork were not too fine for the horses which displayed their owners' grandeur on the streets of San Francisco and along the neighboring

drives. A story is told of one who visited the show rooms of
Thomas Day & Company to select a chandelier of silver and
crystal which would be worthy of the drawing-room of the residence he was planning on Nob Hill. The salesman whom he
encountered combined enthusiasm and obsequiousness in correct proportions but evidently lacked the necessary admixture
of intelligence.

"That is a beautiful, a magnificent production of our own
artists and workmen," he said, standing back to admire the
silver filigree and pendant crystals of the chandelier which he
was displaying. "You couldn't do better. Our workmen are
all artists. They rival or surpass anything produced in the
world. Why, only yesterday I sold a chandelier almost precisely like this to———" and he named the latest multimillionaire
of the Comstock.

"Where is he going to use it?" the prospective customer
asked with rising interest.

"Oh, in his new stables," said the salesman. "They are to
be the finest in San Francisco, and of course that means the
finest in the world."

That was the order of the day. Any man who aspired to
social, professional or business success with the nabobs of the
West maintained and appeared in public with horses and
equipages which were worthy of blue ribbons in any horse show
in the world. Horses were imported from Arabia, carriages
from England and France, harness from the leather workers
of Florence. Lucky Baldwin imported the first four-horse
English coach to come to San Francisco, and created a sensation when he tooled his own matched four along the fashionable
drive known as the Point Lobos road.

It was a gay and colorful life, speeding into the spring of
1875. But it could not satisfy Lucky Baldwin's appetite for
new ventures, new thrills, greater activity. The picture of a
semi-tropical paradise which had sprung full-grown to his mind

at his first sight of the beauties of the San Gabriel Valley had been only temporarily obscured by the minor panic encountered upon his return to San Francisco. With stocks booming again the vision returned with new force.

Why not go south again, buy eight or ten sections of that lovely landscape and build the paradise that he had pictured? He had watched the Comstock shares leap and fall and leap again to the tune of uncounted millions over a period of fifteen years. He himself had accumulated millions. But he had narrowly escaped being destroyed with lesser men on several occasions, chief of which was the brief panic just passed. He recognized the mining stock-market as a gamble in which the winners usually seemed to play with marked cards.

Baldwin, at heart, was not a gambler. He was a product of the soil, of the fourth generation of Baldwins who had earned their living from the virgin soil of the American frontier. Though his own wealth had come largely from the mining stock-market he had greater faith in the land. Comstock shares were high again, but again they might drop. He sold his control of the Ophir for a reported five million dollars, and again traveled to southern California to realize his dream and establish his fortune in the land which he believed could not depreciate.

In the sensational ruin of the mining-stock business which was to follow, many persons maintained that Baldwin's sale of his chief holdings at almost their peak prices was just another indication of his luck. He himself insisted that the sale at that time was the result of deliberate reasoning and sound judgment.

Again in southern California, he journeyed once more through the San Gabriel Valley to Bear Valley, to examine his mining properties there, and again was moved by a vision of a great irrigation project which would make that desert blossom. He had plenty of money available. He purchased six thousand acres at a few dollars an acre, with additional water rights from which he hoped to develop the land. In the San Gabriel Valley he was thrilled as upon his first visit.

Most of the land, he found, was held by half a dozen owners, some under the original Spanish grants and some by later sale or patent. Louis Woolfskill, a rancher, owned a few hundred acres. Juan Mateo Sanchez owned the Rancho Potrero Grande the Potrero de Felipe Lugo, and La Merced, the latter being largely rough hill land apparently unfit for anything but sheep pasture. William Workman, of the Los Angeles banking firm of Temple and Workman, held the forty thousand undeveloped acres of the Puente Rancho. Harris Newmark, the leading wholesale grocer and ranch produce dealer of southern California, owned several thousand acres of the most beautiful woods and meadows sloping down from the Sierra Madre foot-hills. That area was known as the Rancho Santa Anita.

Lucky Baldwin chose it as the home ranch of the vast estate which he visioned. Immediately he bought the Woolfskill property for ten thousand dollars. Then he bought the adjoining acreage of the San Francisquito at a low figure. Having learned that the wholesale house of H. Newmark & Company owned the coveted Santa Anita property, he then turned to them.

"I'd like to buy that Santa Anita ranch of yours, Mr. Newmark, if you are not asking too much for it," he said after a long preliminary discussion of weather and crops, as was his customary approach to a business proposition.

"We are not anxious to sell," said Newmark.

"I'll give you one hundred and fifty thousand dollars," said Baldwin. "Cash!" and he tapped a tin box carried under his arm.

Newmark shook his head, smiling. Baldwin was disappointed and indignant. "How much then?" he demanded.

"One hundred and seventy-five thousand," said Newmark.

It was Baldwin's turn to shake his head, but he did it without smiling, and stalked out of the room. He hung around town for a day or two, hoping for a call from Newmark, but received none, and went out again to look over the San Gabriel Valley. He found himself more in love with it than ever, and returned to Los Angeles prepared to pay the one hundred and seventy-five thousand dollars asked by Newmark. Again in Newmark's office with his tin box under his arm, he announced his decision.

"I'll give you one hundred and seventy-five thousand dollars for that ranch, Mr. Newmark," he said, after the usual preliminaries.

"It's two hundred thousand," said Newmark quietly.

Baldwin was shocked and grieved. And as a side-light on his character it should be remembered that he had just sold his Ophir holdings for five million dollars, and had that amount of money—twenty-five times the price asked for the ranch—available in cash.

"Two hundred thousand," Newmark repeated. "Next week it will be two hundred and twenty-five thousand."

Baldwin leaped to his feet, turned his back and strode out of the office. On the sidewalk he bumped into his attorney, Reuben Lloyd, who had made the trip south with him.

"By gad, Lloyd!" he burst out indignantly. "That fellow in there is asking me more than twenty-five dollars an acre for that sheep pasture out in the San Gabriel Valley."

"I thought you said it was rich soil, grow anything, plenty of water, fine trees, fine view, fine climate, everything marvelous."

"I did. But two hundred thousand dollars! By gad, that's a lot of money."

Lloyd grinned, and tapped the tin box under Baldwin's arm. "You've got it, ten or twenty times over. Go back in and buy the land. Don't forget he knows the Southern Pacific and the Santa Fe railroad are both going to build through there. He knows that just as well as you do. He'll put the price up another twenty-five thousand next week."

"By gad, that's what he said he'd do. I believe he would. He's already raised it from a hundred and seventy-five." Baldwin wheeled, reentered the office and plumped his tin box down on Newmark's desk. "I'll take that ranch for two hundred thousand," he said.

"Two hundred and twenty-five thousand," said Newmark, with a twinkle in his eye.

"That's next week," said Baldwin. "I want it now."

Newmark looked him over quizzically. "Oh, very well."

Baldwin opened the tin box, counted out twelve thousand five hundred dollars in currency and asked for a receipt. "That will bind the sale until I can examine the title," he said.

Newmark agreed. In his reminiscences of sixty years in southern California, published nearly half a century later, he states that that tin box contained several million dollars.

The one hundred and eighty-seven thousand five hundred dollars balance was paid over in a few days. Baldwin deposited forty thousand dollars in the Temple & Workman bank, engaged a crew of Mexicans under a capable foreman, outlined preliminary work of improvement, and returned to San Francisco.

For a moment his luck deserted him. He made a huge deposit, stated in various reports at from one million five hundred thousand dollars to three million six hundred thousand dollars in the Bank of California. The records have been burned. There remains only circumstantial and somewhat conflicting evidence of the exact amount of the deposit.

It is known that in that year, some time after the purchase of the Santa Anita ranch, he came to the separation of the way with his second wife and in settlement gave her one million dollars and the Baldwin home at 410 Geary Street, San Francisco. It is known that he had another one million dollars available for another purpose. It is known that he was able in the same year to complete the Academy of Music, more widely known as the Baldwin Theater, a part of the new hotel structure, and then the finest theater west of New York. It is known that he found funds for the planting of orchards and vineyards, the digging of wells, the building of reservoirs and irrigation lines, the clearing and planting of fields, and similar improvements on the new rancho. It is known that he had ample funds available to travel eastward again, to gain new laurels as a patron of the tracks, and to buy brood mares to stock the racing stables already planned at Santa Anita.

At the Saratoga meeting he picked up Josie C. and Maggie Emerson, thoroughbred Kentucky mares, and shipped them west. Returning to California by way of Kentucky he stopped at Alexander's stud farm near Woodburn and bought six fillies, Jennie D., Blossom, Clara D., Santa Anita, Glenita and Ophir. The eight, with the two stallions Grinstead and Rutherford, previously purchased, were the start of one of the most successful racing stables ever developed in America.

It was to give Lucky Baldwin as much fame as his affairs with women were to give him notoriety, as his millions were to give him power, and as his new land holdings were to give him a permanent place in the history of the West as a pioneer subdivider, promoter and developer of southern California.

But in the meantime a catastrophe impended. The word reached Baldwin by telegraph while he was still in the East. A second rumor that the big bonanza on the Comstock had been exhausted brought panic to the market. Baldwin promptly wired to draw four hundred thousand dollars from his account at the Bank of California. Reuben Lloyd wired back that the bank had closed its doors one hour before the arrival of his draft.

Baldwin answered: "Protect my interests, but do nothing to hurt Ralston." Then he followed the message as quickly as the trains could take him.

But it was too late to save William C. Ralston, cashier and general manager of the bank. Before Baldwin's arrival, the bank directors had met, discovered that Ralston was at least one million five hundred thousand dollars short in his cash, and arbitrarily deposed him. Two hours later his body was found floating in the bay. The affairs of the bank, of the city of San Francisco, of the Comstock region, and of almost the entire Pacific Coast were in chaos.

And Baldwin had from one million dollars to two million five hundred thousand dollars in the closed bank. Joseph L. King, historian of the San Francisco Stock and Exchange Board, and at that time an active broker, puts the figure at one million dollars. H. H. Bancroft, the historian who interviewed Baldwin for his *Chronicles of the Builders,* says two million dollars. H. A. Unruh, Baldwin's confidential business man for thirty years and executor of his estate, says two million five hundred thousand dollars.

Whatever the exact amount, it was a staggering blow to Lucky Baldwin. His investments probably were strung out as thinly at that moment as at any time in his life. He still owned some shares in the Comstock, and saw them lose thirty per cent. in a day. Immediately the stock exchange closed, and the shares could not be sold at all. He had already put two million dollars into the new hotel, and needed a million and a half more to finish and furnish it. He had committed himself deeply in the Bear Valley and San Gabriel Valley properties in the southland. He had invested nearly one hundred thousand dollars in race-horses. He was threatened by a suit for divorce which was soon to cost him more than a million. Almost every bank in San Francisco had closed with the closing of the Bank of California. The panic spread to southern

California, and by the time Baldwin reached San Francisco the Temple and Workman bank, carrying his account in Los Angeles, also closed its doors. Business was paralyzed.

"By gad, I'm not licked yet," said Baldwin.

Immediately he went into conference with his lawyers, Reuben Lloyd and Michael Reece.

"What have you done?" he demanded of Lloyd.

"I asked Ralston what was the actual condition of the bank," Lloyd explained. "That was an hour after it closed. He said, 'You and I have had several transactions, and I always told you the truth, didn't I?' I said, 'Yes, sir, I think you always did.' He then said, 'There is dollar for dollar in this bank for the depositors, if properly managed, but very little for the stockholders.' Believing that, I went to Sharon and suggested the idea of subscribing money and putting the bank on its feet. He eagerly seized the idea."

"You did just right," said Baldwin. "Let's go to work at it."

And go to work they did. Immediately they encountered difficulty in the opposition of D. O. Mills, president of the closed bank. Mills preferred to throw the bank into bankruptcy. Sharon, Baldwin and a few prominent stockholders were inclined to believe Ralston's statement to Lloyd that there was dollar for dollar in the bank's resources for the depositors. And that was what Baldwin wanted. He was not a heavy stockholder at the time, if indeed he owned any stock, but he had a million or two million dollars on deposit, tied up by the closing. He needed that money badly to complete the new hotel, to expand and improve his southern holdings, to settle the difficulties which he was encountering with his second wife.

If the bank could be reorganized and hasty liquidation could be prevented, Baldwin hoped to get his money out. Sharon, who knew more about the situation in the Comstock than any one except the bonanza firm of Mackay, Fair, Flood and

O'Brien, also felt that the bank must be reopened. The bonanza firm was threatening the monopoly of the bank ring even before the closing, and was taking advantage of the situation to seize control. One feature of their plan was to start a bank of their own.

The issue developed into a race between arrangements to reopen the Bank of California and to establish the Nevada Bank of San Francisco under control of the bonanza firm. Sharon, Baldwin and Baldwin's attorneys spent their days hurrying around the financial district of San Francisco soliciting subscriptions to finance the reopening of the bank, and spent their nights in conference upon ways and means. D. O. Mills was argued into agreement to subscribe one million dollars. Sharon agreed to subscribe one million dollars. Baldwin agreed to subscribe one million dollars. Lloyd subscribed one hundred thousand dollars. Others came in as their means and inclination dictated. The reorganization plan was completed.

It had the sympathy and approval of almost the entire Pacific Coast. The business of the West had leaned upon the Bank of California as no such area has ever leaned upon a single bank. When the prop failed, business crashed. Only by restoring the prop could business be restored. Baldwin realized that as clearly as any one, and acted accordingly.

The new Nevada Bank won the race by one day, opening for business with ten million dollars capital and a board of directors which included Mackay, Fair and Flood, on October 4, 1875. But that was just another bank, though a tremendously rich one for the time. The Bank of California was the symbol of prosperity. When it reopened for business the following day, San Francisco celebrated with informal parades, firecrackers, and general demonstrations of joy.

Some timid depositors lined up to withdraw their funds. Baldwin shouldered his way through the line, carrying two sacks of gold, all he could struggle under. He dumped them clinking and ringing on the receiving teller's counter. The line at the paying teller's window broke to get a better view of the great piles of double eagles. The money was counted and stacked in gleaming heaps in full view of the crowd.

"Mr. E. J. Baldwin, Lucky Baldwin, president of the Pacific Stock Exchange, who already has two million dollars in this bank, adds forty thousand dollars in gold to his deposits," the teller announced dramatically.

"Good enough for me," remarked one creditor waiting near the paying teller's window, and left his place.

"Lucky Baldwin?" another questioned aloud. "Well, if Lucky Baldwin can do it, I'd like to go along with him," and he left the withdrawal line to join the increasing line of depositors.

Confidence was restored. The bank regained its feet, though it never regained its ascendency. Mackay, Fair and Flood had seen to that. They had taken full advantage of the opportunity afforded by its closing. With vast quantities of gold and silver coming daily from their big bonanza, all they had to do was to cart it to the new mint in Carson City, and they were independent of any bank. Promptly they used the opportunity to seize the Bank of California's monopoly of the mills, the transportation, the timber and the rich supply business of the Comstock. In the six weeks of the Bank of California's suspension, the bonanza firm had become the kings of the Comstock. Their Nevada Bank was but one feature of their sudden astonishing rise to power.

But before the public became aware that the new bonanza kings had supplanted the bank ring as dictators of the Comstock, the San Francisco Stock and Exchange Board and the Pacific Stock Exchange, sired by Baldwin, reopened, simultaneously with the Bank of California. The panic was over. Comstock shares again boomed.

Doubtless Baldwin took advantage of the opportunity to increase his cash resources. There is evidence of that in the developments which followed immediately in southern California. The Temple and Workman bank in Los Angeles had suspended when the Bank of California closed. F. P. F. Temple and William Workman, his father-in-law, appealed to Baldwin for a loan which they hoped would tide them over their difficulty. Though nominally bankers, they were of the type of the old Spanish haciendados from whom Temple was descended, large landowners with an almost feudal attitude toward their tenants and business clients.

I. W. Hellman, shrewd banker and financier, had been associated with Temple in the '60s, and had left him and started the Farmers and Merchants Bank because, he said, "Mr. Temple's only qualification in a borrower was that he must be poor. I saw that doing a banking business on that basis would soon leave me poor also, and I dissolved the partnership."

Lucky Baldwin had had some dealings with the Temple and Workman bank in the year prior to its suspension, and evidently had a clear idea of the character of its management. So, though he was willing to lend the money for its reopening, he protected himself adequately. The loan, of two hundred and ten thousand dollars, should be secured by a blanket mortgage not only on the Temple and Workman real estate but on that of their friend Juan Mateo Sanchez. The interest was to be figured at one and one-fourth per cent. per month, compounded monthly.

Temple asked Sanchez to agree to the mortgage. They were friends of long standing, and men of similar character, wealthy, generous, untrained in the go-getting school of business which had developed Baldwin's shrewdness from childhood, perhaps to the damage of ethics and conscience. Sanchez was anxious to accommodate his friend, but was a little doubtful of the wisdom of the step. He consulted his friend Harris Newmark, head of the wholesale house which dealt with most of the ranchers of the southland at that time.

"I felt convinced that Temple and Workman's relief could be but temporary," Newmark wrote in his reminiscences many years later, "and so I strenuously urged Sanchez to refuse; which he finally promised me to do. So impressive was our interview that I still vividly recall the scene when he dramatically said: '*No quiero mirir de hambre!*' I do not wish to die of hunger! A few days later I learned, to my deep disappointment, that Sanchez had agreed, after all, to include his lands."

Sanchez owned the great barren tract known as the Rancho La Merced, the Potrero Grande, and the Potrero de Felipe Lugo. Temple and Workman owned the Puente Rancho of forty thousand acres, a half-interest in the Rancho Las Cienegas, the Temple Block in Los Angeles, now the site of the city hall, and other property on Spring Street. All of this vast domain within a day's ride on horseback from the Los Angeles plaza went to secure Baldwin's loan of two hundred and ten thousand dollars at one and one-fourth per cent. per month, compounded monthly.

As Newmark had warned, and as Baldwin doubtless anticipated, the Temple and Workman bank failed. Temple suffered a stroke of paralysis and died a lingering death. Workman committed suicide. Sanchez died a poor man. Lucky Baldwin, busy with his development of the great show ranch of Santa Anita, busy with the completion of the Baldwin Hotel, busy with the settlement of separation from his second wife, busy with his racing stable, busy with innumerable other activities including the satisfaction of the women who were flocking to dig a bit of the gold for which he was now famous, allowed the mortgage to run almost to the limit under the statute of limitations. Interest at one and one-fourth per cent. per month compounded monthly was building up his profit rapidly enough to suit the most grasping usurer.

At last suit was brought to foreclose. With the exception of the Temple Block, which was bid in by Newmark and Company, nearly all the land involved went to Baldwin to satisfy his judgment. Now he was a landowner extraordinary. Thousands upon thousands of acres were his. A new vision opened.

Chapter XIII

SPORTING LIFE

Completion of the Baldwin Hotel had been delayed by the scarcity of money due to the Bank of California's suspension and Baldwin's million-dollar subscription to its reorganization in the summer of 1875, but when business began to pick up, the theater which was included in the hotel structure was rushed to completion. It was, as its owner had promised, the finest thing of its kind west of New York. Red plush upholstery, velvet hangings, gilt scrolls and filigree work in the decorations gave it precisely the effect which the gay rich San Francisco of the day approved.

It was cleverly arranged to display the beauty and riches of its patrons as well as the merit of its performances. There were too many beautiful women, too many pearl necklaces and diamond tiaras, too many sable and ermine cloaks, too many diamond studs for stiff white shirt bosoms in San Francisco then to be adequately displayed in half a dozen theater boxes. A dress circle was arranged, above the orchestra circle, in lieu of a golden horseshoe of boxes, to give the theater patrons an opportunity to disclose their own magnificence. Baldwin had the instincts of a showman, though he himself was inclined to be shy.

The opening night, late in the fall of 1875, was an occasion of brilliance never forgotten by the seventeen hundred persons who filled the theater to capacity. Incidentally it set a precedent which was maintained as long as the structure stood, both in the quality of performances and in the smartness of audiences.

The opening performance was of *Richard III,* with Louis James and James O'Neill as the stars. Others as great or greater were to refute even Shakespere's wisdom in the succeeding years. Time was to prove them not "a poor player that struts and frets his hour upon the stage and then is heard no more," but artists whose names have grown greater with the years since their passing. No great actor or actress in those gay days had really "arrived" until he had played in the Baldwin Theater.

Sothern and Mansfield took the parts of Cholmondeley and Chevrial, Modjeska and Maurice Barrymore played *As You Like It,* Edwin Booth, who had been a boy in the mission district in the '50s, was welcomed home as San Francisco always welcomed the home-folks who had become great, and his performance of Hamlet was a triumph. Fanny Davenport played Cleopatra. Lillian Russell there added to the fame of her figure and her voice. Mrs. James Brown Potter and Kyrle Bellew played Romeo and Juliet. Wilton Lackaye's Svengali filled the house to overflowing for weeks with Mabel Gilman singing *Ben Bolt* in the wings as the first step in her own spectacular career. John Drew and Ada Rehan contributed their parts to the Baldwin's fame.

And among those who observed and applauded was—no reader could ever guess. Who but Jeremiah Garoutte, friend of Elias Baldwin's childhood, now a prosperous stockman in the Sacramento Valley. Jerry had been rediscovered by his boyhood admirer. A satiny team of matched horses with silver-mounted harness and carriage met Jerry and his family at the ferry building and carried them in state to the theater. There the boy Elias marked the boy Jerry for the envy of the crowds with the gift of a box which through succeeding years he was free to occupy, though statesmen and bonanza kings might plead in vain for seats.

Friends might repudiate Baldwin as he gathered scandal

with his wealth; Baldwin might alienate friends; but he seldom forgot them. The bond with Jerry Garoutte, revealed at the opening of the Baldwin Theater, is illustrative.

But great as was the sensation and the triumph of the opening of Baldwin's Academy of Music, it was only an incident in that crowded year. Witness the list of activities: the establishment of his racing stud at the newly purchased ranch of Santa Anita, the recovery from a panic on the Comstock, the founding of the Pacific Stock Exchange and his own election to its presidency, the journey to the racing centers of the East and the purchase of brood mares for his racing stables, the collapse of the Bank of California with its loss of millions, its reorganization and recovery of millions, the financing of the Temple and Workman bank in Los Angeles with a mortgage which was to make him the most notable landowner and pioneer subdivider in the state, the opening of the Baldwin Theater and the pushing of work upon the palatial Baldwin Hotel, and through it all the philandering which brought about a separation from his second wife and a settlement upon her of one million dollars and the home.

Surely George Kennedy must have been right. "Baldwin had more things to do in an hour than any man I ever knew—and did them."

Next to the hotel which was to be a tangible monument to his rise from an Indiana cabin, race-horses probably were Baldwin's greatest enthusiasm at the moment. Mollie McCarthy was the first star of his stables. Others of his horses were gaining fame upon the San Francisco tracks, but Mollie McCarthy had turned in such performances as began to make her name and that of her owner known among breeders, trainers and sportsmen generally throughout the country. Baldwin became convinced that no horse living could beat the mare over a killing four-mile course.

He matched her against Frank Harper's Ten Broeck for a

twenty-thousand-dollar side bet at Churchill Downs, Kentucky, and traveled east with her and her jockey and trainer to view the race. The mare was out in front at the start, running easily in perfect form. Down the stretch at the first circuit she led by ten lengths. Down the stretch at the second circuit she led by six lengths. Into the last turn on the third circuit she was still leading. But Ten Broeck was creeping up. At the distant turn the mare faltered. Ten Broeck shot ahead and took the rail. Baldwin shook his head, lowered his glasses and turned away. He knew horses. Mollie McCarthy was through. Baldwin walked out of the grandstand without waiting to see the finish. Ten Broeck galloped on to victory. Kentucky cleaned up on California money that day.

"By gad, I'm not licked, even if that horse is," said Baldwin, and set about to buy and breed better horses. He added several to his string in Kentucky and went on to New York.

It was the year of the Centennial Exposition in Philadelphia. No Californian could visit the East in that year without visiting the exposition. Baldwin had a double purpose in attending. He wanted the circus-day thrill of the crowds and spectacle, and he wanted ideas and furnishings for the hotel in San Francisco which was nearing completion.

He stopped at the Continental Hotel, and there met Jim Marvin, a genial and efficient young man whom he had met before as clerk of the famous Fifth Avenue Hotel in New York, where he had registered on numerous occasions.

"There's a man here whom you ought to meet, Mr. Baldwin," said Marvin. "Maybe you already know him. He was in Virginia City in the early days."

"Then I suppose he's broke," said Baldwin, without enthusiasm. "What does he want? Grub-stake?"

"No, he doesn't want anything," said Marvin, smiling. "He's doing pretty well himself, though not so well as you. His name is Sam Clemens."

"Never heard of him," said Lucky bruskly. "I don't like to meet people. They all want something. They think I'm an easy mark."

"Maybe you've heard of Mark Twain," Marvin suggested, still smiling.

Baldwin shook his head; then brightened. "Oh, yes; he used to be a reporter on *The Territorial Enterprise* in Virginia City. He wrote under the name of Josh for a while. I knew him." He laughed aloud. "I remember once he rigged up a game on a friend of his." He laughed again at the memory. "One of the stores had just got in a load of watermelons from the Sacramento Valley. This, what's his name, Mark Twain, was always broke. He got this friend of his, another reporter, to steal one of the melons piled in the front of the store and toss it to him on the sidewalk so that he could get away around the corner with it before the storekeeper could notice. The other reporter went into the store and Twain stood outside. And when the other fellow tossed out the melon, Twain just let it go, and it smashed to pieces on the sidewalk. Twain just turned away as if he hadn't had anything to do with it, and walked along without cracking a smile. The other fellow certainly had a lot of explaining to do to that storekeeper. Twain was a joker all right. That was a good one." Baldwin laughed again. "What's he doing now?" he asked.

"My heavens, man," said Marvin, "where have you been? He's a famous lecturer, and getting to be a book writer."

"Oh," said Baldwin, with a trace of contempt, "a writer. Well, I s'pose that's all right. I read the newspapers myself. No time to waste on books. I guess I can get along without meeting him again. He'd probably want a tip on the market, or to have me carry some stock for him."

"Here he is now," said Marvin suddenly, catching sight of a loose limbed man in a wrinkled linen suit, with a great shock of hair, and a stub of cigar under a drooping mustache. "Mr.

Clemens; here's an old acquaintance of yours from Virginia City. Mr. Baldwin, Mr. Clemens."

The two men shook hands, studying each other with shrewdly inquiring eyes. "I hear you're getting famous, Josh," said Baldwin at last.

"I know you are," said Clemens. "I read in the paper this morning that you were here to buy some swell stuff for your new hotel in San Francisco."

"Well, I thought I'd look around," said Baldwin.

"I just saw a clock in the jewelry and silver exhibit that you ought to have," said Mark Twain. "It was made by Tiffany. It's the daddy of all the clocks; just won first prize. It not only tells the hours and minutes and seconds but the turn of the tides, the phases of the moon, the price of eggs and who's got your umbrella."

Baldwin grinned. "How much?"

"Twenty-five thousand dollars."

Baldwin's grin faded. "By gad! For a clock!"

"Yes," said the humorist, "no hotel is complete without one. The Baldwin ought to have the best." He threw away the stump of his cigar and dragged another from his pocket. "Have a cigar," he offered.

Baldwin inspected the offering, shook his head, and produced one of his own. "Baldwin ought to have the best," he said.

An hour later he had purchased the twenty-five-thousand-dollar Tiffany clock, which was to be one of the wonders of the new hotel. It failed to tell who had the lost umbrella, but it did record the time, day, week and month, tides and phases of the moon with precision and good fame. A safe by Herring Brothers, the most elaborate thing of its kind yet constructed, also a winner in the exposition, was also purchased for the hotel. Carpets from the notable factories of Philadelphia at a cost up to twenty-five dollars a yard were ordered to supplement foreign importations at thirty dollars a yard. Furniture and draperies were ordered both from Europe and from American manufacturers. A dozen pianos were purchased for use in the public parlors and in a few of the most elaborate private suites. Silverware was ordered from Tiffany. Linen and glassware were in keeping. A million dollars went into the furnishings of four hundred rooms.

Chadwick, of the Willard Hotel in Washington, was engaged as manager. Jim Marvin was induced to take the job of chief clerk. Baldwin returned to the Coast in good humor, despite his great disappointment at Churchill Downs. It was well that he did. Bills for the completion of the hotel structure were assuming unpleasant proportions. Baldwin made an audit and discovered that his personal representative on the job had padded the pay-roll to the extent of fifty thousand dollars.

"Throw him out," he said to his counsel.

"Aren't you going to prosecute?"

"Has he got the money?"

"No; he lost it in the market."

"Then what's the use of prosecuting? Takes more money. Throw him out."

Similar incidents, illustrative of Lucky Baldwin's attitude toward incidents past, are scattered through the record. The past was past to Baldwin, to the day of his death. Only the present and the future were important. He seldom reminisced. He always planned. If stolen goods could not be recovered, the loss was written off and forgotten. Why prosecute?

A man named Fitzgerald, night clerk in the hotel for a time, was found to be stealing and selling silverware. Jim Marvin caught the theft and reported it to Baldwin. Baldwin seemed indifferent. Marvin took the subject up directly with the night clerk. Fitzgerald laughed in his face.

"How do you suppose I got this job anyway?" he demanded.

"I've often wondered," said Marvin.

"Well, I'll tell you. I used to work for Baldwin in the livery-stable on Commercial Street. One night I saw him get into a quarrel with a stable hand and slam him over the head with a shovel. The man appeared to be dead. Baldwin thought he was dead, and still thinks so. I was the only man who saw it. Baldwin don't dare to fire me."

"I see," said Marvin. "You're a blackmailer too."

Fitzgerald thumbed his nose. "Baldwin don't dare to fire me," he repeated.

Marvin meditated. He did not believe the story, and finally reported again to Baldwin. Baldwin was undisturbed.

"Is he still stealing?" he asked.

"I think he is," said Marvin.

"Tell him I said to stop it. If he doesn't stop it, I will."

A night or two later more silver disappeared. In a week a policeman showed up at the desk where the night clerk had just gone on duty.

"We've got a full report on you from the Boston police," the officer said. "You've got a record there as long as my arm. You came out here with a well-known prostitute and thief known to the police as Gentle Annie. We've got her record too. My orders are to tell you to get out of this hotel, and get out of town. And do it now."

The night clerk vanished. The thefts of silver ceased.

On another occasion a friend with whom Baldwin was having one of his infrequent drinks at the ornate bar of the hotel called his attention to a headlight diamond in the necktie of a bartender who had been on duty only a few days.

"That fellow is too prosperous, E. J.," said the friend. "I happen to know that when you hired him he was broke. Now look at that diamond. He must be knocking down on you at a great rate. You'd better fire him before he breaks you."

Baldwin grinned. "Why fire him now? I'm just getting him rigged out."

That was Lucky Baldwin at the age of fifty. He never got over it. Money in his pocket was cash, to be hoarded and guarded to the bitter end. Money in the bank, in securities, in personal property, even in real estate, was a vague thing, intangible and impersonal. He could write a check or a hundred checks with an almost childlike indifference as to whether there were sufficient funds in his account to cover, but he clung to a roll of two or three thousand dollars in his pocket as if it were all that stood between him and starvation.

Two stories of his later life illustrate the point. In the course of his development of his great southern land holdings he maintained a bank account in the convenient town of Monrovia, which, incidentally, he had been instrumental in founding. Mr. Bartle, manager of the bank, was on good terms with Baldwin but was constantly annoyed by the rancher's propensity to overdraw his account, and this while Baldwin owned many thousands of acres of the richest land in the state.

Meeting him in the bank one day, Bartle called Baldwin behind the cashier's wicket and showed him a stack of twenty or more checks, all of which were overdrafts. "Look at these checks, Mr. Baldwin," he said. "There isn't any money in your account to cover them. It might not be so bad, but you've been crowding them in here like this for months. We can't run a bank that way. It's a nuisance. What shall I do with these checks?"

Baldwin drew himself up with dignity, but Bartle caught what he thought was a twinkle of amusement in the hazel eyes. "Why, Mr. Bartle," he said, "I'd certainly send them back." And that was that. It illustrates Baldwin's attitude toward money he could not see or feel.

The opposite characteristic, of his unyielding grip upon cash in his pocket, is clear in the memory of Mrs. Julia Baldwin, widow of Lucky's cousin Charles, who managed the Las Cienegas ranch for many years.

LUCKY BALDWIN

"A party of us who were visiting at Santa Anita were going into Los Angeles one evening to the theater. Two rigs brought us from the house down to the station at Sierra Madre where we were to buy our tickets for the train. That was long before automobiles. E. J. was in the second rig. That would give all the rest of the party an opportunity to buy his ticket instead of his having to buy theirs.

"I was there first, and went to the ticket window to get my own ticket. It was closed. The agent evidently was still away at his supper. But on the ledge I saw a pocketbook. I picked it up and found it stuffed with bills. A minute or two later the window opened, and I bought my ticket and handed the pocketbook to the agent, suggesting that whoever had left it there probably would be back looking for it.

"When Mr. Baldwin arrived in the second rig with the rest of the party I told about finding the money. A minute later I felt him brushing the back of my coat and skirt with his hand.

"What are you doing, E. J.?" I asked.

"He grinned. 'I'm just brushing the hayseeds off of you,' he said. 'You certainly are a hayseed, letting all that cash go.'

"It was funny. He would entertain dozens of persons, lavishly, but when any one got into a train or street-car with him he was always too busy with his newspaper or something to find the fare until after they had paid. He was always generous in a poker game if there were girls or women playing, but there again it was poker chips, not cash that he was handing out, though he knew they would be cashed in eventually. And while he was perfectly willing to give a girl a stack of chips if she had lost hers, he played the game pretty tight himself."

Symbols of money, as in the protested checks, appeared to mean almost nothing to him. The cash itself, even if it were only a five-cent piece for carfare out of a pocketbook containing many hundreds of dollars, was something to be rigidly conserved. Half a dozen persons who knew him intimately have told me of this trait of character in a man worth millions. It was emphasized as he grew older.

Perhaps in 1876 he was too busy to make such a point of saving the nickels while he spent the thousands. Returning from the Centennial Exposition he stopped again at the old home in Indiana, visited his sister Evaline and her husband at New Carlisle, and induced them to return with him to California.

The big bonanza was at its peak. The Comstock was producing at the rate of several millions a month. Every one seemed to have money. Work on the show-ranch of Santa Anita was rushed along, almost regardless of expense. Baldwin was too busy with the completion of the hotel, his work in the mining stock exchange, the breeding, training and racing of horses, and numerous personal affairs including one with the eighteen-year-old beauty, Jennie Dexter, whom he had met in Virginia City, to spend much time on the ranch.

He engaged as manager one Dick Kelly at a salary of sixty dollars a month and a promise of a great future. He gave Kelly enough orders to keep him busy for months, orders for tree planting, well digging, reservoir building, irrigation systems, construction of stables and a training track and so forth.

Water rights in the canyons of the Sierra Madre were purchased or filed upon. Dams and conduits were planned to conserve and distribute the water. Mexican, Chinese and white laborers were employed and housed on the ranch. Chinese labor was paid one dollar a day, Mexicans twenty-five dollars a month and board, white Americans up to thirty-five a month and board. A man with a double team of good work horses could be had for three dollars a day. A great deal of work could be done under such a wage scale, and Baldwin saw to it that a great deal was done.

Orange groves and vineyards were planted and irrigated. Gardens were laid out and cultivated to beautify the setting of the comfortable ranch house which he planned. Ponds were built for beautification and irrigation. Grain-fields were cleared and plowed. Stables were erected for the thorough-breds, and cabins built for the housing of the laborers who preferred to live on the ranch. Baldwin planned each detail and left the execution to Kelly.

Then he hurried back to San Francisco to keep his eye on the sources of all this expenditure. With his sister Evaline and her husband Thomas Fawcett and their daughter Virginia still his guests, he stopped at the Ralston Hotel. Clara Mathis Snyder Doble and her husband, Budd Doble, joined the party there. Doble leaped suddenly into fame temporarily greater than Baldwin's by driving Goldsmith Maid to victory in a trotting race which is still a classic in the history of harness races.

An exhibition by the great mare and her famous driver was arranged at Salt Lake City. Baldwin always found time for such an event as that. He took the entire party to the Mormon capital, and renewed the brief acquaintance which he had formed with Brigham Young twenty-three years earlier in negotiations for the sale of his wagon loads of tea, brandy and tobacco. But then he had been an emigrant, one of thousands passing through the frontier city, as shabby, lean and unprepossessing as the others except for the fact that he had something to sell which the Mormons could use. Now he was a man of millions with a name becoming nationally known.

Brigham Young respected millions. He realized their power. He invited Baldwin and his party to a state dinner. Probably Baldwin was flattered, though he was not at all awed. For that matter, he never was. He was no snob. He had no inferiority complex. It is in the record that "he kidded Brigham Young about the number of his wives." Too bad that the verbatim record of that table talk has not been preserved. Baldwin might have qualified as an expert.

Doubtless it was a gay affair, if somewhat rasping to more delicate sensibilities. But delicate sensibilities were not something for which Lucky Baldwin was to become famous. The party returned to San Francisco and Baldwin was busy until after the Christmas holidays, completing the selection of furnishings for the hotel, which was to open in the following April.

After the holidays the entire party traveled again to Santa Anita, where the Mexicans entertained them with a barbecue that was a revelation to the Indiana-born Fawcetts. The improvements on the ranch were taking form. Baldwin looked them over, gave orders to keep Kelly and the three hundred workmen busy for another six months, and hastened back to San Francisco—straight into the worst financial panic the West had ever known. Compared to the panic of 1877, the earlier panics growing out of the Comstock gamble, even including that which had closed the Bank of California, were nothing.

The others had been due to rumors that the mines were exhausted. This was due to the fact. Since the reopening of the Bank of California and the establishment of the Nevada Bank of San Francisco by the bonanza kings, the city and the entire Coast, not to mention many eastern and some European capitalists, had engaged in a mad frenzy of speculation in Comstock shares. Such speculation had seemed to be justified by the fact that the two big bonanza mines were hoisting millions of dollars' worth of ore, and paying dividends of more than two million dollars a month, while half a dozen other mines were producing richly. A majority of the twenty thousand owners of real estate in San Francisco had mortgaged their property to speculate in the Comstock. Credit was strained to the breaking point.

In that situation, early in 1877, Consolidated Virginia, the first of the two big bonanza mines, passed its regular monthly dividend of one million and eighty thousand dollars. The market crashed. Soon the California, second of the big bonanza mines, passed its dividend. The valuation of the two mines dropped one hundred and forty million dollars in three months. A tenth of the population of San Francisco was reduced to pauperism.

Baldwin was deeply involved. He needed a million dollars to complete the payments for construction and furnishing of the new hotel, now almost ready to be opened. He needed cash to keep up the pay-roll of two or three hundred workers on his southern ranch. He wanted to maintain and improve the racing stables and stud-farm which he had started. He wanted to marry Jennie Dexter as soon as divorce from his second wife permitted. He wanted to save what he could out of the crash of such shares in the Comstock as he still held.

"By gad, I'm not licked yet," he told his sister Evaline as he escorted the Fawcett family to the train for return to their home in Indiana. "Don't you worry. I'll straighten this out."

Straightway he went to the Bank of California and interviewed William Alvord, the president who had succeeded D. O. Mills, and Thomas Brown, the cashier who had succeeded William C. Ralston.

Despite the fact that Baldwin was a stockholder and director in the reorganized bank, they met him coldly. The bank had survived the market crash but had tightened up like a clam to conserve its resources. Baldwin was already acquiring a reputation of being poor pay, a reputation which was to persist and grow to the end of his life, despite his wealth. Also he was acquiring a reputation for defiance of the conventions, though the wide-spread newspaper publicity of such defiance was still in the future.

Alvord and Brown were conventional bankers, perhaps a little sanctimonious. Probably they disliked and distrusted the unconventional Baldwin. Certainly they were unimpressed by the glamour with which popular gossip had surrounded him.

They knew something of the extent and variety of his commitments. And the tragic results of Ralston's over-extension, promotions and speculation in that very bank were still fresh in their minds. They refused to lend Baldwin any money on any security he could offer.

But Baldwin knew the business situation in San Francisco—none better. He knew that the Nevada Bank, organized by Mackay, Fair and Flood less than two years earlier, had plenty of money, whether or not any one else on the Pacific Coast had it. That bank had been the bonanza kings' depository for the millions extracted from the big bonanza, and the additional millions squeezed from the Comstock through their monopoly of milling, transportation, lumber, water, and all other supplies. In fact, he knew it was this concentration of wealth in the hands of the bonanza kings rather than the cessation of Comstock production that had made the effects of the panic so disastrous.

He called upon his old friend Flood, with whom later he was to become involved in a bitter quarrel and battle. At that moment they were on friendly terms. Baldwin had fought Mackay, Fair, Flood and O'Brien before they became known to the world as the bonanza kings, just as he had fought Sharon and the bank ring. But that was all in the day's work. He had always been an individualist in the market, buying, selling, holding, on the strength of private information and judgment, without becoming involved in pools or conspiracies. So Flood welcomed him pleasantly. What arrangements they made are not in the record.

But Baldwin was able, while thousands of men who had been wealthy were begging handouts, to complete the financing and open the hotel which he had designed as a monument to his name. That was in April, 1877, the saddest period in the history of San Francisco until April, 1906. With a tenth of its population living upon charity, and half the others barely able to avoid it, the city was in no mood to have wealth and luxury flaunted in its face. And the Baldwin Hotel represented wealth and luxury.

The twenty-five-thousand-dollar clock recommended by Mark Twain was typical of its furnishings, its architecture and its atmosphere. Of a style of architecture then called the French renaissance type, with mansard roof surmounted by cupolas and towers, it was ornate and spectacular. A most elaborate and expensive portfolio of views and description issued by the management is before me. It seems worthy of some quotation as much for its revelation of the tone of publicity of that day as for the facts and description offered.

"Not only is it an imposing structure on the thoroughfare from the ferry landing, but it is equipped with everything that ingenuity has yet devised for the comfort of its guests, while there is a lavish richness in its detail that charms the eye and strengthens the sense of its completeness. The Baldwin, among the many vast possessions of its owner, is his particular care and pride. He studies to add to its convenience and attractiveness, and to the end that it shall maintain its place as the peer of any hotel in the land. . . . He calls upon the decorator for a touch here and there, when to the less interested observer no such touch is necessary. . . .

"The main entrance is on Powell street. It is here that the visitor will note the first of those striking decorations that greet the eye at every turn. The outer doors swing between panels that might be taken for colored glass, did not the scrutiny their radiance invites show them to be more of crystals and stones; some as Nature's mysterious process produced them, and others cut into flashing facets. Pale Amethyst contrasts with the deep glow of the Ruby. Purple, Blue, Yellow and intermediate shades have been wrought into a design, the plan of which seems adrift in a kaleidoscopic confusion of color. . . .

"Immediately at the left of the entrance is the lounging room. . . . Paintings on glass illustrating incidents in the life of Mr. Baldwin. One is the scene of his crossing the plains. . . . The second represents vividly an attack by Indians. . . . The third is the dying struggle of a huge grizzly, wounded by hunters and harassed by dogs.

"The bar room is next beyond that devoted to billiards. . . . The wide frieze is embellished with the heads of horses, with whips and spurs, and with horseshoes—omens of the owner's likings, and his proverbial good fortune. The glittering array of glass and silver, the French plate, the stuffed leather chairs, the long mahogany bar itself would naturally be expected. The surprise is in the novelties that do not essentially pertain to the establishment. . . . In front of the mirror, perched in huge bouquets are two birds. Hark! They are singing; the little throats throb with melody, the heads turn from side to side, the tails are aflutter as though with the ecstasy of music. But these songsters bespeak only the cunning of human ingenuity; their motion is mechanical, their notes borrowed from metal reeds; they are toys, but they come from Paris, and such toys are not bought to amuse children. . . ."

And so it goes through seventy-odd elaborately illustrated pages. It was a spectacular monument to a spectacular character, strangely in keeping. But it was not a propitious moment. Knowing what is known of the sad business situation in the San Francisco of that day, it must be assumed that the gala opening was none too gay. Nor were the months immediately afterward.

Jim Marvin, who had been lured to the first chief clerk's job by Baldwin, is authority for the statement that a parlor, bedroom and bath with three meals, American plan, could be had for four dollars a day. "And the food cost us three dollars and a half," says Marvin. Well it might. The hotel boasted the services of one of the most famous French chefs of the time, Auguste Artot, who had learned his trade abroad, and perfected his artistry at Delmonico's, New York. There was nothing but the best.

Lucky Baldwin had his monument, which was to contribute to the gaiety and epicurean reputation of his city for a score of years, but which at the moment threatened to crush its builder, and eventually did almost literally crush him. In the meantime, however, other interests pressed.

CHAPTER XIV

STRAINING CREDIT

LUCKY BALDWIN was proud of the monument that he had completed at the time of San Francisco's worst business depression, though he was disappointed by the briefness of acclaim and the limitation of patronage. But he did not pause in his stride. His energy was unimpaired. Always, he looked ahead.

Virginia City, apparently crushed by the exhaustion of the big bonanza, required his attention if he wished to save anything out of the collapse of such mining shares as he still held. By careful investigation and wise trading he had not only survived but profited from two earlier mining-stock panics. He threw himself into the task of doing so again. And in the course of frequent visits to the Comstock his attention was attracted to the possibilities of Lake Tahoe, which he had passed scores of times since his first westward passage with a pack-train in 1853.

Now, cruising the timber around the shores of the lake with a thought of compensation for his recent losses in the mines, he stopped at a small resort known as "Yank's." "Yank" was Ephraim Clement, from the state of Maine, who had homesteaded a section on the lake shore and added to the homestead by purchase until he owned one thousand acres. There he operated a summer resort with accommodations for forty guests.

A magnificent pine forest stretched back from the shore of the great blue lake at Yank's. For several days Baldwin had tramped through what had once been similar forests, now ugly barren wastes of cut-over lands and burned slashings, stripped first by the bank ring and later by the Mackay-Fair-Flood-O'Brien monopoly to provide the millions upon millions of feet of timber required in the mines. The magnificent sapphire which was Lake Tahoe was no longer set in the pure green gold that Baldwin had first seen, but in marred and tarnished brass. The wastful havoc wrought in the virgin forests roused Baldwin to fury. For a moment he forgot profits, and the wide extension of his own business interests and obligations, already too broad for safety.

"By gad," he roared to Yank, "it's a shame and a crime! Some one will be cutting this timber next," and he waved to the thousand acres of great tall pines.

"Mebbe," said Yank, shrewdly non-committal, rolling a pine-needle between thin lips.

"By gad, I'll buy it myself!" Baldwin shouted.

"Mebbe," said Yank.

That was the sort of trading Baldwin understood. His anger cooled, and his enthusiasm was hidden. But within a year he owned Yank's thousand acres, changed the name to Tallac, improved the resort facilities, and began cautiously to buy adjoining timber and shore lands from sheep men, squatters and others until he owned eight thousand acres. The name of Tallac was to become great upon the mountains.

Outwardly undisturbed, though actually in difficulties because of the lack of profits from the great hotel in San Francisco, Baldwin in the following year built the Tallac Hotel, raising the capacity of Yank's crude resort from forty to four hundred guests. Throughout his life the lake was to be one of his favorite retreats, as it remains to-day a favorite retreat of his descendants.

At the age of fifty he had added another obligation to the many which filled his days and strained his bank-account and his credit. Now he had real property from the San Bernardino

Mountains to the top of the Sierra—six thousand acres in Bear Valley, fifty thousand acres or more in the vicinity of Los Angeles, eight thousand acres at Lake Tahoe, business property in San Francisco and Los Angeles—and no money. It was a situation that was to keep him hopping for another thirty years.

Still he found time for personal affairs that, except for his wealth, might never have advanced to the publicity of print. For instance this, from *The San Francisco Alta* of February 24, 1878:

"The fair but forgetful Lennie, who has been imprisoned since the 11th of February on a charge of perjury made against her by E. J. Baldwin, was yesterday afternoon brought before Judge Morrison on a writ of habeas corpus obtained by her counsel, L. E. Bulkeley and John M. Coghlan, who appeared in her behalf at the request of some benevolent ladies of this city. Mr. Bulkeley remarked that neither he nor his associate counsel knew Miss McCormick, and cared nothing about the merits of her case against Baldwin; they believed her to be illegally imprisoned, and therefore moved for her discharge. . . ."

Though contemporaries probably were interested in the scandal, the point of greater interest to an investigator into the life and character of Lucky Baldwin is hidden between the lines. It rests in the fact that "some benevolent ladies of this city" were interesting themselves in the affair, and were more concerned with getting the young woman out of jail than they were with the merits of her case against Baldwin or of Baldwin's defense. Their interest was sentimental rather than ethical.

What they wanted was to get Lennie McCormick out of jail. They chose to ignore the charge of perjury. It made no difference to them that the girl might have thrown herself upon Baldwin. Perhaps she had not. They assumed that she had not. They were defending all womanhood, their own virtue and the virtue of their daughters. But their action and the attendant publicity started building Baldwin's reputation into that of an ogre from whom all young women should be protected. They ignored the fact, revealed repeatedly through succeeding years, that not all young women wanted to be protected from a man worth millions.

The incident served merely to strengthen Baldwin's complete indifference to public opinion and defiance of conventions. He continued with his loves as with his business, an individualist. The McCormick case out of the way, he found time to marry the pretty childish sweetheart, Jennie Dexter, big-eyed and tiny-footed, to whom he had been devoted since his separation from his second wife. The bride was nine years younger than the bridegroom's first daughter. Their first and only child was named Anita.

The Daily Alta of March 11, 1879, printed the following:

"On Sunday evening a few personal friends of E. J. Baldwin, Esq., accompanied by the Grand Opera House Orchestra, serenaded that gentleman and his accomplished bride at their residence, No. 1217 California Street. . . . Prominent among the numerous guests were Sergeant Sharp, D. W. Lake, Alex McAboy. . . ."

It seems that Baldwin was as indifferent to social distinction 'as he was to other evidence of public opinion. He was making no effort to compete socially with the bonanza kings or the railroad barons. If Sergeant Sharp, D. W. Lake and Alex McAboy were "prominent among the numerous guests," it seems certain that the gathering was not one to excite the society reporters who had filled one-fourth of the entire news space of the San Francisco papers with an account of a party given by William Sharon in the preceding year. Sharon's list of guests included such names as Leland Stanford, Collis P. Huntington, James G. Fair and a score of others still famous in

America's so-called high society. Baldwin's guests would now
be difficult if not impossible to identify.
Did Lucky Baldwin care? He did not. He lived his life
to suit himself. And with the great pressure of wide-spread
business obligations upon him it was a life too busy to be
concerned with conventional social aspirations.

The year in which the serenade was reported was occupied
by the planting, under Baldwin's personal supervision, of the
first walnut orchard at the Santa Anita ranch, another pioneering step in the development of California agriculture. The
new hotel at Tallac was built, also under Baldwin's personal
supervision. The racing stables at the ranch were further extended. The financial difficulties of the Baldwin Hotel required close attention. Hiram Augustus Unruh, nephew of
Baldwin's first wife, was engaged to assist in the hotel job.

With creditors clamoring, taxes mounting, business still depressed by the collapse of the Comstock, Baldwin was put to
it to hold his own. In that strained period, doubtless, was
founded the reputation which grew steadily through the
years—a reputation of never paying a bill without pressure,
frequently carried to the extent of a court judgment. Jim
Marvin, chief clerk of the Baldwin the first five years of the
hotel's operation, tells a couple of incidents in illustration.

"The Baldwin owed Shroufe and McCrum, wholesale liquor
dealers, nine thousand dollars on a bill for whiskies, cordials
and imported wines. The liquors had been consumed. Our
cellars were low, containing little but some of the California
wines produced on Baldwin's own ranch at Santa Anita, and
raw brandy produced at his own distillery. Shroufe and Mc-
Crum had demanded payment again and again, and at last
had cut off the hotel's credit. We needed the liquors to keep
up the reputation of our bar and dining-room, but they needed
the money. At last they sued and levied an attachment on the
hotel safe.

"Then Baldwin went out somewhere and got the money. It seemed that he generally could when the pressure was sufficiently strong. He paid the bill and the attachment was released. His delay and apparent indifference of course had been a trial and a nuisance to the liquor house, but apparently he never thought of that. As soon as the bill was paid he went straight back to Shroufe and McCrum.

" 'Gentlemen,' he said, drawling a little as usual, 'now that we are all squared up and my credit is good, I wish you would send up ten thousand dollars' worth of assorted wines and liquors to the hotel. Here is a list.' And, by heaven, he got the goods.

"Another time he was so badly pressed for cash that he literally pleaded with the Bank of California for a loan of one hundred thousand dollars. The hotel was mortgaged and I guess everything else he owned was in the same fix. The bank wouldn't give him the money. He came back, scratching his head.

" 'By gad, I'm not licked yet,' he said to me after sitting quietly behind the desk for a while. 'Jim, you come with me.'

"We went back to the bank together, and he made a proposition that all the receipts of the hotel should be impounded in the safe under my absolute control until they amounted to enough to pay off his note for one hundred thousand dollars. On that arrangement the bank gave him the money. It wasn't a week later before he came to me in the office one afternoon and told me he wanted twenty thousand dollars from the safe.

" 'But I can't do that, Mr. Baldwin,' I said. 'I've given my word to the bank to hold every cent of this money for them until your note is paid.'

" 'By gad, that's right,' he said. And that was the last I heard from him until the note was paid. But he was mighty hard up, though he owned thousands of acres of the finest land in the state. The hotel was losing a lot of money. We gave too much for our rates, and the overhead was too high, and there was too much competition from the Palace, recently completed by Sharon. Business was bad and San Francisco couldn't support two such fine hotels. Two or three times while I was there between 1877 and 1882 I remember the help struck because they weren't paid their wages. Sometimes the management had to get out and rustle up the pay-roll before we could serve a meal or get the beds made.

"Baldwin was a peculiar man. He was shrewd and persistent but he was poorly educated, and he was shy. His reputation for being a gay dog with the women was given to him by the women themselves rather than earned, though I believe he seldom refused what they offered. I knew him well there at the hotel for years, and I made up my mind that they were chasing him a lot more often than he was chasing them. I've seen them in action, and I've seen him. I'm ninety-one years old now but I can remember what a come-on eye looked like. A lot of them thought Baldwin was an easy mark, and he found that they were.

"He was shy with men too, when he didn't know them. I remember once when John A. Rice of Chicago and Charles Leland of Albany, two of the leading hotel men of the East in their day, were stopping at the Baldwin. I thought E. J. ought to know them and they him, and when I saw him in the lobby I rushed out to grab him and introduce him. When he understood what I wanted he began to stall. 'I can't do it, Jim; I'm awful busy. Here, you take a dollar and buy them a drink. Explain how busy I am,' and he hurried out of the lobby as if he were afraid some one would show him up."

In that year, 1879, the United States returned to the gold standard which it had abandoned in the desperation of its financial difficulties after the Civil War. San Francisco was learning to get along without the influx of millions from the Comstock, which had ceased with the exhaustion of the big bonanza. Business prospects were a little brighter, but Baldwin was still pressed for money.

The fame of his fortune had dimmed. Too many persons knew that he was paying his employees more regularly with promises than with cash. Too many were learning that his credit was poor. Among those who knew or suspected the situation were the newspaper men. They realized that the ill fortune of a man long supposed to be lucky was news. The downfall of a prominent man, whether popular or otherwise, is always news. And Baldwin certainly had been prominent. Probably also the influence of "some benevolent ladies of this city" was making itself felt. In view of the facts, there may have been a bit of gratified malice in a Los Angeles dispatch to *The Daily Alta,* published on August 12, 1879·

"For a few days past there has been a rumor in the air that the U. S. authorities were about to make an important seizure of the property and person of a violator of the revenue laws whose position and capital had heretofore served to exempt him from suspicion of attempting to defraud the government. Yesterday the mine was exploded and Lucky Baldwin's distillery and warehouse and wine vaults at the Santa Anita ranch were seized and he was placed under arrest on the charge of refilling stamped packages of brandy. Mr. Baldwin was brought into the city by Marshal Dunlap, and will have a preliminary hearing tomorrow before Commissioner Whiting."

The story created a sensation. Two days later *The Alta* followed it with another:

". . . Mr. Pensioner, who has been for the past three years Mr. Baldwin's distiller, testified that it had been the custom to refill stamped packages with liquor that had paid no tax, the same being done by the direction of the proprietor, said packages being for retail purposes owned by and being carried on in the interests of Mr. Baldwin. This had been the regular practice ever since the (commissary) store was opened for business, and was discontinued six weeks ago. Mr. J. A. ("Dick") Kelly who has been in the employ of the defendant, also testified substantially to the same facts, and further that in a conversation with Mr. Baldwin at one time, Mr. Baldwin said that 'he was paying the government well enough, and it stood him in hand to get the best of them when he could.' Upon this testimony Commissioner Whiting held the accused in the sum of $3,000."

The situation threatened to become serious. There were a great many persons in the state at that time, envious and otherwise, who would have enjoyed seeing Lucky Baldwin's luck turned sour. But the apparent seriousness of the affair prompted closer investigation which resulted in the following editorial comment in *The Alta*:

"The more the facts of this case are disclosed the more are we impressed by the hardship imposed upon Mr. Baldwin by the whole prosecution. . . . It appears that Julius A. Kelly, a distant relative, had received many favors from Baldwin and had been appointed superintendent of Santa Anita. Kelly started the store on the ranch and sold the liquor. Kelly it was who ordered the refilling of stamped packages. The clerk was under his sole orders. Difficulty arose between Baldwin and Kelly. Kelly was fired. He and all his relatives who had lived without cost on the ranch were sent away.

"Internal Revenue Agent Gavitt, whose prosecutions of San Francisco merchants are well remembered and whose mistakes and tyranny led to his recall from the Coast, about this time turned up in Southern California and saw a chance to make trouble for an innocent and wealthy man, and political capital for himself in the discharged Kelly. A bargain was made and Kelly was appointed a government officer. Kelly hastened to the Santa Anita ranch and was told by the clerk in charge that he was simply carrying out Kelly's former orders. Kelly swore out a complaint and had Baldwin arrested for an offense of which he was ignorant and innocent. . . .

"The amount that it is claimed the government has been

cheated out of was $200. Mr. Baldwin expends more than four times that amount each month for charities. The risks he would take in such an evasion of the revenue laws are fine and imprisonment and seizure of property worth from $30,000 to $40,000."

That story in *The Daily Alta* should be analyzed in the light of what had gone before and what was to follow. The abrupt change of attitude on the part of the editor from the rather gloating announcement of Baldwin's arrest would indicate that some pressure had been brought to indicate that Lucky was not yet down and out. That is revealed in part by the casual reference to Baldwin's expenditure of more than eight hundred dollars a month for charities. So far as I have been able to discover, that is the only statement of Baldwin charities in more than a hundred newspaper stories about the man between 1879 and 1909. It seems doubtful that a man of Baldwin's reputation could give away a thousand dollars or so in cash each month without it being known and recorded. So one may guess that the editor of *The Alta* was trying to square himself by a little flattery.

And newspaper editors seldom flatter failures. In this affair *The Alta's* omission of further facts concerning Kelly is also illuminating. J. A. Kelly was the same "Dick" Kelly whom Baldwin had first hired to manage the new ranch and oversee its development. He had been engaged at a salary of sixty dollars a month in charge of work employing several hundred men, and this salary had never been increased as promised, and had not always been paid. True, Baldwin had allowed Kelly to house and feed family connections at the ranch, but he had not made good his original promise to improve the man's own situation. The housing and feeding were in line with Baldwin's characteristic disregard of symbols or material of wealth while he clung tenaciously to the cash—when he had it. No apology for Kelly is intended. The facts are emphasized for added light upon Baldwin's character.

LUCKY BALDWIN

That character, already in training for a multitude of law-suits to come, now revealed itself by ignoring all the publicity involved, and turning his defense over to Hall McAllister, prominent San Francisco legal and social light. Evidently the lawyers of that day were as adept in the art of procrastination as lawyers of a later day. The case was postponed and delayed for months. Finally Baldwin was indicted on a charge of removing one thousand gallons of distilled spirits from his Santa Anita distillery without paying the manufacturer's internal revenue tax.

In the following January the case came to trial. McAllister pointed out that only twelve barrels of brandy, of twenty-five gallons each instead of one thousand gallons were involved. The total tax bill would have been two hundred and seventy-two dollars. The lawyer emphasized the petty nature of the alleged fraud, withered the witnesses with his contempt, intimated a conspiracy of revenge on the part of Kelly, and won the case. The jury was out only fifteen minutes, and returned with a verdict of "not guilty."

Fifty years later Jim Marvin told me that it cost Lucky Baldwin one hundred and fifty thousand dollars to keep out of the penitentiary. If it did, the money must have gone to counsel. It was not in the verdict. And it is extremely doubtful that it, or any large part of it, went to counsel, though Baldwin already was known as a profitable client, and in the course of time was to pay far more than one hundred and fifty thousand dollars for legal services. At that difficult period of his affairs he was obtaining much of his legal advice on a typically Baldwinesque basis.

Fremont Older, veteran editor of half a century of San Francisco journalism, makes the point. "Henry E. Highton and Colonel Kowalski, two of the bright and shining lights of the San Francisco bar, were living in the Baldwin Hotel. Baldwin, always eager to get something without paying cash for it, made it a practice to stop either one of them in the lobby or in the bar when he needed a legal opinion, and inquire casually concerning a hypothetical case. Highton or Kowalski would give an opinion and go their way.

"At the end of the month, when statements for board, rooms and bar bills were rendered to the lawyers, they in turn would make out bills for legal advice, sufficient to cover the hotel's bill against them. It was a standing joke among all the lawyers in San Francisco."

There is little doubt that the story is true. It would have been typical of the Lucky Baldwin of that day. And Highton if not Kowalski had a reputation of being as good an actor in his own behalf as he was in behalf of a client. Byron Waters, veteran lawyer of San Bernardino, who served Baldwin in numerous suits growing out of the Bear Valley activities, and who once defended him in a suit brought against him by Highton, tells another story to the point.

"H. A. Unruh, nephew of Baldwin's first wife, was employed in the hotel. Baldwin had evidently discovered that he was paying a pretty high price in board, rooms and bar bills for the occasional and casual legal services, and had put a stop to the practise. Still Highton allowed the bills to pile up. Baldwin ordered Unruh to collect. Again and again Unruh failed, or obtained merely a fraction of the amount due.

" 'That old man must have you hypnotized,' Baldwin told Unruh one day. 'You're responsible for collections in this hotel, and yet you allow him to occupy the best suite in the house, order all his meals from the dining-room, buy the most expensive liquors in the bar, and pay practically nothing.'

" 'Poor old Highton; he's up against it,' Unruh defended. 'The old man is sick. Why, I go up to his room to dun him, and he tells me he's sick, and he looks sick, and he hasn't even enough money to buy medicine.'

" 'And I suppose you buy it for him,' said Baldwin.

" 'Well,' Unruh shifted uneasily under his employer's scrutiny. 'I can't let the poor man die for lack of a little medicine, can I?'

"Baldwin laughed, and called to Colonel Kowalski, who happened to be passing. 'Colonel,' he said, 'Highton owes us a lot of money, and Unruh here is too soft-hearted to collect it. He says Highton is broke and sick and about to die for lack of medicine. What do you think about that?'

" 'I think he's a damned liar,' said Kowalski pleasantly, 'and a good actor. He's just putting it over on you, Unruh. He's as healthy as a horse.'

"Unruh didn't think much of that. He was from Indiana. His indignation stirred at the assertion that he was being tricked. 'By gad,' he adopted Baldwin's favorite oath, 'I'll go up and collect that bill if I have to choke it out of him.'

" 'Wait a minute,' said Baldwin, knowing Unruh. 'I just want to lay a little bet with the Colonel here that you won't get it. And to make sure you don't show us your own money instead of Highton's when you come back, turn out your pockets now and show us how much you've got.'

"Unruh displayed forty-three dollars, and started with indignation and determination toward Highton's suite. Kowalski and Baldwin lounged and chatted for half an hour. Finally Unruh reappeared, hastening across the lobby, and was out in the street before they could hail him. A few minutes later he was back, and they caught him on the way to the elevator.

" 'Did you get the money?' they demanded.

"Unruh's expression of distress gave way to one of puzzlement. Then he remembered. 'Oh!' he said.

" 'What's that you've got in your hand?' Baldwin demanded.

" 'It's a bottle of medicine for Mr. Highton.' Unruh smiled feebly and sat down.

" 'Turn out your pockets,' Baldwin ordered.

"Unruh, shamefaced, turned them out. His forty-three dollars were gone.

"Baldwin roared with laughter. 'You see, Colonel? He not only failed to collect the bill, but evidently he gave Highton all the money he had.' Unruh, red with embarrassment, admitted the truth.

" 'Highton's a great lawyer,' said Kowalski.

" 'And a great liar,' said Baldwin, still chuckling.

" 'Well,' said Kowalski."

Two years later Hiram Augustus Unruh was installed as business agent and general superintendent of Baldwin's great ranches in the South, and served in that capacity until the final distribution of the Baldwin estate.

But in the meantime shortage of ready cash was pressing Baldwin to use his ingenuity to hold his wide-spread properties and develop them to a point of profit. The Tallac Hotel, built in 1879 and first operated by Sharp Brothers who had been known to Baldwin as operators of the Arlington Hotel in Carson City, and then by Captain Gordon, had failed to pay expenses. Baldwin leased the property, together with all his interests at Lake Tahoe to M. Lawrence and G. L. M. Comstock. Immediately the property began to pay.

It was money for which Baldwin had urgent need. For instance, the gas bills at the Baldwin Hotel were running up toward two thousand dollars a month, and these were bills which could not be stalled off by any hard-luck story. It was too easy for the gas company to turn off the supply. Baldwin had a better idea. He built his own gas works, and was soon selling five hundred dollars' worth of gas monthly in addition to supplying the hotel.

The Santa Anita Ranch and adjoining property in the South were now producing richly. The Santa Anita dairy alone was turning out two thousand pounds of butter a week. The vineyards, winery and distillery were supplying far more of their products than could be sold in the South. The truck gardens and orchards were producing. Shipments from the San Gabriel station in the first year after the extension of the Southern Pacific railroad to that point included 43,856 boxes of oranges and lemons, 384,460 gallons of wine, 54,946 gallons of brandy, 174,750 sacks of grain.

The completion of the railroad put the Baldwin ranches within practical reach of the Baldwin Hotel. The food bills were promptly reduced, and the profits improved. Still all was not easy going. Probably some city politicians were looking for their rake-off. Baldwin had never been a politician, and had never been notably generous to them. It was another phase of his independence.

The board of supervisors rescinded the permit under which he was operating a steam engine in connection with his gas plant, and immediately Fire Marshal Durkee arrested him on a misdemeanor charge. When a man is believed to be down, a kick is indicated. A second charge, of manufacturing gas from crude petroleum within limits prohibited by the board of supervisors, was lodged against him. There had been an explosion in his gas works which had injured two employees, caused a loss of three thousand dollars, and directed a great deal of unfavorable attention to what was declared to be a public nuisance. Baldwin succeeded in settling both cases, but added neither to his reputation as a public-spirited citizen, nor to his profits.

And in that year also, a tragedy, perhaps the saddest in his life, came upon him. Jennie Dexter Baldwin, still hardly more than a girl though her daughter Anita was several years old, sickened and died. She was, if the memory of numerous persons who have testified concerning Lucky Baldwin's private life can be trusted, the one great love among his many purported loves. It is certain that he was proud of her petite beauty.

Throughout the remainder of his life, while other women were petting, pursuing and suing, and men were damning, he treasured in a cabinet that attained almost the sanctity of a shrine in his Santa Anita home, a pair of the tiny shoes and a pair of the tiny gloves of this sweetheart-wife.

Jennie Dexter Baldwin died in the Baldwin Hotel on November 16, 1881, at the age of twenty-three years and six months. It was a sad ending to one of the most difficult periods in Baldwin's career. But it did not prevent more sensational affairs. Gun-play was soon to climax less conventional passions.

CHAPTER XV

FLAMING LOVE

THE available records indicate that Lucky Baldwin was one who could treasure a sentimental memory as he treasured a pair of tiny shoes, and at the same time solace himself with other affairs. Two sentimental interests remained after the death of his young wife. The first was his affection for his little daughter Anita. The other was in his granddaughter Rosebudd Doble, petite and winsome as Lucky approved, in contrast to the somewhat flamboyant pulchritude of her mother.

The granddaughter, Rosebudd, was older than the daughter, Anita. Rosebudd, named in part for her father, Budd Doble, was born in the Baldwin Hotel in the first year of its opening. The grandfather was fond of the child, and occasionally found time to play jacks with her on the floor as he did with little Anita, but a contemporary newspaper comment states that "if ever Lucky Baldwin had a soft spot in his heart it was for his wife Jennie Dexter and his daughter Anita."

Probably he was seeing little of Rosebudd at that time. Clara had separated from Doble after four or five years of married life and had divorced him because, as she testified later, "he wanted me to keep house and I wanted to live at a hotel. So he left me and took Rosebudd." It was not much of a shock to Baldwin when, a year after the death of his wife, his daughter married her fourth husband, an opera singer known as Harold, whose real name, Stocker, she bore through the rest of her life. They were a marrying family. Anita was to have two husbands, Clara four, and Lucky himself was to have four wives, with a well-defined but unsubstantiated rumor of a fifth, not to mention numerous sweethearts and breach of promise and seduction suits.

But in the first year of his widowerhood he appeared to devote himself, so far as publicity reveals, more strictly to business than to romance. H. A. Unruh was established as general business agent in the southern California estates, which, with the foreclosure of the Temple, Workman and Sanchez mortgages now aggregated many thousands of acres.

Lucky Baldwin needed money. He tried to cut off the drain upon his resources occasioned by lack of business in the Baldwin Hotel by leasing that property to H. H. Pearson, so that he could concentrate his attention upon the task of wringing a profit from the southern ranches. He had given a right of way through the Santa Anita property and near-by lands to the Santa Fe railroad, then building into California. In the deed was a provision that all passenger trains should stop on signal at his station. With this railroad service he hoped to be able to stimulate the colonization of tracts of his land, and sell off small plots to settlers from the East or Middle West.

Iowans and others who now make up a majority of the residents of southern California perhaps would not like to believe that even indirectly they owe their present homes to a man of Lucky Baldwin's character. They move on a more conventional moral plane. But it is likely that, but for Lucky Baldwin, their invasion of the Pacific Coast might have been delayed for another generation. He started it, ahead of its time, and kept it going. He was America's original realtor. He was southern California's first great real-estate promoter.

Witness some of his advertising in the days before advertising became a nationally-recognized profession. Remember that this was advertising such as had never been done before, for the sale of land which had cost him one-tenth of the price he asked:

"This land, including water, in 5 to 20 acre tracts, clear and ready for the plow, $250 to $400 an acre; 25 per cent cash, balance at end of six years; interest 8 per cent per annum. Must be planted to citrus fruits within one year. Epidemic diseases, poisonous insects, tornadoes, cyclones, earthquakes and thunder storms are practically unknown. An average of more than 300 sunny days makes it possible to work in the open air without injury to health. A comfortable house, hard finished, of four to six rooms, can be built for $600 to $700. The principal products of the valley are fruits, (citrus and deciduous) grain, vegetables, nuts, wine, brandy and petroleum. Five acres of foothill or ten acres of valley land, after trees are in bearing, will give an income of $1000 to $3000 a year net.

"Organize a club of ten, send one of the number to select, plant in trees, and care for from 100 to 150 acres, and in from four to five years the club members will have an income paying property suitable for homes, which will justify pulling up stakes and locating where the advantages are so great. To such clubs advantageous terms will be given, and every possible assistance rendered."

In real-estate promotion Lucky Baldwin unquestionably was ahead of his time; and equally without question he knew his stuff. In reply to one prospect who protested that $200 an acre for some unimproved ground was too much, he answered indignantly: "Hell! We're giving away the land. We're selling the climate."

His first sale of importance was made in 1881 to Nathaniel C. Carter, who also was an advanced real-estate promoter, though lacking Baldwin's resources and never to equal his fame. But Carter also had vision, and finding Baldwin in need of ready cash succeeded in buying eleven hundred acres of the wilder portion of the Santa Anita upon the Sierra Madre foot-hills. This he subdivided, and established the village of Sierra Madre, the name of which he appropriated from a neighboring colony with poorer facilities for publicity than his own.

At the same time Baldwin was pushing his own promotions. Still he found time for the thrills and profit of horse-racing and, as gun-play was soon to prove, for dalliance. Gossip concerning the Lucky Baldwin amours, which had been increasing in sibilance ever since he had been rated a millionaire, suddenly exploded into print. Let *The San Francisco Call* of January 5, 1883, tell it:

"A WOMAN'S REVENGE

"LUCKY BALDWIN SHOT BY HIS YOUNG COUSIN, VERONA

"Yesterday at 10:10 o'clock a young woman who calls herself Verona Baldwin, a cousin, shot E. J. Baldwin through the left arm at the level of the heart as he was leaving his private dining room on the second floor of the Baldwin Hotel. She fired from behind him at a distance of six feet, without warning. She was immediately disarmed and arrested.

"Baldwin walked to his rooms, bandaged his arm with towels and awaited a doctor. The girl, in jail, said: 'He ruined me in body and mind. That is why I shot him.'

"The wound is not very dangerous. Reuben H. Lloyd, Baldwin's attorney, was summoned at once. The girl, about twenty-three, known as Fannie, is a tall brunette, of slight build, large hazel eyes, and good looking. She told a *Call* reporter:

" 'I ought to have killed him. Yes, I ought to have killed him at the ranch.'

"She says she was employed by Baldwin on the ranch as a school teacher and he assaulted her and then had charges of improper conduct brought against her and had her fired. 'He was afraid that I knew something that might be damaging to him, and he made these charges so as to impeach my testimony should I ever appear as a witness against him.' . . . 'I did not try to kill him. I hit him just where I wanted to, for I am a good shot and never miss anything I aim at. But it would have been far better if I had killed him.'

"Baldwin's attorney said: 'What I know about the case is this. Mr. Baldwin placed her in the school on the ranch; and all the people on the ranch live in a large house there. At the time this woman was dismissed there was on the ranch a certain doctor, the guest of Mr. Baldwin. One evening a servant named Silas reported to Mr. Baldwin that he had accidentally entered one of the rooms and had surprised the doctor and Miss Baldwin there. Upon this Mr. Baldwin ordered the doctor to leave the ranch, and Miss Baldwin was dismissed. Miss Baldwin while on the ranch was on friendly terms with a man named Garvey who had made a claim to some of Mr. Baldwin's land in Los Ángeles county. . . .

" 'Some time ago Miss Baldwin came to my office and said she would kill Mr. Baldwin unless he gave her some money. She wanted to pay a premium for $50,000 life insurance.' (Lloyd suspected a suicide plan) 'She also sent letters to Mr. Baldwin asking for money, and once he gave her $20 to pay her fare to Oregon. At another time she wanted to obtain $100 from him. At that time she threatened to kill Mr. Baldwin.' "

Lloyd later added the information that three days before the shooting the girl and Baldwin met in the attorney's office, and the conversation seemed to be upon a business basis. Probably it was. The prompt acquittal of the young woman when Baldwin declined to testify against her, and her immediate removal to what was then Washington Territory, might have been interpreted as indicating a settlement out of court. But the scandal was not so easily subdued.

Lucky Baldwin's amours had broken into the public prints, and they remained there, through this and that. Three years later the same young woman reappeared with a threat to sue Baldwin for the maintenance of the child whom, she insisted, he had fathered. That threat also was hushed quickly, and again the girl vanished, only to reappear in the news a third time when she was found to be violently insane and was committed to the state asylum at Napa by Judge Lucien Shaw.

FLAMING LOVE

At the hearing the young woman denounced Mrs. Watson, matron of the Girls' Home where she had applied for aid, and struck Doctor Cochran, one of the examining physicians, twice in the face.

"The poor victim of Lucky Baldwin's heartlessness," according to *The Los Angeles Times* report, "referred to him in comparison with Mrs. Watson, saying that he was a million times better than her, who had refused to give her bread when she was in want and sick."

When the court ordered her to be removed to the state institution she screamed that she was of British royalty on British soil, and they could not send her to an asylum.

"It scarcely admits of a doubt that her present pitiable condition results from actual want and almost starvation," *The Times* report concludes.

The whole affair did nothing to improve Baldwin's reputation, though it did much to extend it. Another echo of the case came shortly afterward when, in the course of a series of the most unrestrained and violent attacks ever made upon any man in public print, Horace Bell, a Los Angeles lawyer and publisher of a sheet which he called *The Porcupine*, printed among the mildest of his denunciations of Baldwin: "Our hellish statutes protected him and enabled him to send his victim to an insane asylum."

In the meantime, however, Lucky Baldwin's reputation as a Lothario was growing even faster than his reputation as a turfman, a multimillionaire and a great landed proprietor and promoter. It would have been rare and racy material even for the tabloid newspapers of half a century later. But, there being no tabloids, even New York's then famous *Herald* gave it space. Witness the following extract from *The New York Herald*, republished in *The Los Angeles Times*, and cited by Baldwin's counsel in support of his appeal for a change of venue in the suit brought by Louise C. Perkins for five hundred thousand dollars damages for alleged breach of promise to marry:

"She (Verona Baldwin) was acquitted about the same time Baldwin took his arm out of the sling and was exiled to Washington Territory. The amorous millionaire had however received a shock, and he went off to Los Angeles to recuperate. There he met still another little brunette, a Miss Lillie Bennett, the child-like daughter of a well known architect. But though very little and very ingenue, Miss Bennett was a canny body, and grey-haired grandpa Baldwin had to make her his tiny wife."

A digression may be permitted at this point to reveal the manner in which this marriage, Lucky Baldwin's fourth, was announced and received in San Francisco, where it was celebrated on May 20, 1884. The fact that there are several errors in *The San Francisco Call's* account of the nuptials, such as stating that it was Baldwin's third marriage, that his first wife was still living in the city with her married daughter, and so forth, is interesting in that it indicates the comparative obscurity in which Baldwin had lived in his first years in the West with his first wife, Sarah Ann Unruh. *The Call's* account, in part, follows:

"A MILLIONAIRE'S MARRIAGE

"WEDDING YESTERDAY OF E. J. BALDWIN
AND MISS LILLIE BENNETT

"Yesterday afternoon at 1:30 o'clock, E. J. Baldwin, the millionaire rancher, stock speculator, and hotel proprietor entered for the third time upon the troubled sea of matrimony. The groom is such a well known figure around town that any description of him is superfluous. Yesterday, however, he seemed to have lost a score or more of his well rounded years, so agile was he in every movement, and so buoyant his spirits during the trying ordeal.

"The new-made bride, Miss Lillie C. Bennett, is his junior by some forty years. She is a pretty demi-brunette of petite figure and winsome ways, the only daughter of the old Forty-niner, A. A. Bennett, the architect who planned the state capitol at Sacramento. . . .

"The ceremony was performed at the residence of the bride's parents at 2323 California street. It was strictly a family party, only a few of their friends being present, but notwithstanding that, the appointments were most elegant. . . . The beautiful marriage service of the Episcopal Church was read by the Rev. R. C. Fonte, Reuben H. Lloyd meanwhile supporting the groom as best man. Mary Morton was bride's maid.

"When the happy couple had been made one, a toothsome collation was served and a pleasant hour spent in discussing the delicacies of the table. . . . After a two months honeymoon the couple will reside at the Baldwin residence, 1217 California street.

"The groom's first wife is still living in this city with her married daughter, Mrs. Ford, at the old Baldwin house at 410 Geary street. . . . At the time of divorce over a million dollars was settled on the lady. Mr. Baldwin's second wife died some twelve months since. She was a Miss Jennie Dexter, formerly of Virginia City, one of several handsome sisters who were well known in this city."

Evidently San Francisco was not to be excited over another Baldwin marriage, whether a third or a fourth. *The New York Herald's* story is a little more dramatic. It continues:

"Scarcely had bride and bridegroom got accustomed to each other's society when still another slim brunette appeared upon the scene with a thunderbolt in the shape of a complaint and a marriage contract. The complaint alleges that as long ago as April 12, 1883, (three months after Baldwin was shot by Verona) Miss Perkins gave herself up to Baldwin on the strength of a signed promise to marry her. No wonder Baldwin staggered and dropped into a chair when the papers were served on him, while the beads of perspiration started on his forehead. . . ."

No wonder indeed, but doubtful. Lucky Baldwin was not of the type to stagger and perspire over a breach of promise or seduction suit more or less. He was becoming thoroughly hardened and indifferent to scandalous publicity. C. C. Goodwin, of *Territorial Enterprise* fame, friend and journalistic associate of Mark Twain, has left this comment in his vivid little book of character sketches, *As I Remember Them*.

"When a great fortune came to him, many an adventuress sought his acquaintance. He knew their object; he was restrained by no sense of propriety, no regard for public opinion, no chivalrous regard for womanhood, and it was not long before he took the blackguard's idea that every woman had her price.

"He was the only man we ever heard of who plead in answer to a complaint filed against him, that his public reputation was such that every woman who came near him must have been warned against him in advance."

The transcript of the appeal for a change of venue on the ground that Baldwin could not get a fair trial of the Louise Perkins suit in Los Angeles continues, in part:

"That affiant would further show that one Horace Bell, who is an attorney practicing at this bar, publishes a newspaper which he calls The Porcupine in which the following false article appears Sept. 10, 1885:

" 'Most of our readers remember that, after Miss Louise Perkins had sued Beast Baldwin for breach of promise of marriage and $500,000, Baldwin through himself, his agents and attorneys, procured a fellow signing his name as Gregory to make a deposition of such beastliness and apparent falsity on its face as to have an effect on the public mind the reverse of that intended. Hellman's Real Estate Journal was paid by Baldwin's attorney for publishing the deposition and it was intended to forestall public opinion against Miss Perkins. It was the most indecent and vile publication ever printed in America. The Police Gazette would not have dared to publish such indecency. For money our prudish neighbor over the way published the vile deposition, and it came back on Baldwin like forty boomerangs, and was of vast benefit to the honest cause of Miss Perkins. . . ."

And so on for interminable pages accusing Baldwin not only of numberless seductions, but of bribery in attempting to defend himself from the results of his alleged lechery.

"All this," said *The Porcupine,* "was published in our most cherished contemporary, the Truly Virtuous Times, in its issue of August 24th."

Continuing, the transcript cites innumerable other published articles attacking Baldwin, which Baldwin's counsel insisted made it impossible for him to obtain a fair trial in Los Angeles County. One such article, published in *The San Francisco Post,* copied in *The Ventura Signal* and recopied in *The Los Angeles Times,* gives the girl's side of the story as follows:

"In the year 1883 Miss Louise Perkins, a lovely damsel of about fifteen years, resided with her parents on a piece of land belonging to Lucky Baldwin, situated two miles from his magnificent country place at Santa Anita. . . . Baldwin visited the parents and met the girl and became her suitor. The girl said Baldwin kept her all one night at Santa Anita. On another occasion at a picnic Miss Perkins was crying, and when some one asked Baldwin what was the matter with her, he replied, 'Oh, nothing. I just asked her to stay all night with me.' "

So the battle raged with columns upon columns of the most violent attacks upon Baldwin, chiefly in *The Porcupine,* but incidentally in many of the other newspapers of the West, and some in the East. The case dragged along for months and at last was set for trial on November 17, 1885. *The Santa Ana Standard* then was moved to editorial comment:

"The defendant came in with an application for a change of venue. He swore the prejudice was so strong against him that he could not get a fair hearing or an impartial jury in the county. Miss Perkins filed a counter affidavit swearing that there were 5,000 men in the county who would do him justice, and stating further that defendant's reputation, while generally bad, was no worse in Los Angeles than elsewhere.

"The Court took the case under advisement. It seems to us that it is a pretty bad admission for a man to make and swear to, that in a county of over 60,000 people he can't find a man willing to do him justice in a legal trial. If his reputation is that bad he had better throw up the sponge and settle the case."

Apparently even Lucky Baldwin's magnificent indifference to public opinion could not remain proof against the unrestrained violence and bitter denunciation and invective of Bell's *Porcupine*. Or possibly his action was based upon the advice of counsel when his appeal for a change of venue was denied. He brought suit against Bell for libel, demanding damages of five thousand dollars on each of twelve counts. But Bell also was a fighter. He answered with an affidavit averring, among other things, that

"Defendant (Bell) alleges it to be a fact that ever since the residence of the plaintiff (Baldwin) in the county of Los Angeles, both before and after the publication complained of, the house in which plaintiff resided in said county was generally and publicly known as 'Baldwin's harem.'"

A sidelight on that detail, which may or may not be taken as a refutation, was still current many years later around the bank in Monrovia where Baldwin transacted some business. Customers and others around the bank at the time of the research for this volume, still remembered vividly the frequent appearance of Baldwin at the bank, driving a four-horse tally-ho from his near-by Santa Anita estate, loaded with pretty girls who were supposed to be his guests at the ranch.

On one such occasion the bank manager previously quoted

in reference to Baldwin's NFS checks, glancing at the bevy of beauty upon the tally-ho, said, "Who are your friends, Mr. Baldwin?" Baldwin drew himself up with his customary dignity. "Those are not my friends, Mr. Bartle; those are my companions."

But in the meantime Baldwin's counsel felt more strongly than ever that he could not get a fair trial of the five-hundred-thousand-dollar suit in a county where such interminable columns of attack and denunciation of their client were being published. They appealed to the State Supreme Court from the order refusing a change of venue. The appeal was denied and on February 2, 1886, a year after the complaint had been sworn to and three years after the alleged seduction, the case came to trial before Judge Hatch in the Superior Court in Los Angeles.

With the possible exception of the Sarah Althea Hill case against the multimillionaire U. S. Senator William Sharon, of Comstock fame, which had its climax in the marriage of that fair plaintiff to her counsel David Terry, and the subsequent killing of Terry by the body-guard of the presiding Justice, Stephen J. Field whom Terry had threatened, the Perkins-Baldwin suit is perhaps the most famous in the records.

Stephen M. White, whose heroic statue still adorns the western façade of the Los Angeles Hall of Justice, was counsel for the girl, aided by W. T. Williams. Lucky Baldwin's array of counsel included the prominent firm of Wells, Van Dyke and Lee, and two others, Howard and Roberts.

Miss Perkins, petite and pretty, made an excellent complaining witness:

"I am nineteen years old. I was sixteen years and five months old when I first met Mr. Baldwin. . . . We moved near Compton in 1882 and lived near Mr. Baldwin for two years. I first met Mr. Baldwin in 1882. My father and I went to see him on business. We met Mr. Baldwin and he said he felt quite well acquainted with me as he had heard Mrs. Dexter speak of me often. He invited me to stay (at the ranch) and I did, for a week, till my father came for me. He afterward came and took me riding several times around El Monte.

"He wanted me to go to San Francisco to spend the holidays. My mother said I was not ready to go. Mr. Baldwin went off without me. That was the time, in January, 1883, when he was shot by his cousin, Verona Baldwin. In March, 1883, I went to San Francisco with him. In April, 1883, he and I were alone in his private parlor. He asked me to marry him. . . . We had a second conversation in the same apartments. He again asked me to be his wife. . . .

"I consented and asked him when it would be. He said in two or three months. I was then sixteen years and six or seven months old. Mr. Baldwin then took a diamond stud out of his pocketbook and said he would have a diamond ring made for me. He took me to Col. Andrews' Diamond Palace on Montgomery street and had my finger measured for a ring. Here it is."

The ring was offered in evidence. It was the ring described in one of Horace Bell's bitter attacks upon Baldwin as "a paste diamond." Abbreviated for newspaper publication, the girl's testimony continues:

"A few days later he took me to Sacramento. Mrs. Dexter told me to go as it would be very pleasant. Mr. Baldwin had told my mother he would protect and advise me as he would his own daughter. We went along to Sacramento and stopped at the Golden Eagle Hotel one night. He said we were the same as married, or soon would be, and that it made no difference as we would be married soon. The next day we returned to the Baldwin in San Francisco and there we met Mrs. Dexter. I went to San José with him and remained over night with him at the Auzerais House. We returned to the Baldwin and I remained there till about the first of May, 1883. . . . I then returned to Los Angeles. . . .

"In December, 1883, I went to San Francisco to go to school. Mr. Baldwin wanted me to go and was to pay my way. His daughter met me and we went to a private house. Mr. Baldwin came on the Sunday following. The next day we had a conversation about my health. I did not see him again until after he was married to Miss Bennett. Then he came into a store to see me. He said he would get rid of his wife and marry me...."

Baldwin, on the witness stand, admitted that he had had improper relations with the girl, thirty-nine years his junior, but denied seduction or promise of marriage. The defense made an effort to show that the girl was not the unsophisticated innocent she pretended to be but on the contrary had had affairs of her own which indicated that she was a precocious adventuress who was using her experience and knowledge of life and of Lucky Baldwin in an effort at extortion. Some evidence of such sophistication and precocity was to be disclosed later, but not in time to effect the verdict.

Stephen M. White, already growing famous as a trial lawyer of rare dramatic ability, summed up the case for the girl with an appeal to the emotions of the jurors seldom surpassed even in a later day. White's impassioned appeal brought tears to the eyes.

"Women, cruel to their own sex, will not look upon her with an eye of charity," said White sadly. "What shall she do? She might be put in a position of competency but she can do nothing. No merchant can employ her because some fine lady customer will not come to the store if he did. She must make a living—she must exist. You cannot life her as Omnipotence did Mary Magdalen. You cannot send her upon the pathway of want. You will not do that although you have it in your power to do so. You can at least say to this community that she was dishonored by the wiles of this man."

The hearts of the jurors were wrung. A verdict calling for seventy-five thousand dollars damages was returned promptly. The court-room broke into applause. But obtaining a judgment against Lucky Baldwin and collecting the money on that judgment were two very different things. He and his attorneys alike always preferred fighting to paying. The case was appealed, and dragged along for months. At last the appeal for a new trial was granted by Judge Cheney on the grounds that the judgment was excessive.

"In examining the record of this trial," said the judge, in part, "we find a number of errors and irregularities, the effect of which, we deem, must have been made to mislead the jury and which could not fail to be prejudicial to the defendant. By patient and careful search we have been unable to find any lighthouse set up on the shore of damages calculated to guide us into a tried and safe harbor. We find no verdict for damages as great as this in American reports, and but one referred to in the courts of England in an action on this nature. To warrant such a wide margin as exists between this and the verdicts of the books we must look for something more than the assumed fact that the defendant is an unusually wealthy man, a millionaire. A man of six millions is entitled to the same legal rights and defenses as one whose bank account shows a few trifling hundreds.

"The plaintiff testified in this case that she was chaste up to the breach of the contract except with the defendant, and in the cross examination of the defendant under the objection of his counsel, he was obliged to answer explicit questions as to his improper relations with the plaintiff in the affirmative. . . .

"All this (including White's appeal to the emotions of the jurors) may be true. I don't know. And setting aside the feelings of a man, as a judge I have no right to consider whether it is or not. The truer it is, the more influence it must have had with the jury, and a verdict of seventy-five thousand dollars being the thunder which followed this brilliant lightning, I am impelled to believe it did prejudice the jury. . . . The motion for a new trial is granted."

Was Lucky Baldwin disturbed? He was not. In *The San Francisco Call* of June 14, 1887, appear two illuminating items, one immediately after the other:

FLAMING LOVE

"The Perkins-Baldwin breach of promise suit was called today. The defendant was not present. Col. Wells stated that the defendant was dangerously ill in Kentucky and asked for a continuance, which was granted for one week."

"St. Louis, June 13.—Mr. Baldwin is enjoying the races in his usual good health."

Anti-climax was to appear shortly. The case was called again, before Judge O'Melveny, in Los Angeles on July twenty-fifth, and this time it was the plaintiff who failed to appear.

Stephen M. White, representing the girl, was shocked and grieved, not to say astonished. Baldwin's counsel had something of the expression of the cat that ate the canary. The newspapers explained. The girl "evidently had eloped since the verdict with one Will Fallon of San José, who had $150,-000, and whose mother was worth $1,000,000. He was living with her against his mother's wishes."

White, with two years' work upon the case behind him, had some right to be shocked and grieved, not to say astonished. His client, out of court, and without consulting or notifying him, had settled the case and signed a complete and legal release of all claims against Baldwin, for a reported consideration of fifteen thousand dollais. White, with a court victory to his credit, got only the razzberry. Baldwin's counsel, with a court defeat against them, got cash.

Lucky Baldwin's personal reputation had been touched up by a new and flaming smear of color. Verona Baldwin had only started the flaming publicity of his loves by her gun-play in 1883. The four years between that detonation and the anti-climax of the collapsing Perkins suit had been crowded. And the Perkins suit was not the last, by any means, although at the time of its settlement he was fifty-nine years old.

There were to be more loves, more publicity and more shooting.

[235]

CHAPTER XVI

MAKING ONE DOLLAR DO THE WORK OF TEN

LUCKY BALDWIN, gray-haired, nearing sixty, with his body bearing the scar of one woman's bullet, his bank-account bearing the scar of a more practical woman's vengeance, and his home sheltering his fourth youthful wife, still had more things to do in an hour than any man alive—and did them. Santa Anita had blossomed under his direction into the great show ranch of California. Rich orchards and vineyards, rolling grain-fields, lovely lakes, winding driveways, tree-lined approaches, a spacious ranch house, stables worthy of the aristocrats of the turf which he was breeding, velvet lawns and gorgeous flowers made the land a joy and a monument. "There is not money enough in the world to buy the four thousand acres of the home ranch at Santa Anita," said H. A. Unruh, Baldwin's friend and confidential business man through the remainder of his life.

Still, in the early '8os, though he owned many thousands of acres of the finest land in the state, he was pressed for cash. Temporary relief came with the completion of the second railroad from the East, the Santa Fe, through the Baldwin property. An influx of visitors and potential home-seekers and investors came with the railroad. Southern California enjoyed its first great real-estate boom. Baldwin turned some of his less productive and less promising acres into cash.

Unruh was proving himself a capable manager of the southern ranches. The Baldwin Hotel in San Francisco was under lease, which while not satisfactory at least relieved the owner of personal management. The Tallac at Lake Tahoe was being operated successfully by Comstock and Lawrence. The mining venture in Bear Valley was not proving a financial success, and Baldwin's interest there was reverting toward his original plan to reclaim his own six thousand acres and other thousands near by, through a great irrigation plan. Competent attorneys were successfully opposing the attacks of young women upon his fortune. Lucky Baldwin had enough time to throw himself into the racing game with as much energy as he had thrown himself into the mining-stock game years before.

Volante, Grinstead, Silver Cloud, Rutherford, Emperor of Norfolk, Rey el Santa Anita, were or were to become names to conjure with upon the race-tracks of America. No detail of feeding, breeding or training was too small to merit Lucky Baldwin's interest. His childhood love of horses and his life-long study of them were rewarded. Upon one trip with his racing string to the eastern meetings he encountered in St. Louis a young negro blacksmith, freed from slavery at the age of eight and trained without pay as an apprentice in a blacksmith shop. The youth had revealed a talent for shoeing race-horses in such manner as to get the best possible performance from them.

To the uninitiated a horseshoe is a horseshoe. To John Isaac Wesley Fisher, a horseshoe was a work of art which could make or ruin a race-horse. The weight and balance of the shoes, to correct or emphasize irregularities in a horse's stride, Fisher argued with Baldwin, could win or lose more races than could honest or dishonest jockeys. Baldwin demanded to be shown, and offered one of his own horses for the experiment. Fisher examined the animal, and watched while a stable-boy rode it a fast quarter to match its own best time. Fisher pulled the shoes and replaced them with others of his own make, differently balanced. The same stable-boy rode the horse again and cut more than a second off its best previous time for the quarter. Baldwin was convinced. He hired the black-smith—for life. A year later, convinced that negroes would make more satisfactory employees on the ranch than the Mexicans and others with whom he was having a great deal of trouble, Baldwin sent Fisher back to South Carolina to bring out a carful of negro field-hands and horse handlers for work at Santa Anita.

"After that," says Fisher, "we not only raised our race-horses, but we raised our own jockeys. Isaac Murphy and Freddy Welsh taught the boys to ride. Every man who knows the names of the big jockeys knows those boys. You bet! Si McLain! My, how that boy could ride a race-horse. And Pike Barnes, and Van Buren. They all won Derbies."

A racing stable is an expensive plaything. Lucky Baldwin was beginning to realize it. There were no big race meetings between San Francisco and Chicago. County fair races, where the interest usually centered in the trotting events, contented the smaller towns. There were long jumps between the big meetings, San Francisco, Louisville, Chicago, Saratoga.

Baldwin discovered that while he was winning many excellent purses and was making excellent profits from his famous stallions at stud, he was sinking in transportation and overhead for his thoroughbreds more than he made. So in 1886, concluding a successful invasion of the leading tracks of the East, he again visited his old stamping-grounds in Indiana, the Fawcett farm and the Unruh farm, and decided to buy acreage where he could quarter his racing stable during the winters. With the assistance and advice of his brother-in-law, Thomas B. Fawcett, he selected one hundred and fifty-four acres near the farm upon which he had been reared, and bought the property from Ransom Hubbard and Henry R. Ranstead. Fawcett was commissioned to build a huge barn on the farm, and look out for the horses through the winters.

Baldwin maintained the place as long as he lived. The

wisdom of his decision, both in reducing expenses of his racing activities, and in saving the horses from the ill effect of too much railroad travel over roadbeds which were not so smooth in the '8os as they later became, was soon to be revealed in the record of the Baldwin stable. It worked as well as the highly skilled horseshoeing by Fisher, and the careful training of both horses and riders. Lucky Baldwin was one of perhaps less than half a dozen racing owners in the history of the American turf who actually made it pay.

In a single season he won fifteen races out of twenty-five starts at Saratoga. Even his most violent detractors, and he had as many as any private citizen who ever lived, never accused him of pulling or faking a race. Lucky Baldwin's horses always were out to win. The Emperor of Norfolk, a son of Grinstead, was first to establish Baldwin beyond question as a leader on the American turf by winning a Derby. Norfolk brought the Baldwin stables forty-nine thousand dollars in a single year. Volante was credited with seventy-nine thousand dollars in a year. And that was real money half a century ago. Baldwin entries won three out of the first four American Derbies at Washington Park, Chicago. Rey el Santa Anita took the World's Fair Derby. Let Baldwin himself tell that story. Research seldom finds him in such a reminiscent mood.

"Snapper Garrison had the mount on Senator Grady, while Fred Taral was up on Domino. Domino was the hope of the East that day, for he was their idol and all their money was on him. When the word was given Domino was off in front, his mouth open and Taral sawing at his head. Rey el Santa Anita was knocked to his knees in the first ten yards and dropped back into last position.

"For the first mile Santa Anita was in next to the last position, just galloping. Domino was sizzling along out in front and everyone thought the race was over. At the end of the mile Van Buren (Baldwin's jockey on Rey el Santa Anita) took the colt out into the middle of the track and turned him loose.

Talk about a finish! I wish you could have seen the way that grand big fellow went to the front. They say that Rey el Santa Anita was the first horse to crack Domino's skull, and he certainly ran the eyeballs out of the eastern favorite that day.

"Taral told me afterward: 'I was pounding along in front with Domino,' he said, 'and all at once I heard a horse coming to me on the outside. I knew it wasn't Grady but before I could turn my head to see, he was by me like a flash and there was that red Maltese cross (Baldwin's silks) staring me in the face. Why, sir, Rey el Santa Anita went by me as if we were tied to the rail. I never saw a horse run such a last quarter in my life.'

"Taral had Domino under wraps until he heard my horse coming, and then there was such a cutting and slashing as you never saw in your life. But there wasn't a chance. Rey el Santa Anita simply galloped to the wire and Van Buren was pulling him up at the finish."

The old man's dark hazel eyes gleamed and sparkled with the memory. The thrill of the race-track was a thrill which moved him to almost his only public expressions of enthusiasm through the sixty-odd years from his first horse race on an Indiana country road until the year of his death.

"What was the hardest race I ever won? The Latonia Derby, won by my mare Los Angeles. That Latonia race was run deep in the mud, and she ran a dead heat with White. They wired me at Kansas City: 'Dead heat. What do you want to do? Split the purse?'

"I wired back: 'No. Run it off.' You see, I knew that mare. They ran it off, and Los Angeles won by a city block."

Since the date of his first sensational appearance on the Point Lobos Road in San Francisco, tooling a matched four from his own stables with the first English coach ever seen in the West, fine horses had been Lucky Baldwin's public pride and joy. His private life was another matter, though frequently he failed to keep it private. Like Lorenzo the Magnificent, he appeared to feel that if he could give the public a spectacle or a thrill of entertainment, his private affairs were none of their business.

He was himself a notable whip, handling four horses to a high tally-ho with the skill of the famous old-time professional fast stage drivers. His carriage horses at Santa Anita were cared for in an elegant stable, set in lawns and approached by drives and walks lined with flowers and shrubbery. Rustic cabins to house the stable help were placed among the oaks on a gentle slope to an artificial lake. The race stock, business-like in contrast, was stabled in plain white-washed box stalls, convenient to the half-mile training track. They were the commercial part of his horse loving. Above each stall was the name of its famous occupant. They were the dressing-rooms of the stars of turfdom: Emperor of Norfolk, Volante, Silver Cloud, Rey el Santa Anita, Gano, Verano, Lucky B, Cruzados, and others which contributed similarly to Baldwin's fame and fortune.

The Santa Anita ranch was a popular objective of tourists. Baldwin was shrewd enough to realize that it was the best possible advertisement of the other lands which he was offering for sale. Partly for that reason, and partly because of his pride in the paradise which he had constructed, he made sightseers welcome, and enjoyed showing them the beauties of the ranch.

"What do you raise on the ranch?" was a frequent question.

"Everything in the world but the mortgage," was Baldwin's smiling answer to all questioners who did not appear to be potential buyers of other Baldwin lands. But the potential buyers also were arriving in numbers since the completion of the Santa Fe railroad. Baldwin was eager to help them in the task of developing their purchases. He was an efficient pro-moter always with an eye to the main chance.

When W. N. Monroe purchased acreage and subdivided it to found the town of Monrovia he immediately met difficulty in selling lots to prospective home owners because of the lack of a public school to attract men with families. He consulted Baldwin.

"There are not enough children living on the tract to force the state or county to establish a school," he complained. "No school, no more children, no more development of the town, no more sales of lots. What to do?"

"That's simple," said Baldwin. And the next day fifteen families, mostly Mexicans from Baldwin's Santa Anita ranch, moved into the district and were housed in tents provided by Baldwin. Overnight there were enough children to require the authorities to establish a school. A schoolhouse and teacher were provided.

Baldwin furnished transportation for the workers back and forth to his ranch, while the children went to school. As fast as new families moved into the new town, established homes and sent their children to the school the Mexican families were recalled to the ranch. Monrovia thrived and prospered, and stimulated further sale of Baldwin ranch plots.

Lucky, appreciating the possibilities of sale of town lots at a price higher than farm plots, took advantage of the general real-estate boom to subdivide and promote as a townsite the area immediately below the Santa Anita ranch, which was to become the thriving town of Arcadia. Crews of laborers planted trees along the roads which were to become city streets. Baldwin himself superintended the planting along the three-and-one-half-mile length of Santa Anita avenue, "the Double Drive" of towering eucalyptus trees which was to grow in fame and beauty long after its sponsor's death. The space between the center rows of seedlings was designed for a bridle path, with broad driveways on either side. Water in barrels was hauled by mule teams from Santa Anita canyon to assure a start of the young trees. Land on both sides was surveyed in sections and the section lines planted with trees. Artesian wells were developed, a water company formed, and the village began to attract attention and settlers.

MAKING ONE DOLLAR DO THE WORK OF TEN

Ahead of his time in his shrewd ability to promote real-estate sales, Baldwin built a hotel, the Oakwood, and promptly made it a mecca for coaching parties. The drive from Los Angeles was just long enough to make it a pleasant objective. Food and drink were of the best. Incidentally the enterprise provided a new market for Baldwin ranch products. Comstock and Lawrence, successfully operating the Tallac Hotel at Lake Tahoe in the summer, moved their entire personnel to the Oakwood in the winter, and gave such service that the fame of the place brought more and more visitors. It cost probably not more than fifty thousand dollars, but for years it gave advertising worth many times that amount to the Baldwin lands, in addition to earning profits, at times astonishing, in its own right.

Meanwhile what appeared to be the best of his other ranches were being developed. Charles Baldwin, a cousin from Indiana, was installed as superintendent of the four thousand acres of the La Cienega ranch, adjoining Los Angeles on the south, and extending over what are now the Baldwin Hills, known to every visitor to the Tenth Olympiad as the seat of the Olympic Village housing the world's finest athletes, and known to the world's dabblers in oil stocks as one of the California oil-fields. In 1885, and for some years thereafter, the hills were a sheep pasture.

Soon Charles Baldwin was able to marry his Indiana sweetheart. Under his management the ranch was improved into one of the leading dairy ranches of southern California, with richly productive vineyards incidental to the dairying business, and the breeding of pedigreed greyhounds as a hobby. Charles and Julia Baldwin prospered with the prosperity of the ranch. Lucky Baldwin, hard as his reputation was becoming, and unsentimental as he was assumed to be, liked to surround himself with members of his family. They in turn were fond of him, and those who still live retain an affection for his memory, even though they may retain no illusions.

[243]

LUCKY BALDWIN

In the midst of his racing and real-estate promotion, and even in the midst of legal difficulties with young women who sought financial or other solace for the favors they had conferred, he found time and inclination to visit his relations in Indiana and welcome them to his home.

His favorite sister, Evaline, and her husband Thomas Fawcett, who with their first daughter had been Baldwin's guests in San Francisco nine years earlier, came to the Santa Anita ranch in 1885 with their second daughter. The daughter, now Mrs. L. H. Rush, of Alhambra, retains vivid memories and a whimsical impression of her uncle's vagaries and characteristics.

"I visited the Santa Anita ranch with my mother and father in 1885 and again in 1905," she says. "Uncle was very fond of my mother, and always seemed to be fond of me. I always got along very well with him. I knew how to deal with him, I guess. I was always careful not to arouse his anger. I didn't want him to speak to me as I sometimes heard him speak to others. He had a violent, bitter tongue when he was aroused, and his language was something to hear.

"He liked a joke on others, but not on himself. I remember once, for instance, when he and I had a game of croquet on the ranch. He loved to play croquet and was a pretty good player, but so was I, and that day I won. Afterward I found a little blank book, without a line written in it, and I wrote on the first page: 'This book contains all you know about croquet.' I gave it to him, and he didn't speak to me for hours.

"But though he liked practical jokes when they were on other persons, he also had a dry sense of humor such as practical jokers seldom have. I remember one instance of that, too. He never went to church, but on Sunday mornings he always dressed carefully in his best black broadcloth frock coat, and went for a stroll about the ranch. One Sunday morning I was walking with him, and said: 'Uncle, you look exactly like a preacher.' He stopped and looked me over, and for a moment

I thought I had made a mistake. Then he stretched out his hand and touched my head. 'The Lord have mercy on your soul,' he said.

"His motto always seemed to be, 'Let the other fellow worry.' He seemed to carry that into all his activities, including his interest in fast horses and pretty women."

Casual acceptance of Lucky Baldwin's amorous peccadillos by his family connections might be interpreted as an illuminating sidelight upon his character. He was to them in truth a Lorenzo the Magnificent, justifying himself so completely by his accomplishments that his sins could be ignored as foibles, and even damning publicity could be scorned.

For instance, in the course of research for this record, I have been introduced by one of the family connections to one of Lucky Baldwin's last mistresses, still a charming, well poised woman. Prior to the introduction I had been told that this woman could and would give me some interesting data concerning Baldwin's life and character. I asked the name and was given one which was unfamiliar.

"What was the nature of her association with Mr. Baldwin?" I asked.

"Well," the hesitation was almost imperceptible, and the voice without intimation of apology, "she was his mistress. But of course——" and the implication questioned only my discretion.

I hastened to give assurance, and the introduction followed. There was not the slightest constraint on the part of either the person who gave the introduction or the woman to whom I was introduced.

On an earlier occasion, two women of the family were awaiting the appearance of Baldwin to take them to dinner and to the theater when a note was delivered by messenger to the room in which they were sitting. One, according to the story told me by the other, apparently as indifferent to conventional personal ethics as Baldwin himself was to public opinion, opened the envelope, read the note and sealed it again, with the smiling remark that they probably would have to go to dinner and to the theater by themselves. The note had contained a woman's invitation to Baldwin to call upon her. Sure enough, when Baldwin appeared and read the note, he asked to be excused from the evening's engagements. Smiling tolerantly, his family guests went their own way and allowed him to go his, apparently with no loss of respect. Within the family he was accepted as able to make laws unto himself.

He could make rules, if not laws, but they were not always satisfactory. The first real-estate boom which had come to southern California with the completion of the Santa Fe railroad had been fine while it lasted, but it didn't last long. Baldwin again found himself land-poor. He was in such desperate need of ready cash in 1889 that he announced that he would retire from the turf. And this despite the fact that his stables contained three Derby winners, and that the newspapers declared he had been "almost phenomenally successful in racing, and is, outside the Dwyer Brothers of Brooklyn about the only horseman who has made horseracing a paying business."

"Yes," Baldwin permitted himself to be quoted in *The Los Angeles Times* and *The San Francisco Examiner*, "I have concluded to retire from the turf at the conclusion of the present racing season. I will not retire without regretting the step, for I take great pleasure in the raising and racing of thoroughbreds, but my business enterprises in California will for the next few years engross my entire attention.

"During the past season I was in the East the greater part of the time, and the result was that my business was conducted in anything but a satisfactory manner."

The public announcement added that he would sell all the yearlings and two-year-olds at the Santa Anita ranch at auction, and continue breeding there with an annual sale of stock.

Something must have come along, however, to relieve the pressure upon him at least temporarily, for the following year *The Times* reported that the Baldwin racers were at Saratoga and would winter in the East to be ready for the following season. The newspaper added that Baldwin's veteran trainer, Bob Campbell, had been dismissed and was succeeded by Tom Reagan. And again the next year a story appeared in print to the effect that thirteen brood mares had been stolen from the Santa Anita stables and that Thomas Reagan, "his trusted turf agent," had sold two valuable horses without authority and disappeared. "Baldwin plans to act through New York lawyers to regain the horses."

Still, though he had continued in racing, he was hard up. Land was not selling and business was not good. Cash was so short that when Charles Anderson, recently arrived from the Middle West, was engaged as bookkeeper and storekeeper at the ranch in 1889, he evolved a system, with Baldwin's approval, of issuing trade orders on the store which passed as currency on the ranch, and to a limited extent among outsiders who could come to the ranch store for their supplies.

Employees upon the ranch, the majority of whom were Mexicans, were virtually in a state of peonage. They were given shelter, permitted to raise a few chickens and occasionally a pig on food obtained without charge from the ranch, but were seldom paid in cash, and then only a fraction of the wages that might be due. Instead of cash they had charge accounts at the general store, which carried a miscellaneous stock of goods from groceries to shoes and an assortment of cheap jewelry. There were no regular pay-days.

When the grumbling of the workers or an occasional threat of bodily violence to Baldwin became sufficiently menacing, Lucky might gather a few hundred dollars in cash and go with Anderson to the store on a Saturday evening. The workers would crowd into the store.

LUCKY BALDWIN

"Dinero! Dinero!" The cry for money would rise above the chatter of those making purchases at the counters. Baldwin would wave back the crowd and beckon a spokesman. Called thus from the immediate support of his fellows the man's assurance would shrink to something like a whine. "We want our wages, señor. *No quiero morir de hambre!*"

"You're crazy," Baldwin would counter pleasantly. "You have plenty to eat. What are you kicking about? You have chickens and a pig. I give you their feed for nothing. You can get groceries and overalls and shoes here at the store."

"Si, señor; yes, but we want our wages. We want to go into the town and enjoy ourselves, a little *fiesta*. You owe us money. We want our pay." The peon's arms would wave, and his eyes flash with excitement.

"Oh, all right, Manuel. Don't get excited. You buy what you need first for your wife and kids for next week, and then we'll see what you have coming to you." The laborer would be pacified momentarily. Aided by a fat wife and hampered by three or four black-eyed, calico-shirted children, he would select perhaps a bag of corn-meal, a string of chili peppers, a mixture of coffee and chickaree, and perhaps a pair of overalls for himself and a yellow ribbon for his wife. Anderson would check up his account against his accumulated wages, and find that he had perhaps fifteen dollars still due. Manuel would renew his demand for cash.

"Fifteen dollars!" Baldwin would exclaim in horrified astonishment. "By gad, that's a lot of money, Manuel! What will you do with fifteen dollars? You will go blow it all in on *tequila*. You will get drunk. You will get into a fight and if you are not stabbed to death you will be thrown into jail. You will not be able to work next week. Your wife and children will starve. You will be a murderer. The padre will never absolve you. I will give you a dollar. You can have plenty of *fiesta* on that, and come back to work next Monday."

"No, no, señor; I want my wages. Fifteen dollar. *Pronto!* You give."

But it was a firm conviction of Baldwin's sixty-odd years that words were cheaper than money. He would argue, and at last perhaps induce the indignant Mexican to buy a jug of molasses and a pair of two-dollar shoes for his wife to reduce the cash obligation, and then dismiss him with two silver dollars. And similar scenes would proceed with seventy-five or a hundred others. Two or three hundred dollars in cash, thus judiciously distributed might quiet the immediate demand for a two- or three-thousand-dollar pay-roll.

Even the higher-ups among the employees were stalled along indefinitely. Anderson himself discovered one day that his arrears in salary had mounted to fifteen hundred dollars. In vain he asked for payment. Baldwin told him what a wonderful future was before him on the ranch, and what profits could be made on the land. "I'll give you a deed to twenty acres there on the flat below La Merced, and take your receipt for the back pay. It will make your fortune."

"No." Anderson had been reared on an Iowa farm. He knew something about land himself. "That land has alkali in it. It's no good," he said.

Baldwin argued in vain. "You're always willing to sell the poor land, the alkali and hardpan, to the help in lieu of wages," Anderson countered. "How about giving me ten acres of that good land in the tract just beyond Monrovia?"

"Oh, no; I couldn't do that, Charley. You know I can get cash for that land. You know I need a little cash just now."

"Well, give me your note for the fifteen hundred dollars. I have a right to interest on this money you owe me."

"Fine!" Baldwin always was ready to give a note. It postponed the evil day indefinitely. So he gave Anderson a note. And on his next day off Anderson selected ten acres of the good land, bought it from Baldwin's agent without consulting

Baldwin, and paid for it with the fifteen-hundred-dollar note. Baldwin's agent could hardly refuse to accept Baldwin's own paper.

"By gad, Charley, that was a slick trick you pulled on me," said Baldwin with no apparent rancor when he learned what had been done. "You're more of a business man than I thought. I'd like to have you make a trip up to Bear Valley with me. That mine and stamp mill up there are no good. Those fellows who are running it are stealing all the profits. I want to develop the irrigation scheme and sell off that acreage."

So together they made the journey to the Bear Valley property, driving from a station on the Santa Fe beyond San Bernardino. On the return trip Baldwin stopped at the same station and asked for a ticket to Santa Anita.

"You'll have to wait eight hours," said the agent. "This next train is a through train. It doesn't stop at Santa Anita."

Baldwin looked the agent over coldly. "It doesn't, eh?" he said at last. "Then give me a telegraph blank." The blank was provided, and Baldwin wrote:

"J. F. Falvey, Superintendent, Santa Anita Ranch. Put 200 men to work at once tearing up Santa Fe tracks through my ranch. E. J. Baldwin."

The local station agent, who was also the telegraph operator, read the message, and his eyes popped. "Oh!" he said. "Oh! You're Mr. Baldwin."

"Yes, I'm Mr. Baldwin; and when I gave the railroad a right of way through my ranch it was with the definite arrangement that all trains must stop there on signal."

"Yes, Mr. Baldwin. Certainly, Mr. Baldwin. Here is your ticket. I'll speak to the conductor."

CHAPTER XVII

MORE GUN-PLAY

LUCKY BALDWIN was hardly more than getting by on his sixtieth birthday. He was in serious need of money, annoyed by unsatisfactory management of his great hotel in San Francisco, forced to defend himself against innumerable suits for money he would not or could not pay, and frequently subject to scurrilous comment in the newspapers. If he grew a little querulous it was hardly more than could have been expected.

But if he was becoming a bit touchy it was not the feeble irritability of an old man. Walking into the ferry building in San Francisco with Harry Comstock, son of the lessee of his Tallac Hotel, he was bumped by a hurrying pedestrian. "Hey!" he said. "What do you mean? Watch where you're going."

The pedestrian stopped and glared. "Who are you talking to? Watch where you're going yourself, old man. Quit blocking the way. If you're too old to keep up with the procession, drop out of it."

Baldwin dropped his suitcase. When the hand came up it was a fist. And it came all the way up to the point of the younger man's chin. That individual's pugnacity vanished in a dazed expression of surprise, and he faded quickly into the crowd while Comstock restrained Baldwin from pursuit and the finishing of the knockout.

Again, stepping from the elevator into the main lobby of the Baldwin Hotel one evening, he found bell-boys, clerks and a bartender standing around in feebly protesting helplessness while one of the young bloods of the town amused himself by knocking the crystal pendants from the great chandelier with a heavy cane. "What the hell!" said Baldwin, and ignoring the stick in the hands of the drunk, swung on the young man's eye.

The young man turned his cane from the pendants toward Baldwin's head. The old man dodged, and landed an upper-cut. While the drunk shook his head to clear it, Baldwin seized him by the collar and kicked him bodily out through the front door into the street. The casual spectators and the over-cautious employees cheered as the hotel owner reappeared from the sidewalk.

"You're fired," said Baldwin. "You're all fired. No wonder this hotel is on the rocks with a lot of lily-livered help around watching quietly while some drunk breaks up the fixtures. You're fired!"

A bartender laughed. "Fine," he said. "Then you'll pay us our back wages."

"Oh, well," said the owner, "get back to work."

"You've lost the stone out of your diamond ring, Mr. Baldwin," said a clerk.

"By gad!" said Baldwin, all interest in the earlier incidents suddenly wiped out. "Now I have got a notion to fire the whole lot of you. That diamond was worth more than the chandelier. If you had kicked that bum out I wouldn't have had to. Scrape up that broken glass around here and see if that stone is in it."

The outer doors swung again and a newsboy entered. "You're Lucky Baldwin, ain't you?" he said.

"Yes; what do you want, bub?"

"When you hit that feller on the ear, I saw this fly," said the youngster. "I just found it in the gutter," and he handed over the diamond.

"Thank you, bub; here's a dollar." Baldwin turned again to the gaping employees. "Get back to work, you loafers."

He was not always so pugnacious. He could still plot and

enjoy a practical joke. Directing the laying of a pipe line at the Tallac Hotel, he noticed a yellow-jacket's hole at the root of a mullen plant where the men had stopped to eat their lunch.

"I've heard that no man in the world could sit on one of those mullen plants for five minutes," he remarked to Comstock, loud enough for the workmen to hear.

"What's that?" demanded a big Irish ditch digger.

"There's something about a mullen plant that makes it impossible for any one to sit on it for five minutes," said Baldwin.

"Shure, that's a foolish idea," said the Irishman.

"Well, if you think so, I'll just bet you five dollars you can't sit on that one there for five minutes."

"I'll take ye," said the Irishman, and plumped himself down on the weeds, and opened his lunch bucket. A moment later he leaped up with a howl, while the black and yellow wasps poured angrily from their nest.

Baldwin roared with laughter.

The easy life in the pine-scented mountain air of Lake Tahoe always put him into the best of health and spirits. Under the efficient management of Comstock and Lawrence the Tallac was an investment which had seldom disappointed him. The income was reliable. He enjoyed the summer influx of visitors, the rides through the pine-shaded trails, the views of the great blue lake, the hunting and fishing in season, the satisfaction of guests attracted by his personally supervised advertising as a pioneer of western summer resorts.

He enjoyed the feasts of wild ducks roasted in a Dutch oven by young Harry Comstock. He enjoyed the gaiety of the young people who surrounded him. He enjoyed the simplicity of the life, rising early, engaging enthusiastically in continuous improvements of the property, sleeping soundly.

He had always been a temperate man, except perhaps in his devotion to business and to women. He had never been a heavy drinker or trencherman. He smoked, with moderation, only the best of cigars. When finally he was advised to reduce even that allowance of tobacco he cut it out entirely, and proved his strength of character to himself by always keeping a humidor of the finest Havanas within easy reach, and never touching them.

At Tahoe he found undiluted enjoyment in the simple life. Pressing debts, impending suits, business problems, even affairs with women could be forgotten in a rarified atmosphere where each day began with a lovely dawning and was filled with natural beauty, healthful activities, unexacting companionship, and closed with a supper of corn bread and milk and a night of perfect sleep.

It always seemed too good to last. And it was. Creditors or lawyers, horse-racing or real-estate promotions, a new love found or an old one forgotten would call him back to San Francisco or Santa Anita.

His reputation of never paying a debt without a court judgment was growing rapidly in these years. And he was adding to that reputation another of not paying even when judgment was rendered if he could appeal from that judgment. Occasionally he was even being cited for failure to pay his lawyers The practise was taking on the appearance of an established policy. A personal friend finally asked him in confidence why he did it, inasmuch as he generally had to pay sooner or later, with court costs added.

"I have to do it," said Baldwin, grinning. "Everybody in the country, including the women, thinks I have millions, and they're all ready to rook me as an easy mark. This is the way I prove they're wrong, and maybe discourage their efforts. I want a reputation of being hard to collect from. If anybody wants anything out of me for any purpose, they'll have to sue."

The list of lawsuits is far too long to enumerate. Their variety is more interesting. A Stockton firm sued for payment on a threshing-machine which Baldwin alleged had broken down before it could be used. The case was carried through the courts for months. Judgment against Baldwin was appealed twice, and finally reversed. The artist who had painted numerous pictures of Baldwin's winning horses and even of his fight with the Indians on the plains in 1853, all advertised by Baldwin as decorative features of his hotel, sued for thirty thousand dollars and was awarded three thousand dollars. The law firm of Silent, Wade and Fitzgerald sued for half their fee for the prosecution of libel suits brought by Baldwin in the course of the Louise Perkins case, and won a judgment. Baldwin appealed, and lost. John H. Temple sued to recover part of the Rancho La Merced, and won judgment. Baldwin appealed, and won.

Suits in which Baldwin appeared, generally as defendant, occasionally as appellant, occasionally as plaintiff, were almost too common to attract attention. Many of them were not even mentioned in the newspapers. But the newspapers were on their toes for more dramatic affairs.

Such a bit of drama appeared to have come in April, 1892, when the marriage of his pretty youthful daughter Anita became known. *The San Francisco Examiner* appeared to chuckle audibly over the story. Its attitude might be taken to indicate that Baldwin was no longer the popular figure he had been in the San Francisco of big bonanza days or even in the days of the opening of the Baldwin Theater and the Baldwin Hotel.

"Lucky Baldwin came to town yesterday," said *The Examiner,* "but he did not have the big tallyho at the depot to meet him. He just came in like an ordinary granger, and did not ask the reporters to be kind enough to put in the paper that E. J. Baldwin, a prominent rancher of Los Angeles County was a guest at the Baldwin.

"He went up to the hotel with a cold hard look in his eye, and a keep-away-from-me-if-you-are-wise air that discouraged advances. The employes of the place were all doing $10 worth of work for $1 salary when he came in. . . .

"Hunger, however, drove him finally to the dining room, and there he was asked by a reporter if he had become reconciled to the marriage of his daughter Anita to his nephew George Baldwin.

"His silence was as full of eloquence as Tom Fitch with a $10,000 retainer in his pocket. . . . He seemed slightly at a loss for language. . . . He is not ordinarily a Chesterfield in manner. . . .

" 'Are you going to resume cordial relations with your son-in-law and daughter?'

" 'I have nothing to do with my son-in-law. The marriage is legal, so far as I am aware, and if I am satisfied with it the public will have to be.'

"Those who expected an outburst on Mr. Baldwin's part are doomed to disappointment. If E. J. Baldwin ever had a soft spot in his heart it was for Jennie Dexter Baldwin and his daughter Anita.

"There was a gleam of satisfaction in Mr. Baldwin's face when he was told that George had been promoted in the county clerk's office."

But that incident was soon to fade into insignificance with the filing of another seduction suit against Baldwin, at the age of sixty-six. Lillian A. Ashley, with an array of counsel that might have done credit to a greater cause, demanded seventy-five thousand dollars on the ground that she had been seduced by Baldwin in San Francisco on March 3, 1893. She exhibited a baby in evidence. Davis & Valentine, Wellborn & Hutton, and Oscar Trippett appeared as counsel for the young woman.

Baldwin promptly branded the suit as extortion, and completed his statement with a typically Baldwinesque touch. "The woman is old and homely. Any one who has seen her would not credit her charge against me." She was in fact, at the time of the alleged seduction, thirty-one years old, thirty-four years younger than her alleged seducer.

H. A. Unruh, Baldwin's confidential business agent, had been warned of the impending suit and had checked up in so far as possible on the young woman's story. She had, he discovered, come to Los Angeles about Christmas of the preceding year with a young man supposed to be her brother, and had taken rooms at 129 South Olive Street. They were almost without money, and soon moved into a single room, where a baby girl was born. At the time Miss Ashley was reported to have said that the baby's father was a Boston man and that she had obtained two thousand dollars from him. When giving information to the bureau of vital statistics, however, she announced that the baby's father was E. J. Baldwin.

Any amour of Lucky Baldwin which advanced as far as the courts was news, and the Associated Press carried Miss Ashley's deposition. "I send you a thousand kisses," wrote Lucky Baldwin to his lady friend in the East, according to this sworn statement.

She was then in school in Boston where Baldwin had first met her and, according to her story, had promised her a golden future, education, clothes and travel, after which improving experiences she was to come West and be his daughter. She did come West, receiving numerous telegrams en route. These she cited:

"Be sure you look for me."

"I will be waiting for you."

"You must come right to the Baldwin Hotel."

On their face they seemed harmless enough—even cautious. And Baldwin did not meet her, she said, but she went to the Baldwin Hotel, and later to San Diego, Coronado and the Santa Anita ranch as his guest. He even gave the brother a job. The baby was born on December 7, 1893. So ended the deposition.

But Baldwin's chief counsel, Henry Highton, was still a competent lawyer. It was two years before the case was brought to trial in San Francisco.

The records of that trial were destroyed in the San Francisco

fire of 1906, but from newspaper accounts and subsequent legal
reports on actions growing out of the original case, it may be
gathered that Lillian A. Ashley was born in Vermont, in 1862.
She was reared on a small stock farm where she developed an
interest in horses which led her to attempt a correspondence
with Baldwin when he had become a national figure on the
turf. While living at the home of a Mr. and Mrs. Thompson
in Boston she induced Baldwin to come to see her. Soon, she
said, she was invited with Mrs. Thompson to come to California at his expense to visit.

Baldwin, however, apparently did not keep up the correspondence. At no time in his life was he much of a letter-writer.
Nor did he provide the necessary funds for the trip. The girl
finally came to California with a Raymond excursion party in
1893. Baldwin, she said, failed to meet her at Covina as
promised, but sent her twenty-five dollars to come to San
Francisco. She was met by Baldwin there and registered at his
hotel as Mrs. Ashton, of Boston. The next day they drove together around the city, dined together in her suite and went
to the theater.

After the theater, she testified, they had supper in Baldwin's
rooms, with plenty of champagne, and Baldwin proposed marriage, saying that he was divorced. They wrote a marriage
contract, she testified, before retiring together to her suite, and
Baldwin took charge of the paper "for safe-keeping."

George Baldwin, a cousin of Lucky, and the husband of
Anita, testified that Baldwin introduced Lillian as his wife.
Evidently the supposed reconciliation between Lucky and his
son-in-law was not so perfect as had been supposed.

"He asked me to say nothing in regard to the introduction
he gave me," George Baldwin testified. "I says, 'How is that;
haven't you got a wife?' And he says, 'Yes, but you can have
as many as you want if you know how to manage it.' I says,
'That is a new one on me; you can do that in Utah but not

in California.' He says, 'Don't say anything about it, George,' and walked away."

Another witness, Stewart by name, testified that he had met the girl in a corridor of the hotel and Baldwin had introduced her as his wife. He (Stewart) was not sufficiently well acquainted with Baldwin to know at that time that Baldwin had a legal wife.

One Wheatfield testified that he thought Baldwin had introduced the girl as his wife, but Baldwin had introduced so many women as his wife that he had got himself "mixed up so on Baldwin's ladies that I could not stand here and swear to any of them . . . as to being his wife or not his wife. He had a manner of introducing them that way."

With two weeks of similar testimony completed in behalf of the plaintiff, Highton outlined the defense: .

"We acknowledge that the defendant may have been familiar with the plaintiff, and may have been the father of her child, but we do say she was not seduced. We claim that the plaintiff is and was an experienced and accomplished adventuress who conceived years ago the scheme of extorting money from Mr. Baldwin, and has persistently followed that intention; that she is not what she seems to be in chastity or anything else; that she is not innocent now and was not innocent at the time of the alleged seduction."

So the defense marshaled its witnesses. John Osborne, an Oregon farmer, testified that he had met Miss Ashley on a train to Boston in 1887, several years before her first meeting with Baldwin, and had stayed with her in a Boston hotel at her suggestion.

J. R. Wood, a private detective, testified that Miss Ashley had attempted to blackmail Col. Alfred A. Pope in Boston and had finally been given two thousand dollars for certain compromising letters and a release of all claims against Pope.

A letter from Lillian Ashley to Lewis Leach, of Fresno, was

offered in evidence to indicate more conclusively that the young woman was an adventuress.

Baldwin himself took the stand and testified that he had met the young woman first in Winchester, Massachusetts, after two years of solicitation by her. Letters were offered to prove this solicitation. He admitted that the young woman was his guest at the Baldwin Hotel in San Francisco, the Oakwood Hotel in Arcadia and the Coronado Hotel in San Diego, registered as his daughter. He denied that he had ever given her any gifts of value. He denied that he was the father of her baby.

The trial dragged on for nearly a month, sordid, dull, uninteresting. Then came drama, swift and flashing.

Lillian Ashley on the witness stand, in tears, under cross-examination. Counsel for the plaintiff and the defendant, leaning forward eagerly, intent upon every word. A small insignificant-looking woman in a shabby dress slipping quietly from her seat, lips pressed tight, eyes alight with purpose, hands hidden in the folds of a voluminous skirt. She was at the back of Baldwin's chair before any one suspected her purpose. And when they did suspect, it was too late for those who saw her to do anything more than gasp at the impending tragedy when she lifted a heavy revolver and leveled it a few inches from Baldwin's unsuspecting head.

The heavy gun wavered as the shabby little woman tugged at the trigger with one trembling finger. It was melodrama, play-acting. A woman gasped aloud. All eyes turned in her direction. The shabby figure of Vengeance with the heavy revolver, finding that she could not pull the trigger with one finger, gripped the gun in both hands, held together as if in prayer, and pulled with both forefingers.

The gun roared. A wisp of white hair flew from Lucky Baldwin's head, and the heavy slug buried itself high in the wall of the court-room. Feeble, inexperienced, incompetent, the woman had jerked the barrel of the revolver upward as she fired.

The court-room was in an uproar. H. A. Unruh leaped toward the woman, seized the smoking revolver and wrested it from her feeble grasp. Attorney Crittenden sprang to the aid of the woman, inadvertently making a movement toward a side pocket as he leaped. No one seemed to know what had happened or what was happening. Unruh covered the lawyer with the woman's gun and Crittenden tried to draw a pistol. Some spectators dropped to the floor as the gavel crashed like pistol-shots and more shooting seemed imminent.

Attorneys Lloyd and Highton seized the guns from Unruh and Crittenden and handed them to court officers. Baldwin himself, suddenly black with anger but revealing not the slightest trace of fear at his escape from death by a fraction of an inch, seized the woman who had tried to kill him. A bailiff led her away, weeping bitterly. Judge Slack cited Unruh and Crittenden for contempt of court.

The melodrama was finished. It was the high light in the Lillian Ashley seduction suit against Lucky Baldwin. The developments which followed could be nothing but anti-climax. The woman who had tried to kill was identified as Emma Ashley, a sister of the plaintiff. According to Associated Press dispatches reporting the affair she was a religious fanatic.

In ill repute as Lucky Baldwin unquestionably was for his affairs with women, Lillian Ashley failed to win her case. Highton proved himself competent when he said the case would be fought out on an issue of law, not of morals. For nearly twenty years Lillian Ashley dropped out of the picture, only to reappear after the death of Baldwin in an equally vain effort to obtain a part of his estate for her daughter, then known as Beatrice Anita Baldwin or Beatrice Anita Turnbull.

The hearings of that subsequent suit were remarkable for two things, the astonishing array of legal talent on both sides, and the comment of Justice Henshaw who rendered an opinion in which five other judges concurred, to close the case for ever. The names of seventeen lawyers, all prominent at the California bar, appear in that final record. Isidore B. Dockweiler, Hutton & Williams, Walter B. Grant and Walter McCorkle appeared for the appellant. Bradner W. Lee, Gavin McNab, Henry T. Gage, W. I. Foley, Gibson, Trask, Dunn and Crutcher, Garret W. McEnerney, Hull McClaughry, James L. Robinson and Walter Rothschild represented the interests of the Baldwin estate.

"Baldwin's own reputation as a libertine, if not national, was certainly more than local, and there is evidence that Miss Ashley knew this," said the court's final opinion. And again: "Wherefore, we indulge the not unreasonable hope that this case will prove the last of a most malodorous brood."

CHAPTER XVIII

PANIC AND DISASTER

THE Lillian Ashley seduction suit was not the only trouble
that descended upon Lucky Baldwin's whitening head in the
early '90s. Indeed, to a man of Baldwin's moral, or immoral,
type it may have been the least of his troubles. Probably his
affair with the fair Lillian was in the nature of momentary
relaxation from what appeared to be far more pressing difficulties.

The great ranches were not paying. The Baldwin Hotel
was not paying. The mine and mill in Bear Valley were not
paying. Virtually nothing was paying. True, he had taken
in some cash from the sale of the Sierra Madre, the Monrovia,
and part of the Arcadia townsites, and had disposed of several thousand acres of farm land. But some of the latter was
coming back upon his hands because of the inability of the
buyers to meet their deferred payments.

Prices of agricultural products had been declining steadily
for several years. The production of gold in America had
fallen away to almost nothing with the apparent exhaustion of
the western mines. The credit of the nation, at home and
abroad, was being steadily deflated. Congress assumed that
the depression of agriculture was due solely to a lack of money
in circulation. As a cure-all such as Congressmen are always
eager to promote in emergencies it had promoted the coinage
of more silver, and provided that the treasury notes which had
supplanted the worthless greenbacks after the panic of 1873
might now be redeemed in silver as well as gold.

Foreign investors who had been buying largely of bonds

financing the great railroad building of this country in the '70s and '80s were afraid that their bonds would be paid off in silver dollars. They began to send them back to America for sale, demanding gold. The bond market collapsed. Gold flowed abroad. The United States Treasury's gold reserve dwindled to sixty-five million dollars. And circulating against that reserve were treasury notes aggregating nearly five hundred million dollars. The nation's credit was on the verge of ruin. Panic swept the country.

President Cleveland, ignoring a Congress which had continued to prescribe the patent nostrum of silver for correction of an economic illness demanding gold, conferred with J. P. Morgan and August Belmont in lieu of any competent central-banking system. They worked out a plan. But in the meantime the business and agriculture of the country were paralyzed.

Lucky Baldwin could not, if he would, pay his bills. Neither could many other persons, for that matter. A situation, duplicated in some of its phases nearly forty years later, developed. Men begged on the streets of every city in the land. Independent and arrogant demands for high wages were forgotten. They wanted food and shelter, and were eager to work for food and shelter.

Those who had always been poor suddenly found themselves on a level with those whom they had envied as being rich. The fact that the poor had not risen, but that the others had been forced down to their level was beside the point. A lifelong incompetent out of a job appears, to himself at least, more admirable than a successful man reduced to poverty and idleness. The failure is accustomed to excusing himself. The successful man is not. The chronic incompetent, in such circumstances, even assumes that the success of the other was merely a matter of luck, now played out. The man who never had it can entertain himself and feed his vanity by matching with lies the tales of his companion in the bread-line who has lost a fortune, and with the added advantage that there is a sense of gain, not of loss, behind the lies.

So Lucky Baldwin discovered that the peons and even the negroes and white Americans working on his ranches considered themselves in better circumstances than many of the business and professional men or independent farmers in their neighborhood. Now it was less difficult to make two hundred dollars in cash cover a two-thousand-dollar pay-roll. But it was far more difficult to get the two hundred dollars in cash. Money disappeared entirely from circulation on the Baldwin ranches.

If a peon wanted fifteen dollars due him on the books to make *fiesta* now he was lucky to get a trade order on the commissary for two dollars instead of the two dollars cash with which he had been placated a few years earlier. Perhaps he took the trade order out and sold it to some one for seventy-five cents. Still he knew he was lucky. He could obtain from his labor a bag of corn-meal, a string of peppers, a calico shirt and a package of tobacco.

There were plenty of men to be found in Arcadia and Monrovia in the great depression which descended upon the nation nearly forty years later who remembered those earlier days and wished that Lucky Baldwin was still dealing out a few groceries in lieu of cash.

"Baldwin kept dozens of families and dozens of single men on his ranches with shelter, food and clothing during all those hard times," says Felix Sandefur, who was associated with Baldwin in the grain business for many years. "It is true that they were virtually in a state of peonage, but let me tell you that a peon on the Baldwin ranch was much better off than a free man on the street in those days. Baldwin was never a slave-driver to his workmen, though he did crack the whip occasionally over his superintendents and others in positions of responsibility.

"The laborers were well housed, and had plenty to eat and something to wear on the Baldwin ranches, while other men begged and starved. Baldwin never fired them, though many of them stole from the ranch and sold the stuff outside for whatever it would bring. In fact it revealed a charitable side of Baldwin's nature that few persons ever gave him credit for. But that was all right with Baldwin. He didn't want credit for charity. He was afraid of it; afraid of the demands which might descend upon him if he were ever known to give away anything in charity. If he ever handed out a dime or a dollar to a beggar, no one but the beggar knew it. But he did keep hundreds of persons from starving—and got a lot of work out of them."

That is the impression which persists around Lucky Baldwin's old haunts to-day. To be sure, the ranches were continuing to blossom under this cheap labor. Fruit, grapes, wine, brandy, grain, blooded horses and cattle, hogs and sheep thrived and multiplied, though the prices they fetched were negligible and Lucky Baldwin seemed always to be broke.

The Merced ranch, rough and rocky, apparently useless for anything but sheep pasturage, swarmed with sheep. One of the most illuminating and characteristic anecdotes ever told of Lucky Baldwin deals with one of the Basque herders on the sheep range. Unfortunately, it would not be permitted in the mails. But the eventual development of the district is a story that would have pinned the nickname of Lucky upon Baldwin if he had not already been known by that name throughout the country.

Because La Merced was nothing but sheep pasture, Baldwin could not sell it. And having held it for years it attained a sentimental value in his mind. Baldwin was that way. Whatever was his was valuable because it was his. The longer he held it the more valuable it became—to him. Whenever a potential buyer of anything approached, his price always went up, whether the item involved were real estate, live stock, grain or something else. He was always, and especially in later life, as H. A. Unruh has given testimony, a "good holder." Only the tremendous pressure upon him for cash, and the fact that Unruh was a very practical business agent, induced him to let loose of any of his real-estate holdings in the Southland.

As time went on the Merced property thus increased in sentimental value as it had failed to increase in market value. When small offers were made for the property Baldwin sought excuses to avoid selling. Finally he struck upon a good one.

"That ground has oil under it."

No one believed him. It is probable that he did not believe it himself, at first. But such a theory would always justify refusal of any price within reason for sheep pasturage, and the land remained unsold. As the statement was repeated doubtless Baldwin himself began to believe it. He held the land. To-day on that land are the Montebello Oil Fields, among the richest in the West.

The same trait of character, the same theory and the same justification to-day are bringing to his heirs the riches of the oil development of the Baldwin Hills section of what was then his La Cienega ranch. And incidentally, a large part of that ranch was sold to a rich real-estate promotion company for one million five hundred thousand dollars before the discovery of oil in the hills, and allowed to revert to the estate when the subdivision failed to prosper.

Yes, E. J. Baldwin was lucky, though he himself persistently and sometimes indignantly denied it.

"A man makes his own prospects," he said in an interview published in *The San Francisco Call* in 1892. "One can make a living where another cannot. You can give one man a two-bit piece and away he goes, and the next time you see him he is prosperous; while another man may have ever so good a start and never get along at all. Some men are good at all kinds of business and can turn their hands to anything, and adapt themselves to circumstances, while others can only do one thing or appear to understand one kind of business; and if they do not have that one thing they are lost.

"I would constantly reiterate the advice of Horace Greeley— 'Go West young man, go West.' You want to go where there is plenty of land and there is plenty of land here.

"Lots of men think they have ability. Perhaps they have, but they wait. You must not do that. You must start at the word, and keep going.

"I started with nothing and since then I have been in every kind of business and succeeded in all. Many times it looked blue but I pulled through by attending well to my business."

But that was in 1892. A change had occurred in the circumstances of American life which Baldwin, typically a part of that life as he had been for sixty-odd years of the development of the vast and constantly extending frontier, did not realize. The frontier had been conquered. The whole area of what is now the United States had been brought under control and for the most part settled. The spirit of the frontier had ceased to be the ruling spirit of the nation.

The day had passed when Americans could escape from their difficulties and start a new life with new promise of independence and prosperity simply by going West. The problems of the nation were new problems, in government, in business, in social intercourse.

Lucky Baldwin no longer personified the spirit of America, though the country still retained some of the best of his characteristics. A settled nation required new political, economic and social organization, with the violence, the freedom, the crudities, the flaunting defiance of conventions removed. The spirit of the nation changed, aspiring not only to money-making but to cultural improvements. Lucky Baldwin did not change. He had lived too long—two-thirds of a century—as an integral part of the frontier. A society which had changed could, and did, condemn a man who had not changed. The reformed sinner is most bitter against sin.

Baldwin dragged through the panic and the years of hard times with difficulty, but with cheerfulness. The lifelong habit of looking ahead, never backward, sustained him. Business was bad but he had learned to stretch a dollar indefinitely by the simple expedient of declining to pay his bills until suit was brought, judgment won, the judgment appealed and sometimes reversed, and the evil day put off as long as possible. He was shrewd and wily. An incident that occurred along about 1905 is revealing. It is told by Will E. Keller, still in the grain business in Los Angeles, who believes he is the only man who succeeded in collecting a bill from Baldwin without a suit in the last twenty years of Baldwin's life.

"With Tom Hayes, Billy Roland and the McDonald Company, I built a grain warehouse near Arcadia," says Keller. "At about the same time Baldwin also built a warehouse. Baldwin came to us and offered to let us use unfilled space in his warehouse in return for operating his property, handling his grain in and out, and so forth. We had the help available in our own plant, and figured we could accept the proposition with some small profit.

"But Baldwin was a mighty shrewd business man. He had estimated the size of his crop almost to a bushel, and had built his warehouse to accommodate it, and no more. So by the time we had received and stored all his grain there wasn't enough space left to put in a single sack of our own. And as fast as he had brought in his grain he had taken warehouse receipts from us and carried them to the Farmers and Merchants Bank, and borrowed on them to the limit. So we were out about two thousand dollars for handling his grain, and couldn't get a cent on it.

"We put in a bill for services. Baldwin wouldn't pay. We didn't like to sue, as he was a big man in the grain business in those days, so we let it run along until one day I met Baldwin's manager, H. A. Unruh, at the races at Agricultural Park.

"Unruh asked me if we wouldn't like to buy some barley. Right then I got an idea, and I said, 'Yes.' The price was right and the next day he began delivering the barley, about two thousand sacks, to our warehouse. When Unruh came to collect I gave him a check for sixty-seven cents and a receipt for the bill we had been trying to collect from Baldwin. The sixty-seven cents was the difference between what Baldwin owed us and what we had raised at the bank on the barley.

"Unruh was the maddest man you ever saw. Of course the whole thing was a little irregular, but it was a typical Baldwin trick, and Unruh knew it. Maybe that was why he was so mad. But it didn't do him any good. We had our money. Of course the story went around among the farmers and grain dealers like wildfire. Baldwin and Unruh knew they would be laughed out of court, and they let it go."

Few such stories of Baldwin's reputation for being chronically bad pay are available concerning the period twenty years earlier when money was rolling in upon him from the Comstock. That phase of his character seemed to grow with the bad luck of the '90s. Few persons were making money in those years, and Baldwin's business interests were widely extended and his obligations staggering.

He had not followed out his decision to retire from the racing game. The farm and winter stables in Indiana were a heavy expense. The Baldwin Hotel in San Francisco was paying little if any profit. The Tallac at Tahoe and the Oakwood at Arcadia were paying little. The reclamation project in Bear Valley had called for large amounts of money, and returned almost nothing. The taxes on his thousands of acres of land mounted high. Farm products brought little. Real-estate sales were almost at a standstill. Such lawsuits as that of Lillian Ashley were expensive, even when he won them.

Debts multiplied despite Baldwin's poor credit rating. Jobs were not much more plentiful from 1892 to 1897 than they were in 1929 to 1933. There were plenty of persons who were willing to work upon the Baldwin ranches and in other branches of the Baldwin business for the bare necessities of life. But even their nominal wages ran up steadily into large sums, and the commissary at the ranch had to be kept stocked. Few would accept the supposedly inferior land which Baldwin offered in small tracts in lieu of wages.

"It ain't worth its salt now, but you take it and hold it and it will make you rich," he told John Isaac Wesley Fisher, the negro blacksmith who had been putting winged shoes upon his race-horses for twenty-odd years.

"No, sir, boss, I don't want that land," Fisher would reply whenever the argument revived. "It's no good. I want my wages, but if you can't pay 'em, I s'pose you can't. Anyway, me an' my family is eatin' reg'lar. I'll just stay on here an' work. I reckon you an' me'll just go busted together."

"Better take the land, Fisher. I tell you there's oil in that land." Baldwin had convinced himself of this by that time, though he had convinced no one else.

"No, thanky, boss. I'll just let my wages pile up, an' some day mebbe you can pay."

So the wages of a hundred employees piled up. But no such arrangement could be made with the tax collector, or the wholesalers from whom he bought supplies for the commissary. One hundred, two hundred, three hundred thousand dollars at a time he borrowed from the Hibernia Savings and Loan Association in San Francisco. He had long since exhausted his credit and even sacrificed the good will of the Bank of California, which he had helped to reorganize twenty years before, and the Nevada Bank to which he had transferred his account at the suggestion of Unruh when the Bank of California had refused to accommodate him.

But he did have property. The Baldwin Hotel and site had cost three million five hundred thousand dollars, and was worth more with the growth of San Francisco through two decades. He still had a San Francisco residence at 1217 California Street. He still had the rich and beautiful ranch at Santa Anita. He still owned several thousand acres of timber and the hotel at Lake Tahoe. He still owned several thousand acres in Bear Valley. He still owned La Merced and La Cienega ranchos and some valuable real estate in Los Angeles. He still owned a great and famous racing stable.

And in effect he was broke, and worse than broke, though always he carried a roll of two to three thousand dollars in currency in his pocket. It was one of his peculiarities. Cash in hand was something to which he clung with a tenacity almost miserly. With two or three thousand dollars in cash in his pocket he could, and did, look the world in the face and tell it to go to hell, even while he was owing two or three millions, and was being publicly denounced as a gambler, a libertine and a dead-beat.

The charge of gambling was never fully justified, though unquestionably he loved a poker game as he loved women. But he was no more generous in one than in the other. He was never a plunger, unless it were in the days of his Comstock operations, and then always he had acted upon first-hand and authoritative information, just as Mackay, Fair and Flood acted. At poker he played for small stakes and played them close. His reputation for heavy play and big winnings might have been due to an incident in the early days of the Baldwin Hotel.

There, seated with a few friends around a poker table in a private suite, some one suggested that they should have some publicity for their sport. Baldwin, seeing only the possibility of a practical joke, agreed and sent a trusted messenger down to the hotel office with an order for all the gold in the safe.

Gold was the currency of San Francisco. The man came back lugging a heavy sackful of twenty-dollar gold pieces. Most of this was stacked in gleaming piles before Baldwin. The rest was scattered on the table to represent the pot. With the stage thus set, a few choice gossips were allowed a peep at the big game. One peep was enough. Baldwin's reputation as a great and lucky plunger at poker was made.

To him it was an amusing joke. Although poker was his favorite indoor sport, with one exception, he preferred to play it with a fifty-cent limit. Lucky Baldwin was canny.

But even his canniness could net him no profit in the '90s. The mortgages held by the Hibernia Bank against his property mounted to $1,688,000 according to records in the San Francisco tax collector's office in 1898. The lien upon the site of the Baldwin Hotel was $900,000. And the building and its furnishings were without insurance. A few thousand dollars had been carried, but allowed to lapse. In such matters Baldwin was indeed a gambler.

And on November 23, 1898, he lost that three-million-dollar pot. The hotel which had been his pride and monument when it opened twenty-one years earlier, burned to the ground.

"The Baldwin Hotel is a ruin. The most tremendous conflagration that has ever happened in San Francisco burst forth shortly after three o'clock this morning," said *The Call*.

Baldwin had left the hotel shortly before the fire and gone to his home on California Street. At daybreak he stood beside the crashing ruins, himself apparently ruined, but to all appearances as steady of eye and firm of jaw in disaster at the age of seventy as he had been in the success of his five-million-dollar profit in the Ophir corner at the age of forty-five.

At last he broke his silence. "By gad, I'm not licked yet," he said to Jim Orndorff, then manager of the hotel, and turned his back upon the holocaust.

The débris burned for days, and daily Baldwin came and looked it over, and went away, striding swiftly, with head high and face serene. Byron Waters, his counsel in much of the complicated litigation growing out of the Bear Valley activities, was in San Francisco on business. When the ruins had cooled sufficiently for closer inspection he walked through them with Baldwin.

"He didn't molt a feather," says Waters. "He was game to the core. His courage never faltered. He never, to the day of his death, lost his enthusiasm. And even on that day he was planning what he would do on the next."

But in 1898, at the age of seventy, Lucky Baldwin needed cash as well as courage. With a heavy mortgage upon the hotel site, he found difficulty in negotiating a sale that would give him some much-needed cash. James L. Flood made an offer of one million one hundred thousand dollars, which was two hundred thousand dollars more than the mortgage. As usual, when it came to the actual wrench of closing a deal for the sale of any of his treasured real estate, Baldwin wanted more. No more was offered. Baldwin planned to build a row of one-story structures upon the ruins, sufficient, he hoped, to pay the taxes upon the property.

San Franciscans who had been assembling in their pearls and silks and furs, their broadcloth and linen for twenty years of display and entertainment at the Baldwin Theater and twenty years of refreshment in the Baldwin bar and dining-room, were indignant. The newspapers denounced the plan as one of coercion to force a higher bid for the property.

"San Francisco has been good to him, and he would repay its kindness with a shanty," said *The Call.*

Flood, however, had a stronger weapon. He was a financial power in the city, and Baldwin owed too much money to maintain his independence indefinitely. Flood induced the "good holder" to relinquish his grip. The sale was made, transferring the site of the hotel to Flood, while Baldwin retained the adjoining and far less valuable Baldwin Annex.

Soon he was suing Flood for eight thousand nine hundred and eighty-eight dollars, alleging that he was forced to spend that much to erect props to sustain his adjoining property against the new owner's excavation for a great office building.

In such straits Lucky Baldwin came to the end of the century. He had had a lot of luck in the past ten years and nearly all of it had been bad. But as he himself was always likely to observe, "By gad, he wasn't licked yet."

At the age of seventy-two, smiling and debonair, he turned to the Far North to rehabilitate his shattered fortunes in the seething gold excitement of Nome.

CHAPTER XIX

STARTING ANEW AT SEVENTY-TWO

LUCKY BALDWIN's invasion of Alaska in an effort to recoup his fallen fortunes at the age of seventy-two in the wild business of the Nome gold-rush was the sort of drama to charm a San Francisco that had been founded on the gold-rush of 1849, and built to sensational prosperity on the Comstock mines. No incident of Baldwin's life has been subject to more romancing.

The picture of a white-haired grandfather, slender and erect as a boy, with eyes that had looked into the eyes of death and still sparkled with life, with hands that had juggled millions and were now almost empty, sailing undismayed into the Arctic to wrest a new fortune from Fate, appealed to the public which had been reading of his successes, his loves, his eccentricities, for decades. It was a picture certain to obtain publicity and to grow with gossip.

For forty-odd years the stories of Lucky Baldwin had been accumulating legendary features. Nearly always, after he began to attain publicity with his millions and his love-affairs, there had been suggestions of more titillating excitements behind the printed stories. Given a dramatic character with millions of dollars, a famous racing stable, a penchant for pretty women, defiant of public opinion, and the imagination of the gossips would do the rest. There are still more stories about Lucky Baldwin that could not be printed than those that were printed.

But the newspapers did the best they could, or the worst, depending upon the point of view. It made no difference to

Baldwin. He stood in his black frock coat and his broad black Stetson hat near the rail of the *S. S. Valencia* as it backed from its berth in San Francisco, his eyes puckered in tolerant amusement, and let the crowds take their own impressions, and the newspapers make their implications.

What of it? Lucky Baldwin had been an individualist for seventy-two years. He had made and spent and lost his own millions. He had taken his fun where he found it. And now he was starting out again, not to pay for his fun, but to have more. He was as clear-eyed and apparently as vigorous as the youths and maidens crowded upon the decks around him. If the public wanted to associate him with those youths and maidens, it was quite all right with him. His individualism was of that rare quality which allowed similar privileges to the rest of the world.

So *The San Francisco Call* could report and imply: "A blonde young woman well known in San Francisco's night life leaned over the rail handing roses to friends with one hand while in the other she grasped a bottle of champagne. Behind her stood Lucky Baldwin wearing his black slouch hat in review." Out of that implication, and earlier stories which had announced that Baldwin had arranged to take thirty young women to Nome with him, have grown legends adding to the Baldwin fame, but unjustified by the facts. To be sure, *The Call*, in the same article concerning the departure of the *Valencia*, did clear up the facts about the thirty young women:

"She sailed at 11:25 a.m., with 450 passengers, among whom was Lucky Baldwin who has spent so many weary days of his life in litigation with fair and susceptible young women. With Baldwin were David Unruh, his manager, A. A. Burnett and R. Ringrose. The former millionaire [note "the former"] takes three portable buildings, five horses, two wagons and an outfit for a gambling house. Ned Foster was to have gone with Baldwin and taken thirty women who were to have been employed by them in a dance hall. A few days ago Baldwin and Foster had a row which resulted in a dissolution of the compact. It was understood that Deacon Jones was going along as floor manager and that he was stowed away in a stack of hams. The ship's officers went carefully through the stack of hams but Deacon was not located. . . ."

Still the damage, if one cares to call it that in view of Baldwin's established reputation, was done. Many persons read newspaper articles carelessly, and misquote them in repetition. Soon a tale was in circulation from mouth to mouth that Lucky Baldwin had sailed for Nome with a whole boatload of young women to show the miners and adventurers a real touch of high life.

Lucky Baldwin, though still very much alive, was already attaining legendary proportions. On the day after the departure of the *Valencia,* the following story appeared in *The Call* under the head-line:

"BALDWIN'S GOOD LUCK AGAIN IN EVIDENCE

"There are indications that the good fortune which attended E. J. Baldwin in his palmy days and from which he gained the title of 'Lucky' has returned to him. At least a large chunk of it is on the way to Nome with him aboard the steamer *Valencia.*

"When he was laying in his supplies for his northern trip he purchased $200 worth of goods from Holbrook, Merrill, Stetson & Co. H. H. Baldwin who also had the gold fever but went north on the *St. Paul,* purchased more heavily from the hardware firm, his bill footing $2,000.

"Grove Ayres and Mr. Merrill with customary generosity . . . sent their big customer a token of appreciation to the steamer, a case of wine and several boxes of dainties. A letter couched in the most touching terms was written to send with the little remembrance. 'Mr.' Baldwin was wished a pleasant journey, a safe return, and all that sort of thing. The hope was expressed that the wine would cheer him on his way.

"It is at this point of the story that Lucky's luck reasserted itself. The drayman who was engaged to deliver the goods knew but one Mr. Baldwin. Lucky was speechless when the package was delivered to him. He concluded that a firm which could afford to be so generous for a $200 order should be advised of his appreciation, and he wrote thanking Mr. Ayres and Mr. Merrill for their kindness. He wrote that if he needed a keg of nails or a package of tacks when he reached Nome he would send them the order and not expect any champagne in return either.

"Both the *Valencia* and Lucky Baldwin and the *St. Paul* with his namesake were out in the stream when Holbrook, Merrill and Stetson received the note. Lucky was emptying a glass to the health of the firm, and H. H., aboard the *St. Paul* was mumbling that they hadn't even said a thank you."

Incidents of that sort, however trivial, were seized upon and given space in the newspapers. They did not allow the legend of Baldwin's luck or the romantic features of his new fling for fortune to die. Communication with Nome was poor in 1900, but promptly upon Baldwin's return with the last steamer before the close of navigation in the autumn the newspapers renewed their comment, and their implications.

"Lucky Baldwin arrived last night from Nome on the Oregon Express from Seattle, having come from Alaska on the S. S. *Valencia*. He is much pleased with the prospects of his northern mines . . ."

And the next day:

"In answer to every query about Nome he says he is going to write a history of the place. Interrupted by Anita and later by a dizzy blonde whom he calls Laura, he still reiterates he is to write the history." Etc., etc.

Few persons, either writing or speaking of Baldwin in the last thirty years of his life, ever neglected to mention a dizzy blonde or a petite brunette, if one could be dragged into the scene. And there is no doubt that frequently they were there. So the legend grew.

LUCKY BALDWIN

This record, however, is fortunate in being able to bridge the gap in the newspaper accounts and perhaps to correct the implications of the press with a first-hand account of the Nome adventure. It is from the lips of one of his fellow-passengers, who had the further advantage of being his business agent on the Alaskan trip. David Unruh, mentioned in *The Call's* account of the departure for Nome, retains a vivid memory of that experience. He is the son of H. A. Unruh, Lucky Baldwin's faithful business agent for thirty years. Educated as an engineer at Boston Tech and Stanford University, he is a man of analytical mind, not denying Baldwin's peccadillos, but sometimes moved to indignation at his defamation, and still loyal to his memory.

"For more than thirty years," says Unruh, "I've been denying and correcting stories that Mr. Baldwin took a shipload of girls with him to Alaska. It is just one of those tales of scandal that spread so widely and rapidly that the truth never could keep up with it. Every little while I meet some one who, knowing that my father was associated for many years with Baldwin's business affairs, tells me a weird and scandalous story of his trip to Nome. I know better. I was there.

"Lucky Baldwin not only did not take a boatload of women with him to Nome, but he did not take one. As his business agent in that venture I knew that none of the women on the ship were either his employees or his intimates. As a private individual of course I knew his reputation as a Lothario even at the age of seventy-two, and as that was none of my business I kept out of his way. The ship was crowded, and I had the steward make me up a bed in the lounge the first night out. The next day Baldwin asked me where I had slept. When I told him he said I was an idiot, and that for the rest of the trip I should occupy the vacant berth in his stateroom. After that I was in touch with him for the entire trip, day and night, and there was no scandal on that trip.

"Momentarily at least, Baldwin was not interested in women, and they were not much interested in him. He was supposed to have lost the millions which had made him the willing object of attention of designing women for many years. And this was a business venture, inspired in part by his desire to recoup his fortunes in the Alaska gold-rush, and in part by a desire to renew his youth in the always youthful spirit of a new and booming mining camp.

"Of course he hoped to locate or buy some promising claims, but he had no illusions about mining. His first experience in Virginia City, nearly forty years earlier, had convinced him that there were as great possibilities of profit in the incidental business of a booming camp as there were in the mines. Also, he knew, he was two years late for the location of the best claims. So he had taken with him more supplies and equipment for business than for mining.

"The outfit included gambling paraphernalia, tables, and so forth, a considerable quantity of liquors for his proposed bar, two ready-cut frame houses, two light wagons, five horses, and a lot of baled hay. As capital he had his customary cash roll of about three thousand dollars and thirty certified checks for one thousand dollars each.

"Well, when we reached Nome it was spread all over the beach and back toward the tundra. There were about twenty-five thousand persons in the camp. The buildings were mostly one-story frame shacks, swarming with cheechakos, gamblers, miners and sourdoughs, with a sprinkling of Alaska Indians and dance-hall girls. There was no wharf at which a vessel the size of the *Valencia* could tie up. We had to lay half a mile offshore and land in small boats, while the cargo was lightered in.

"Baldwin handed me ten thousand dollars in checks and told me to go ashore and buy a site for his buildings. For some inexplicable reason, or lack of reason, he never looked upon checks as money, although he had paid cash for them and could get cash or anything else in return. He handed me that ten thousand as so much paper, though he wouldn't have parted from his roll of currency without a battle to the death.

"Well, I went ashore and found the town all huddled together in a maggoty mass. The liquor and gambling interests centered around Wyatt Earp's 'Second Class Saloon,' advertised throughout the North as 'the only second class saloon in Alaska.' A few blocks away from Earp's saloon, in any direction, business simply petered out, and gave place to cabins and shacks occupied by the residents of the camp, good, bad and indifferent. I couldn't get a piece of vacant property within reach of the business center. The best I could do, and that for eight thousand dollars, was to buy two lots, well out toward the edge of town.

"When that was done I went back to the ship and we had our freight taken ashore in lighters. The baled hay was piled up on the beach, back from high tide, to form a temporary corral for the horses, while the workmen put up the buildings. Baldwin and I sat on the hay and watched the horses and the job.

"Reaching into my pocket for my pipe tobacco I found a handful of horse manure. I knew the old man pretty well, and I didn't say anything, though I noticed an extra pucker around his eyes when he glanced at me. We went on chatting and strolling about a little, and finally I found a chance to pull the same trick on him. When he happened to put his hand in his own pocket and found out what was there, he didn't bat an eye. Baldwin was always game. He never weakened.

" 'Well, by gad,' he said, and threw the handful at the nearest horse, 'that damned horse dropped his manure right in my pocket.' He wouldn't have let on for a million that I had turned the tables on him. He did love a practical joke.

"A few days later, after we had got the houses up, and had

decided not to open the bar and gambling outfit out there on the edge of town, Baldwin decided to go into the interior and look for claims. We packed a four-ton load on a two-ton wagon, and started out, Baldwin on horseback. There were about three miles of tundra, boggy and treacherous, back of the town, cut by streams and spotted with bottomless areas. It took us two days to do that three miles, and then we abandoned the wagon and packed to Salmon Lake, sixty miles north, where some new diggings were being opened.

"Baldwin went only half-way. He met us on our way back, and accepted our report that there was nothing at Salmon Lake that would interest him. Then he headed back to Nome on his horse. I was slogging along on foot, with a pack, and it was mighty hard going. I couldn't keep up. Baldwin would ride ahead, and then wait for me. When I reached him he would kid me a little and ride on again. Finally he pulled a soda-water bottle full of port wine from his pocket and showed it to me.

" 'That's good port,' he said. 'It's from the Santa Anita ranch. You know how good it is.'

" 'Yes.' I did know, and my tongue fairly hung out for it. I was all in.

" 'Well,' said Baldwin, 'if you catch me, I'll give you a drink,' and he rode ahead again.

"He was still the practical joker; sometimes very practical. I never did catch him. But I got back to Nome. And that was about all I did do.

"We were too late into Nome. We couldn't buy any worthwhile prospects, and we couldn't even open the bar and gambling house with any prospects of success so far from the center of town as we were. The gambling outfit was never even uncrated. The bar was never set up. We went out on the last boat that fall, leaving Ringrose as caretaker.

"When we started back the next spring, Baldwin was ill. There was a woman with him on that trip. The gossips were partly right about that. But they were not entirely right. She was a nurse, and a good thing she was, too. By the time we reached Seattle the old man was so bad off that he had to be taken off the boat and she went back to California with him by train."

Incidentally, to digress a moment from Mr. Unruh's narrative, that nurse was a very pretty nurse, and young. I saw her thirty-one years later, and she was still a pretty woman, with the small hands and feet and trim figure which Lucky Baldwin always admired.

"So I went on alone to close up the business," Mr. Unruh continues. "And when I arrived at Nome a friend came out to the steamer and told me that a frame-up of the crooked officials who infested the Alaska gold-fields and camps at that time, affording the theme of such popular stories as Rex Beach's *Spoilers*, had turned all our property, including liquor, gambling equipment and even houses over to a phony receiver on a trumped-up charge of tax evasion or something of the sort.

"As soon as I could get ashore I went straight to the United States marshal and asked him about it. He said that there was a legal claim for twenty-five hundred dollars against our property, but if I would deposit a ten-thousand-dollar bond to protect the claim, the property would be released. Imagine, a ten-thousand-dollar bond to cover a twenty-five-hundred-dollar fake claim. And I didn't have the ten thousand dollars.

"I went to Wyatt Earp and asked his advice. He got hold of one or two business friends and arranged the bond. When I took it to the marshal he said it was no good. He would have to have twenty thousand dollars' worth of gold-dust. I went back to Earp. He was mad. But he got together the twenty-thousand dollars' worth of gold and gave me a man to lug it to the marshal's office, where I got a receipt and the property was released.

"Then I sold the stuff for a profit of between fifty and

sixty thousand dollars. Wyatt Earp refused a cent of pay for his accommodation. He said he was more than satisfied to put a crimp in the grafting of that crowd of crooks. A lot of persons were not as lucky as I in the dealings with them. They got their twenty-five hundred dollars' graft out of me, but they failed to get the twenty times that much that they had schemed for. I couldn't sell the land, but we leased it to the first telephone company established in Nome."

That was the end of Lucky Baldwin's last adventure in the mining camps. To the public, which had acclaimed the rise and derided the fall of his fortunes, it was anti-climax. But now his fame was greater than his fortune. It could not be destroyed.

Back again on his Santa Anita ranch, his temporary illness overcome by skilled nursing, he applied himself with all his old energy to the task of restoring his tottering finances.

"By gad, I'm not licked yet."

Resources and reputation were in a sad way, but energy and courage were undiminished. Witness a Pasadena dispatch in *The San Francisco Call:*

"Lucky Baldwin still has his nerve with him. . . . He has been developing water on his ranch and arrived Sunday to see how things were progressing. J. L. Breen, a ranch employee, had received a jug of whisky by express from a friend and was making merry. He wanted J. McDonald, a man said to be eighty years old, to take a drink. He attacked the octogenarian with a knife, it is alleged. Thereupon George Gould interceded and was felled by an ax. He was not killed. The bystanders were afraid to touch the drunken man.

"Just then E. J. Baldwin came and taking in the situation, he drew a gun. McDonald and Gould lay upon the ground. Breen was threatening to commit murder with an ax. Gould had blackened his eye and McDonald's blood was on his shirt front. Baldwin presented his revolver and declared he would shoot if the man did not submit to arrest. Baldwin held Breen covered until Deputy Sheriff Hosmer could be summoned from Sierra Madre."

It was not a simple matter to write off such a man, even though the newspapers had begun to refer to him as the "former millionaire." Real estate and agriculture were a little better in the early 1900s than they had been in the '90s, though still nothing to boast about. The "free silver" specter which had frightened national business for several years had been laid with the defeat of Bryan for the presidency. The ill effects of the panic of 1893 had been partly overcome. Theodore Roosevelt was president. Big business, though disturbed by "trust-busting" activities, was no longer staggering blindly. Alaskan gold and the new Nevada mining prosperity that began with Tonopah were making themselves felt. The nation as a whole was more cheerful and hopeful than it had been for a long time. California, among others, felt the uplift. Lucky Baldwin, owning thousands of acres of heavily mortgaged land, also felt it.

By hook or by crook he managed to pay the taxes and hold on to most of his property. With thirty thousand sheep, three thousand cattle, five hundred horses, five hundred mules pasturing and multiplying on his acres, he generally had something to sell to meet the most urgent demands upon him. If this were not enough, he was able to put one hundred thousand gallons of wine and thirty thousand gallons of brandy on the market each year. Vast quantities of grain, fruits and walnuts were being harvested annually. Prices were not what he wanted, but they were something.

Lucky Baldwin refused to be discouraged. He sold his crops, disposed of a little real estate at the best prices he could get, and kept down his overhead by dodging or indefinitely delaying payment of all bills he could dodge or delay. He worked ten hours a day, drank sparingly, smoked not at all, ate corn bread and milk for his supper as he had been doing for years, conserved his health, and still found time to play croquet with his guests, to sit in a mild poker game at his Oakwood Hotel, to travel frequently back and forth between his Los Angeles and San Francisco and Lake Tahoe properties, to drive his four-in-hand with the tally-ho load of girls from the ranch to shop in Monrovia, to breed, train and race his horses, and to enjoy himself as few men in their seventies have enjoyed themselves.

But his affairs were dangerously extended. Witness two newspaper items in 1904:

"E. J. Baldwin yesterday filed a renewal of mortgage to the Hibernia Bank for $1,375,000 in the Recorder's office. The security given is the Baldwin Annex property, holdings in the Western Addition, and his home in Los Angeles."

"Yesterday E. J. Baldwin assigned to the Hibernia Bank for the further security of a promissory note in the sum of $1,375,-000 . . . all the rents, issues and profits received in leases and agreements made by Baldwin on his properties upon which the loan was issued, until such time as the debt is paid."

Such necessity, such a situation, might have been expected to disturb the even tenor of life for a man past seventy-five. Not Lucky Baldwin.

"By gad, I'm not licked yet."

Unperturbed and unregenerate, he continued to welcome and entertain his guests with the same smiling hospitality, superior wines and liquors, tally-ho and carriage drives, hard-fought games of croquet and poker, and more personal attentions, with which he had been entertaining them and himself for half a century.

Even a new son-in-law, Hull McClaughry, one of his counsel in the famous Perkins suit, second husband of his daughter

Anita, was made welcome, in so far as the public knew, in marked contrast to the earlier son-in-law, his young cousin George Baldwin.

John Mackay, richest of the bonanza kings, with his wife and daughter, a notable figure in the high society of New York, Paris and London as well as a leader in the big business of America, dropped in to pay a visit. There had been occasions in the bonanza days when Baldwin and Mackay were strenuous opponents in their efforts to get the best of each other in the mining stock-market. But evidently there were no grudges held.

Mackay was welcomed and entertained at the ranch, and appeared to enjoy his visit. Baldwin could be a charming host when he cared to take the trouble. It is too bad that the reminiscences of the great days of the big bonanza and the great battles of the stock exchange which must have filled many an evening of the visit could not have been preserved. But the evenings were not all spent in reminiscence.

Among other features of entertainment Baldwin took Mackay to a concert given by the great violinist, Jan Kubilik. They agreed that the classic compositions were all well enough but that the highest point reached by the artist was in his rendition of *Annie Laurie*.

Perhaps Lucky Baldwin was growing old. But he at least did not suspect it. There was life in the old dog yet.

Chapter XX

ROMAN HOLIDAYS

LIFE on the Santa Anita ranch was peaceful—too peaceful—
for a young man in his seventies. Poker and croquet and
charming guests were all very well in moments of relaxation,
but they could not completely satisfy a man who had had a
hundred things to do every hour for half a century and had
been doing them. Money troubles and lawsuits had become
so commonplace that Baldwin could brush them aside as easily
as he brushed aside the pestering flies when he sat beneath
the oaks of his beautiful gardens.

He craved action. And what Lucky Baldwin craved, he got.
Action was available in several forms. One, which had stood
near the top of his interests for sixty years, was horse-racing.
His stables still boasted some of the fastest horses in the
country. Chief of the lot at the moment perhaps was Cruzados,
son of his famous Emperor of Norfolk and Atlanta II, bred
and trained under his personal supervision, as everything on
the ranch was bred, trained or otherwise improved.

Cruzados had sprinted to fame in his first race as a two-
year-old at Tanforan, covering the half-mile in forty-seven and
one-half seconds. The next year the colt had won eight
races out of twelve starts, placed three times and was third
once. Such a showing had revived all Baldwin's enthusiasm
in the racing game which he had followed and fostered throughout his adult life.

Casting around for something to occupy his attention between the tasks of operating a business which employed several
hundred workers, the earning of taxes on fifty thousand acres

of property and interest on a debt of $1,375,000, the general supervision of the summer hotel at Lake Tahoe and the winter hotel at Arcadia, the entertainment of guests, a few family affairs, and other time-consuming odds and ends, Lucky Baldwin decided to build and operate a race-track of his own, as an adjunct to his racing stables.

The Baldwin Hotel had not proved the imperishable monument to his fame that he had hoped it would be when he had planned its three-million-five-hundred-thousand-dollar magnificence thirty years earlier. A racing plant that might outshine the fame of Saratoga would be better. No sooner decided upon than undertaken. Los Angeles was already race-horse conscious. Indeed it had been so since the days of the dons.

Graybeards still talked of the great race between José Andres Sepulveda's Black Swan and Pio Pico's Sarco, a nine-mile classic that had brought every don, peon and pioneer from within a hundred miles to the starting and finishing post on San Pedro Street, near the city limits. Sepulveda had imported Black Swan from Australia to defeat the California favorite. Part of the Black Swan's training grind was the five-hundred-mile road trip under saddle from the incoming ship at San Francisco to Los Angeles.

The Sepulvedas bet five hundred horses, five hundred mares, five hundred cows, five hundred calves and five hundred sheep upon the outcome. At the starting-point the wife of José Andres untied a huge handkerchief filled with the fifty-dollar octagonal gold slugs which were current in California in those days, and distributed them to her attendants to bet on the race. The rich and the ragamuffins alike bet everything they could lay their hands upon—money, live stock, saddles, wagons, houses, lands, hats, shoes and cigarettes. And Black Swan galloped in with the profits.

With so worthy a background the Los Angeles prior to invasion from the Middle West had retained an eager interest in horse-racing. Agricultural Park had proved a popular course. Lucky Baldwin saw no reason why his contemplated racing plant at Santa Anita should not be more so. The Oakwood Hotel, near the site of the projected track, was already a popular and profitable gathering-place for coaching parties and others with money and a taste for good dinners, a whirl with the tiger, and incidental entertainment. The Villa Clara, operated near the gates of the Baldwin estate by his eldest daughter, was a rendezvous of the young bloods of the day. Arcadia, and incidentally Lucky Baldwin, ought to be able to profit from the additional activities of the race-track.

But others than Baldwin saw potential profits in a modern racing plant. The promoters of Ascot Park, on the edge of the city, perhaps had more cash or better credit than Baldwin. They beat him to the barrier. The region could not support two tracks. Once again Baldwin's plans received a thorough drenching with cold water. He shook his head and set his teeth.

"By gad, I'm not licked yet."

He completed the surveys for his own plant, tucked the blueprints away for future use, and looked about for more entertainment. What better on a fine January day than the chariot races at Tournament Park, a feature of the Pasadena Tournament of Roses. The Circus Maximus had little on this.

To be sure, the charioteers were clad in togas of cheese-cloth instead of silk and linen, but they were just as red and blue and yellow, for all that, and one or two of them at least had the advantage of a full quart of Cyrus Noble whisky, whereas the Romans probably had had to be content with wine, and Ben Hur perhaps with water. Perhaps the chariots were not of gold and ivory, but who would stickle for such details when the fours abreast were galloping madly around the track, eyes staring, nostrils flaming red, hoofs pounding, chariots leaping and careening behind them, brilliant cheese-cloth togas flying in the wind, while the drivers, barearmed and burly, leaned upon their reins, balanced themselves upon the bounding floorboards, and plied their lashes in a heart-breaking finish. Take it from *The Pasadena Star,* an eye-witness account:

"The thousands of spectators stood in almost breathless silence as the fiery steeds swept past the grandstand, and after the final race had been run and MacWiggins was declared the victor the enthusiasm knew no bounds, and the winner was carried from the course on the shoulders of his admirers."

Or go back to the start for the complete thrill:

"E. T. Off, pale faced and encased in a flowing toga of blue cheesecloth, got into his chariot behind four fast greys. Mr. MacWiggins in orange climbed in behind four bays, one of which was attached to the chariot with ropes, the leather traces having given out. Off had beaten C. C. West; MacWiggins had given the dust to F. E. Turner, in the preliminary heats.

"Now the winners met, Off pale as a statue and MacWiggins, brother of the owner, brown as an old pocketbook as they paraded in front of the stand. There was cheering. And then some more cheering. The two chariots clattered up the track and faced the starter. Off looped the reins around his white hands. MacWiggins, the owner, lit another Mexican cigarette. MacWiggins, the driver, threw away the straw he had been chewing.

"They're off! Everybody in the stands is on his feet and stays there. Down the line come the chariots, swaying from side to side, the horses at top speed. In the stand a judge leans over to say 'Go!' They go. . . ."

Lucky Baldwin got a kick out of that. He would. When the race was finished, and MacWiggins with his orange cheesecloth toga and his four bays had been declared winner, Lucky Baldwin was "rarin' to go." It had been a day of thrills, but it had lacked one thing to make it complete, the Baldwin colors in the toga of the winner, the Baldwin horses, four abreast, in that last thundering sweep of horses and chariots down the track between the roaring thousands.

Baldwin had watched the preliminary heats with as much interest as he had watched the final, and had picked C. C. West, a strapping young giant with the arms of a galley slave, the grin of a devil and the reckless daring of a quart of Cyrus Noble whisky, as the best potential charioteer among the four. To be sure, West had been eliminated in the preliminary heats, but Baldwin, knowing both horses and men, had attributed the elimination not to the driver but to his steeds. He called West over, red toga and all, and made a proposition.

"You'll drive again in the next races?" he demanded.

"If I can get something to drive besides those plow horses," said West, grinning.

"You've got 'em," said Baldwin. "Take your pick of my stables."

"Oh, man!" West beamed. "We'll walk away with it then." But his grin faded an instant later. He too was a sportsman. "But you understand, Mr. Baldwin, horses that run in a race like this probably will never be any good for anything else again."

"Take your pick," Baldwin repeated. It was the gesture of a Roman senator, fit ending to a Roman holiday. There were more to come. Messala and Ben Hur had little on these Tournament of Roses charioteers. The wrecking of Messala's chariot was an incident that could be repeated. Witness *The Star's* account of the race of January 1, 1906:

"With a frightful runaway from the start, a thrilling climax came to the first heat of the first event of the chariot races at Tournament Park this afternoon when E. T. Off of Los Angeles, who was driving his own chariot, was thrown to the ground and seriously injured. The horses were in reality running away like mad from the start of the race and came dashing down the home stretch uncontrolled and uncontrollable. A caballero, grasping the situation, rushed for the maddened horses, grasped at the reins of the nearest animal, which veered and threw itself on the pole of the chariot which struck into and precipitated Off to the ground after hurling him many feet into the air. The chariot was wrecked and the infuriated animals dashed on, but were stopped by caballeros some half mile away. . . .

"West, driving Baldwin horses, but in his own name, won the second heat from Michel by a chariot length in one of the most exciting races ever witnessed."

"That was nothing," West told me with a grin twenty-six years later. "The horses always ran away. We trained them to run away. At least I trained the Baldwin horses to run away. They were running horses, remember, not harness horses. Mr. Baldwin and I would select a four for the race, with a couple of reserves for emergencies. I'd hitch them up one at a time to a breaking cart, and let them go hell-bent around the track. Sometimes they'd take off straight across country in spite of everything I could do to hold and guide them. We wouldn't put the four together to a chariot more than once before the race. We wanted them to be scared, and they were scared, and they ran that way."

Rivalry grew bitter between drivers, owners and horses. Better and better horses were employed in the contests. The Baldwin stables, even with West's skilled but reckless driving, were not always in front. In the meeting of 1908, West with Baldwin horses almost duplicated one part of the most famous chariot race in fact or fiction.

Driving against P. B. Michel, he was a few feet behind on the rail at the first turn of the course when his right-hand horse tripped on the whiffletree of Michel's chariot and went down. Running madly, the other three horses dragged the fallen animal until it broke from the harness. West, "with superb horsemanship," according to the eye-witness account, "retained his footing on the careening chariot, stopped his team, and returned to the stands on foot."

Raising his whip, his toga fluttering in the wind, he saluted the judges and bowed low to the shouting crowds. The judges declared that Michel had cut in too soon on West, being less than a chariot's length in advance, and gave the race to West on the foul.

The time for the course had been cut from 1:57 credited to E. T. Off as winner of the first race in 1904 to 1:38½ credited to West with Baldwin's horses five years later. But runaways, accidents, charges of foul play and so forth were making the tournaments almost too much of a Roman holiday. The sport was ended. It had served its purpose for Lucky Baldwin—thrills toward the end of his days.

After all, there was greater profit and a more sustaining interest in legitimate horse-racing for a man nearing eighty years of age. He had not abandoned the idea of a magnificent racing plant on his Santa Anita ranch when Ascot had temporarily dashed his plans. When the extension of the municipal boundaries of Los Angeles included Ascot Park, and thereby put the track out of business as being a gambling resort within the city limits, Baldwin was ready to go. The Santa Anita track opened in December, 1907.

"Lucky Baldwin has realized the greatest ambition of his life," said *The San Francisco Call*. "Nearly eighty years of age, he has suffered many reverses and achieved many successes, but the climax of his career, his fondest hope, was the establishment of a modern racing plant on his famous ranch, Santa Anita.

" 'I desire no other monument,' said Baldwin when the first day's races at his new track had been run. 'This is the greatest thing I have ever done, and I am satisfied.' "

It is something to have achieved one's fondest hope, to have accomplished the greatest thing one has ever done, and to be satisfied at the age of seventy-nine; no matter how unimportant the actual achievement may appear to others. But that exultation was brief. The next day the same newspaper carried this item:

"Emperor of Norfolk, winner of the American Derby, and one of the greatest race horses and sires in the history of the American turf, died of old age this morning at Lucky Baldwin's Santa Anita ranch. The closing hours of the famous stallion's life presented a unique and pathetic spectacle. When word was sent out that the Emperor was dying, racing men who are at Santa Anita track gathered in numbers at the Baldwin stable and the grand old horse passed away like a king surrounded by his court. Lucky Baldwin was overcome by grief. He said he would bury Emperor of Norfolk on his ranch and erect a monument to his memory."

The man who had made and lost millions, won and broken hearts, defied convention, shown the way for agriculture and real-estate development in southern California, and furnished more newspaper copy throughout the United States than any private citizen of his time, was growing sentimental. It was almost his only sign of age. How little he had suffered from the years or been changed by them was revealed one day at the ranch store.

John Wiggins, one of the oldest employees on the ranch, who had finally accepted some acreage in lieu of wages long accumulated, met Baldwin one day at the store where Baldwin had driven in his buggy with one of his favorite guests, a pretty girl still in her teens. I have the story from her.

"E. J., I want some money," said Wiggins, before Baldwin could alight from the buggy. Wiggins was approximately the same age as Baldwin. "You owe me money, and I want it."

"Well, John, I don't know," said Baldwin, temporizing as usual when any demand for money was made. "You know times are hard. I'll have to see about it."

"See about nothing. I want my money, and I want it now. You've turned over some dry land to me and I can't irrigate it. I got to have some money to put up a windmill."

"Oh," Baldwin smiled with relief. "Is that it? Hell, John, there ain't going to be any wind this winter." And with that he stepped down from the buggy and waved Wiggins and the incident away with a gesture.

"By God, I'll take it out of your hide," shouted Wiggins, and swung wildly.

Baldwin swung back. In an instant they were in a clinch, falling, rolling and fighting in the dust. Baldwin's girl companion screamed for help. A clerk and two or three loafers rushed from the store, and with considerable difficulty separated the octogenarian battlers. That was Lucky Baldwin, a great-grandfather, at an age when conventional men are supposed to be setting up their treasures in Heaven.

With the same young woman, less than twenty years old, he was at dinner one evening in the then-famous Van Nuys Hotel in Los Angeles preliminary to an evening at the theater to see David Warfield put on his first southern California performance of *The Music Master*.

"I'll bet you five dollars that you cry when you see this play, E. J.," she said.

"I never cry at plays. The only play ever worth crying at was *The Black Crook*, with Clara Morris. Now there was a play, and an actress. Too bad you couldn't have seen it."

"Well, I've been hearing of it all my life," said the girl. "But I'll bet you five that you cry at *The Music Master*."

In parenthesis perhaps it should be noted here that the young woman speaking was the only one of the tally-ho loads frequently accompanying Baldwin on his visits to the bank in Monrovia who maintained a personal account in that same bank where Baldwin was so frequently overdrawn.

"It's a bet," said Baldwin. "I know Warfield. He used

to be a call boy in my theater in San Francisco. I hear he's a good actor now, but he can't make me cry."

A man approached from another table. "Is not this Mr. Baldwin?" he said.

"Yes, and you're David Warfield. I'm glad to see you again. This young woman," he waved toward his guest, "has just bet me five dollars that I'll cry at your play to-night. You know damn well there's never been a play in history that was worth a tear, except maybe Clara Morris in *The Black Crook.*"

Warfield smiled. "Maybe not, Mr. Baldwin," he said.

"Come and see. You've seen them all. I haven't seen you since your own theater burned. That was a loss to San Francisco. I'm sorry." He walked away.

"Of course I started to cry even before the curtain went up," the young woman told me twenty-five years later. "I had read the play. But at the end I got a smile. Mr. Baldwin never turned his head toward me, but he slipped a five-dollar gold piece in my hand. 'You win,' he said.

"Mr. Baldwin knew all the best actors and actresses. I remember once Mrs. Leslie Carter and her husband, Mr. Paine, were guests at the ranch. For entertainment one evening we went over to the Oakwood to play roulette. Mrs. Carter took Mr. Baldwin by the arm and dragged him up to the table. 'You're lucky,' she said. 'I want to hold on to you while I place a bet.'

"She put down a five-dollar piece. The wheel clicked. The dealer handed her back a hundred and eighty dollars.

"Mr. Baldwin was never so satisfied with his own luck. He always insisted that it was work that brought him success. When he bet it was backing his judgment, not his luck. I remember once at the track. Cruzados was to run that day. He had been hurt the year before and had been on pasture nearly the whole year. But I had talked with the trainer and others, and I thought he would win. He was quoted at seven to one.

When I told Mr. Baldwin he said he didn't believe the horse was ready. He'd been out of the running too long. But I was confident and told him I was going to bet twenty-five dollars, and asked if he didn't want me to put down a bet for him.

"He hesitated a minute, and then gave me fifty dollars. 'If he wins,' he said, 'you bring my half back, you understand?' He was willing to take that much of a chance, but he wasn't willing to let me spread his winnings around. He was that way. Cruzados galloped in at seven to one. E. J. was as pleased as a child, though it was about the only childlike trait I ever saw in him, unless it was his affection for his pet parrot.

"Every one around the Santa Anita ranch, and even in Arcadia, knew that parrot. It seemed to be as fond of Mr. Baldwin as he was of it. He used to say it was the reincarnation of some woman he had loved. It used to ride around on his shoulder and fly loose over the whole ranch. Once in a while a hawk would get after it. It would streak for home as fast as it could fly, yelling 'Pa! Pa! Pa!' at every beat of its wings.

"It was jealous too. At the Oakwood Hotel there was another parrot named Gene, usually kept in a cage. Polly used to fly over to visit Gene. One day she came into the hotel and found Mr. Baldwin petting Gene. She just squawked once, 'Pa!' and turned around and flew for home. She never went to the Oakwood again, and it was days before she would have anything to do with Mr. Baldwin.

"But she was true to him. Once when he had to go to San Francisco on a three-days trip Polly disappeared. Rosebudd and I were at the ranch, and we hunted all over for that parrot. We knew Mr. Baldwin would be broken-hearted if anything had happened to her. But we couldn't find her, and at last we gave up. We had quite a discussion about it when we drove to the station in the buggy to meet him. We did hate to tell him. Finally, I agreed to do it. We thought he might take it from me with less of a scene.

LUCKY BALDWIN

"He got into the buggy and we started back to the ranch, and I was just starting to tell him that Polly must have been caught by a hawk at last when bang came something on the buggy top, and Polly herself swung over the edge and looked at us. 'Pa!' she said, and fluttered in to perch on his shoulder. It seems impossible, but she must have been waiting in those trees near the station for him for three days. My, that was a relief.

"Mr. Baldwin was an extraordinary man. It wasn't only the parrots that knew that. I remember once when he and I were at dinner in the Van Nuys and he got word from Tobin of the Hibernia Bank in San Francisco that the bank was going to foreclose a million-dollar mortgage on his property. He shook his head, and his eyes hardened, and his jaw set.

"'By gad,' he said, 'I'll show 'em. I've been through four panics, 'thirty-seven, 'seventy-three, 'ninety-three and 'seven, and I've ridden 'em all. By gad I'm not licked yet.'

"He was seventy-nine years old then, and he wasn't licked. He never was licked. He raised enough of the money in some way, through a man named Charles Canfield, I think, to hold off the foreclosure. He always looked ahead. He always carried on."

But time was limited now. Lucky Baldwin was nine years past his Biblical allotment. He was still working ten hours a day, and finding time for the entertainment of guests, the excitement of the races upon his own race course, the management of his ranches and other business activities.

Two more years went by. The long drives to his outlying properties were getting to be a burden. On the way past La Merced one day with Harry Comstock seated beside him, his spirited team of trotters took fright and attempted to bolt. Baldwin gritted his teeth, braced his feet and pulled on the reins. He held the horses to the road, but they tore ahead at a run. Comstock, knowing his man, braced himself and kept silent. Gradually the team slowed.

"You've got 'em now, E. J.," he said. "Mind if I take the reins?"

"Might pull 'em down a little, Harry," said Baldwin, panting with the effort he had made.

Comstock seized the reins beyond Baldwin's hands, and pulled the horses to a slow trot. Baldwin sighed and sat back.

"Not so easy as it used to be, Harry," he said at last. And that probably was the only confession of age he ever made.

"You're wasting a lot of time driving over these roads, E. J.," Comstock suggested diplomatically. "You ought to get an automobile to save time. They're making them pretty good nowadays. You could save a lot of time and money and energy if you had an automobile."

Baldwin, his breath still coming hard from the effort of his struggle with the team, considered the suggestion.

"I've thought of it, Harry," he said at last. "I rode in one once, and I can see that they have some advantages, but I don't like the smell of the damn things. I prefer horses. And besides, I can't afford one."

A few months later it was to be disclosed that Lucky Baldwin owned property worth several million dollars at that time.

"But there's oil in those hills, Harry," he went on, waving toward the rocky sheep pastures which he had been holding for more than thirty years. "When I bring in oil on that land, maybe I'll get me an automobile."

Not long afterward, Lucky Baldwin missed a day at his race-track because of a cold. For almost the first time in his eighty-one years he gave orders to ranch superintendent, storekeeper, trainers and others from his bed. When routine business had been disposed of he called John Isaac Wesley Fisher, the negro horseshoer who had been putting winged shoes upon his race-horses for thirty-seven years.

"John," he said, "I want you to look over that filly that we're pointing to win her next race. I watched her trial yesterday and I thought her stride wasn't quite what it ought to be. She's overreaching with her hind feet. You fix her up. I want to win that race, and the filly can do it if she's right. Now straighten up these pillows. I want to get out to-morrow to watch her."

But to-morrow Lucky Baldwin was a sick man. A few days later, he struggled painfully to one elbow.

"By gad, I'm not licked yet," he gasped. Ten minutes later he was dead.

It was March 1, 1909. Lucky Baldwin had crowded eighty-one years full of more things to do in an hour than any man of his day, and had done them, grave and gay, constructive and destructive, praiseworthy and scandalous.

CHAPTER XXI

THE LUCKY BALDWIN TRADITION

SUCH a name, such fame and such fortune as Lucky Baldwin's could not die with its owner. Hardly had his body been consigned to the family mausoleum in Cypress Lawn at San Francisco when the scandals were renewed and extended.

But Baldwin had had more than half a century of experience with courts and litigation. He had not been such a fool as to believe that his far-flung business interests, coupled with his reputation of innumerable affairs with innumerable women, could pass without a struggle. In the year before his death he had conferred for weeks with his personal counsel, Bradner W. Lee, in the drawing of a will intended to be impervious to the attacks which he believed would be inevitable.

That this precaution was wise and well-founded was to be revealed through five years of litigation and eventual settlement. And in the end his fortune was distributed precisely as he had intended it to be distributed. Even in death he had not been licked.

All of California, parts of Indiana, New York and the racing centers of the country awaited the announcement of the will's provisions with eager curiosity. They were not disappointed. A new sensation, in line with what a scandal-loving public had hoped for, appeared with the filing of the will for probate.

Baldwin had a third daughter, never before acknowledged. She was named in the will as Mrs. Zelda Selby, but not otherwise explained, though the will admitted Baldwin's parentage. "I declare that I have no issue now living other than my said three children hereinbefore named, (Clara Baldwin Stocker,

LUCKY BALDWIN

Anita Baldwin McClaughry, Zelda Selby) and that there are
no children living of any deceased child of mine. . . ."
The newspapers lost no time in announcing further identification of Mrs. Selby. "She is Mrs. Rozella Selby, twenty-five,
wife of David F. Selby of Selby Brothers, confectioners, 1057
Washington Street, Oakland," *The Call* reported on March
fourth, the fourth day after Baldwin's death. "Mr. Selby holds
a written document penned by Baldwin acknowledging Mrs.
Selby as his daughter. The will gives Mrs. Selby acreage worth
about $50,000."
The following day Mr. Selby was quoted in *The Los Angeles
Examiner* as saying that his wife's mother was Martha Agnes
Fowler, also known as Bertha Fowler, a San Francisco girl,
who was said by Selby to have been legally married to Baldwin,
making his fifth wife.
In view of the fact that the young woman was reported to be
twenty-five years old, and therefore must have been born in
1884, three years after the death of Baldwin's third wife,
Jennie Dexter, and the year in which he married Lily Bennett,
who was named in the will as his widow, the public was left to
draw its own conclusions as to the accuracy of the Selby statement. In any event there was no doubt that Baldwin had recognized a daughter whose existence as such had been unknown to
the public for twenty-odd years. The identification of this
daughter's mother and the legitimate or illegitimate details
of her relationship to Baldwin were not made so clear.
Two days after *The Examiner's* statement, *The Call* announced that a threatened will contest had been compromised,
Selby stating that his wife had won concessions from Clara
Baldwin Stocker and Anita Baldwin McClaughry. The report added that certain authorities declared the beneficiary had
little standing in court and that threatened scandal as well as
a provision in the will for cutting off contestants had made the
compromise easy. The public was forced to be content with

[304]

that. Almost the last Lucky Baldwin scandal died of inanition. Perhaps the quick forgetting of the subject was due in part to the greater interest in the amount of the famous estate and the details of its distribution. H. A. Unruh, Lucky Baldwin's friend, distant kinsman and faithful business agent for thirty years, was named executor. His first estimate of the value of the estate, according to the press, was roughly $25,000,000. Three months later the official inventory, covering several hundred typewritten pages, fixed the total value at $10,930,801, including 1,691 parcels of real estate valued at $10,612,025, and 2,564 items of personal property valued at $318,776.

The bulk of the real estate was to be divided equally between two daughters, Clara and Anita, with a share of about five hundred thousand dollars in community property to go to the widow, Mrs. Lily Bennett Baldwin, residing in San Francisco. Included in minor bequests were Mrs. Selby, Mrs. Elizabeth Rush who was the daughter of his favorite sister Evaline Fawcett, Charles Fawcett, Rosebudd Doble Mullender and H. A. Unruh.

With so much made known, other would-be heirs began to flock in. Three days after Baldwin's death *The San Francisco Examiner* stated that "a man said to be from New York arrived in Arcadia yesterday with the express intention of contesting the will." It was not long before names and dates began to appear. Even a life as crowded as that of Lucky Baldwin could hardly have included all the activities and connections alleged. But they all made newspaper copy, keeping the Baldwin name before the public, and maintaining and extending the Lucky Baldwin tradition.

One William C. Rutan even announced that Lucky Baldwin was not and never had been the E. J. Baldwin whose name was signed to the will. According to Rutan's claim, his own father had joined the original Baldwin emigrant party at Council Bluffs, Iowa, on the first western trip and had assumed Baldwin's name and identity after E. J. Baldwin had been shot, killed and buried on the trip. Rutan himself, he said, was Clara Baldwin Stocker's half-brother. It was an entertaining bit of publicity but it produced nothing except an added fillip to the Baldwin tradition.

Mrs. Mary Baldwin Morin, of Freeport, Illinois, announced a claim to a sister's share in the estate on the ground that she and E. J. Baldwin were both children of William and Nancy Baldwin, Virginians who had settled at New Diggins, Wisconsin, where they had fifteen children, of whom E. J. was one of the eldest and she herself one of the youngest. That story got about as far as Rutan's claim.

Mrs. Rose M. Wyatt announced that she was a granddaughter of the testator, her grandfather, George W. Baldwin of Otter Creek, Indiana, having assumed the name of E. J. Baldwin on his first trip to California in "1851." There he married a second time, she asserted, and her mother and Clara Baldwin Stocker were half-sisters.

Mrs. Laura P. Alsip claimed a legitimate daughter's share in the estate on the ground that prior to 1850 E. J. Baldwin was known as William H. Baldwin, and that under that name he had married one Ophelia Henderson of Chillicothe, Ohio, September 9, 1845. She declared she was born of that marriage in 1848, and that Baldwin and her mother lived together until 1853 when Baldwin abandoned his wife and changed his name to Elias Jackson Baldwin. For lack of evidence, at the request of her counsel, the claim was dismissed.

The Lucky Baldwin tradition was maintained.

Lillian Ashley, who had figured in one of the most sensational cases ever brought against Baldwin in life—the case in which her sister had missed accomplishing his death almost literally by a hair—appeared in behalf of her minor daughter, claiming a granddaughter's share in the estate. All the old scandal was rehashed in the trial. It failed with the others.

THE LUCKY BALDWIN TRADITION

And four years after the death of Lucky Baldwin, Judge Rives in the Superior Court of Los Angeles handed down an order for final distribution of the estate. Lucky Baldwin's world-famed luck had extended to his heirs. The value of the estate had doubled in the four years of delay and attendant litigation.

The actual value at the time of distribution was ten million dollars more than the original appraisal, so that the two chief heirs, Mrs. Clara Baldwin Stocker and Mrs. Anita Baldwin McClaughry, received approximately ten million dollars' worth of property each in addition to more than two million dollars previously turned over to each by the administrator. In accordance with an agreement made with the heirs the court awarded H. A. Unruh as executor and Bradner W. Lee as counsel one hundred and eighty thousand dollars each for their work. Incidentally the court praised Unruh most highly from the bench for his superior handling of the task.

And even then the luck of Lucky Baldwin had not run out. The ten million dollars' worth of property left by a man who had seemed on the verge of ruin when he journeyed to the Far North to begin life anew at the age of seventy-two, had not only grown to more than twenty millions four years after his death. Four years later the Merced sheep pastures, despised for forty years except by Baldwin, came into production as the Montebello Oil Fields, one of the richest in the West. In another seven years derricks were sprouting and oil flowing on the Baldwin Hills, where the sheep of his La Cienega ranch had been grazing for nearly half a century. The millions divided among his heirs were increased again.

The Baldwin luck was maintaining itself with the Baldwin name and the Baldwin tradition. Baldwin Park, Baldwin Lake, Baldwin Avenue, Baldwin Hills, Baldwin this and Baldwin that, the name holds its fame throughout the Southland. The Baldwin tradition still holds and thrives, more than one hundred years after his birth. In some respects it has been improved upon.

Endowment of the Clara Baldwin Stocker Home for Women by Lucky Baldwin's eldest daughter, who died in 1929 at the age of eighty-two, leaving an estate of some ten million dollars, bears witness to a spirit of philanthropy in the second generation which was never notable in the first.

The Orthopedic Hospital in Los Angeles could speak a similar good word for the second generation in the person of the second daughter who has contributed generously to its support. The University of California's agricultural department is still carrying on and improving the breed of prize stock presented to the farm by that same daughter, Mrs. Anita Baldwin.

Lucky Baldwin started something when he won that first horse-race on a country road in Indiana. The Baldwin millions, the Baldwin name, and various features of the Baldwin fame and character carry on. As this is written the newspapers throughout the United States are announcing that the race course on the famous Santa Anita ranch is to be rebuilt and reopened as a modern racing plant at a cost of one million dollars, sponsored by Anita Baldwin in defiance of conventional opposition. Lucky Baldwin certainly would approve of that.

He was Lucky Baldwin, perhaps the outstanding individualist of his generation in America—indifferent to convention, scornful of public opinion, defiant of restriction, acquisitive, energetic, immoral, successful according to his lights. His character was his own, as his success was his own. He did as he pleased, and gladly conceded the same privilege to the rest of the world. His was the spirit of the frontier, which was the dominating spirit of America throughout the two-thirds of a century of the country's greatest growth.

By gad, that spirit isn't licked yet.

THE END

NEVADA GHOST TOWNS & MINING CAMPS ILLUS-TRATED ATLAS by Stanley W. Paher, photographs by Nell Murbarger. This companion to the all-time Nevada favorite features 54 new maps and more than 460 previously unpublished pictures by the famous photographer. Available as two paperback volumes or a combined hardback edition.

NEVADA GHOST TOWNS AND MINING CAMPS, by Stanley W. Paher. Large 8-1/2 x 11 format, 492 pages, 700 illus., maps, index. About 688 ghost towns are described with directions on how to get to them. It contains more pictures and describes more localities than any other Nevada book. Nearly every page brings new information and unpublished photos of the towns, the mines, the people and early Nevada life. Now in 11th printing, it is the best seller of any book on Nevada ever published and it won the national "Award of Merit" for history. Cloth with color dust jacket.

LAKE TAHOE: THE LAKE OF THE SKY by George Wharton James. This reprint of the classic 1915 work came out in the summer of 1992. For information on Tahoe's varied history — its Indians, towns, first automobile routes, steamer travel, early twentieth century recreational activities, first explorers, the lake's various names, its physical and geological characteristics, as well as its flowers, birds, animals, trees and plants — this is your book. Editor Stanley Paher has inserted over 100 historic Lake Tahoe photographs throughout the text, including two pages of pictures of Meeks Bay Resort.

TAHOE HERITAGE: THE BLISS FAMILY OF GLENBROOK, NEVADA by Sessions S. Wheeler with William W. Bliss. This new book has created a sensation since its recent release. An account not only of a truly remarkable family but of Lake Tahoe from its earliest days. D. L. Bliss formed the Carson and Tahoe Lumber and Fluming Company in 1873 in order to supply the lumber for the Comstock mines. In order to bring logs from all points on the Lake to Glenbrook (the millsite), Bliss purchased the iron-hulled steamer, *Meteor*. In 1876 it was said the *Meteor* was the fastest inland steamer in the world. Bliss later built the passenger ship *Tahoe*, the Lake's most luxurious vessel, constructed the railroad between Truckee and Tahoe City and created the Tahoe Tavern, a resort hotel which attracted society's elite. When reading about the reasons for the closing of the Glenbrook Inn, it is a rare individual who can fight back tears of sadness. The California State Park down the road from Meeks Bay Resort is named after D. L. Bliss. Through his brilliant business ability, he made the resorts of Lake Tahoe among the most widely known in the world. A first-class book!

ORDEAL BY HUNGER, by George Stewart. 328 pages, illus. Well written classic history of the snowbound Donner Party in the California Sierra. The party suffered inconceivable hardships, and some individuals resorted to cannibalism. A perennial best-seller.

HISTORY OF THE DONNER PARTY, by C.F. McGlashan. 260 pages, illus., maps. Subtitled "a tragedy of the Sierra," this book originally issued in 1880 is the first presentation of the facts of the 1846 emigrant trek. Author McGlashan based his book on letters and personal interviews with survivors.

PATTY REED'S DOLL, by Rachel Laurgaard. 143 pages, illus. Adventures of the Reed family, including 8-year-old Patty who carried a tiny wooden doll, amid the Donner emigrant party of 1846.

RAILROADS OF NEVADA AND EASTERN CALIFORNIA by David F. Myrick Volume I, North, 472 pages. • Volume II, South, 496 pages. This comprehensive record of more than 80 railroads is just as much a faithful history of the region as well. The principal mines and mills and their production are scrupulously detailed, together with the personalities who created them. Maps visually orient the reader to the locales and situations described. It is an accurate and reliable travel guide for readers who choose to explore the railroad routes of yesteryear. Myrick's remarkable collection of 660 scarce, early photos of long-vanished trains, towns, and mining operations as well as numerous maps, contribute to this magnificent two-volume compendium of historical lore.

PREWAR WOOD, Carol Van Etten's first volume on the marine history of Lake Tahoe, is an excellent collection of information regarding Tahoe's pre WWII speedboats. A classic source of valuable information for owners and would-be owners. Excellent section on Fred O. Kehlet and Meeks Bay. Loaded with pictures.

LAKERS AND LAUNCHES, second volume in the series by Ms. Van Etten, came into print in 1992. This work focuses on launches, cruisers and sedans and illuminates the social elements of life at the lake in the early part of this century. Contributors include darel Kehlet, Fred Kehlet and Jean Kehlet Russo. Full of pictures including the Meeks Bay Mystery Sedan.

GEORGE WINGFIELD OWNER AND OPERATOR OF NEVADA, by C. Elizabeth Raymond. 368 pages. Major biography of one of the most significant and controversial figures in Nevada history.

MY ADVENTURES WITH YOUR MONEY, by George Graham Rice. 334 pages, 110 illus. Here are the memoirs of get-rich-quick financing of central Nevada and Death Valley mines, with interesting anecdotal material. Author capitalized the stocks of Goldfield, Greenwater and Rawhide mines, listed them on the national exchanges, and reaped the profits until convicted of mail fraud in 1911.

GOLD IN THEM HILLS, by C. B. Glasscock. 330 pages, illus., map. Intro. by David Myrick. Author saw the reversals of fortune, had a part in the frenzies, experienced the hardships. Chapters 2-4 tell the development of early Tonopah; chapters 5-17 discuss Goldfield's freighting, high-grading, big mines, society and the fast-talking promoters. Greenwater and Rawhide also are included. This informally written book will surely be enjoyed by all who love old Nevada. Color cover.

SILVER SYNDICATE PRESS
"Publisher and Distributor of Books Dealing With The Old West"

Write:
POST OFFICE BOX 71226, RENO, NEVADA 89570